To Dian

Love,
Margy

Margaret Turner Taylor
March 2021

I Will Fear No Evil

Other books by
Margaret Turner Taylor

TRAVELING THROUGH THE
VALLEY OF THE SHADOW OF DEATH

SECRET IN THE SAND

BASEBALL DIAMONDS

TRAIN TRAFFIC

THE QUILT CODE

I WILL FEAR
NO EVIL

MARGARET TURNER TAYLOR

This book is a work of fiction. Many of the names, places, characters, and incidents are products of the author's imagination or are used fictitiously. Any resemblance to actual events or locales or person living or dead is entirely coincidental.

Copyright © 2020 Margaret Turner Taylor
All rights reserved. This book or any portion thereof may not be reproduced or used in any manner whatsoever without the express written permission of the publisher.

Llourettia Gates Books, LLC
P.O. Box #411
Fruitland, Maryland 21826

Hardcover ISBN: 978-1-953082-03-9
Paperback ISBN: 978-1-953082-04-6
eBook ISBN: 978-1-953082-05-3
Library of Congress Control Number: 2020925285

Cover photo by Martha and Edward Jenkins
Photography by Andrea López Burns
Cover and interior design by Jamie Tipton, Open Heart Designs

*This book is dedicated to
Orlena Scoville and to Bacalhoa,
the home she loved.*

CONTENTS

Prologue xv

CHAPTER 1
Market Day in Guernica 1

CHAPTER 2
Building a Refuge in Eastleigh, England 7

CHAPTER 3
At First Sight 14

CHAPTER 4
No Ordinary Evening 21

CHAPTER 5
Anna Goes to England 25

CHAPTER 6
I am a Jew 30

CHAPTER 7
Going Home to Portugal 37

CHAPTER 8
Bacalhoa 42

CHAPTER 9
War Is Coming 50

CHAPTER 10
Everything Changes 59

CHAPTER 11
Death and Mourning 67

CHAPTER 12
Captain Max 77

CHAPTER 13
A New Challenge 86

CHAPTER 14
Everything Changes Again 101

CHAPTER 15
And So It Begins 112

CHAPTER 16
Allies in America Join the Fight 119

CHAPTER 17
The Escape Route 127

CHAPTER 18
Hiding Children Isn't Easy 138

CHAPTER 19
There's a Place for Us 148

CHAPTER 20
The Game's Afoot 158

CHAPTER 21
Bottles of Wine 167

CHAPTER 22
Bless the Little Children 175

CHAPTER 23
Arriving in the Land of the Free 186

CHAPTER 24
The Underground Is Underway 194

CHAPTER 25
By The Sea 203

CHAPTER 26
Full House 219

CHAPTER 27
Saving Emerson   228

CHAPTER 28
The Wolfram Prize   237

CHAPTER 29
Chasing Ghosts   253

CHAPTER 30
Max meets Annalise   268

CHAPTER 31
Aboard The *Anjo*   276

CHAPTER 32
Trouble in Virginia   286

CHAPTER 33
The Treasure of Shinkolobwe   296

CHAPTER 34
Visiting the Past   303

CHAPTER 35
Healing Emerson   314

CHAPTER 36
Preparing the Table   327

CHAPTER 37
Goodness and Mercy   337

Author's Note   343

Acknowledgments   351

About the Author   353

BACALHOA

The photograph on the front cover of *I Will Fear No Evil* is the real façade of the Quinta Palacio da Bacalhoa as it appeared in 1998. The photograph on the back cover is the view from the loggia.

PROLOGUE

*"The only thing necessary for the triumph of evil
is for good men to do nothing."*
EDMUND BURKE

None of us chooses the world into which we are born. We do not choose our families. We do not choose our countries of origin. We do not choose our time in history. Some of us are lucky and some of us are not. What we do have are the choices we make with the lives we have been given. Some of us are brave. *I Will Fear No Evil* is a story about people who have tremendous courage.

This is a story about people who might have chosen, if it were possible, to have been born during another time and in another place. Given the randomness of fate, they had the daring to live and love in the times and places they were given, and they rose to the challenge to do the right thing in a world where new evil revealed itself on a daily basis. They found courage within themselves. They discovered that they could be brave, that they could act in the face of danger, that they could do good deeds and make a difference. Even in a very frightening world, they could become heros. Each one lived by the words: *I Will Fear No Evil*.

Chapter 1

MARKET DAY IN GUERNICA

April 26, 1937

Anna and her little sister Beatrice ran to their uncle's bakery stall. It was market day, and Uncle Theo always let them have the leftover pastries he hadn't been able to sell. For the past few months, there had been scarcely anything left at the end of the day.

The war in Spain with its rationing and shortages had been devastating to the Basque people whose land was rugged and not that productive under the best of circumstances. Market day was disappointing these days, and most of the merchants quickly sold out of the few vegetables and bars of soap they were able to gather together to display in their stalls. Anna's uncle somehow managed to find a little sugar, a few eggs, and some white flour, when no one else in Guernica and the surrounding towns could find any of these things. Some people said Theo smuggled his ingredients from France or Portugal.

Before the war, Anna and Bea could look forward to pastries filled with rich vanilla custard or covered with chocolate glaze. Now, they were lucky to have a scrap of dough with some sugar and cinnamon on top. Anna knew her uncle made these dough cookies especially for them. These confections were not really leftovers that hadn't sold, but were made by Uncle Theo so that she and Beatrice would have something special to eat on market day. It was just 4:30, time for the market to close. Theo hugged the girls and handed them each a scrap of dough. He looked sad, Anna thought, that he didn't have anything better to give them. They sat down on the curb beside the stall to eat their pastries.

Anna was never sure, when she looked back on that day, what she had noticed first. The destruction came so quickly and so unexpectedly that the sounds and sights ran together in her memory. The past many months of Spain's civil war had made all children too familiar with the realities of airplanes overhead and the bombings these airplanes brought. Today there was something different about the roar that came from the skies. Anna heard one airplane and didn't pay much attention to it. Then she realized there were too many planes that flew in formation and screamed overhead. The sound of the airplanes grew, louder and closer than they'd ever been before.

Anna's instincts told her this was not the usual bombing they had come to expect, and it was going to be very bad. She pushed Bea under Uncle Theo's table. There was no time to find a safer place. She covered her little sister's body with her own and told her not to worry, that it would all be over soon. Usually the bombing raids lasted just a few minutes, but on this day, the storm of death from the sky was unlike anything the town of Guernica had ever seen before.

Wave upon wave of planes dropped their deadly cargos on the marketplace. Fire fell from the sky. The planes flew so low, Anna thought they would surely strike the awning that covered her uncle's pastry stand. She thought that if she raised her arm above her head, she might be able to reach out and touch one of the German planes as it strafed the market square. The planes flew that close to her and little Bea. Anna hid her eyes and squeezed her arms around her younger sister. The noise was deafening. The swirl of wind that the low-flying planes created, swept everything on the market tables into a cyclone of food and vegetables and death. Bombs exploded, one after another. They fell without remorse and blew everything to smithereens.

Anna heard her Uncle Theo cry out. She looked up in time to see him blown apart, into a hundred pieces. His arms and legs and pieces of his body flew everywhere in all directions. Nearly paralyzed with shock, Anna dragged Bea closer to the curb of the street. She knew that small rise of stone would not protect them, but she sought that hopeless spot of shelter out of desperation. A flying piece of shrapnel struck Bea in the neck. The little one screamed and bled until she died in Anna's arms. Anna held her and continued to protect her little sister's lifeless body as death rained down around them, on and on and on.

The carpet bombing was nothing like any attack even these war-weary citizens of Guernica had suffered. Wave after wave of the Condor Legion, a unit of the German Luftwaffe, spewed their weapons of apocalypse down on this spiritual capital of the Basque nation, destroying with impunity its children, its old people, and everyone else and everything in their path. What the incendiary bombs did not kill, the strafing from low flying planes murdered with machine guns.

At long last, the endless punishing of unbearable noise and relentless bombing and killing from the airplanes dissolved into blessed silence from the sky. The only sounds Anna heard now were the screams of horror and cries of pain from those who lay wounded and dying in the streets. Anna dragged her sister's corpse beside her as she moved through the carnage to try to reach their home. She struggled with the body and refused to give up trying to take her dead sister to a safe place — the sanctuary where their parents would surely make everything all right again.

Finally, Anna reached her street and looked for her house. It was gone, leaving only a pile of rubble that burned and smoldered. Nothing was left of the place where she and Bea and her parents had always lived. Nothing at all remained except charred timbers and ash. A priest whose cassock was covered in blood and dirt pried Anna's fingers from her dead sister's body and lay Beatrice down in the middle of the street. One of the neighbors, whose house was also burning, grabbed Anna to keep her from running into the ruins to try to find her mother and father. Anna kept insisting she had to find her parents. She began to scream when someone told her that her parents had died when a bomb exploded in their house.

Anna didn't remember when she stopped screaming. When she finally had screamed until she could scream no more, Anna was silent. She grew quiet after that market day in Guernica, and it seemed as if she had taken a vow never to speak again. Her eyes were dead. Her face was blank. She looked at no one, and she saw nothing. She was lost to the world around her.

The priest who had taken Bea's dead body from her, carried Anna to an aid center outside the Carmelite Convent. The nuns had set up a tent hospital to treat the victims of the horrible Guernica tragedy. When a doctor finally came to the cot where Anna lay and examined her, he declared her to be physically unhurt except for a few cuts and bruises and some minor burns. Because Anna refused to speak and would not even say her name, she was assumed to be an orphan and a mute.

She was transferred to a hospital in Bilbao. Nurses and others who came to visit her exclaimed that it was a miracle Anna had lived and had no serious injuries. Anna could not understand why this miracle, that seemed to have something to do with her, was greeted with happiness. Anna knew that everything about her that mattered was in fact already dead. Her heart was dead. Her soul was dead. Everyone she had loved was dead. She stayed silent and numb inside.

From the hospital, Anna was sent to a home for orphans and displaced persons. The people there bathed her, dressed her, fed her, and cared for her. Anna still did not speak. One day, a priest came and took Anna and some other children away from the home. The man pinned a cardboard sign on Anna's thin jacket, put a beret on her head, and took her to an overloaded boat which she boarded with crowds of other children. The priest told her she was going to England.

Anna was told she was one of the lucky ones. Of the many thousands of children who had lost their families in the Spanish Civil War and in the bombing of Guernica, she had been selected to participate in The Beret Project. These dislocated young people would be sent to England to a children's camp that was being established especially for them. Each child wore the distinguishing beret that identified her or him as a member of this group of a fortunate few. They waited and waited until the *Habana*, the ship that would carry them across the Bay of Biscay to a new life removed from the conflicts of the Iberian Peninsula, received permission to take them to England.

Their non-combatant status in the Spanish Civil War did not allow Britain's government to accept refugees from the conflict, even children who were orphans. The British could not offer transport, refuge, funds, or anything at all to those who wanted to escape the ravages of war. Private funds were raised by concerned British citizens; the Beret Project was financed completely with donations. The British government contributed nothing to this humanitarian effort. Four thousand children finally made the historic voyage on the *Habana*, a broken-down vessel that was on its final crossing.

They arrived in Eastleigh, England and were housed, fed, clothed, and received medical care in the camp established on private property and organized and run by volunteers. These children would find temporary and permanent homes among the generous people of the British Isles and spend the years of World War II in Britain.

Chapter 2

BUILDING A REFUGE IN EASTLEIGH, ENGLAND

MAY 1937

Katharine Marjory Stewart-Murray, the Duchess of Atholl, hurried to gather her luggage as the taxi stopped at the curb. She was late and absolutely could not miss this last train of the day to North Stoneham. She handed the driver a fistful of money and rushed into the crowded station. She knew she'd overpaid, but she didn't have time for him to make change. Her mission was too important to risk missing her train. A porter approached her, wanting to take her baggage, but Kitty was a strong and independent woman, even in her sixties. She preferred to make the train on time, even if she had to carry her own valises.

A young woman was hurrying beside her, and Kitty realized they were running for the same train. The young woman threw her own bags onto the train, saw that Kitty was also boarding, grabbed Kitty's bags, and handed them up into the first class car. She jumped up into the train and pushed their bags out of the way as she gave a hand to Kitty to help her up the steps. They exhaled in relief just as the whistle blew and the train began to move out of the station.

"Thank you, my dear, I appreciate the help. I was worried that I was going to miss this last train to North Stoneham, and I might have done so without you."

The young woman replied in her American accent, "I always promise myself that I'm going to have my things packed the night before, call a taxi with plenty of time to spare, and be at the station way ahead of when the train is scheduled to leave. Of course, that never happens, and it seems I am always rushing to make the last one of everything."

The two women proceeded down the aisle to find their compartments. "I am just the same way," Kitty replied. "I always plan too many things that I want to do, and I never allow myself enough time to do all of them. You would think I would have learned by now to better manage my time and my life."

The women were both ticketed to the same compartment. "I'm Kitty Stuart-Murray." She introduced herself as they stowed their luggage on the racks above their heads.

"I'm Emerson Taylor Cabot from Connecticut ... in the United States. My problem is that too many things are important to me, and I try to do them all. I always am running out of time, of course."

"And what of importance brings you to the North Stoneham train this afternoon?"

"What brings me here today is probably one of the most important and significant things I've ever wanted to do. I mean, what I am hoping to do in Eastleigh. I'm going to help build a camp for the children who are coming over from Spain — the orphans who have been displaced because of the terrible war going on there. So many children were left without homes and families when those bully Germans, who aren't even supposed to be fighting in Spain, bombed the Basque town of Guernica. I'm in England studying economics at Oxford, and I have become quite concerned about what is happening in Spain. In the States, we didn't hear much news about the Spanish Civil War. The newspaper reports the really horrible things that happen, but most of the time the war is ignored as if it were happening on another planet. Since I've been in England, there is ever so much more news about what is going on there. It is just across the water after all. The bombing of Guernica was such an unspeakable tragedy. When I heard that a ship full of children might be allowed to come here and that a camp was being built to house them, I decided Oxford and economics could get along without me for a few days. My grandfather taught me how to do carpentry work, and I am really pretty good with a hammer and saw — especially for a woman." Emerson's smile was sardonic. "So here I am on my way to help build the camp for the refugee children."

Kitty was intrigued and captivated by this young American with the unruly yellow hair and the contagious enthusiasm. If Kitty herself had not already also been on her way to work on building the exact same camp for the displaced children, Emerson Cabot from Connecticut in the United States would have convinced her to sign up. Kitty was the President of the National Joint Committee for Spanish Relief. "How did you hear about the Beret Project?"

"Oh, so you know about the children who are coming and the urgency of getting this camp built for them as quickly as possible? I have heard that the British government might not let them come. I don't understand that at all. How could they turn away children? These are children who have lost everything. Most of them are orphans whose parents have died in the war. I know it has to do with Britain's non-intervention policy and not taking sides in Spain and all of that. But have they no humanity?"

Kitty laughed and marveled at the idealism of youth and the "can do" attitude of Americans. "My thoughts exactly. I think we are going to be able to get the government to agree to allow them to come. We have formed the Basque Children's Committee, and we hope to be able to provide enough private financial support so that Britain's neutrality will not be compromised."

"You know a lot more about this than I do. You're in charge of something that has to do with the camp and the children, aren't you? Here I am telling you all about it, and I am preaching to the choir."

Kitty loved the way Americans were so forthright with their opinions. "Yes, my dear, I am kind of in charge of some of this project. Mostly people want me to find money for them, but I am on my way tonight to be certain the building of the camp that will receive the children is progressing as quickly as possible. Until we have the facilities finished and are ready to receive the children, we cannot give the go-ahead for their ship to leave Spain. We are doing everything we can, and we are doing it all as fast as possible. We have to convince my government that this can be done without the British taxpayer's contributions."

"I am so happy to meet you and to know that the camp and the whole project are in such good hands. You must tell me everything that I can do to help."

Kitty could see that Emerson was wearing an expensive wool coat and practical but extremely well-made shoes. She was traveling first class and was studying abroad at Oxford, so she must be a young woman of some financial means. "My committee and I are ever so grateful for your help. I am sure that we will find many ways for you to contribute — including the use of your carpentry skills. There are many elements that we are trying to coordinate to get the children here. The most difficult seems to be the political aspect of things. But isn't that always the way ... bureaucracies and bureaucrats and politicians and silliness like that blocking our desire to do good deeds? However, I think we are going to prevail. In fact, one of your American diplomats has been a great deal of help in applying pressure to my own government. He's a lawyer and assigned to the American Consulate in London. He knows all about immigration law and international neutrality. He is taking our case to the British bureaucracy and explaining to them how this can be done without compromising Britain's precious non-intervention status. He is quite a wonder. You will have to meet him. And so today, I meet another young American who is eager to help us in our crusade — and a female carpenter at that. We are thrilled to have your help."

"I'm so heartened to hear that the technicalities and the practicalities are all being addressed. We will get this done. When do you think the children will arrive?"

"One of the members of my committee, Leah Manning, who works for Spanish Medical Aid, and my dear friend Edith Pye are coordinating the effort to get the children aboard the ship in Bilboa. Edith is working on behalf of the Society of Friends, the Quakers. They are all depending on me to finish building the camp and raise the money so the children can leave Spain. I keep telling them I am working as fast as I can, but they are working in a war zone. Of course, nothing can happen fast enough when it comes to getting children out of harm's way. They have a ship, an ancient one, called the *Habana* that used to make runs between Spain and Cuba. It's an old wreck, but we are hoping it will hold up for one last trip across the Bay of Biscay. Originally, we were expecting to bring about a thousand children across, but the number keeps growing every day. It is almost impossible to turn away an orphaned or injured child when there is the possibility of saving a life. I think we are talking about bringing more than three thousand children at this point. I worry about that ship, but that is not the department about which I am supposed to worry. I am supposed to worry about things at this end of their journey."

"I've always been good at worrying about things. I will do your worrying about the *Habana* for you. That will leave you free to focus on worrying about the camp and the money." Emerson gave Kitty a smile.

"Where are you staying in Eastleigh? Do you have a reservation at a hotel?"

"Oh, yes. We were told we had to make our own arrangements and pay for our own food and lodgings and transportation if we intended to volunteer. One of my friends from Oxford, who was hoping to travel here and help out, had a reservation at a hotel in Eastleigh. She came down with a bad case of flu and couldn't make the trip. I was delighted to take her place and her hotel reservation. I have money, you see, to pay my own way," Emerson said this somewhat sheepishly as if she was embarrassed to admit she wasn't impoverished.

"We wish we could house and feed the volunteers, but the fact is, we don't have the beds or the funds for that. So your willingness to pay your own way is greatly appreciated," Kitty, a wealthy woman in her own right, understood and admired Emerson's reluctance to flaunt her privilege. "To use your words, we will make this happen, Emerson. With friends like you and dear Peter, our diplomat from America helping out, how can we fail?"

"Peter?"

"Peter Mullens is the lawyer from the American Consulate who is working night and day to help us overcome the legal and political obstacles. He is so dedicated to this mission. You will like Peter. I worry about him sometimes. I don't think he remembers to eat and sleep."

"I always remember to eat," Emerson assured her.

"So do I," Kitty laughed. "Speaking of which, I think it is time for a hearty English tea. What do you think?"

"I absolutely agree with you. I love scones." The women proceeded to the lounge car for their tea.

Chapter 3

AT FIRST SIGHT

May 1937

*E*merson woke up early the next morning, anxious to get to work building the camp for the Basque children. She dressed in long pants, a warm sweater, and her anorak. It was May, but if it rained, she knew it could be cold. She went to the hotel dining room for the English breakfast that was included with her room rate. She loved the hearty food she knew would be served and was especially grateful for it today, as she knew she would be working hard this morning. As she looked around the dining room, she tried to guess, based on the way they were dressed, which of her fellow breakfast eaters were headed for the camp. It was drizzling outside when she left the hotel and began her walk to the area where the camp was being built. She was happy to have waterproof rain gear, wool socks, and Wellington boots to keep her warm and dry.

Several other young people were heading in the same direction, and she caught up with a group and introduced herself.

They were all energetic and full of enthusiasm, anxious to get started doing something useful. They talked about how terrible things were in Spain. Why couldn't the Germans and their Luftwaffe mind their own business and leave Spain alone? As they made the last turn in the muddy road, they were surprised with the breathtakingly beautiful sight that greeted them. Quite a few lovely domed white tents were already built and ready for the children. How had so much been done in such a short time?

The tent city with the graceful round tents was unexpected. Emerson had expected small brown military structures made of drab canvas — utilitarian but without charm. This place would surely lift the spirits of the children when they saw it for the first time. These tents were like wonderful clouds. From a distance the campground resembled the set up for a wedding, a fancy party, or even a heavenly circus.

The volunteers were galvanized, and they were thrilled to be joining the effort to help build such a cheerful place. Emerson decided whoever had organized it all was quite efficient because so many of the tents had already been completed. She knew the builders of the children's camp were under great pressure to complete the facility as quickly as possible. The ship that would bring the displaced children to England, the *Habana*, was not able to leave Bilbao until it received word that the camp was completed and all the money to support the orphans had been raised.

Emerson and her group were questioned briefly about their skills and assigned to work groups. They worked hard all morning in the rain, but no one complained. Mid-morning hot cups of tea and consommé were brought around with what the English called biscuits. They looked like cookies to Emerson's American eyes. The refreshments were a nice touch and helped to keep spirits high. At 1:00 the volunteers were called to a central tent for a substantial hot lunch. Whoever was in charge was taking good care of their workers. The day ended for Emerson's crew at tea time, and a late crew took over. The late crew were local people who had just finished their day jobs and were coming to work for several more hours on the camp. Emerson welcomed the chance to go back to the hotel, have her tea, and rest. At the end of the day, she looked forward to a warm fire and getting out of the rain.

The next few days passed quickly, and the camp was near completion. The number of children who were expected to arrive increased daily, so more and more tents had to be built. Emerson was thinking about returning to Oxford and her studies when she ran into Kitty, the woman with whom she had shared a train compartment on her way to North Stoneham. Kitty was one of the organizers in charge of the entire camp project and an exceptionally important person. Emerson was thrilled to see Kitty again, and Kitty was delighted to find that Emerson was still in Eastleigh.

"Have you had your tea?" Kitty asked Emerson when they met in the lobby of the hotel. Emerson's hair was damp and frizzled, and she looked particularly disheveled. She'd been climbing under the wooden platform bases of the tent structures to check that bolts and screws were tightened. Her boots were covered with mud, and her clothes were wet and dirty. She'd been working hard.

"I was going to go to my room and have tea sent up," Emerson wasn't really embarrassed by what a mess she was because she knew Kitty understood that she had been working at the camp.

"Please, have tea with me. We have something to celebrate, and I have someone I want you to meet. I know you feel like you ought to change clothes, but I have a table by the fire. You will warm up soon enough," Kitty knew that Emerson had been working all day in the rain and was amazed that she still looked quite beautiful, even soaking wet. "Have you had a good experience building the camp?" Kitty really wanted to know. She'd been one of the leaders of the effort to bring the children to England. She had tried to keep her volunteers happy and to give each one work they were able to do and wanted to do.

Emerson began to tell Kitty how good she felt about participating in the children's camp project and how fun and rewarding it had been. She'd completely forgotten how she looked, how wet and unkempt she was. They sat down at the tea table and began to drink hot tea and eat sandwiches and cakes. Emerson was giving such an enthusiastic account of her past few days, she didn't notice that someone was standing behind her, listening intently to every word she had to say. Kitty noticed him, looked up, and smiled at the young man who stood behind Emerson. "Peter, you are finally here. I am so glad to see you and so grateful for everything you have done for us. Come and sit down, and we will tell Emerson our good news."

Peter walked around Emerson's chair and looked down at her riot of yellow curls and bright blue eyes. "Peter, this is my friend Emerson Cabot. She's from Connecticut. We met on the train earlier this week, and she has been doing carpentry work at the camp. She has just been telling me stories about how the work on the tent construction is progressing." Kitty could see the curiosity in Peter's eyes as he looked at Emerson.

"Emerson, this is Peter Mullens, the American diplomat whose praises I have been singing. Peter has been helping us with international law and Britain's pesky neutrality position. He has been working tirelessly to get authorization for the children to travel here from Spain." Kitty watched Peter as he put out his hand to shake Emerson's. Kitty could see that he was charmed by this young woman whose cheeks were red from the heat of the fire and who glowed with the joy of participating in a project that thrilled her.

"It is a pleasure to meet a fellow American, Emerson. Everyone here is grateful for your hard work and for taking time out of your life to help us build the camp in Eastleigh." He smiled down at Emerson and could not seem to take his eyes away from the somewhat disheveled and very lovely young woman. Kitty's eyes twinkled.

Emerson looked up as Peter spoke to her. He towered over her as he stood beside her chair and shook her hand. Emerson was caught completely off guard as she looked up into blue eyes much like her own. Peter's hair was dark, and he was dressed in a beautifully tailored dark gray suit. This was the elegant and cosmopolitan diplomat whom Kitty held in such high regard. Emerson might not have guessed Peter was an American had she not heard his soft Southern accent. Emerson thought he was simply gorgeous, but it was his smile that really captivated her. She could tell he was an awfully intelligent and serious man. But underneath his professional demeanor, she could sense he had a passion for life and would be fun to get to know. "It's a pleasure to meet you, Peter. You are a much more important cog in this wheel than I am. I'm just a worker bee, hammering away with wood and nails. I understand you have been trying to untangle the red tape that's been preventing our children from coming to England."

Peter sat down at the tea table, and Kitty smiled to herself as she poured tea for Peter and handed him the plate of sandwiches. She might as well not have even been there. She realized she was watching something quite special. At this moment, these two young people had eyes only for each other. One is rarely able to observe what might be called "love at first sight" as it is happening, but Kitty was pretty sure she was looking at that very thing right here and now, around this tea table.

Peter was from Virginia and was a Consular officer at the United States Embassy in London. Emerson told Peter she had grown up in Connecticut and gone to school in Massachusetts. A waiter interrupted them and said that Peter had a telephone call. Peter excused himself and went to take the call. Emerson wanted Kitty to tell her everything she knew about Peter. Kitty asked Emerson if there was any special man in her life. Emerson's eyes turned dark and sad for a moment. She said there had been — a long time ago, but there wasn't anyone now.

All of a sudden Emerson realized what a wreck she must look like. She exclaimed to Kitty about her appearance and stood up to excuse herself so she could go to her room. "Oh, dear, Kitty, I look a fright. What must Peter think of me — a bedraggled, soaking rat with a nest for hair?"

"You look marvelous, my dear, and Peter thinks you do as well."

"I need a bath and clean clothes and lipstick. I am going to my room this minute."

"I think Peter will be disappointed when he returns from his telephone call and finds that you aren't here."

"Tell him he can call me on the hotel telephone — if he ever wants to speak to my mess of a self again."

Kitty laughed as Emerson flew out of the hotel lounge. Peter came back from his telephone call, and the look of disappointment on his face was obvious when he realized Emerson was no longer there. "She said to call her on the hotel telephone if you ever wanted to talk to her again. She was embarrassed because she thought she looked terrible. I told her she looked perfectly lovely, but she went to her room to make repairs."

"She said I could call her on the hotel telephone? Of course, I want to talk to her again. Do you think she would have dinner with me tonight? How long do you think she is staying in Eastleigh? The camp is pretty much finished. Do you think I can convince her to stay longer?"

"I am certain she would love to have dinner with you tonight. And I think I have an idea about how I can talk her into staying a few more days. Leave that to me, Peter. Get on the telephone and call her room." Kitty did not believe in matchmaking, but in this instance she felt the match had already made itself. She just needed to lend a bit of a hand.

Chapter 4

NO ORDINARY EVENING

May 1937

Emerson stepped from the lift into the hotel lobby. "Here I am, Kitty. I am as ready as I'm ever going to be." Kitty almost gasped with surprise as the enchanting young woman greeted her. She almost didn't recognized Emerson. Kitty had only seen her in travel clothes and in work clothes. She had never seen Emerson dressed for dinner, with her hair composed, and with make-up on her face. Emerson wore a navy blue wool dress with a scoop neckline and long sleeves and a beautiful string of pearls that matched her pearl earrings. Emerson apologized for her flat shoes, saying she hadn't thought she would need heels on this trip and had only thrown in the navy blue dinner dress because one of her flat mates had said, "you never know."

"My dear, you look beautiful, just beautiful. The dress is lovely. Peter will be surprised to see how nicely you 'clean up' as you Americans like to say."

Emerson laughed and said she hoped Peter would notice a difference between the way she looked tonight and the way she had looked at tea that afternoon. Kitty and Emerson walked through the lobby and saw Peter sitting at a table in the hotel bar. Kitty was going to have a drink with Emerson and Peter before her dinner meeting with some government officials. There were papers to sign that would allow the *Habana* to leave port from the Spanish Coast and sail for England tomorrow. Kitty and Peter had a few details to work out before Kitty met with the powers that be. Even if she had not had a dinner meeting, Kitty would have found an excuse to leave Peter and Emerson alone for dinner.

Peter stood up and came to greet the women as they entered the bar. Peter could not take his eyes off Emerson who really did look splendid. Kitty hoped Peter would be able to focus on the business they had to take care of and was not entirely under the spell of the goddess in the navy blue dress. He took Kitty's hand and seated her at the table. Emerson seated herself and smiled at Peter.

"You look lovely – both of you look lovely tonight." He said to them, but his eyes were on Emerson alone.

"Peter, let's get down to it so you and Emerson can have a nice dinner. I will meet with my bureaucrats, and everything will be settled to clear the *Habana* to sail in the morning. You will be happy to know that I have finally found all of the money to satisfy the requirements of the British government. Each child will have a specified per diem to fund expenses, and it is the amount required to allow the children to come to Britain. Officials have had a tour of the camp and given their approval of the program we designed for taking care of the displaced little ones. Here is the list of our benefactors who have pledged money to pay the children's expenses. I have made a copy for you in case any of the legal proceedings get snarled."

Still smiling at Emerson, Peter took the papers from Kitty and said he was sure it was all in order. He asked what they wanted to drink and went to the bar to order for them. "Peter is a serious man, but I have rarely seen him completely speechless. Emerson, he is very taken with you. Please do me a favor and remind him to eat. He gets so caught up with a project that he forgets he needs to attend to mundane things like food."

"He is quite handsome isn't he? I hope he's not already taken by some brilliant, gorgeous deb from Virginia. That would be just my luck."

"I don't think you have to worry about that with Peter. I have known him for a few years, and he has never mentioned having a woman in his life."

Peter returned with their drinks, and they toasted to finally getting all the paperwork in order and all the construction work completed. They toasted the children who would be arriving in a few days. They toasted the volunteers and the benefactors who had made it all possible. Kitty packed up her briefcase and gave them each a peck on the cheek. "Have a wonderful dinner, my dears." She had a huge grin on her face as she walked back to the lobby and entered the meeting room of crusty old men whose favor she had to curry to get her project one step closer to success. She wondered from time to time what Emerson and Peter were talking about.

Peter and Emerson decided to dine in the hotel that evening. Somewhere after the soup and before the cheese course, they both realized this was no ordinary dinner date. They stayed talking at their table over coffee until the dining room staff finally had to politely ask them to leave as it was after midnight.

Emerson had decided she would take Kitty up on her offer to help with the children when they arrived at the camp. Peter had to return to London, but he promised he would be back for the weekend. He said good night to Emerson when he left her at the lift. He offered his hand, but Emerson ignored the handshake and put her arms around him and gave him an enthusiastic kiss. They held on to each other a little longer than was necessary, and the usually serious Peter had a big smile on his face as he left the hotel to return to London.

Chapter 5

ANNA GOES TO ENGLAND

MAY 1937

A nice young woman held Anna's hand as they boarded the Habana. The woman spoke Spanish and tried to engage her in conversation, but Anna remained silent as they found a spot on the overcrowded ship. The woman offered Anna a sandwich and an apple, but she did not take any of the food. Except when the friendly woman took her to the toilet, Anna stayed exactly where she had been put and never moved during the rough passage across the Bay of Biscay. Bad weather made many of the children and adults seasick, but Anna had not had anything to eat or drink and was not ill. When the ship finally docked, Anna's travel chaperone took her hand and led her off the ship to a bus that would take her and the others to the children's camp in Eastleigh, England.

Anna looked out the window of the bus and was surprised to see how green and beautiful this country called England was. She was moved from place to place and ate only when someone held the food up to her mouth and told her she had to eat. The sight of the white tents, one of which someone had told her would be her new home, led Anna to believe that she had finally died. Surely this city of beautiful round white structures was heaven, and she was thankful that she would soon see Bea and her mother and father. She wondered in which of the magnificent tents she would find her family. She was sure that God would reunite them all in the same tent.

Anna realized soon enough that she was still very much alive and was assigned a cot in one of the tents. Other girls who were about her same age came to the tent to find their own cots. The girls tried to talk to Anna. A few of them even spoke the Basque language, but Anna stared straight ahead and seemed not to notice that anyone was speaking to her. Anna was bathed and given new clothing, and a doctor examined her. A nurse, who accompanied the doctor on his rounds, read from a file and explained that Anna was mute and perhaps also deaf as she had not spoken to anyone since she had been taken from the streets of Guernica. The doctor suspected that her mutism did not have any organic origin but was probably a result of the trauma she had endured. Anna was not the only child in the camp who would not speak.

The next day, a young woman with curly yellow hair and a big smile came to Anna's tent and brought a picture book and a folding chair so that she could sit beside Anna's cot. "Hello, Anna. My name is Emerson, and I'm going to read you a story. I don't know much Spanish, and I'm sorry that I don't know any of the Basque language. But I am going to read from a book with lots of pictures. Even though I will be reading to you in English, maybe we can communicate through the pictures." Emerson realized she needed to know more Spanish to be able to have even the slightest chance of getting through to this sad and silent child. Emerson had learned a little conversational

Spanish during the summer she'd spent in Mexico when she was at boarding school. She promised herself that she would study her Spanish vocabulary and try to find out more about Anna's life.

Emerson had read the file that the camp had on Anna's history. They were taking the word of a local priest in Guernica that her name was even Anna. The scarce information in her file said that Anna's whole family had been killed in Guernica during the attack by the German Luftwaffe's Condor Legion. It said that Anna had tried to save the life of her younger sister and had carried her sister's dead body through the town to try to find their parents. A priest had pried Anna's small hands away from her sister's corpse. When Anna found out that her home had been destroyed and that her parents as well as her little sister were dead, she had screamed for hours. Then she had become completely silent. She had not spoken again since that terrible day. After reading the story of Anna's tragedy, Emerson vowed that she would learn enough Spanish to be able to speak to Anna in a language the little girl could understand. More than anything Emerson wanted to be able to break through Anna's silence and bring her back to the world of the living.

Peter spoke several languages – Spanish, French, and Portuguese among them. Peter and Emerson were spending as much time together as they could manage, and Peter found a Spanish tutor who could help Emerson learn Spanish more quickly. Emerson returned to Oxford and her studies during the week, and every Thursday evening she took the train to North Stoneham to spend time with the children. She found she was putting more hours into learning Spanish than she was studying political economy. She bought children's books with simple Spanish words to read to Anna. Emerson read to several other children during her weekends at the camp, but the always silent Anna was the challenge Emerson was determined to turn into a success. Weekend after weekend Emerson sat beside Anna's cot and read to her. She sometimes would take Anna's small hand in hers and just sit there with her in silence.

"I know you are terribly sad because you have lost your family," Emerson said slowly and carefully to Anna — in Spanish. Emerson had practiced her short speech with her language tutor and was anxious to see if she could reach Anna by sharing some of her own personal story. "I know how it feels to lose your family. My own mother and father were killed in an automobile accident when I was nineteen. I've never had a brother or a sister. When I heard that my parents were dead, I wanted to die and thought I would die. I didn't think I would ever be able to find a reason to live again. So I understand something about how you are feeling."

Emerson thought Anna moved just a little when she told her about her own family tragedy. Emerson kept on with her Spanish words. "Finally, I realized that my parents would not have wanted me to give up on living. I knew they would want me to think about the life I had ahead of me. I tried so hard to find reasons to think of the future. I tried to think about what I could do with my life, rather than always thinking about what I had lost. I am sure your parents would also want you to find a reason to embrace your life and your future. They would want you to speak."

Emerson had not tried to hug Anna before because the doctors had warned her and the other caretakers against it. But Emerson realized she herself needed the comfort of a hug after telling Anna the story of her own loss. When she put her arms around Anna, Emerson could not keep her own tears from flowing. She rarely spoke about the loss of her parents and the emotional devastation it had brought her at the age of nineteen. She verbalized it now only in a foreign language to a little girl who had suffered her own unspeakable loss and who Emerson was not sure could even hear her, let alone understand her. Emerson had not realized the impact that giving her speech to Anna in Spanish would have on her own psyche. She sobbed as she held onto Anna. Anna slowly reached for Emerson's hand and squeezed it. Emerson squeezed back. They had found a common bond in their sorrow.

Chapter 6

I AM A JEW

1937-1939

Maximillian Meyerhof had grown up in Frankfurt, Germany as the son of an influential rabbi with a large congregation. Max's father Joachim had realized early in Hitler's rise what a threat the Nazis were to all the German people, but especially to the Jews. Joachim had read Mein Kampf and urged Max to read it. Max's father told him that evil people like Hitler almost always tell you ahead of time what they intend to do. A man of conviction and courage, the rabbi had spoken out quite publicly against the Nazis— to the congregation at his synagogue and to the wider Jewish community in Frankfurt and in Germany. Rabbi Meyerhof had authored several anti-Nazi articles for Jewish publications.

After the Nazis enacted the Nuremberg Laws of 1935, all Jews in Germany were negatively impacted by the things that Rabbi Meyerhof had been telling them would happen. Rabbi Joachim Meyerhof, in addition to being a wise teacher, took on the almost mystical persona of one who could foresee the future. The Jewish community listened, and the rabbi became even more outspoken. Jews began to liquidate their property and leave Frankfurt. The Rabbi's family and congregation urged him to leave Germany, but Joachim was a determined man. His wife might even have said he was a stubborn man. He refused to leave the country he loved, and he refused to dampen the fervor of his words of warning to his fellow Jews about the intentions of the Nazis.

The Gestapo had visited him at his synagogue and warned him not to speak out against the National Socialist government, that he was placing himself and his family in danger with his criticism of Hitler. Joachim's family discussed what options they might have. Max, his two younger sisters, and their mother had decided that their first choice would be for all five of them to leave Germany together. They knew Joachim would not leave, and they did not want to leave without him. They admired the rabbi's courage and his self-imposed mission to speak out against evil. The entire family agreed that they would support his decision to stay in Germany. The rabbi continued to fight with his words.

Unbeknownst to the children, Joachim, at great cost, had obtained French passports for the entire family — himself included. If things became too threatening, they could all leave Frankfurt and go to France. The rabbi decided to share the secret of the French passports with his son Max and showed him where the precious documents were hidden in a secret compartment in the bookcase of the rabbi's study. Also in that secret place were packets of German, French, and British currency, along with information about significant family money which had been transferred to several banks in America — in case the Meyerhofs ever needed to start their lives over again in a new country.

One day while the family was having tea together, the Gestapo had burst into their home and killed everyone in the family except Max who was just nineteen years old at the time. Max's little sisters were tortured before being murdered. Max escaped certain death by jumping through the second story window of his home. While making his escape, he was shot in the arm and thigh. In spite of being badly wounded, he was able, against all odds, to outrun and hide from his pursuers. Dr. Jacob Engelman, the Meyerhof's family physician, secretly treated Max's gunshot wounds and saved his life when Max developed a deadly infection.

Max and Dr. Engelman escaped together from Germany with the help of a friend who had been a Catholic all his life but who had been reclassified as a Jew because he had a grandmother who might have been born a Jew. Max and Dr. Engelman escaped to Belgium and lived there during the last months of 1937 and the first part of 1938. Max had sustained permanent damage to his arm because of the gunshot wound. The physical therapy Dr. Engelman had insisted on had given him back almost full use of his damaged leg. No matter how hard he tried, he would never be able to recover full use of his right arm. The most difficult part of Max's recovery was not coping with his physical disabilities. Max struggled to come to terms with the loss of his family and the horrifying brutality that had surrounded their deaths. Max woke up in the middle of the night screaming and crying, and it took everything Dr. Engelman could do to bring Max back to sanity from his own personal hell.

A young man of only nineteen when his family was murdered, Max was determined to exact revenge for his loved ones by devoting the rest of his life to fighting the Nazis in every possible way he could find to fight them. Max had always wanted to go to sea, but he'd never thought he would have the chance to pursue that kind of career. Fluent in three languages, Max's education had been a strictly classical and intellectual one. If his life had turned out differently, he would have become a college professor or a rabbi like his father.

Max was excellent in math and understood business with an instinct unusual for someone so young. Max became obsessed with the idea that he wanted to sail on a tramp steamer or a cargo ship and to learn all he could about the shipping business. He eventually wanted to own and run his own shipping empire. The idealistic Max wanted to deliver Jews to Palestine on his fleet of ships. Max recognized better than most the importance of moving Jews out of Germany. He pushed himself "to get on with his life."

Dr. Engelman was anxious to get on with his own life and had been offered a position at a hospital in London. He was reluctant to leave Max until Max was ready to live on his own. Max was still a young and somewhat vulnerable young man, but he was extraordinarily intelligent and committed to his life's plan. When Max was able to secure a position on a cargo ship, the decision was finally made for Dr. Engelman. They said tearful goodbyes. They promised to stay in touch and to reunite after Hitler had been destroyed. They knew, as did everyone in Europe who would open his or her eyes, that war was on the horizon.

Max held a French passport that said his name was Maximillian Boudreaux. That was the name he had assumed in Belgium and the name he adopted as his business name for the future. Max legally changed his last name to Boudreaux and became a Frenchman. He left Maximillian Meyerhof behind forever. Dr. Jacob Engelman and Max Boudreaux went their separate ways. These two Jewish refugees were the lucky ones. Most of the millions of other Jews who could not leave Europe would not be as lucky as they had been.

Max lied to the Captain of the Portuguese cargo ship, the *Coracao de Anjo*, the ship on which he took his first job at sea. Max lied about his age and about his experience. Max talked a good game and learned fast. He convinced Captain Breno Sousa that he could do the job. In fact, Max had been hired to do difficult physical work aboard the *Anjo*. Partly because of his permanently disabled arm and partly because of his youth and inexperience, the lifting and the long hours were almost impossible for Max. He struggled to keep up with the seasoned sailors who had been doing hard labor for years. But he never complained, and he pushed himself to do what was required of him — until he became exhausted to the point of becoming ill. Max's first voyage was from Antwerp to Lisbon, not a particularly long run. Captain Sousa was impressed with Max's determination and how quickly he learned, but it did not take long for him to realize that Max was not the experienced sailor he had claimed to be.

Max was taken off the ship in Lisbon and cared for at the home of the ship's Captain. A gruff and tough but kind man, Breno Sousa saw something in Max and decided the boy was worth saving and encouraging. Sousa's wife, Inez, cared for Max until he recovered from the pneumonia that had almost killed him. Max began to learn Portuguese during his convalescence, and he never gave up on his dream of returning to sea. Captain Sousa did not know Max's reason for being so determined to become a sailor, but he talked to Max about training for a position on board a ship so he would not have to lift heavy cargo. It was obvious that Max was intelligent and well-educated, and Sousa encouraged him to study to become a navigator. Even when Max was eventually well enough to return to the ship, Sousa encouraged him to continue his navigation training. Sousa's own navigator was nearing retirement age, and Sousa promised the position to

Max when that time came. Max lived with Sousa's family and continued his studies.

The Captain took Max under his wing to teach him what Max so desperately wanted to learn — everything there was to know about ships and the shipping business. Max was determined to learn to be the best navigator who sailed the Atlantic and the Mediterranean. This career path seemed the only possible way he would ever get back onto a ship as a member of the crew. Sousa talked to Max about what it took to become the captain of a ship. When the *Anjo* was in port, he took Max on board the *Anjo* and showed him how to operate the ship and steer from the bridge. He taught Max how to negotiate for and load cargo, hire crew, and do all the things a ship's captain needed to know. Max, always a quick learner, eagerly absorbed every piece of this valuable knowledge.

When Sousa was away from port on a cruise, Max continued studying to become a navigator. He also began to spend time hanging out at the Lisbon docks and keeping his eyes and ears open. He was anxious to understand the intricacies of the shipping business and how to bid on and secure cargoes and all the other machinations, financial and personal, that were required to be a success in this complicated arena. Always an avid reader, Max studied everything he could about navigation as well as about shipping and international finance. He became fluent in Portuguese, his fourth foreign language. He decided he needed to learn Spanish as well, since Spain was so close to Portugal.

Captain Sousa did a great deal of business with Spain even though the Spanish Civil War had been going on for years. When that war finally ended, Sousa's ship visited Spanish ports more frequently. Finally, Max convinced Captain Sousa that he was ready, and the young man was thrilled to be able to accompany the *Anjo* on its next voyage out of Lisbon.

The date of departure for his first stint as the ship's junior navigator was set for September 1, 1939. Max had worked hard to prepare himself and was eager to embrace his new life. But the beginning of another war was destined to drastically changed Max's world again. The Nazis invaded Poland, and German U-boats were everywhere at sea, hiding and causing trouble wherever they could find a ship to sink.

Chapter 7

GOING HOME TO PORTUGAL

1938

Emerson and Peter had known each other for only a few months, but they were in love. There was no reason why they shouldn't marry. Peter was thirty and Emerson was twenty-five. Emerson was finishing her studies at Oxford, and the decision was finally made for them when Peter found he was to be posted to Lisbon for his next diplomatic tour. Peter had a large extended family living in Virginia, but Emerson had no family living anywhere. They decided to be married in London. Peter went on ahead to take up his new posting at the U.S. Embassy in Lisbon and find a place for the newlywed couple to live in Portugal.

Emerson knew that Peter's family was well-to-do, just as Peter knew that Emerson came from a wealthy family. They had never really talked about their finances, and it didn't seem to be an issue until Peter began looking for a house to buy. He wrote enthusiastic letters to Emerson about how much he loved the area outside Lisbon — especially a town called Setubal. Peter wanted Emerson to come to Setubal. He wanted Emerson to see the place he had fallen in love with and hoped to buy for them. Emerson told him she trusted whatever choice he made and that she wanted to be surprised. And indeed, she would be surprised when she finally arrived at her new home, a home which could accurately be described as a palace.

While Peter was buying an estate in Portugal and getting settled into his new position at the embassy, Emerson finished her exams at Oxford and arranged for their wedding. She missed Peter when he was away and couldn't wait to be married. Peter had written to his family in Virginia and told them all about Emerson. They knew that Emerson had no family living in the States and understood why Peter and Emerson wanted to be married at a simple ceremony in London.

War in Europe was an ever-present threat, but Peter's parents wanted to make the trip to England for their son's wedding. With Neville Chamberlain and Adolph Hitler carving up Czechoslovakia during the summer of 1938, Peter's parents took a risk that there would not be a war and that the *Queen Mary* would indeed sail in August.

Rachel Friedman Goodwin, Emerson's dearest friend and roommate from Smith College, lived in Boston with her husband who was in rabbinical school. Rachel was writing the dissertation for her Ph.D. in psychology at Harvard. Emerson had been the maid of honor at their wedding three years earlier and wanted more than anything for Rachel to come to London for her wedding. But luck would have it that Rachel was four months pregnant with her first child, and because of complications with the pregnancy, she'd been told by her physician that she was not allowed to travel. Rachel was terribly disappointed to miss the wedding. Emerson had wanted her dearest friend in all the world to share this important event with her. They had written each other at least twice a week since their graduation from college. They were now separated by the Atlantic Ocean, but they remained as close as sisters. Emerson knew that Rachel would be with her in spirit on her wedding day when she married Peter Mullens.

Emerson arranged for their wedding to take place at an Anglican chapel in Mayfair. Peter's family had visited London in the past and always made their reservations to stay at Claridge's Hotel. Emerson decided that the reception following the wedding would be held at Claridge's. Peter had told Emerson that his parents were the antithesis of ostentatious and did not enjoy anything that was overly elaborate or fussy.

Emerson and Peter met his parents and his younger sister, Alice, who had also decided to make the trip, when they arrived in Southampton, England in late August of 1938. Emerson had known ahead of time that she would like Peter's family. She realized that anyone who had raised and had been an influence on the character of the wonderful person she had fallen in love with would be extraordinarily kind. Peter's parents were delighted with their new future daughter-in-law, and Peter's sister immediately bonded with Emerson.

No one who was with the couple for even a few minutes could doubt that they adored each other. There was an electricity between them that said to anyone who was watching that these two were star struck lovers. Peter was tall and serious with dark hair, and Emerson was small and talkative with blonde hair. They made a handsome pair, and their happiness seemed to embrace everyone who was around them. Peter's parents were especially thrilled to see that Emerson was able to make Peter laugh and relax. They had never seen their serious and ambitious son so happy.

Peter and Emerson invited Kitty to their wedding. If it had not been for Kitty, the two would never have met. They were eternally grateful to her for their good luck. They were privileged to know this extraordinary women. Kitty was proud of herself for introducing these two Yanks and was thrilled to be included as a guest at their wedding. Emerson's flat mates and a few special friends of Peter's from the American Embassy were invited.

On a gloriously sunny morning in early September, Emerson and Peter were married at the chapel in Mayfair. Emerson wore a floor length, white silk wedding gown with long sleeves and a long train. She had splurged on her dress, and the lace inserts in the bodice resulted in a creation that was the perfect blend of tradition and up-to-date elegance – much like Emerson herself. Her cathedral length Portuguese lace veil was a gift from Peter. Peter was speechless when he saw Emerson walking down the aisle. He was amazed that this breathtakingly beautiful creature had agreed to be his bride. The wedding ceremony was short, and the luncheon reception afterwards at Claridge's was elegant and simple.

Emerson and Peter caught the boat train from London to Paris for their honeymoon. Peter was taking leave that was due to him — in spite of the critical international situation which had all diplomats and all countries on edge. The couple was gloriously happy to be together. Because of the Civil War in Spain, it was not advisable to travel through that country, and commercial aircraft would not fly over Spain. The newlyweds made their way to Lisbon from Paris by way of the train to Marseilles and then by plane from Marseilles to Lisbon. It was a long, circuitous, and somewhat arduous trip. After traveling all day, Emerson and Peter spent their first night in Portugal at a hotel in Lisbon.

Emerson was anxious to see her new home, and Peter could hardly wait to show it to her. The next morning a hired car drove them to Setubal. The countryside was glorious on this September day. Finally, as they drove through a grove of dense trees, a large stone palacio appeared. Emerson did not suspect that this was the 16th century quinta that Peter had purchased, an estate called Bacalhoa. She was stunned when the car stopped, and she realized this ancient and imposing building which stood in front of her was her new home.

Chapter 8

BACALHOA

1938

Bacalhoa had been built by the King of Portugal for his mother. It definitely was not a small place, not at all the "cottage" that Emerson might have envisioned. It came with acres of grounds, a vineyard, and a glorious garden with a huge pool in the center. A wall, that must have been built originally for protection, surrounded the palacio and the gardens. Made of stucco and stone, the wall had been mended and repaired repeatedly over the years, but it enclosed Bacalhoa in a way that made those inside feel secure from whatever might be happening in the rest of the world.

Emerson knew the estate came with servants, and having had a glimpse of the size of her new home, she wondered how many people were required to keep this house and these grounds in such wonderful condition. It was truly a magnificent, even a magical place. Emerson was overwhelmed with the grandeur of it all. Peter was so delighted with the property he had bought for their first home together, how could she fail to be thrilled as well? "I thought your family wasn't into fancy and elaborate," Emerson was honestly wondering.

"Emerson, this place has tremendous history. How often does one get to live in a home that was built before Columbus set sail for America? When you see the inside, you will fall in love with it."

"Peter, it is truly amazing, without question, and I love it even before seeing the inside, of course, because you love it. But it is just the two of us, and it is so much more than we really need. I am quite breathless."

"After seeing what happened to those children from Spain, I decided I was going to carpe diem and live a more expansive life than I have in the past. Knowing you has taught me how to love with great passion, and I fell passionately in love with this place. I want us to have a long and full life here and bring lots of children into the world. I want to fill up all the bedrooms." Even as he was saying this, the small wrinkle in Peter's forehead might have gone unnoticed in the presence of his enormous smile. Emerson saw the fleeting element of worry in his face but decided it was because he was afraid she wouldn't like Bacalhoa.

"Can we afford to live in a castle or a palace or whatever this is? I cannot even imagine how much this must have cost."

"Of course we can afford it. I am the most prudent of men when it comes to finances. I consider this place an investment as well as a place to live. I am investing in the future of Portugal. Even if I am posted to another country in my career, we will always have Bacalhoa as our home." Peter continued telling Emerson about their quinta. "It was built during the transition from Medieval to Renaissance architecture and therefore has style characteristics of both periods." He went on and on as they climbed the stairs to the main entrance. "It even has its own chapel off the master bedroom suite."

"Peter, living in the country is going to be marvelous, but what about your work at the embassy? It took more than an hour for us to drive here from Lisbon. We had to wait for the ferry to cross the Tagus. You will have to drive *at least* two hours every day just going to and from work. Is living in Setubal worth that?"

"I have considered the long drive and have decided it will actually work to my advantage. I have a driver and a car, and I will be able to do two hours' worth of work undisturbed by any person or by the telephone. I will get more done during those two hours of the day than I will get done in all the rest of the hours that I spend in my office at the embassy. If I have an early meeting, I can eat breakfast in the car. It is more than worth it to me to be able to live at Bacalhoa." Peter was adamant. Peter was in love.

Peter swept Emerson into his arms and pushed open the heavy front door as he carried her over the threshold of their new home. Emerson decided she would love this enormous pile of stone no matter what condition it was in and no matter what the heating bill turned out to be. She knew she was married to the most wonderful man in the world, and that was all that mattered to her. Peter was brave to decide to invest in Portugal. It was a relatively poor country compared to other European nations. It shared all of its land borders with Spain which had been fighting a horrible civil war for the past several years. If wise and careful Peter was willing to take a risk and buy this Portuguese landmark, how could she fail to fall in love with the place?

Emerson was once again overwhelmed when Peter gently put her down so that she was standing on her own two feet. The entrance hall was huge. It had stone floors and walls, and there were hand-painted tile accents on the walls of the sparsely furnished room. "The quinta comes with some furnishings which I bought when I bought the property, but we will need to buy some additional pieces and do a good amount of sprucing up with slipcovers and draperies and such."

"How do you know about things like 'slipcovers and draperies and such,' Peter? I thought you were all business and not a homebody at all."

"You underestimate me, darling. I know many things about many things. But right now I'm tired. Let's have our lunch and take a nap."

They entered the dining room, which in itself was a work of art, and Bacalhoa's nine servants stood there, lined up in a row beside the table to meet Emerson. Peter seemed to know them all and was delighted to introduce his new wife to the staff. They were smiling and nodding their heads. Emerson shook hands with each one, smiled, and said "Bom Dia" as she repeated each name. The woman at the head of the line spoke to Peter in Portuguese. Emerson's Spanish language tutor at Oxford also knew Portuguese, and when Peter had received his posting to Portugal, Emerson had begun to learn Portuguese. Even though it was a Romance language like Spanish, it had been more difficult for Emerson to learn.

"Magdalena says you are even more beautiful than I told her you were. She said you look like an angel with your halo of golden hair. Magdalena is the housekeeper and speaks English. She doesn't think her English is very good, and she is looking forward to practicing it with you. You will be spending more time with her than with anyone else on the staff."

Magdalena was about thirty-five years old and small and slim with olive-colored skin and dark eyes. Her black hair was streaked with the slightest hint of white and was drawn tightly back from her face into an intricate knot arranged at her neck. She wore a black skirt and a beautifully embroidered starched white blouse. She looked quite professional. Emerson could tell that Magdalena was intelligent and had everything and everybody at the house under control. She and the housekeeper would get along just fine.

"Please tell Magdalena and everyone else that they are to speak to me in Portuguese. I want to learn the language which is spoken in the country where I have chosen to make my home. I will make lots of mistakes, but the best way for me to become proficient in Portuguese is to speak it as much as possible. I am honored to meet each one of these people who work so hard to keep Bacalhoa running in good shape." In addition to Magdalena, Emerson met Benadina, the cook; three housemaids; a laundress; and three gardeners. Peter explained that there were additional outside workers who took care of the animals and worked in the vineyard and at the farm.

"Animals? Vineyard? Farm? What have we gotten ourselves into, Peter? What kinds of animals?"

"A few chickens and goats and sheep. Some pigs, cows. Nothing big. But there is a barn where we could keep a few horses if you want to ride."

"Let's eat lunch and take that nap. This is a lot for me to absorb all at once." Emerson nodded and smiled as Peter dismissed the servants to go back to their work. It seemed that Magdalena also served the food at the table, and she asked them to be seated. The table was long and could easily seat at least eighteen or twenty or more. The table was covered with the most beautiful white tablecloth Emerson had ever seen. She touched the hem of the cloth and appreciated the feel of the fabric. Two places at one end of the table had been set with many pieces of heavy silver flatware and several wine glasses. Magdalena spoke to Peter, and he translated for Emerson.

"Magdalena wanted us to have our first meal in the dining room. She realizes that with just the two of us, we may not want to eat every meal at such a large table. She says that in good weather we will probably want to enjoy most of our meals together on the covered loggia."

Magdalena brought cold tomato soup with small pieces of cucumber and tomato and cubes of bread in it. It was nicely seasoned, and Emerson said she could have this soup every day for lunch. Magdalena was pleased and said she would pass the compliments along to Benadina who took great pride in the meals she prepared. The next course was potato salad and grilled prawns which were enormous and delicious in their lemony sauce. Emerson, who had eaten bland Connecticut potato salad all of her life, wondered how the Portuguese cook had transformed this dish into something special and incredibly delicious. There was a flan with fresh fruit, a salad course, and finally cheese and crackers. "I can't eat like this for lunch every day, Peter. I am so full right now I think I will burst. All I want to do is lie down and go to sleep." Emerson made sure that Magdalena knew how much she had enjoyed the delicious meal. Magdalena said a few words to Peter.

"Magdalena guessed that you enjoyed your lunch because you didn't leave one bite in any bowl or on any plate." Peter laughed, and Emerson so loved to hear him laugh. "It won't be like this every day. The cook and Magdalena wanted to prepare something special for our first meal here at Bacalhoa ... as a kind of celebration. Benadina wanted to show off some of her cooking skills. You and Magdalena and Benadina will plan all the meals from now on, if you want to do that. Let's have a tour of the rest of the quinta and then take our nap."

The lounge opened off the front hall and also opened into the dining room. Americans would call this lounge the living room. It was a long and elegantly appointed room. There were some wonderful antique pieces of furniture as well as several overstuffed pieces, most of which were in need of refurbishing. One bedroom wing held four large bedrooms and two somewhat modern bathrooms. The other wing held the library, an office, and the master bedroom suite with its sitting room, a large bathroom, a dressing room, and even a small chapel off the bedroom.

Although it was a palacio and quite grand, the scale of the rooms was not so huge that they felt cold or intimidating. The ceilings were high, but something about the proportions of the rooms or the way they were furnished scaled them down to human size. Emerson felt the warmth of the castle during her first tour and realized she did not have to worry about living in a drafty, unwelcoming place. When they finally reached the master bedroom with its large and welcoming bed, Emerson was more than ready to collapse. Peter was worn out as well. Emerson was surprised that he was also ready for a nap as he had always seemed to have more energy than she did. Usually when she was ready to quit, he still wanted to go and go and keep on going. She was glad he was willing to slow down today.

While Emerson was in the dressing room changing out of her travel clothes, someone had quietly turned the bedspread back. Their bed was beautifully made with fine, white embroidered Portuguese linens. Emerson had never seen bed linens as lovely as these and ran her hands over the strong, soft linen fibers. She could tell the sheets had been laundered many times, to make them as soft to the touch as they were. The embroidery and cut work on the bedspread was as exceptional as the work and attention to detail she had so cherished in her wedding dress.

Peter was already sound asleep in the bed when Emerson lay down beside him. They slept most of the afternoon. The newlyweds woke as the sun was going down and made love for the first time in their new home. They were still tired from traveling, and Peter asked to have dinner brought to the sitting room of their bedroom suite. Emerson realized that she was going to have to become accustomed to a very different life here in Portugal. There was a new language, a new house — if you could call it a house, all the new servants whose names she was trying so hard to remember, new food, new bedlinens, new everything. Her new husband was the only thing that was familiar to her in this foreign place where she had landed.

Emerson wrote long letters to Rachel every day and eagerly awaited the post that brought Rachel's letters to her. There was so much to tell Rachel about her life in this beautiful but remarkably comfortable home. Emerson told her friend that it all might have completely overwhelmed her if she had not felt so safe with Peter. Emerson shared stories of her insecurities and embarrassment as she learned to deal with her servants. People in the United States had help in their homes, but most people did not have a large staff of servants. Emerson was intimidated by the expectation that she would run this large palace and know what to say to all of these people who worked for her.

Rachel's letters to Emerson were full of anticipation over the birth of her child and the difficulties of her pregnancy. She said her obstetrician had told her she might be having twins. Rachel's life had understandably become focused around the new baby or babies she would be bringing into the world. She wrote about moving to her own larger home and decorating the nursery. She talked about baby names and how she was searching for the perfect nursemaid to help her when the baby arrived. Emerson wished Rachel were closer so that they could see each other, but their friendship sustained them both as they adapted to the changes and the challenges in their lives.

Chapter 9

WAR IS COMING

1938

War in Europe was coming, and it was coming soon. As destructive as the war in Spain had been, when the rest of Europe finally went to war, it would be many times more terrible. One day at the end of September, shortly after Emerson had arrived in Portugal, Peter came home early from his job as a consular officer at the United States Embassy in Lisbon. He was as down as his new wife had ever seen him. Peter almost always had a positive attitude, even when conditions in the world looked terribly bleak.

This particular day, Peter had just received word that Neville Chamberlain, Britain's Prime Minister, had given the Sudetenland to the Nazis and had declared "Peace for our time." The Czechs had not even been allowed to participate in the negotiations that had decided the fate of their own country. Peter was furious and discouraged. He had been working very hard with the American diplomatic team to pressure Chamberlain to be tough and stand up to Hitler. In the end, Chamberlain had given in to Hitler's bullying. To believe that Chamberlain would do otherwise had probably been a fools' errand from the start, although, of course, Peter hated to believe himself a fool. Several times Peter had stayed overnight in Lisbon talking to Washington and London on transatlantic telephone calls and sending and receiving cables. He came home to Bacalhoa on October 1, 1938 and collapsed on the couch in his study.

Emerson was concerned at this uncharacteristic behavior and brought hot tea and some of Benadina's shortbread cookies. She wanted Peter to talk to her and not just brood in his study and ignore her. "He is a thug and he is evil and he is bent on destroying Europe." Peter sounded disgusted and desperate. "He won't stop with the Sudetenland. He has already taken back the Rhineland and gobbled up Austria like it was an hors d'oeuvre. He won't stop until all of Europe is ablaze. What can the Americans possibly do to stop this world war from coming? Portugal will try to remain neutral, so it will be an important place for diplomacy. But I don't see any way of stopping this madman Hitler except with a horrible war."

Emerson had never seen Peter so distraught. His face was gray, and he looked as if he hadn't slept in days and weeks. "Peter, you have been working way too many long hours, and you need to rest. Kitty warned me that you sometimes forget about food and sleep because you become so serious about your work. I promised her I would be sure that you remembered to eat and rest. I have failed in my promise to Kitty. You will not be any good to anyone, if you don't take care of yourself. You are going to go to bed right now and go to sleep. You and I are going to the boathouse for a picnic tomorrow. You are not allowed to go in to work for at least three days."

In addition to the grounds and gardens that surrounded Bacalhoa, there was the farm that belonged to Bacalhoa.

The farm was a mile farther out in the countryside. There were also property rights that included a small piece of beach on the Atlantic coast. Many of the castles and palaces in Portugal came with non-contiguous waterfront properties. In addition to the small cove with its beach, Bacalhoa had a boathouse and a boat of some kind. Emerson and Peter had not yet had a chance to fully explore their beach real estate. Peter had seen it before he bought the quinta, but Emerson had never been there. She was anxious to visit the cove and the boathouse. She needed a change of scenery for herself and a day away for Peter.

Emerson got her picnic the next day, and she and Peter laughed together as they explored the beach and the dilapidated boathouse that sat beside a small tidal cove on the Atlantic Ocean. They even tried to start the outboard motor on the boat that must have been sitting abandoned in the boathouse for a decade. There was no gasoline in the engine, and even after filling it with gas, the engine would not start. It would take some serious work to get the old boat up and running. They had their picnic by the water and made love on the blanket before they fell asleep. As they were packing up the car to drive back to Bacalhoa, one of their gardeners came cycling down the lane from the main road. He had ridden his bicycle all the way from the quinta to tell Peter to come back at once for a telephone call. So much for Emerson's imposed days of rest.

When Peter heard that he had an emergency telephone call, his shoulders slumped visibly. He knew it would not be good news at the other end of the telephone line. They loaded the bicycle, the picnic basket, and the blankets into the car, and all three hurried back to Bacalhoa where Peter made the telephone call. He was going to have to go to the embassy for meetings. He still looked so tired, and Emerson was terribly worried about his lack of energy since they'd arrived at Bacalhoa. Peter allowed the worries of the world to become his own personal worries. His engagement in and his intense concern about current affairs was one of the reasons Emerson loved him, but it was also a terrible strain on Peter and on their relationship —especially now that war was threatening to erupt.

When she accepted that Peter was going to be spending more and more of his time in Lisbon, Emerson decided to take on the project of refurbishing her home to make it more modern and more to her taste. She loved the stone walls and floors and the colorful Portuguese tiles. Each room had gorgeous rugs which must have been made to order for the large rooms. But the bathrooms all needed updating. Emerson made plans to have some family furniture shipped from her home in Connecticut. She arranged to have the good pieces in the palacio reupholstered and slipcovered. She ordered new draperies made for some of the rooms and shopped for lamps and other things to make the place her own.

She hoped it would cheer Peter to see her enjoying and working on their home. New upholstery and new colors would make the rooms more cheerful and welcoming. Emerson needed a project, and she threw herself into redecorating her surroundings. She enjoyed giving her large and beautiful home a makeover, but she worried all the time about Peter who could not seem to tear himself away from his responsibilities at work.

One of Peter's jobs as the embassy's consular officer was to issue visas to people who wanted to travel to the United States. There were the daily refugees from Spain who poured into Portugal to escape the destruction of the civil war and wanted to continue to travel on to the U.S. There were Portuguese citizens who were anxious to go to the U.S. to live with relatives who had already emigrated. There were those who wished to cross the Atlantic to try to make their fortunes in the New World. In addition to going to the never-ending meetings during which American diplomats and diplomats from other nations talked and talked about what they were going to do to put a stop to Adolph Hitler, Peter had his usual work of deciding who would be granted U.S. visas and who would not. His days were so filled with crisis meetings that he brought most of his regular visa work home to Bacalhoa and did that work in the evenings in his office next to their bedroom. He pretended to show some interest in the work Emerson was doing with the house, but she could tell his heart wasn't in it.

It was already late October, and Emerson was organizing an American Thanksgiving dinner for the few new friends they had made in Setubal. Peter was going to invite some colleagues from the embassy. Emerson and Peter had attended a few formal parties at the American Embassy, but Emerson was not really fond of formality and embassy protocol. She wanted to support Peter in everything he did, so she gracefully and cheerfully attended whenever Peter asked her to accompany him to these events.

Peter's parents and sister had been touring the British Isles and Scandinavia since Emerson and Peter's wedding and were coming to Bacalhoa to visit for several weeks before returning home to America. They would be guests at the quinta during the Thanksgiving holiday. Emerson wanted most of her "sprucing up" to be finished before they arrived.

Magdalena was enthusiastic about the new fabrics and furniture that gradually made their appearances in the rooms at Bacalhoa. Emerson often asked Magdalena's opinions about what colors and patterns to select. Magdalena had excellent taste and could recommend which designs were in keeping with Bacalhoa's style and would fit in with the traditional styles of Portugal. Emerson's language skills were improving, and she was thrilled to be able to speak a few words to her servants about their duties.

One evening in early November, Peter was especially upset when he returned from Lisbon. The night before, in Germany, the Nazis had destroyed Jewish businesses, homes, and synagogues and had arrested hundreds of Jews for no reason at all in cities all over that country. The Nazis had tried to pretend this "night of broken glass," which was being called Kristallnacht, had been a spontaneous outpouring of anger by the German people against the Jews. Everyone knew this wasn't true, and Peter was discouraged because there was really nothing anyone could do to stop the crimes against humanity that the Nazis were committing inside their own country.

It became clear that, after annexing the Sudetenland, Hitler was going to take the rest of Czechoslovakia. It seemed there was nothing that could be done to stop him. Peter could not imagine that any country really wanted a war, but he told Emerson that the British and the French felt that war against Hitler appeared to be inevitable. He told her that sooner or later the Americans would be into it as well. Peter drank several glasses of port after their dinner that night and fell asleep with his head down on his office desk. Emerson understood Peter's feeling of powerlessness because she also felt powerless. There was nothing she could do or say to help ease her husband's fears and fury over the deteriorating situation in Europe.

Emerson had asked that one of the Bacalhoa farm's turkeys be fattened up for the Thanksgiving feast. She also had ordered a special ham for the dinner and had collaborated closely with Benadina about the Thanksgiving menu. It was to be a combination of American traditional foods and Portuguese favorites. The number of guests was growing, and soon all twenty seats at the dining room table were promised. It would be Peter and Emerson's first dinner party as well as their first time to entertain Peter's parents.

Emerson taught her cook to make sweet potato biscuits and pecan pie, and Benadina was thrilled with these additions to her culinary repertoire. Emerson had learned to make the biscuits and the pies during holidays she'd spent in Baltimore, Maryland with Rachel's family. Emerson was happy to share her American culture and cooking with Benadina. Emerson and Benadina agreed on three kinds of stuffing – one recipe made of corn bread for Peter's parents, the celery and onion white bread stuffing that was Emerson's tradition, and a Portuguese oyster stuffing that Benadina announced would be better than the other two put together. And she was right about that. All the Americans had second and third helpings of the rich, flavorful mixture of Portuguese bread, oysters, butter, garlic, broth, and seasonings which Benadina said was a family secret from hundreds of years ago. She was not about to disclose a thing. There were vegetables of every color from Bacalhoa's gardens and too many desserts to count. Once Benadina started with the sweets, she lost track of how many she was making. Peter poured wine made from the grapes grown at Bacalhoa.

The Thanksgiving dinner was a great success, and the Americans were delighted to have a traditional American feast with a Portuguese twist. Emerson had worried needlessly about the turkey. It had been surprisingly tender. Everyone left the table completely stuffed and thankful. Peter was proud of his wife, and Emerson was overjoyed that the event had been able to bring a smile to her husband's face and to his eyes.

Peter's family decided to stay at Bacalhoa for the Christmas holidays. Having come such a long way and considering all that was happening in Europe, they did not know when they would again be able to travel to Portugal. Peter's father, Peter Senior, had organized the gardeners to find and cut down a large pine tree and bring it to the quinta. They set it up in the center of the lounge, and Emerson, Peter's mother Charlotte, and his sister Alice bought and made tree ornaments. They enjoyed decorating the quinta for Christmas, and Magdalena and the other servants loved with the way the Americans made each room into a Christmas celebration. Emerson was determined that her first Christmas with Peter would be one they would always remember, and she worked hard to make the house, the meals, and the gifts special.

The newlyweds hosted a festive Christmas party and served English Wassail. American, British, and Portuguese guests were invited to the refurbished palace with its enormous Christmas tree and evergreen wreaths with red bows at every door and window. Emerson and Peter invited everyone they knew and quite a few they didn't know. They invited their neighbors and the Americans and Brits who lived in villas nearby. They invited Peter's colleagues from the embassy.

They invited their next door neighbor Dr. Robert Carmichael who was a physician from England. Everyone said he was a wonderful doctor who had lost his wife a few years earlier. A handsome and charming bachelor, others had invited him to dinner and to parties, but the rumor was that he was still in mourning. To Emerson's surprise, he accepted their invitation and actually showed up at their Christmas party. Emerson made a special point of greeting him. You never knew when you would need the doctor next door.

Emerson served the special recipe for English Wassail that she had tasted and come to love when she'd lived in Britain. It was a hot drink of fruit juices and cider and spices and rum. Benadina had baked and cooked for days to produce a beautiful and delicious banquet of holiday food. Sweets and savories abounded. Peter had hired a small jazz combo that played Christmas carols, mood music, and dance tunes, and everyone had a wonderful time.

Emerson indulged herself and had a floor length red velvet dress made to wear to the party. Her hair had grown long, and she wore it on top of her head with red velvet ribbons woven into the elaborately arranged braids. She wore a simple diamond necklace that had belonged to her grandmother. Emerson looked stunning. She found she enjoyed entertaining. She especially enjoyed the way Peter looked at her that night with love and adoration and a hint of amazement in his eyes. Emerson wondered if he was surprised with her competence as a hostess, with the way the red dress made her skin glow, or with how good her hair could look when the hairdresser spent hours taming it into a civilized hairdo.

Peter relaxed for the night and was a charming and gracious host — proud to show off his palace and his beautiful and brilliant wife. They were happy that night like they had been at the beginning of their courtship. Emerson prayed that it would last but knew that once Peter went back to the embassy, he would revert to his serious and conscientious self and would begin to worry about the world again.

Before Peter's family left to return to America, they expressed their concerns to both Peter and to Emerson about Peter's health. He was terribly thin, and the dark circles around his eyes never disappeared. Peter was a grown man, and he realized that his parents loved him and were not criticizing him. They were concerned about him. Peter, too, was worried about his health, but he would never allow Emerson or his parents know of his own unspoken concerns. Peter knew he lacked the energy he used to have, the energy that previously had made it possible for him to plow ahead even when he was exhausted. He was finding he had to push himself harder and harder every day. He could not understand why his energy had left him. He was a young man in his thirties but some days he felt as if he were old before his time.

Chapter 10

EVERYTHING CHANGES

1939

When Peter's parents and sister left after the New Year of 1939 arrived, Emerson experienced a letdown. She attributed this to having been so busy over the Christmas holidays. Portugal's winter weather was very different from what Emerson had experienced during her years growing up in Connecticut or her years at school in England. Portugal's subtropical climate guaranteed there would be never be a white Christmas, but Emerson was surprised that it rained more than half the days during the months of December and January. Sometimes it seemed to her that it rained every day. Fires in the lounge, in the dining room, and in their bedroom and sitting room helped chase away the dampness. But they could no longer have cocktails or breakfast or any meals on the loggia. Emerson was happy when there was even part of a sunny day.

Emerson's best friend Rachel, who lived in Boston, gave birth to fraternal twins in January. Rachel's mother,

Naomi Friedman, had sent a telegram to Emerson to announce the arrival of the baby boy and baby girl. The birth had been difficult and had required a Cesarean section at Massachusetts General Hospital. It was several weeks before Emerson had a note from Rachel herself. Rachel said she was completely exhausted all the time, but her babies, David and Esther, were amazing. The note was much shorter than her usual long and thoughtful letters, and Emerson realized that Rachel had moved on to another phase of her life, a phase that did not include the time to write long letters and to philosophize about life as she had done before the babies were born. Rachel was right in the thick of living her life and no longer had the luxury of analyzing, pondering, and writing about it.

Peter's return to work continued to consume him. Even as the civil war in Spain was winding down, Adolph Hitler became bolder and more terrifying. The world grew ever more anxious as it watched his seemingly insatiable appetite for land and power threaten to play out in Europe. Everyone was on edge, waiting for something else to happen. Emerson was terribly worried about Peter. He came home late for dinner, and if there was some kind of a crisis, he sometimes did not come home at all. Emerson knew he had moved a cot into his office at the embassy and slept there when he didn't have time to come to Bacalhoa to sleep.

One morning in March, Peter brought her coffee and sat down on the bed beside her as she drank it. He had not been home last night when Emerson had gone to bed at 11:00 p.m. Peter seemed almost out of breath as he began to tell her about his previous day's work at the embassy. Emerson was delighted to see Peter in the morning, or in fact, any time lately. Some days he left so early and stayed so late she didn't see him at all.

Peter was telling her about what had happened in Germany. She already knew that giving the Sudetenland to Germany had fatally weakened the rest of Czechoslovakia. The German Wehrmacht had moved into Bohemia and Moravia and occupied what remained of the country. Hitler had claimed all of Czechoslovakia as German territory. Peter told Emerson he had been working extraordinarily hard to keep this from happening and was devastated that he had not been able to prevent Hitler from taking over the rest of that vulnerable country. He put his head down on Emerson's lap and wept. Emerson had never seen Peter cry, and she had no idea what to say to him as he completely crumbled with despair. She held him until he finally lay down beside her and went to sleep.

He did not wake up for more than 24 hours. She tried to wake him to make him eat and drink something, but he just told her to leave him alone. She knew he needed rest and was thankful to see him sleeping, but she was worried. She decided to call the English doctor who lived next door. He had been trained in Scotland and was said to be an excellent physician. He had moved to Portugal because his wife had been ill and needed a warmer climate than England could provide. Unfortunately, only two years after they'd moved to Portugal, his wife died from chronic lung disease at the age of 32. Everyone had been worried that Dr. Robert Carmichael would leave and return to England. His patients were delighted when he decided to stay in Portugal. When Emerson called him, he told her he would come to Bacalhoa later that afternoon.

After examining Peter and listening to his heart and lungs, Dr. Carmichael asked Emerson to come into the bedroom so that he could talk to both of them together. He asked them to call him Robert.

"I'm sorry to say that I am afraid Peter may have a heart condition, a very serious one. I am a general practice doctor. I would like for him to go to England to have an examination by a cardiac specialist. I know the trip back to Britain is not an easy one, but I think the American Embassy will provide transportation for Peter to go for an examination and possible treatment. I will make some telephone calls and write a letter of recommendation if necessary. Peter, I don't think you should go back to work until you are able to get a diagnosis. That is my advice, and I will work with you and with the American Embassy to be sure this happens."

Emerson had not been expecting this news at all. She had been prepared to hear that Peter had experienced a nervous breakdown as the result of overwork, not that he had a heart condition serious enough for him to have to return to London to see a specialist.

"I can't possibly go to England. It's becoming harder and harder to travel anywhere, and I am needed at the embassy, more so now than ever with all that is happening day by day in Germany and Czechoslovakia."

"You have to go, Peter. Your heart condition could be very serious. It needs to be seen to immediately — no matter what the little Austrian bully is doing this week. I think you need to be ready to travel in the next few days. I know the American Ambassador personally and will speak to him, with your permission." Dr. Carmichael was firm with his patient.

Peter was so tired and so ill he did not have the strength to argue. Emerson agreed with the doctor and told Peter there was nothing to discuss. He was going to England, and that was that. Three days later, Peter was aboard a military transport plane on his way to a hospital in London for tests. Emerson was heartsick with worry and wished more than anything that she had been able to accompany him. She wondered if Peter would tell her the truth about what the heart specialist found. She did her best to stay busy and prepare herself for whatever the news about Peter's health would be.

Peter stayed in the London hospital for three weeks. There were many tests and consultations with England's best cardiac specialists. Then Peter was transferred to what the British call a nursing home where he received several weeks of convalescent care and treatment. Most of this treatment was designed to force him to rest and eat well. He needed to recover his strength and stamina. Peter hated being away from Portugal. He hated not being able to do his job at the American Embassy, and he missed Emerson and Bacalhoa terribly.

During the time Peter spent in England, the Spanish Civil War finally ended. In a radio speech which aired on April 1, 1939, General Francisco Franco claimed victory. The last of the Republican forces had surrendered on March 31st when the Nationalists finally seized control of all Spanish territory. This outcome had not been unexpected. Great Britain ended their policy of neutrality on February 27, 1939 and officially recognized the Franco regime. Although those who feared and mistrusted Franco had hoped for a different ending, Franco's victory had been inevitable for some time. Everyone on all sides seemed to be relieved that the long and brutal civil war was finally over.

Emerson had spoken with Peter on the telephone a few times, and at last he told her he was returning to Lisbon. Peter had not told her what the heart specialists had said to him, and Emerson was concerned that no news was not good news.

Emerson had hoped that when she saw Peter again, he would look more rested, healthier, and stronger. She tried not to let her disappointment show when he returned home in early May. She ran to her husband and wrapped her arms around him. She could see that he was even thinner than he had been when he had left for England. His face was an alarming shade of gray. Emerson was frightened and prepared herself to hear what Peter had to say about his heart condition.

On their drive from the airport to Setubal, Peter asked about Bacalhoa and the servants and what she had been doing. He was just making conversation and putting off the inevitable discussion they would have about his health. When they finally reached their home, Peter was too tired to eat dinner and went directly to bed. Emerson had to wait until the next morning to hear whatever Peter was going to tell her.

Peter brought her coffee in bed and sat down next to her to talk about what he had learned in London. The news was serious. Peter was suffering from congestive heart failure and there was little that could be done to reverse the course of his disease. The heart specialist thought that Peter had been born with some kind of heart defect that had gone undiagnosed. The difficulties of his job and Peter's habit of pushing himself and not resting when he was tired had stressed his heart until it had become seriously damaged. Peter was devastated to have to give this news to Emerson. She had missed him so terribly while he was away and was so happy to have him back. Then to hear that there was nothing that could be done to help him was shattering. She was the one who cried this time while he held her. She pulled Peter back into their bed and begged him to make love to her. She finally fell asleep, and when she woke up, Peter had left for Lisbon.

They made some changes in their lives. Peter left for work later in the morning, and he tried to come home earlier, at least in time for dinner. Emerson insisted that Peter eat well, and they went to bed early each night. On weekends, they took short walks and did all the things the heart specialists thought might help prolong Peter's life. As spring turned into summer, Emerson found herself wanting to sleep later and later, and she began to take a nap almost every afternoon. She tried to hide her morning sickness from Peter until she was sure about her pregnancy. She wondered if Peter would be happy to hear they were expecting a baby. Peter had once upon a time said he wanted to fill up all the bedrooms at Bacalhoa with their children, but that had been in another lifetime, before Peter's heart had started to fail. As her waistline thickened and her clothes became tighter, Emerson knew she would have to tell Peter soon.

The situation in Europe grew increasingly grave over the months of the summer. It looked as if Poland would be the next country to fall to Hitler and the Nazis. Britain and Poland had entered into a Common Defense Pact. This agreement, which guaranteed that Britain would come to the defense of Poland if it was attacked, was an attempt to pressure Germany to back off its feared and anticipated invasion of Poland. The Pact was signed on August 25, 1939. Peter was still trying to work at the Embassy, but he had grown weaker as the summer progressed.

Emerson planned a picnic to the boathouse for a Saturday in late August. She was almost four months pregnant and was anxious to tell Peter since the doctor in Lisbon had confirmed to her that all was well with the pregnancy. Emerson asked Benadina to prepare all of Peter's favorites for their picnic, and Peter made an effort to eat something and to enjoy the outing. The ancient boat had a new motor which worked perfectly. Emerson tried to tempt Peter into taking it out for a short ride inside their cove, but he was too weak to climb into the boat. Emerson knew she was losing Peter. She was determined to savor and cherish this day and every day she had left with her beloved husband. She knew their days together numbered very few.

They were resting on their blanket. "I have a surprise for you, Peter."

"I don't really like surprises, but your surprise may not be as much of a surprise to me as you think it is. The only thing I don't know is why it has taken you so long to tell me."

Emerson threw herself into Peter's arms. She didn't want him to see the tears she couldn't keep from rolling down her face. "Are you happy about the baby?" she asked him when she could find her voice.

"Of course I am happy, my darling girl. I have wanted children to fill Bacalhoa since I first laid eyes on it. And I have known you were the woman I wanted to give birth to my children since I first laid eyes on you." Peter's voice caught with emotion as he tried to continue. "I am worried that I will not be alive to see the birth of this child or …," his voice trailed away.

"You will see the birth of this child, Peter, you must!"

It should have been the happiest time of their marriage, but Emerson now realized that Peter probably would not live long enough to share the much-anticipated event with her. She began bargaining with God to allow Peter to stay alive long enough to see their child who was to be born in February of 1940.

Chapter 11

DEATH AND MOURNING

1939-1940

Peter decided to stop going to the Embassy after Emerson told him the news about her pregnancy. On the first day of September, they learned about Hitler's invasion of Poland from a BBC broadcast over the radio. In the next few days, England and France declared war on Germany. Emerson had the radio moved from the lounge to their bedroom. Peter was no longer able to get out of bed, but he wanted to hear the news of what was going on in the world. Dr. Carmichael came to Bacalhoa every day to see how Peter was doing. He told Emerson that Peter did not have much time left. Emerson already knew this in her heart, but hearing it out loud from someone else, especially from Peter's doctor, hit her hard. It was painfully obvious that Dr. Carmichael hated to have to confirm her worst fears.

She was determined to put on a cheerful and positive face, and nothing could take her from Peter's side. They had their meals in their bedroom. Emerson ate because she knew she had to, but Peter stopped eating altogether and had to be coaxed to take even a sip of water.

Emerson awoke In the middle of the night in late September and listened to Peter's labored breathing. She knew the end was near and clung to this man, this love of her life, the father of her unborn child, the most dedicated patriot she'd ever known. She talked quietly to the semi-conscious Peter about their courtship, their lives together, the child they would have, and all the things she could think of that had made her love Peter so dearly. Finally, when the gray dawn arrived, he slipped softly away — away from the world he had worked so hard to save, away from his beloved Bacalhoa, and away from the woman whom he had loved and who had loved him so much. Death would come to Europe, more death than anyone could ever imagine. Death had already come to Bacalhoa and to Emerson's life. It brought more sorrow than she thought she could possibly bear.

Peter's family had known he was dying and had written goodbye letters to him. They had spoken with him several times over the transatlantic telephone. They had decided not to try to travel to Portugal to see him before he died. They did not think they could make the trip in time, and the threat of war had made any and all travel decisions impossible. In September of 1939, it was out of the question for them to cross the Atlantic Ocean.

Emerson arranged a small funeral service and scattered Peter's ashes in the garden at Bacalhoa. This had been Peter's request. He had also asked her to promise to raise their child in this home he had bought when his life was full of so much hope for the future. How could Emerson say anything except "yes" to her dying husband? There were letters to write and people to see, lawyers and others, until she had taken care of every practical detail of Peter's life and death. Peter's estate was settled, and Emerson could no longer avoid facing the life she had to live without him. That life seemed to stretch out in front of her forever into the future. How could she get through one hour or one day of that terrible loneliness, let alone the infinity of the rest of her life? Every waking moment, she reminded herself that she had to keep going because she was carrying their baby, the child who would always be the living legacy of her dearest Peter.

She thought about going back to the United States to have the baby. Medical care was so much more advanced in New England than it was in Portugal — even with the British Hospital in Lisbon. If she could possibly find a way to return to America, she was afraid that once she'd left, she would never come back to Bacalhoa. That would break her promise to Peter. No one was traveling in the fall of 1939. All sailings of the great ocean liners that crossed the Atlantic had been cancelled. It was not safe to be at sea when German U-boats had promised to torpedo any ship they encountered.

It was as if Europe was paralyzed as the world waited for the next shoe to drop. Europe's "phony war" of the Autumn of 1939 reflected the shock and fear that hung in the air of everyone's life. Emerson struggled to maintain some kind of daily routine. She took over the paperwork and finances of running the estate. She wrote long letters to Rachel and tried not to fill them with self-pity. Emerson's grief was magnified when Rachel wrote to tell her that her own dear father had died of a stroke at the age of fifty-nine.

Emerson made herself look forward to giving birth to Peter's baby, but even her pregnancy had begun to feel like a burden. Dr. Carmichael came to see her and told her he was concerned about her depression. He said depression was to be expected given the circumstances, but Emerson seemed to be getting worse.

Emerson made herself eat because she knew the baby needed nourishment. She tried to sleep because she knew she had to sleep for the baby's sake. One morning in October she woke up and found herself lying in a pool of blood. She knew she was losing the baby. Dr. Carmichael came immediately and sent her by ambulance to the British Hospital in Lisbon. He wanted to have a specialist from London flown in to see Emerson. But Emerson was beyond fighting and beyond caring. The specialist from England might have been able to make it to Portugal eventually, but because of the war, he would not arrive for weeks. It was already too late to save the baby.

The obstetrician at the hospital in Lisbon told Emerson her baby had been a girl and had died at a gestation of about twenty-two weeks. He could not find any reason for the miscarriage and told her he thought she would be able to have as many children in the future as she wanted. Emerson heard all of this as if it were being said to someone else. Was that doctor really talking to her about having as many more children as she wanted? Emerson didn't cry or grieve for her lost child. She was too numb to feel anything. When she was well enough to leave the hospital, Dr. Robert Carmichael arranged for a car and driver to take her to Bacalhoa. Magdalena met her at the door and took her to her bedroom. Emerson would not leave that room again for a very long time.

Dr. Carmichael visited Bacalhoa several times a week during the long winter of 1939 and 1940. He tried to talk to Emerson. He brought a psychiatrist from Lisbon, a Jewish doctor who had left Vienna when the Nazis had stolen Austria from its people. Dr. Benjamin Meyer tried for many weeks to get Emerson to talk to him. He finally gave up. Magdalena bathed and fed and cared for Emerson. Every morning, she brought Emerson freshly squeezed orange juice from the orange groves at Bacalhoa. She had Benadina make food that

Emerson used to enjoy. Magdalena cut up her meat and urged Emerson to eat. One day Emerson would slowly feed herself, and the next day Magdalena would have to feed her with a spoon. Magdalena found music on the radio — music that Emerson and Peter used to enjoy. She read to Emerson and did everything she could to coax Emerson into showing an interest in anything at all. She talked to Emerson and told her about growing up on the grounds of Bacalhoa. Emerson's body grew thin, and her hair grew long. Her hair lost its luster and her skin became as pale as a ghost's. Weeks became months, and the months became many.

Rachel wrote to Emerson, and Dr. Carmichael read the letters to her when he came for his visits. He wrote back to Rachel and told her about Emerson's severe depression and complete withdrawal from the world. Rachel had loved Emerson like a sister since they had both been seventeen and were roommates at Smith College. When Emerson's parents had been killed in a car accident, Rachel's parents had stepped in and become Emerson's family. She spent every vacation with Rachel at her home in Baltimore. Rachel's father was successful in the world of finance, and her mother was a well-respected attorney. They took Emerson into their home and into their hearts and loved her as they loved their own daughter. Rachel and Emerson were sisters in every way but blood. Rachel longed to do something to rescue her cherished "sister" from her catatonic depression. Winter became the spring and summer of 1940. The fall of 1940 arrived at Bacalhoa.

One afternoon, Dr. Carmichael arrived at Bacalhoa carrying a basket covered with a small pink blanket. Magdalena shook her head when she opened the door for Dr. Carmichael. She let him know, as she did each time he arrived, that Emerson had not shown any improvement since the doctor's last visit. Then she saw the basket and lifted the small piece of pink wool.

There in the basket, asleep, was a tiny, fuzzy ball of white, a puppy so small it could fit into the palm of her hand.

Dr. Robert Carmichael explained. "It was Rachel's idea. Emerson had a West Highland White Terrier as a pet when she was a child. She loved the dog beyond belief. The dog ran away one day and never came home. Emerson's family never found out what happened to their 'Lily,' and they never got another dog. Emerson used to talk to Rachel about Lily when they were friends in college. Emerson always wondered what had happened to Lily — why she had run away, if she had been stolen, if she had been run over by a car. Rachel thought perhaps having Lily come back might spark something, anything, in Emerson. This is our last resort short of electroshock therapy. If there were any way to get Emerson to Boston, that's what we would do. Rachel says they have made some advances in using electroshock treatment for people who are as depressed as Emerson is. The Atlantic Clipper Pan American Flying Boat is a possibility, and Rachel's mother might be able to get Emerson on one of them eventually. Naomi Friedman has connections, but every seat is in demand right now. We thought we would try the puppy first. Rachel worked for weeks to find just the right dog and paid a small fortune to have her brought to me from Scotland. Let's hope she does something good for Emerson."

Magdalena reached into the basket and picked up the Westie. "Of course this little one is not house trained. She's too young yet, but I have done this before and can do it again. No problem. If Emerson doesn't respond to the dog, we will keep her here anyway. The castle needs a 'white knight' to guard its doors." Magdalena loved animals and had missed having a pet at Bacalhoa. She had already adopted Lily.

Emerson was sleeping when Magdalena entered the bedroom and put the tiny dog on her pillow. The puppy immediately went for Emerson's face and began licking it. Emerson woke up with a start and looked around for the source of the disturbance. Dr. Carmichael and Magdalena watched as Emerson's eyes got big with an expression of surprise. Emerson had spoken only a few words at a time during the past few months, and no one expected a miraculous recovery.

"Lily, is that you? I wondered where you had gone. I was so sad when you left me, and I am so glad to see you again." Was Emerson living in the past? Dr. Carmichael was concerned that she seemed to think the new puppy was the long lost Westie from her childhood. Magdalena, who didn't follow the English sentences completely, was just happy to have Emerson speaking again — whatever she was saying.

Emerson played with and fussed over the puppy until Magdalena decided that Lily needed to go outside for a few minutes. Emerson watched with alarm when Magdalena left the room carrying the dog. Seeing her concern, Magdalena said, "I'm just taking her outside. We will be right back." When Magdalena returned, Emerson reached out her arms for the puppy and snuggled back into the bed with Lily curled up in the hollow of her neck. That night Lily showed a great deal of interest in Emerson's dinner of sliced lamb and roasted potatoes. Emerson gave Lily small pieces of meat and ate almost everything on her own plate. Magdalena was beginning to be hopeful that Lily would help Emerson find her way back to the land of the living.

Lily demanded that Emerson play with her. She was a puppy and could not sleep all the time. Emerson threw the ball for Lily, and one day, when Lily could not get the ball out from behind a chair, Emerson got out of bed and retrieved the ball. It was the first time she had been able to get out of bed of her own volition and without assistance since she had returned to Bacalhoa after she had lost the baby. One late September day in the fall of 1940 when the sun was shining, Magdalena asked if Emerson would like to accompany her and take Lily for a short walk in the garden. Magdalena put a cape around Emerson's shoulders and slippers on her feet, and Emerson walked outside her bedroom suite for the first time in more than ten months. Magdalena knew that Emerson was going to recover.

Dr. Carmichael still came twice a week and was delighted to be able to engage Emerson in a conversation. She had such a fine mind, and he was relieved to see she had regained some interest in events and ideas. They discussed the progress of the war and what had happened in Scandinavia, in the Ardennes, in Belgium, and in France. Emerson cried when Robert told her about the retreat and the heroism at Dunkirk. Emerson did not remember that Robert had already told her, at the time these events had actually taken place, about the fall of France and that the Nazis had marched into Paris in June. Emerson cried again when she remembered that the last time she had been in Paris, she had been on her honeymoon.

Emerson wanted to be brought up to date about everything that had happened, everything she had missed. Emerson and Robert talked about the Nazis, the position of the United States and its pacificism, about Lend-Lease. They talked about the neutrality of Portugal. Emerson listened to the radio daily to hear details of the London Blitz and the latest about the Battle of Britain.

Emerson called England to find out first hand from Kitty Stuart-Ramsey if Anna, the Basque orphan Emerson had tried so hard to reach at the children's camp, was going to be safe. Kitty reassured her that Anna was out of harm's way and told Emerson she would personally keep an eye out for Anna's welfare. Anna had been adopted by a family in Northern England. Anna had begun to speak again. Anna was going to be fine. Everyone was terrified that Germany would invade Britain. The world held its breath. In 1938 when Neville Chamberlain had sold Czechoslovakia out to the Germans, Kitty, in an act of protest, had resigned her seat in Parliament. She assured Emerson that Sir Winston Churchill was the strongest and bravest of leaders and that he was exactly the man who could lead Britain, no matter what the Germans decided to do.

Kitty had written to Emerson after Peter died but now expressed her condolences over the telephone with a catch in her voice. She told Emerson how much she had admired Peter and that when he died, the world had lost a staunch defender of freedom and an extraordinarily fine young man and patriot. Emerson asked Kitty to stay in touch with news about Anna, but she could not bring herself to tell Kitty about the baby she had lost.

Emerson began to look forward to Dr. Carmichael's visits, and one day she asked him to stay to have a drink with her before dinner. A few weeks later, she invited him to stay and have dinner with her. Their friendship established itself with regular visits. Although Peter had been dead for more than a year, in her heart, Emerson still felt married to Peter. She did not notice that Robert lingered over her hand when he greeted her and wistfully watched her graceful movements as she poured their after-dinner coffee. Magdalena noticed that Robert Carmichael began to bring flowers or candy when he arrived for his weekly visit, but she knew that Emerson was not ready to move on from her marriage to Peter. Dr. Carmichael realized and respected this, too. He was a kind and patient man and friend.

In June of 1941, they heard the news that everyone in Europe had been speculating about for months. The Germans had invaded Russia. Operation Barbarossa was a reality, and the only consolation in the news was that it almost guaranteed that Germany would not invade Britain — at least not yet. Robert and Emerson agreed that Hitler's decision to attack the Soviet Union was a bad one. It was a strategic disaster that Robert said would be the final nail in Hitler's coffin. "He made a terrible decision when he opted to turn on the Russian Bear. The Bear has had Old Man Winter protecting his land for hundreds of years, and no one has ever been able to defeat that one. Hitler has always been a mad man, but he has been able to keep his grandiose delusions in check until now. It is just a matter of time."

Emerson hoped with all of her heart that Robert was right in his analysis and that the "matter of time" would be less rather than more. They knew there were long years of war ahead, but it seemed that perhaps for the first time, the little Austrian might have made a critical error. They could only hope that the Russian winters would defeat the Nazis as they had so many others who had tried to conquer that vast and mysterious land that now choked under the death grip of Joseph Stalin's evil.

Chapter 12

CAPTAIN MAX

SEPTEMBER 1939

Captain Sousa delayed the sailing of the *Coracao de Anjo* until he could gain some understanding of what the war would mean for his business and for the *Anjo*. Were the U-boats going to torpedo every ship they found at sea? What would happen to insurance rates for his cargos? Could he put his crews at risk? Everyone in the shipping business was asking the same questions. Things began to sort themselves as the Germans laid out their rules for what would be considered an enemy ship and what would be considered a neutral ship. Since Portugal had declared itself a neutral country, at least for the time being, ships sailing under the Portuguese flag should be safe from German U-boats.

Max finally sailed as the junior navigator on his first voyage with the crew of the *Anjo*. Having studied and prepared for so long in anticipation of this day, he worried that when the time came, he might not be able to live up to his own and Captain Sousa's expectations. He need not have worried. He was a great success and even became something of a hero when he was able to guide the ship around rather than through a storm that other ships had warned them about over the ship's radio.

After delivering a cargo of industrial and consumer goods to Brazil, they had taken on a cargo of bauxite and were sailing back to Portugal when they encountered their first German U-boat in the South Atlantic. Captain Sousa had all the proper paperwork, and because the *Anjo* was sailing under the flag of a neutral country, he was not alarmed when the U-boat surfaced and the Germans demanded to come aboard. Sousa directed Max and the first mate to go below and stay out of the way of the U-boat officers. Sousa had correctly guessed that Max was not really the Frenchman he claimed to be, and he knew that his first mate was a real Frenchman who loathed the Germans. Sousa wanted to keep the two of them out of the way of trouble, and Sousa's decision saved their lives. Sousa and the senior navigator stood on the deck of the *Anjo* to receive the Germans.

The German U-boat Captain decided he did not like the looks of the papers Captain Sousa presented to him. The manifest said the bauxite was bound for Lisbon, but the Nazi was suspicious and suggested that perhaps Sousa intended to deliver his cargo to Britain. Bauxite ore was the essential ingredient for making the metal aluminum which was the material out of which airplanes were manufactured. Not only did each side in the war want to accumulate as much of this strategic material as they possibly could, they also wanted to keep the other side from having any. No bauxite; no airplanes.

In spite of Sousa's objections, the Germans moved to occupy the *Anjo*. Sousa challenged the seizure of his ship, and the U-boat Captain placed Sousa in handcuffs when he protested.

The *Anjo*'s navigator objected when Sousa was handcuffed. The U-boat officers removed Sousa and the navigator from the *Anjo* and held them aboard the German submarine. When the U-boat had first been sighted, the *Anjo*'s radio operator had immediately sent out an SOS message to ships in the area. The *Anjo* was not equipped with any guns to defend itself. Captain Sousa had arranged for defensive artillery to be installed as soon as the *Anjo* returned to Lisbon, but he had decided to make this one run to Brazil and back without any armaments on board.

In spite of having sent out a radio message, the reality was that the *Anjo*'s crew was completely alone in the middle of the ocean. The chances of another ship coming to their rescue were miniscule. The crew of the *Anjo* had to decide if they should make a run for it or if they should surrender and take their chances with the Germans. With their much-loved Captain Sousa and the *Anjo*'s navigator being held as hostages on the U-boat, the crew believed their ship was doomed. They were certain the Germans would take command of the *Anjo* and its cargo and imprison the rest of the crew. If they did not try to get away from the U-boat, they felt there was little chance that any of them would survive to see Lisbon again.

The first mate consulted with Max, and they decided to make a run for it. There was no chance they could rescue Captain Sousa or the navigator. The crew of the *Anjo* quickly subdued the two German sailors who had been left behind to stand guard aboard the Portuguese ship. The two were tossed into the water and struggled to stay afloat as the *Anjo* pulled away from the German submarine. The U-boat would either come after them, or it would fire a torpedo at the *Anjo* and destroy it. The first mate took over the ship, and Max stepped in to navigate. They all wondered how long it would be before the Germans sent a torpedo after them. The only thing they thought might save them was that they hoped the Germans wanted their valuable cargo of bauxite.

The crew was just turning the *Anjo* around when they saw a single, small plane appear on the horizon. As it came closer, they tried to see what markings were on the mystery plane. Traveling at full speed to try to escape the U-boat, the men aboard the *Anjo* knew they could never outrun the plane. If it had a swastika on the side and was a German plane that had been sent as back up for the U- boat, they were done for.

The crew of the *Anjo* watched as the plane went for the U-boat, opened up full bore, and blasted the U-boat with all of its fire power. Although the *Anjo* was concentrating mainly on making its own escape, the men on board were fascinated with what was happening in their wake. They cheered when the plane dropped what looked like several bombs that landed in the center of the U-boat. The U- boat was fatally wounded, and the *Anjo* sailed on its way as the German submarine listed and began to sink.

They deliberated what to do about attempting to rescue Captain Sousa and the *Anjo*'s navigator who were on board the U-boat. They realized that both of them had probably been killed when the German submarine was bombed. As they made the decision to continue moving away from the sinking U-boat, they all grieved for their beloved Captain Sousa and for their long-time navigator.

The anonymous plane which had come to their rescue, flew over the *Anjo* and dipped its wings in acknowledgement before it took flight back towards the horizon from where it had miraculously first appeared. The *Anjo*'s radio operator had sent an SOS, but where had the plane come from? The crew was mystified as they did not think they were close enough to land for any plane to have found them. How had this plane, which had appeared out of nowhere, known where they were?

How had the plane been able to find and save their ship, alone in the ocean like a needle in a haystack? The plane was a mystery that was never solved. It did, however make for an exciting story when the sailors gathered in the bars of Lisbon and Marseilles and told tales of their exploits and their brushes with death. The tale of the ghost plane that had appeared by the Grace of God to find them in the middle of the ocean, save the *Anjo*, and take down a U-boat, became legend.

Returning to Lisbon was not a difficult maritime feat. The first mate commanded the ship as well as anyone could have. Max earned his stripes as a navigator, and the rest of the voyage was uneventful. Returning to Lisbon without Captain Sousa's body or the navigator's body was heartbreaking for the crew and for Max in particular. Many of the crew had sailed with the two men for years and were devastated by their loss. Max had begun to look to his mentor Sousa as he would to a father. Sousa's kindness and direction had allowed Max to realize his dream of earning a living at sea. What could he possibly say to Inez, Sousa's wife, who had taken Max into their home, cared for him when he was ill, cooked for him, and loved him? Mrs. Sousa had treated Max as she would have treated a son of her own.

Max told Inez Sousa the details of her husband's death and comforted her in her sorrow. Max arranged for the funeral and took care of the Captain's estate. He learned that the *Anjo* was heavily mortgaged, and that Sousa had barely been able to make the payments to keep his ship from being repossessed. Max knew that, before the war, his own German family had deposited significant wealth in banks in the United States, and he asked the Captain's wife if she would be willing to sell the ship to him. Because he was so indebted to the Sousas for their kindness to him, Max paid off the note on the ship and also gave Mrs. Sousa the full price for the *Anjo*. He felt he owed at least that much to her and to her husband who had given him the opportunity for a life at sea.

At the age of twenty-one, Max Boudreaux owned the Coracao de *Anjo* outright and took over as its captain. The crew was shocked at this turn of events, that the very young and very inexperienced junior navigator was now their boss. But they liked and respected Max, and they were happy to stay on under the new owner's command. The ship's first mate received an increase in salary as he was essentially now doing the job of master of the ship. Max was pleased with the way he'd been able to use some of his family's money, and he found himself that much closer to his dream of transporting Jews to Palestine.

Only the former first mate who was now the new master of the *Anjo* knew that Captain Sousa had, just weeks before his death, signed an agreement to transport a secret, special cargo destined for New York City in the United States. Sousa had agreed to deliver the risky and dangerous shipment because it was the only way he could save the *Anjo*. The payment he was promised for this one trip would allow Sousa to hang on to his ship a little longer.

The agreement to carry the clandestine cargo across the Atlantic had been arranged in the strictest confidence with a Belgian mining company. Captain Sousa had finalized the contract with the Union Miniere just before the Germans marched into Poland in 1939. Sousa had confided what few details he knew only to his first mate. Now master of the *Anjo*, the former first mate's loyalty to Captain Sousa's memory made it imperative that the *Anjo* honor the agreement. Max also wanted to honor this agreement that had been so important to Sousa, but the details and the timetable for complying with the terms were vague and uncertain. It was an agreement that hung over Max's head and lent considerable doubt about the sailing schedule of the *Anjo*.

Finally, in the Spring of 1940, Max received word that the shadowy cargo of Captain Sousa's contract with the Belgian mining company from the previous year was ready to be to be collected from a secret destination. The *Anjo* would sail to Portuguese Angola, to the port of Lobito. Angola was a Portuguese colony in Africa, and the *Anjo* routinely on-loaded and off-loaded cargos at Lobito which was a regular port of call for Portuguese ships. Max could not imagine what was so special about this particular cargo and this particular voyage.

The *Anjo* was under orders not to disclose to anyone where they were picking up their cargo or where the cargo was headed. Max trusted his crew to honor these instructions although Max could not understand why all the secrecy was necessary. To be sure, the *Anjo* did not make many runs to New York City, but this Atlantic crossing was turning out to be something quite different from any previous voyage the *Anjo* had undertaken. They were to sail into Lobito under darkness, load their cargo, and sail out of port before dawn. Because the *Anjo* was a Portuguese ship sailing into the port of a Portuguese colony, there should not be much paperwork or any holdups in loading the cargo. Max assumed this was one of the reasons the *Anjo* had been chosen for the special assignment.

The *Anjo* arrived at Porto Lobito after dark, as specified. There was another freighter which had also just arrived in port. Hundreds of steel barrels were quickly loaded onto both ships directly from the railroad cars of the Benguela Railway. Lobito, on the Coast of the Atlantic Ocean, was the sea terminus of the strategic Benguela Railway which extended deep inland to the heart of the African continent. The railway traveled through the Katanga Province of the Belgian Congo. Max supervised the loading of the barrels onto his freighter. He estimated that he was taking on several hundred barrels which comprised approximately six hundred tons of ore. The barrels loaded onto the *Anjo* and onto the other ship were stamped simply: "URANIUM ORE --- PRODUCT OF BELGIAN CONGO."

The uranium ore had in fact come from a place in the Belgian Congo known as the Shinkolobwe mine. The cargo the *Anjo* had just acquired would one day make history, although it would be years before anyone would find out about it. Both freighters were loaded and left Porto Lobito before the sun began to rise on that May morning in 1940. Max and his crew were taking the *Anjo* and its cargo to the United States. Arriving days later in the Port of New York, Max's cargo was unloaded and taken to a three-story warehouse in Staten Island where it would remain anonymous for several years — until it was needed to bring about the end of World War II.

The *Anjo* had originally been fitted with a few passenger berths that were sometimes used when someone wanted to accompany a cargo or just wanted to travel the world on a freighter. Max had the passenger quarters refurbished so that he could carry fifteen people comfortably and twenty-five not so comfortably. In the city of Lisbon by the summer of 1941, there were a great many refugees who would give anything to leave Europe. There were also thousands of Jews who were even more anxious to escape the advancing Nazi death squads.

The *Anjo* did not want for cargo or for passengers. The wartime demand for ships was such that even a mediocre businessman would have been able to turn a profit in the shipping business. Max learned quickly and did extremely well. He accepted cargos to and from ports in the Mediterranean, and he told his crew that they would be doing some quiet transporting of refugees who wanted to reach Palestine. Armed with its new weapons on deck for protection, Max felt his ship was as safe as it could be in a world gone mad with war.

Chapter 13

A NEW CHALLENGE

1941

One week in November of 1941, Robert telephoned to let Emerson know he would not be able to make it for dinner on their usual night and asked if they could reschedule. Robert came to Bacalhoa for dinner every Thursday night without fail, but he was a busy practicing physician and was sometimes called away to take care of an emergency. Emerson understood these disruptions, but there was something that worried her about the tone of Robert's voice that night when he told her he could not keep their dinner date. When he arrived the next night, Emerson could see that he was preoccupied and worried about something. They were close friends, and Emerson did not hesitate to question him about why he was so obviously not himself.

Robert paused a long time before he spoke, "There are terrible things, horrifying things going on in the Third Reich and everywhere in Europe. These appalling events are more frightening than I can begin to comprehend. At first I refused to believe my sources inside Germany, but now I have seen and heard the proof and cannot deny that the atrocities are true."

"Of course, we know that Hitler is a horrible little man who has ravaged Europe with his ambition and his insanity. What could be worse than Nazis? I cannot imagine. What atrocities?" Emerson wanted to hear what new event was so disturbing to Robert.

"What is worse than Nazis are Nazis who are engaged in genocide."

"Genocide? We hear all kinds of unsettling rumors about what is going on inside Germany … but genocide?" She was honestly shocked and disbelieving.

"The Nazis first started rounding up gypsies, the insane, and political foes such as communists, and putting them in work camps, also known as concentration camps. That went on for years, even before the war began. Now the Nazis have begun to arrest Jews in all the nations they've conquered. Jews are being sent to these concentration camps. There are camps in Germany – in Dachau and in Flosenberg and lots of other places. They are building camps in Czechoslovakia and in Poland and everywhere they have taken over. These terrible places are named for the towns where they are built, but mark my words, these names will one day be associated for all time with the worst manifestations of evil. The Nazis are building these camps as fast as they can. They are transporting Jews to the camps on trains. German generals are battling over whether trains will be used to take Jews to the camps or will be used to carry soldiers and armaments to the fighting front in Russia."

"I know they are making Jews wear the identifying Yellow Star of David pinned to their clothing, but what is the reason for putting them in camps? Are they treating them as criminals — without trials?"

"Oh, my dear Emerson, it is ever so much worse than that. These camps are not really work camps or even concentration camps; they are extermination camps, death camps. The Nazis killed the gypsies, the retarded, and their ideological enemies in order to achieve Hitler's goal of 'purification of the master race.' Now they are gathering up Jews and taking them to the camps in order to get rid of them. And I do mean to get rid of them completely — to eliminate them, to murder them. The Nazis are committing mass murder of Jews, and no one seems to be able to do anything about it. No one in the outside world believes that this really could be happening in Germany and in the other countries Germany now rules. But it is happening. I know these things to be true, without question."

"Mass murder? That sounds so extreme, so unbelievable. How can you be certain about the things you're hearing? Maybe these are rumors or propaganda or exaggeration."

Robert closed his eyes and pushed his hair back over his head as he searched to find the words he wanted to say. Emerson put her hand on his arm in an effort to reassure him that it was all right to tell her the things he was trying so hard to find a way to talk about. "Please tell me, Robert. I want to know about it — whatever it is. Don't protect me by withholding the truth."

Robert never showed his vulnerability, and he never let Emerson see that he might be discouraged. As Robert now struggled to share his fears with her, Emerson was touched. She realized how much she cared for this extraordinarily brave man. He was always so strong, so in control, so sure of what to do. Emerson was caught off guard by the tenderness she felt for her dear friend. She wanted him to tell her anything that was troubling him.

"There is a place in Ukraine called Babi Yar. It is on the outskirts of Kiev. Recently, thousands and thousands of Jews were murdered there and buried in a mass grave." Robert paused and took a breath. "The Germans captured Kiev in September of this year, and the Einsatzgruppen that occupied the city conceived a plan to murder all the Jews of Kiev. Can you imagine that — all the Jews in the city of Kiev, all the Jews in an entire city? And for no reason other than that they are Jews?"

"An order was posted in Kiev stating that on September 29, 1941, all Jews were to report to a location near the Jewish cemetery outside the city, to the Babi Yar ravine. They were told to bring with them all their valuables and only those few personal belongings they could carry. The authorities said the Jews were going to be relocated temporarily, and failure to report would be punishable by death. Over the next two days, most of Kiev's Jews went to the cemetery as they'd been told to do. The claim that they were being relocated was a lie. They were marched into the woods, and their valuables and other worldly possessions were taken from them. They were ordered to strip naked and lie down in a long, deep ravine. The occupying Nazi military forces, with the help of the local police, machine gunned Jewish men, women, and children where they lay. Bodies on top of each other piled up in layers until the ravine was filled with the dead. There were tens of thousands of Jews murdered and buried in the mass grave.

"Hardly any were able to escape being killed. Only a few were able to outrun their murderers and hide in the woods. Others lay among the corpses and pretended to be dead. One man watched his wife and children as they were cut down by the machine guns. He stayed completely still in the piles of dead bodies and hoped the men with the guns would think he was dead. After dark, he dug his way out of the corpses and the dirt which had been heaped on top of the dead bodies. He was able to save himself.

"With incredible determination and hardly any food at all, he made his way out of Ukraine and across Europe. He hid on board a freight train that was heading west to France, and he made it to Paris last week. He was close to death when he reached his cousin's house. His cousin is a rabbi in the City of Light. The survivor of this unbelievable mass execution told the rabbi what had happened in that terrible place of Babi Yar. Unfortunately, the escape from Kiev and his journey across Europe with little food or water had ruined his health. The rabbi's Ukrainian cousin died of pneumonia shortly after reaching Paris. When he'd heard the story about what had happened in Kiev, the rabbi and his family decided to leave France immediately and try to reach America. Their path to freedom was through Portugal, and that rabbi was at my house earlier this week."

"I am in complete shock and quite sickened to hear this story. I'm having a really hard time taking it in. It's difficult to believe, but you are so convinced yourself that it is true, you have convinced me. You have the rabbi's testimony, so you have reliable and irrefutable information that these terrible things have happened. As difficult as it is to believe that the scope of Nazi evil extends as broadly and as deeply as you have said it does, how can one possibly now doubt it? I don't understand why the Nazis want to kill these people? And what could they possibly have against Jewish children? I know the Nazis are horribly anti-Semitic, but they are violating the Geneva Convention and every other tenet of international law, not to mention every law of morality and humanity. Why has there been no outcry from the Allies? From the Americans? From everybody? Why don't the Jews who have escaped tell the world what is happening in these camps? About what has happened at Babi Yar? And why is it happening? Are the Germans killing the Jews just because they are Jews?

I can't really believe that. What reason can there be for this mass annihilation?"

"Believe it. It is all too true and is probably even worse than we know. Hitler despises the Jews. He wants them all out of Europe — through emigration or through his extermination camps. He wants to purify the Aryan race. Of course he is insane, but he is managing to succeed in spite of his insanity."

"I do want to know about this, but it is difficult for my mind to take in anything so horrible. Can the German military be conspiring in this kind of thing? Has mankind gone completely mad?"

"The Germans are going to great lengths to keep their killing a secret. One reason I know about the atrocities is because I have been working with the Allies in a confidential capacity. I have wanted to share my activities with you, but I did not want to put you in danger. Because Portugal is technically neutral, I have had to be extremely careful about what I say and what I do. I'm a British citizen, and I believe the German officials who are now everywhere in Portugal are keeping a close eye on me. I fear that the Portuguese PVDE are also watching me. Although the PVDE pretend to be in charge of border patrol and immigration, everyone knows they are in fact Salazar's secret police agency. Many of my fellow Brits went back home when the war started. I decided to stay here, thinking I could do some good in Portugal, to fight the Nazis in my own way."

"Thank goodness you didn't go home. I could never have recovered from my terrible depression without your help. If you had not conspired with Rachel, I would not have my precious Lily." Lily was always at Emerson's side or in her lap. Lily was always happy to greet Robert when he came for dinner. Robert knew that Lily, as well as Rachel and Magdalena, had brought Emerson back to the world.

"So you have been doing whatever it is you are doing since the war began? And what does this have to do with the Nazis murdering Jews in the Third Reich and in Ukraine?" Emerson was intrigued. This was a side of Robert Carmichael about which she knew nothing at all, and she wanted to hear more.

"Among other things, I help to move RAF and other Allied pilots who have been shot down, in France and Belgium and Holland. They travel through Vichy, through Spain, to Portugal, and eventually return to Britain. I call them my flyboys. I won't give you details about how all of this happens. It is complex, convoluted, and very, very secret. Even I don't know the particulars about how they make the journey from occupied German territories to freedom. The French, Dutch, and Belgian resistance groups pick them up when they are shot down, and there are many people involved in the long and circuitous route these men must travel to be returned to Britain. In spite of their arduous ordeals, they are always in a great hurry to get back into the cockpit and begin bombing the Germans again.

"I know about the concentration camps because once in a while we also have the chance to help someone who has escaped from one of those horrible places. These few fortunate escapees contact the underground and are passed along their path to freedom, by way of the same routes the pilots take. At first I thought, as you did, that it could not be happening, but unfortunately it is all too real. I have spoken with a few of the Jews who have escaped from the camps, and they have told me first-hand what is happening there. The story about the atrocity at Babi Yar was told to me personally by the rabbi from Paris who was at my house a few nights ago."

"Why have you not mentioned this to me before? I wish you had told me about what you are doing. This is extraordinarily brave and patriotic of you. I salute you. And I always want you to tell me what is going on and what is worrying you." Emerson again felt the pangs of tenderness for Robert that surprised her, and she desperately wished she could do something to comfort him.

"I'm sorry, Emerson; I have already said too much. I needed to talk to someone about this, but I should not have burdened you with it. There are so many tragic stories, I don't even know where to begin. There was a Jewish child who escaped with her father from one of the camps. They were both handed along the escape route and ended up at my house yesterday. The child was so malnourished and ill she could not possibly survive. She died in my office. That is another reason why I had to reschedule our dinner and why I have been so preoccupied tonight. I apologize. I had no right to expect you to listen to all of this, and I am afraid I may have put you in danger."

"Don't be silly. You are my dear friend, and although I am horrified to hear these terrible stories, you must share things with me. I don't consider myself to be in danger, and even if I am, I can handle it. I do not fear evil Nazis. I want to fight them like you are doing. Tell me what I can do to help. I am always happier if I have a worthwhile project to keep me busy. I've been drowning in self-pity long enough. It is time for me to start thinking about making a contribution to the war effort instead of dwelling on my own losses. Everyone is losing loved ones these days. I am not unique and wouldn't mind if you reminded me of that from time to time." Emerson smiled her best smile and looked directly into Robert's eyes to let him know she really did understand and was very serious about wanting to help. "You are so dear to me, Robert. You have stood by me and comforted me through terrible times. I want to do the same for you. You can talk with me about anything. I want to do whatever I can."

"There is nothing you can do right now — except to keep all of this confidential. I am giving some thought to trying to find a way to get Jewish children out of France to Portugal. These will be the rare lucky ones who are able to escape from Nazi-controlled territories. But they have no place to go from here. There are so many Jewish refugees in Portugal. They are desperate to get on a ship leaving Portugal for South America or the United States or Palestine. Many have no have letters of transit or the money needed to book a passage. The demand for ways to leave Europe far exceeds the supply, and Lisbon is full of crowds of displaced persons — both Jews and non-Jews. Portugal's neutral status is still holding, but Portugal's President, Antonio De Olvera Salazar, does not want to challenge the Germans too directly. Everyone knows that the Germans, and also the Gestapo, are operating here and spying here. They are spying on me. I will say again that I am afraid that the PVDE are also watching me. I check my house regularly for listening devices, and I never say anything over the telephone that could be interpreted as anything except exactly what it sounds like it is."

"Why do you think the PVDE is spying on you? I am sure you are right about the Nazis. The Nazis are spying on everybody, but why would the Portuguese want to spy on you?" Emerson was having a difficult time understanding why the PVDE, the feared and dreaded arm of Portuguese law enforcement that everyone thought of as the "secret police," would be interested in Robert. The PVDE was Portugal's less evil version of the German Gestapo.

"Portugal is in a difficult position in this war. It constantly walks the dangerous tightrope of international diplomacy and attempts to be as evenhanded as it can be with both sides. Salazar can be viewed as a fascist in a way, but not really. Based on ideology, he might be expected to be an ally of Francisco

Franco or Adolf Hitler. But he has decided, for a number of practical and economic reasons, that it is important for the Republic of Portugal to retain its neutrality on the world stage. It is an extremely delicate balancing act. Because I am a British citizen, I am under constant suspicion. I am de facto allied to Britain, and to make matters worse, I am secretly and actively working for the British and Allied cause. Only a few people know about my activities, but I am, in reality, operating as an agent for one of the combatants in the war. I am a threat. I'm a very small threat to be sure, but a threat nonetheless — to the Germans and to Portugal's neutrality."

Emerson knew her Portuguese history and felt certain Portugal would always be a British ally. "I know that Portugal and England have been allies and trading partners for hundreds of years. They have been affiliated for centuries, even before they formally signed an alliance in 1373. That's quite a long time to be friends. No nation would treat such an historic relationship lightly. Isn't the Anglo-Portuguese Alliance the oldest and longest-lasting alliance in history still in force between any nations? Aren't you protected in some way because Portugal values its long-standing relationship with Britain? Aren't all British citizens welcome and safe here?"

"This ancient treaty has protected both countries for centuries, and Salazar is struggling to honor this precious bond. He has been public and emphatic that he will not turn against Britain. However, I don't think this alliance would protect me personally, especially if it was discovered that I am helping Allied pilots escape from Europe. Aside from whatever threats may come to me, I believe it is in the interests of international stability for Portugal to maintain its neutrality." Robert was somewhat concerned about his own personal safety, but he was more worried that Portugal would be forced to take sides in the war.

"Of course, to be honest about it, Portugal has profited from the conflict as well as suffered because of it. Portugal exports sugar and rubber from its colonies to Allied and neutral countries as well as to the Axis powers. Portugal sells whatever it has to the buyer who has the money to pay for it. Business is business. Profits are to be made. One of the most important pawns in this complex game of economic and military chess is the element of Wolfram. Portugal is blessed with a significant percentage of the world's supply of the rare commodity. Germany has none of this critical ore, which is also known as tungsten, within its own national boundaries or in any of the countries it has conquered. Germany has to buy all the Wolfram it uses from other countries. Portugal sells Wolfram to both the Germans and the Allies. This has put Portugal in the middle of a tug of war — quite literally."

"I have heard people talk about Wolfram and what an essential element it is, but I don't really understand why it is so important to the Germans." Emerson knew a great deal about politics and economics. She was less confident about her knowledge of chemistry and metallurgy and wanted to learn more.

"Portugal and Spain are the only countries that can supply Germany with Wolfram. The rest of the world's Wolfram supply is found in countries that are aligned with the Allies. Wolfram is a critical component in hardening steel. It is absolutely essential in manufacturing Germany's tanks and guns and other implements of war. Germany doesn't have any of their own, and they must have it to conduct the war. Germany is a tough customer. They would like to have all of Portugal's tungsten, and they would prefer that Portugal never sell an ounce of it to the Allies. You can see that President Salazar is in an impossibly difficult spot. Germany is constantly threatening to invade Portugal if Salazar doesn't give them what they want." Robert was knowledgeable and realistic about the threats Portugal faced and the difficulties of keeping the country out of the European war.

"Surely that would never happen? Germany has its hands full right now. It occupies most of Western Europe and is in a more than challenging fight with the Soviet Union." Emerson knew that the Germans threatened everybody, but she had not realized before what pressure Portugal was under from the Nazis who wanted to occupy and control everything.

"I have learned never to say never when it comes to these Nazi beasts and their leader. You asked what all of this has to do with me and why I fear the PVDE. The Nazis put pressure on the Portuguese Secret police to be an extension of the Gestapo. Sometimes the PVDE cooperates and gives the Germans what they want. Sometimes the PVDE won't go along. They are also walking an extremely delicate path. I suspect that there are several factions within the PVDE and that these factions have their political leanings. Some in the PVDE are more sympathetic to the Germans and want to be of help to the Gestapo. Other factions are more careful about remaining neutral and want to focus primarily on Portugal's security and safety." Robert had a great deal of insight into the workings of Portugal's secret police organization. If he was concerned about it, so was Emerson.

"Do you really think you are in the sights of the Nazis and the PVDE? How could they have found out about what you are doing?" Emerson was somewhat skeptical that the threat from the PVDE was real. She had always regarded that group of bullies as a force with which she need not concern herself. Clearly she needed to readjust her thinking.

"I am British, and therefore I am the enemy — at least to the Germans. I think I am protected here because the Portuguese honor my British citizenship, but one never knows. Some of my work involves bringing people through Spain. I don't ever actually go into Spain myself anymore, but I work with people who constantly travel through that country. The Allied pilots and others travel through Spanish territory. Portugal's relationship with Spain is and has always been another sensitive issue for Salazar. These two countries have had a long and sometimes extremely contentious relationship — throughout hundreds of years of history. You can see, just by looking at a map, that Portugal finds itself in a precarious position with regard to Spain. Salazar treads a careful and complicated path with Portugal's close and much larger, richer, and more powerful neighbor. Portugal ostensibly maintained official neutrality during Spain's Civil War, but Portugal is a victim of its geography vis-a-vis Spain. The truth is, Salazar's authoritarian regime supplied Spain's General Francisco Franco and his Nationalists with ammunition, logistical help, and volunteer forces during the Spanish Civil War. Franco demanded Portugal's help in the conflict. Spain constantly threatens Portugal, and Salazar is always on guard to try to discourage any aspirations Spain might have about taking over its much smaller neighbor to the west. The man is doing quite a brilliant job, in my opinion. I do not agree with all the decisions he's made, but Portugal is still neutral. It has not been invaded by Spain or by Germany. Maintaining neutrality is extremely difficult. It can also be very profitable."

Robert did not like fascism or authoritarianism, but he loved Portugal. He supported Salazar because he knew the country's President was doing what was necessary for Portugal to survive in a difficult world. Robert was a man of principal and practicality, and Emerson could tell he was cautious and conflicted about his support for Salazar.

Emerson was overwhelmed with the all the information Robert had just shared with her. She realized that maintaining a country's neutrality required exceedingly delicate diplomacy and international maneuvering. She previously had taken Portugal's neutral status in the war for granted. She had not fully understood until now how vulnerable Portugal was and how easily its neutral position could collapse. This made her wonder how safe she was at Bacalhoa. She realized that no one was ever totally safe, no matter where they were — especially in a world that was tearing itself apart

The most disturbing revelations Robert had made to her were about what was happening with the Jews in the countries Germany had conquered. It was still difficult for her to believe that such atrocities could really be happening in the places that were now controlled by the Nazis. How could human beings do these things to other human beings? It would take her some time to absorb and accept the reality of all that Robert had divulged.

Emerson was terribly worried because Robert believed the Germans, or the Portuguese, or both were spying on him and perhaps listening in on his telephone calls and on conversations inside his house. However, she did not doubt for a second that Robert was telling her the truth. He was not an alarmist and would never tell her something that he did not believe to be true. Because Emerson knew this about Robert, she had to accept what he had said with all the veracity it implied.

Robert looked completely exhausted and defeated as he left Bacalhoa that night. Emerson had never seen him like this. She knew her words could do little to change anything. She hoped that listening to Robert's concerns had lightened his burden and provided him with the release he'd needed. His eyes were full of sorrow as he lifted Emerson's hand to say goodnight. He was such a proper gentleman, and he always kissed her hand when they ended their evenings together. Before she really thought about what she was doing, Emerson put her arms around Robert and held him close for a few seconds. She kissed him on the cheek. She didn't want to let him go. She realized she enjoyed the close contact with this man who had always been her friend. When she closed the door of Bacalhoa behind him, Emerson thought she might have seen a slight smile on Robert's face and maybe even a twinkle in his sad eyes.

Chapter 14

EVERYTHING CHANGES AGAIN

1941

In spite of the fact that a war was raging all over Europe, Emerson decided during the fall of 1941 that she was going to celebrate the holidays this year. She planned a small Thanksgiving dinner for a few friends, many of whom she had not seen in more than two years. Most of her expat friends and Portuguese friends had known her as part of a couple. They had sent flowers and food and notes of condolence when Peter died. She had written thank you notes in return. When a year had passed since Peter's death, a few people had begun to invite her to small dinners and cocktail parties. Magdalena had declined these invitations for her, saying that Emerson was not yet ready to attend social events. The truth was, Emerson had been so depressed, she was not able to get out of bed. Sometimes she had been unable to feed herself.

Emerson decided not to include the embassy crowd in her Thanksgiving party this year, as that would bring back too many painful memories. Planning the menu and writing the invitations to Thanksgiving Dinner gave her some pleasure, and Robert was delighted that she was looking forward to seeing people. He served as her informal host, and the Thanksgiving feast was a success. It gave Emerson confidence that she could engage with the world again, at least her small world of friends in Setubal and Lisbon. She started making plans for Christmas.

On the first Sunday in December, Emerson and Robert drove into Lisbon for a late lunch at one of the restaurants they both enjoyed. Emerson looked radiant, dressed in a well-tailored black cashmere suit with a bright yellow and blue silk scarf tied around her neck. The city was packed with refugees who filled the streets and cafes and waited in desperation for their luck to bring them a way to leave the continent.

It was a warm and sunny day, especially for Lisbon in December, and after lunch, Emerson and Robert took a long walk. Emerson drifted off to sleep in the car later that evening as Robert's driver chauffeured them back to Setubal. They had not yet reached Bacalhoa when Robert gently touched her shoulder and told her she had to wake up, that there was news she needed to hear. She blinked her eyes open and focused on Robert's face which was anything but the usually calm and collected face she had almost always known him to present to her and to everyone. He was upset, and his concern was obvious.

"Emerson, I have bad news that has just been broadcast on the car radio. The BBC just reported that the Empire of Japan has bombed Pearl Harbor in Hawaii. Most of the Pacific Fleet of the United States Navy has been destroyed. I am so sorry. It looks like you Yanks will be in it now, too."

"Oh, my God, no. How could this happen? Was it a surprise attack? Why didn't we suspect it was coming? Were many

Americans killed? Maybe I need to go back home to Connecticut and join the war effort?" Tears began to roll down Emerson's face as she thought of the dead Americans who had perished in the attack. "I love my country. We are at war now, and I want to do something to help. Do you think we are in the war with Hitler, too, or just with that nasty little Hirohito?"

"You are asking me questions I can't answer, my dear. But I am sure the United States will be all in against Hitler as well as against the Japanese. You know, Emerson, when Britain declared war on Germany in 1939, I thought that perhaps I should return to England and do my part there. However, I decided I might be able to do just as much good, and perhaps more, working for the Allied cause from Portugal. It was the right decision for me, and I know I have been able to save some lives by staying here. So, take your time, and think things through before you decide to go back to the States. It will be even more difficult and dangerous to cross the Atlantic now than it was before, and I can think of quite a few ways you could help the Allied cause without returning to Connecticut."

"I am stunned by this terrible news, but I guess I knew we would be in this mess sooner or later. To be attacked in the Pacific, in Hawaii, and so unexpectedly is such a shock. Or maybe it was not so unexpectedly. I have been out of things for way too long. I need to be more in touch with what is happening in the world. We were having such a lovely day. I can't bear to think about all those young sailors at Pearl Harbor who died. I have to do something to help. I can't just stay home and have tea and write letters. I have resources, and I am smart and tremendously over-educated. There must be something I can do that will make a difference."

Emerson's chance came sooner than she could have expected when Robert called her on the telephone three nights later and asked if he could come to Bacalhoa at once. It was after eleven o'clock, and Emerson was just about to turn out her reading light and go to sleep. Lily was snuggled down in the duvet snoring softly. Emerson told Robert that of course he could come right over. She knew he would never ask to see her at this time of night unless he had a good reason. She put on her dressing gown made of soft blue wool and went to open the front door herself. There was no need to wake Magdalena just to open the door for Robert.

He was obviously upset when he arrived. Robert was usually perfectly dressed in his expensive hand-tailored English suits and shirts. He was always the correctly groomed British aristocrat. But tonight he was disheveled, and he had blood on his pants and shirt. His coat was not buttoned. His hair was soaking wet from the rain. He stood at the door while he talked to Emerson. "Emerson, I am so sorry to bother you at such a late hour, but I desperately need your help. As I've told you, I am being watched, and I am worried that the Germans and their agents suspect that I've been helping British fliers and other refugees flee France."

"Please come in out of the rain and cold, Robert. There is no need for you to stand out there talking when you could be in here with me in front of a warm fire."

"I don't want to come in, and I can't stand out here any longer — in case someone is watching me right now. The last thing in the world I want to do is put you in danger, but I have a small child in my car who has been seriously hurt. The child is a little French boy. He's five or six years old and has a gunshot wound in his leg. I have just removed the bullet and stitched up his thigh. It would not be safe for him to stay at my house, and he was not able to continue on the 'underground railroad' with the rest of his group of refugees. Is there any way you could keep him with you for a few days until he is well enough to travel? I hate to ask you, but I don't know what else to do. No one knows that I have treated this gunshot wound, and I don't think anyone saw me carry the child to my car. If you agree to help me with this, I will drive my car around to the rear of your property. I'll bring the little boy to you through your garden's back gate. Can you meet me at the dining room doors? Is there anywhere we can make up a bed for the little fellow — somewhere out of the way where no one will see him?"

"Of course, I will help you. I will take him in. I can hide him from everyone else, but there is no way I can keep his presence a secret from Magdalena. She notices everything. She notices when I put my shoes in a different spot. She would know there was a little boy in this house in two seconds. No, she would know it in one second."

"You can trust Magdalena. She has been helping me return the pilots to England for almost a year now. She is a discreet and willing friend to the Allies."

"My Magdalena is one of your operatives? Why am I always the last to know anything around here?"

"It is always need to know, and you have not needed to know until tonight. Now you do need to know. I will meet you at the French doors that open from the dining room out into the garden." Robert left and returned to his car. Emerson locked the front door and hurried to meet the doctor and his patient in the dining room. She thought the small chapel off of her own bedroom suite would be a good place to make a bed for the child. No one ever went in there, and there was no entrance to the chapel except through her bedroom. It would be perfectly quiet. Somewhere there was a folding wood and canvas camp cot that would make a suitable bed for the small boy. It was stored in a closet — if she could just remember which closet.

Emerson met them in the dining room. Robert carried the

little boy in his arms, walked quickly through the house, and put him down gently on Emerson's bed. Lily roused herself, sniffed at the bandage on the boy's leg, then snuggled down beside the unconscious child. She put her chin on his arm. Animals always know when someone needs comforting. Emerson gave Robert a towel to dry his hair and sent him to look for the camp cot, while she brought clean sheets and blankets to the chapel. The small patient never woke up during the process of transporting his sleeping and bandaged body from the car into the house and then to the cot in the chapel. Emerson guessed that Robert had given him something to relieve his pain and help him sleep. Removing the bullet and cleaning and stitching the wound had to have been painful.

Robert gave instructions about the boy's care and finally and reluctantly left Bacalhoa as he had arrived — back out into the rain by way of the dining room doors and the garden's rear gate. Emerson suspected that Magdalena would know all about the boy and what was happening before the child woke up the next morning. Emerson was tired after all the late-night activity and was happy to be able to return to her own bed and go to sleep.

The next morning, Magdalena brought two breakfast trays when she came to Emerson's room. Emerson took her own tray, and Magdalena went to check on the child.

"He speaks only French, Miss Emerson, and I don't know many words of French. Doctor Carmichael says you speak French, so you will have to converse with this little one and tell me what he wants. Doctor Carmichael will be here shortly to see him, to change the bandages on his wound. The child is still sleeping, so you have time to finish your breakfast."

Emerson ate and dressed quickly. She decided to put on long pants and a warm sweater. It was cool in the chapel, and bending down to care for a child who was lying on a cot would be easier in work clothes and sturdy shoes than in her usual daytime dresses. She went to the chapel when Magdalena took the boy his breakfast tray.

Her French was rusty, but she had studied it for many years in school. The vocabulary required for this interaction would not be difficult. "Good Morning, my little one. My name is Emerson. You are a guest in my house, and I am honored to have you here. You have had an injury to your leg, and Doctor Carmichael will be here soon to change your bandages. How are you feeling? Does your leg hurt?"

The boy stared at Emerson and then smiled when he saw Lily standing beside her. "What's the name of the dog?"

"This is Lily. I named her Lily because she is so white — like the flower. She is friendly and likes children very much. This is Magdalena who has brought you some hot chocolate. It is delicious and just the thing to warm you up and make you feel better. Please tell us your name so we know what to call you."

"I am Pierre LaFontaine, and I live in Lyon. I don't remember coming to this house, and I don't remember how I hurt my leg. Who is Doctor Carmichael? I like Lily."

"Pierre, it is so nice to meet you. We will talk about all of this with Doctor Carmichael when he arrives. Dr. Carmichael took care of the wound in your leg and brought you here to my house. Magdalena has made you some eggs and some delicious toast with butter and raspberry jam. You can eat all you want. There is more." Peter shoveled the food into his mouth, as if he hadn't eaten anything in days. By the look of his thin little arms, Emerson suspected that he had not eaten well for a long time.

Magdalena went to open the door for Robert Carmichael and told him their patient's name was Pierre. Emerson was happy to see that Robert looked rested and ever so much better this morning than he had the night before. He was once again impeccably dressed, and his usual composure had returned. He hurried through Emerson's bedroom into the chapel.

Robert's French was fluent, and he was eager to talk to the boy. "And how is our patient today? I understand that your name is Pierre. I am Doctor Robert Carmichael, and I want to tell you what happened to your leg. You received a gunshot wound to your thigh. I don't know how or when or why you got shot, but I had to take the bullet out of your leg and clean the wound. Then I sterilized it with antiseptics to keep the germs away, and then I stitched the wound back together. I will have to check to see if you are healing and put a clean bandage on your leg twice a day. It might hurt some when I take off the old bandage, but it is necessary to change the bandages often to keep you from getting an infection." Emerson acknowledged that Robert's French was in much better shape than hers, and having the doctor speak so effortlessly in his native tongue obviously pleased Pierre. Emerson suspected that Robert's work with the Allied flyboys and the resistance fighters from France had made it necessary for him to brush up on his French.

"Do you know who shot me? Why would anybody do that? I really don't remember anything except I was walking and walking and then hiding in a hay wagon and then walking some more. I was with some other people, and we found a shed in the woods and went in there to sleep. I was so tired. I couldn't walk any more. I don't remember anything else after going to sleep in the shed. I wish I knew who wanted to shoot me." Doctor Carmichael worked quickly to change the bandages and clean the wound. Pierre winced a few times, but he was a brave little boy and didn't cry out in pain.

"The person who shot you probably wasn't intending to shoot you at all, Pierre. He was probably trying to shoot something or somebody else and hit you by mistake. I am just glad that a kind, strong man was able to carry you from the place where you got shot to my office so I could take care of your leg."

"I am glad of that, too. Now I am tired and want to go back to sleep. I ate a lot of eggs and toast for breakfast. I will be fine, if I can eat more food like this." Pierre put his head down on the pillow and went back to sleep."

"He will want to sleep most of the time for the next few days. I have given him medication for the pain. I'll come twice a day to check on how he's doing and change the bandages. Be sure you wake him up to eat and drink and to go to the toilet. He needs lots of fluids, and you may have to force him to drink more than he really wants to drink. Under better circumstances, I might have tried to put an intravenous line in his arm to keep him hydrated, but we don't have those better circumstances. You will have to keep him hydrated by making him drink a lot of water." Robert Carmichael gave more directions about the pain pills and the sulfa medication he was giving the boy to ward off infection. Emerson was worn out from listening to all the instructions and watching Robert clean the wound and change the bandages.

"I would never have made a nurse, I'm afraid. I will leave that to Magdalena and to you, Robert. Do you want some breakfast or some coffee?"

"I would love a cup of Benadina's excellent coffee." Robert loved everything Benadina made, not just her coffee. "I don't know what I'm going to do with the boy when he is well enough to leave. There is no regular schedule for the fliers to come to my house. They just arrive when they arrive. I have no idea when another group will come through or if they will be able to take the boy with them. He may have to stay here with you for a while. It won't be hard to keep him hidden while his leg is hurting and he is sleeping most of the time.

But once he begins to heal, he will want to run around and go outside. He's a child, and he needs to run and play. But he cannot be allowed to appear in public. He doesn't have any papers, and the Germans will definitely have begun to watch you and Bacalhoa now that the U.S. is in the war against them. Portugal is still neutral, and the Germans can't legally do anything to you. But I know of several people who have just 'disappeared' into thin air. I know the Germans were responsible, but there will never be any way to prove they did it. That's why I must be so careful not to arouse suspicion. And now you must also be just as careful and not do anything at all out of the ordinary. I am terribly sorry to put you in this position, but you did say you wanted to do something to help. This is a wonderful way to help — by saving the life of a small boy."

"I am happy to keep him here as long as he needs to stay. I don't know about the servants. I will leave that to Magdalena. She adores children, and I know she will see to it that he has everything he needs, including some exercise. I am already planning a picnic to my boathouse, and I think Pierre will enjoy that — when he has recovered sufficiently to walk outside. We will manage. I'm a 'can do' kind of person. You know the story about how Peter and I met, when I volunteered my carpentry skills to help build the camp for the Basque and Spanish orphans."

"Emerson, I am sure you can do absolutely anything you set your mind to. We will figure this out. The underground brings people to me who have gunshot wounds and other kinds of injuries, as well as those who are ill. That is how I can be the most help to the resistance. I am happy to do everything I can, but I just don't know what to do when we have children who are not able to travel on their own. We might have to wait until who knows when for the next group to arrive so they can take the child with them. We keep our activities and people completely separated, and I have only one name and contact telephone number. That telephone number is to be used only in case one of us is captured and tortured. We can't reveal what we don't know. I purposely don't want to know about the other stops along the escape route, but in this situation I would like to have someone to call for guidance."

"We can handle it, Robert. It's one small boy. If you can keep him on the road to recovery, I can keep him hidden and safe … and well-fed. This is not a difficult assignment." Emerson smiled at Robert. She was happiest when she was needed.

Chapter 15

AND SO IT BEGINS

1941-1942

Because of the widening of the war and the entry of the United States into the world conflict, Emerson did not feel like having a Christmas party or decorating everything as elaborately as she had planned to do before Pearl Harbor was attacked. She did set up a Christmas tree and dug out the decorations she and Peter's mother and sister had made and collected years before, for that first and only Christmas Emerson and Peter would celebrate together at Bacalhoa. That had been in December of 1938, and now it was Christmas of 1941. Could three years have passed? Emerson had missed almost an entire year, mired in grief and depression. It did not seem possible that Peter had been gone for more than two years.

Pierre was curious about the tree. He said he had seen them in the houses of his Gentile friends and in the house where he lived with his French Catholic "family" and pretended he wasn't Jewish. Emerson knew Pierre was Jewish although

Robert had never told her that he was. Emerson had spent years celebrating holidays with Rachel's family and knew the ceremony of the Seder and about Chanukah and all of the Jewish Holidays. She wondered where she could discreetly find a menorah.

She talked to Pierre about her good friend Rachel and about how Rachel's family had informally adopted her when she had lost her own parents. Pierre's eyes filled with tears when Emerson told him her story. Emerson hugged him and said she understood how lonely it could feel not to have a family any more. She said many of the same things to Pierre in French that she had said to Anna in Spanish at the children's camp in England when Anna had been too sad to speak.

Emerson told Magdalena that she wanted to celebrate Chanukah for Pierre's sake. Magdalena nodded and said she would take care of it. A few days later, she appeared with a menorah, nine candles, and several small gifts wrapped in blue and silver paper. "You are truly amazing, Magdalena. How do you do it?" Emerson believed Magdalena could do anything.

Magdalena smiled an enigmatic smile and said, "I have connections. Don't ask."

Emerson, Magdalena, and Robert cared for Pierre until his leg was healed and he was walking again. On a sunny day in January, Emerson and Magdalena loaded the car with a picnic basket in the back seat. Pierre hid on the floor with Lily under a blanket. Lily thought it was a great game and kept licking Pierre's face as they lay together in the back of the car. Bundled up in boots and a heavy coat with a muffler around his neck, Pierre was using a crutch, but he loved walking close to the water and gathering shells on the beach of the small cove. He had begged to be allowed to go for a ride in the boat, but there was no life vest small enough for Pierre. Emerson asked if he knew how to swim. He said he did, so she promised that when he no longer needed his crutch and the weather was warmer, she would give Pierre a ride in the boat. She wondered where in the world she would be able to find a life vest that was small enough for the boy.

Pierre had made friends with all the servants by the time the New Year arrived. Benadina in particular loved Pierre because he had such a good appetite and was so enthusiastic about everything she cooked for him. She loved the excuse to make cookies which Pierre devoured as soon as they came out of the oven. Emerson suspected that Lily was also receiving her share of warm cookies. They would all be sorry to see Pierre leave when the time came. Emerson knew she was becoming too attached to Pierre and dreaded the day when he would have to go on his way. But she knew he had to go, and she would continue to work for that. A plan began to form in her mind.

Emerson reminded Robert about a story he had told her a long time ago, about a Jewish physician who had left Frankfurt and moved to England to begin a new life after escaping from the Nazis. This physician had fled Germany with a young man who worked on a cargo ship that sometimes came to Lisbon. It turned out that the young man now owned the cargo ship. Emerson wanted to know everything about the young ship's captain.

"Dr. Jacob Engelman arrived in England in the spring of 1938. He was staying with friends of mine, and I met him when I visited their house in London. I was fascinated by his story. He had left everything behind when he fled his home in Frankfurt. He was ahead of so many others when he realized he had to get away from the Nazis. He wanted to practice medicine in England, and I was able to find a position for him with a medical group which is associated with the hospital in London where I used to work. He's an excellent doctor, and the medical community in London is fortunate to have him working there. Doctors are always in short supply, and even more so with the war. He and I exchange letters once in a while. I will write to him and ask him about his friend Max. I believe Max stays in Lisbon when he's between sea voyages. I have to say I am curious why you want to know all about this Max, the ship's captain."

Emerson had cleaned out her husband Peter's desk many months earlier and had come across the blank visa forms. Peter had so carefully prepared and signed these visas for the people who were lucky enough to be allowed to go to the United States. A visa for the United States was like gold to any refugee. It had not occurred to Emerson to return the remaining blank forms or the medallion stamp that gave the visa its proof of official validation. She had made no effort to give these things back to the embassy, and no one from the embassy had bothered to ask her for them. Peter had stopped using them when he'd become too ill to work, even from home.

After Peter had died, someone from the Embassy had delivered several boxes from Peter's office in Lisbon. Peter had packed the boxes himself when he'd realized he was not going to be able to do his job any longer. Emerson had put the boxes in a corner of his study and ignored them. She'd not been able to bring herself to unpack Peter's things.

One day after Pierre had come to Bacalhoa, Emerson decided she had the courage to find out what Peter had brought home from his office, what he had packed in the boxes. Because she had been told that he'd packed them himself, she wondered what he'd felt was important enough to bring to Bacalhoa rather than leave at the embassy. Emerson found quite a few special books she knew had been important to Peter. She was happy to have these things her husband had loved. She found some personal correspondence that she set aside to look at later, and she found several maps of Portugal with markings on them in Peter's handwriting. If she had hoped for some personal letter or a note, she was disappointed. When she opened the last box, she knew this was the important one. It was the heaviest box. She could not lift it and had to drag it out of the corner of the room to remove the packing tape.

Inside was treasure of the most valuable kind. If she had seen the contents of the box even one year earlier, she might not have realized the importance of what Peter had chosen to save from his days at the American Embassy. There was no note of explanation in the box, but Peter had brought her a great gift. He had brought hundreds and hundreds of blank visas, the transit letters that would allow many people who wanted to travel to the United States the chance to do so.

Emerson had always believed that Peter was able to look into the future and predict what was going to happen. He'd told Emerson there was nothing mystical about this ability, that he had no crystal ball. It had to do with knowing what was going on in the world and based on that, being able to use his analytical brain to tell him what the future was likely to hold. Peter was the best informed person Emerson had ever known. He read everything, and he read all the time. He seemed to know so many things that had nothing at all to do with his job.

Emerson could not help but wonder if Peter had brought these blank visa forms home with him because he thought he might be able to use them in the future. Perhaps he had known he would not be able to use them himself, but thought Emerson would be able to put them to good use. Maybe he'd hoped that she would find a way to do something worthwhile with these pieces of paper.

It was the discovery of the visa forms that started Emerson's mind going in a thousand different directions. It became obvious to her how this valuable commodity, these blank visas, could be turned into safety and freedom, even life itself, for those who longed for and so desperately needed it. She had the paperwork, the official documents to make it happen.

She could provide Pierre an official document that would allow him to enter the United States and live in freedom. This was her dream, to give Pierre the life he deserved to have in the best country in the world. The next challenge was to find a way to get Pierre across the Atlantic Ocean to the United States, to Boston. She lay awake at night as she formed and then reformed her hypotheses. If she could make it work for Pierre, maybe she could make it work for others.

Emerson had found herself growing overly attached to Pierre. She loved having him around the quinta and could not imagine the place without him. What would Lily do? What would Magdalena do? What would she do? She had been formulating in her mind a plan to ask Rachel to adopt Pierre and to raise him as her own child. As much as Emerson wanted to have him with her forever, Pierre could not stay in Portugal. His blonde hair and blue eyes had allowed him to live as a French child in a Catholic family, but he was French and had been smuggled into Portugal. He did not have papers that allowed him either to enter Portugal or to stay here.

Emerson would have adopted him in a minute if she could possibly have found a way. The next best thing was to send him to the United States, to her dearest friend and "sister" Rachel. Rachel had two small babies of her own, but Rachel's family and her husband's family had more than adequate economic means. Rachel now had a nanny to help with her children, and if she would agree to adopt Pierre, Emerson would pay to hire a second nanny if that was what was necessary.

Robert had warned Emerson not to mention anything about Pierre in her letters to Rachel. Since the United States had entered the war, he had concerns that the Portuguese secret police, the PVDE, might be opening Emerson's mail and listening in on her telephone calls. He was also concerned that, because of Emerson's friendship with him, she might have come under suspicion. He warned her that communicating with people in the U.S. might put her at risk with the Portuguese government or the snooping Germans. He offered to arrange to send her important letters in the British diplomatic pouch. Someone in England, a friend of Robert's who worked in the British Foreign Office, would airmail her letters to the U.S. from London. Emerson knew that the diplomatic pouch was sacred and would not be opened or searched by the Portuguese.

Emerson knew what she had to do and began composing her letter to Rachel. She realized that at some point, they would need to use a code when writing their letters back and forth to each other and in their telephone calls. Until the attack on Pearl Harbor, Americans had been insulated from the war in Europe. Now it seemed that everyone in the U.S. wanted to do something to help with the war effort. Rachel had been knitting bandages and doing other things that bored her. Emerson hoped she could convince Rachel to participate in her plan to save lives — starting with saving Pierre's life.

Chapter 16

ALLIES IN AMERICA JOIN THE FIGHT

January 1942

*E*merson spent a long time composing the letter she sent to Rachel. She described Pierre and how he had come to live at Bacalhoa. She told Rachel how attached she had become to the little boy and that he could not stay in Portugal. In her letter, Emerson wondered if there was anyone Rachel trusted enough to adopt Pierre and made the point that it would have to be a very special family because Pierre was such a special child. Emerson did everything but ask Rachel to take Pierre into her own household.

In a separate letter, Emerson explained what she had learned through Robert about the plight of the Jews in Germany and German-occupied countries in Europe. Emerson asked Rachel how much was known in America about the death camps. She told Rachel about the blank visa forms and the official seal Peter had left with her. Emerson outlined her plan to try to bring Jewish children out of Europe through Vichy France to Portugal and send them on to the United States. If she could get the children to the United States, Emerson asked Rachel if she could find American families who wanted to adopt these children. Emerson wanted to be sure that when a child arrived in the U.S., there would be a family already waiting for him or her. If enough adoptive families could not be found, Emerson's plan could not get off the ground.

Emerson explained to Rachel about the significance of the quotas the U.S. was imposing on official Jewish immigrants and that her orphans would be entering the country with an official visa but outside the prescribed legal quota system. Emerson told Rachel frankly that what she proposed was to smuggle the children into the United States. Emerson described her hopes of finding a regular and reliable way to deliver the children to America and asked Rachel to talk to her mother, who was a lawyer, about Emerson's plan. Rachel's mother would be needed to help with legal matters, particularly with the adoptions.

These children were refugees and would not have birth certificates or identity cards or any official paperwork to prove they even existed. The children had nothing from their former lives and would arrive in the U.S. with just the visas issued by Emerson and a homemade identity card with a photo. The visas would be real entry permits and would have the official seal, but the legality of the paperwork with regard to the entry of the children into the United States ended there.

The children would be entering the United States secretly and would proceed to their new families completely under the protection of private citizens. No officials at any level of government could know anything about Emerson's lifeline to America. No matter how important it was and no matter how many lives it might save, Emerson did not know if Rachel and her mother would be willing to go outside the law for this cause. Rachel's mother was an experienced lawyer. She would be placing her career and perhaps even her own freedom in jeopardy by helping in this extra-legal effort. Emerson laid it all out for Rachel and asked Rachel to do the same for her mother. Emerson pulled no punches in explaining that what they would all be doing would technically be against the law.

Importantly, it would not be just logistical and legal difficulties they would encounter. Even if there were an adequate number of families who wanted to adopt the orphans, some of the children had suffered terribly during the destruction of their families and communities and the round-up of Jews in Europe. These children had lost their parents. They knew all about the death camps and were constantly in fear of being sent to one of those horrific places. Some of their parents had died traveling to the camps, and more had died after reaching their destinations. Some of the children had witnessed the murders of their family members. Some of these children had been sent away by their own parents, in anticipation of the round-up of Jews, to live with non-Jewish families. Some of them had lived with Catholic or Protestant families and had been forced to pretend to be Gentiles. They'd had to deny their Jewish religion and their Jewish heritage.

Most were malnourished, and some were ill with chronic diseases. Some were psychologically disturbed or depressed. Even if an orphan was lucky enough to arrive in Portugal, sound of mind and sound of body, that child might speak only Dutch or Polish or some other language scarcely ever heard in the United States. Emerson did not want to minimize to her friends the difficulties of undertaking a project such as the one she was proposing.

Emerson realized that Rachel knew how quickly children could learn. The adopted refugees from Europe would learn English easily, and most would thrive in school once they had enough to eat and clothes to keep them warm. The most important thing that would facilitate their adjustment to life in a new country was, of course, the love and support a welcoming American family and community could and would extend to these little ones. This acceptance and the security of having a home would make all the difference in their transition to freedom and new lives.

Emerson had her fingers crossed that Rachel and her mother would want to make a commitment to save these children. Emerson wanted to do all she could, but she realized her efforts were just a drop in the bucket of what ought to be done. She might be able to save only a tiny fraction of those who needed to be rescued, but it was better to save a few than to do nothing at all.

It seemed like she waited forever to receive answers to the letters she'd sent. She knew her letters had traveled in the diplomatic pouch from the British Embassy in Portugal to the Foreign Office in London. She knew someone there had sent her letters, via airmail, from England to the United States. She had instructed Rachel to write her back by sending an airmail letter to Robert's friend at the Foreign Office in London. That friend would forward the letters in the diplomatic pouch to the British Embassy in Lisbon in care of Robert's friend there. This friend would see that letters were delivered to Robert, and Robert would bring the replies to Emerson. It was a laborious and circuitous route, but Emerson had explained to Rachel that the Portuguese secret police were watching people and opening domestic and foreign mail. The Germans were always up to something nefarious, like listening in on telephone calls and kidnapping people and making them disappear. Emerson realized they needed an easier, more efficient way of sending and receiving information. She began working on a code they could use to expedite their communications.

Emerson's patience had been truly tested as she'd anxiously waited for a reply from Rachel, but when a letter finally arrived, it was more than worth the wait. Rachel told Emerson that, after she had delivered the twins by Cesarean section, her physician had warned her not to become pregnant again. Rachel was an only child and had been devastated by this news. She had always wanted a large family. Rachel asked Emerson if she thought Pierre would fit into her own family. Rachel wanted to adopt Pierre and hoped Emerson would agree. Emerson wept with joy when she read Rachel's letter. This is exactly what she had hoped would happen.

Rachel was also enormously enthusiastic about helping to place Jewish orphans in the United States and already knew of several families who were eager to adopt children. She explained to Emerson that it was difficult for Jews to adopt children through church-affiliated agencies in the United States because of religious differences. Most children were put up for adoption by the Catholic Church and other Christian charities. They were strict about allowing their charges to be adopted only by other Catholic or Protestant families. Some Jewish religious organizations provided adoption services, but this was on quite a small scale. Most adoptions within the Jewish faith were handled privately.

Because of several organizations to which she belonged through her husband's role as a rabbi and through her own contacts, Rachel had a network of rabbi's wives and other connections all over the United States. She was certain she could find enough families to take all the Jewish orphans Emerson could manage to send across the ocean.

Emerson had not really given the financial aspect of her operation much thought, but Rachel volunteered that, once the children arrived in the United States, she and her mother would handle all the costs of transporting the orphans to their new homes and buying them the clothing and other things they needed. Rachel told Emerson that her mother Naomi had written to Emerson about her proposed role as a legal advocate for Emerson's project. When she read this, Emerson's heart sank as she was certain that Rachel's mother was too much of a legal ethicist to ever think about going outside the strict rules she imposed on herself. Emerson was afraid that Naomi Friedman would never step outside the law, no matter how urgent or important the cause. Emerson was surprised and heartened when she received Rachel's mother's letter.

Naomi Friedman was a brilliant legal scholar. She had fought hard to be recognized in a man's world and was a respected attorney. She had a thriving private law practice in Baltimore, Maryland. She had welcomed and loved Emerson as her own child when Emerson's parents were killed in a car accident when Emerson was in college.

Naomi's letter to Emerson began with a heartfelt expression of gratitude for the possibility that Pierre might become part of Rachel's family. Naomi told Emerson what Rachel had not said about how really desperate she had been when she was told she should not try to have any more children. Naomi said the letter from Emerson describing Pierre and wanting to find him the best possible home in America had been like a tonic for Rachel. Knowing she would be able to adopt a little boy that Emerson had come to love so much had given Rachel a new outlook on life.

Naomi was also grateful that Emerson had given the bright and energetic Rachel a project into which she could throw herself — searching for and selecting good homes for refugee children. Naomi herself was even more enthusiastic than Rachel had been about the effort to save the orphans.

Naomi knew exactly how to arrange the adoptions of these refugees, even without a birth certificate or other official paper work. Naomi had arranged a number of private adoptions in Baltimore and knew the bureaucratic ropes. Each child would arrive with "valid" entry papers, and that was all Naomi would need to make the rest of the adoption process happen. Naomi told Emerson she was honored and excited to be able to work on this humanitarian effort. She said she had been feeling her law practice was no longer as much of a challenge for her as it had been, and she'd been looking for a way to help the war effort. She shared with Emerson that, in her long career as an attorney, she felt the upcoming rescue project would be the most important work she would ever do. Emerson's letter outlining her proposal to relocate the Jewish orphans in America had come at just the right moment for Naomi as well as for Rachel.

Naomi knew exactly where the children could be delivered once they reached U.S. territorial waters. Naomi had many friends and acquaintances in powerful places. She had connections who possessed great wealth and owned significant real estate all over the East Coast. Naomi described a place on the Eastern Shore of Virginia that had water access to the Chesapeake Bay. This potential landing spot for the children was owned by a close friend of Naomi's, and she was certain her friend would be delighted to do his part to welcome the small refugees from Europe.

Naomi had visited her friend's beautiful property several times and knew it would be the ideal spot for the children to safely and surreptitiously arrive by water and disembark in the United States. The area was remote and underpopulated. There was little if any law enforcement presence in the area. Access from the Chesapeake Bay would be ideal for a small boat. Naomi felt it would work as the place for the children to come ashore and begin their new lives. Emerson had no idea where the remote estuary that Naomi had chosen was located.

But if Naomi was advocating for this location, Emerson knew that Butcher's Creek, Virginia would be the perfect spot for the refugee children to first set foot onto the free soil of her wonderful country.

In addition to her ideas about how the children's clandestine arrival in the U.S. could be arranged, Naomi had already figured out how the children would be transported, housed, and cared for on their way to their new homes. Naomi had physicians lined up to give the children physical examinations and shots and any medical care they might require as soon as they got off the ship. Naomi knew how to obtain ration books for the children and how to buy extra food from farmers in the countryside.

Naomi had never acknowledged that there were any boundaries to keep her from being successful in a quest. Naomi had always been a dynamo, and Emerson was filled with relief and gratitude because she knew that between Rachel and Naomi, everything at the other end of the orphan's journey would be handled beautifully by these two superbly capable women.

Now all she had to do was find a ship that would carry the children from Portugal to the Chesapeake Bay. She had no doubts that Robert would be able to follow through with his end to arrange to bring the children out of Vichy France. For the first time, Emerson began to see her plan coming together and had realistic hopes that she would be able to save children who had no hope of a better life, or in some cases, the hope of any life at all. She would save her precious Pierre, and she would save as many others as she possibly could.

Chapter 17

THE ESCAPE ROUTE

February 1942

Robert and Emerson were being chauffeured to Lisbon in Robert's car for the dinner meeting. It was February, and the rain was bitterly cold. Emerson would not have come out on a night like this for any reason other than to further her plans to rescue the children. Robert had contacted his friend Dr. Engelman in London, again through the diplomatic pouch. With great difficulty, they had finally been able to arrange a meeting with Max Boudreaux, the owner and captain of the Portuguese cargo ship, the *Coracao de Anjo*. Emerson and Robert were desperately hoping that this man and his ship would be an answer to their prayers. They had invested more optimism than they should have that the *Anjo* could become their way of transporting children out of Portugal to freedom in America.

Robert and Emerson realized that any association between themselves and the ship's captain must be kept completely secret.

If there was trouble of any kind, it would be better if there were no connections to be discovered. This is the way Robert's escape route for the Allied airmen worked — with each part of the operation knowing as little as possible about the other parts. Emerson and Robert were going to Lisbon to talk with Maximillian Boudreaux. They were meeting at a quiet restaurant run by friends of Max's. It had been arranged in such a way that no one would see them together as they presented their plan to Max and made their plea for him to help them.

Finding the obscure café was not easy, but at last they arrived and ran through the rain under an umbrella to reach the entrance. Wet and chilled to the bone, they were greeted by a blazing fire in the fireplace and taken to a table covered in white linen set next to the fire. There was no one else eating in the restaurant that night. A strikingly handsome young man stood up to greet them. Emerson could not believe how young he looked. Could this possibly be the owner and captain of a cargo ship? Maybe this was the owner's son?

They introduced themselves and ordered before-dinner aperitifs. Delicious small pastries were served as a first course. Emerson noticed that the young man's right arm was not fully functioning. She wondered what had happened to him. She didn't think it could be a war wound, but in a way, it was exactly that. If Emerson had known how Max received his injury, she would have agreed that it definitely was a war wound. The war against the Nazis had begun early for Max.

Max's fight had started many months before the rest of the world knew it was at war. The young man insisted that Emerson and Robert call him Max, and he assured them that indeed he was the owner, the navigator, and the captain of the ship called the *Coracao de Anjo*. He told them that the previous captain and owner had been taken from the *Anjo* and held aboard a German U-boat that had gone down in the Atlantic. The former first mate had taken over the actual duties as the *Anjo*'s master.

Dr. Jacob Engelman had vouched for Robert and Emerson, so Max was willing to tell them a little about his own recent experiences, transporting Jews to Palestine aboard the *Anjo*. He seemed to welcome the opportunity to talk about these things with people he knew he could trust with his stories.

He told them he had been transporting cargo throughout the Mediterranean since purchasing the *Anjo* in 1939. Only his crew knew that he also carried, along with his manifested cargo, a number of Jews who had arrived in Portugal from all the countries of Nazi-occupied Europe. He welcomed as many as his ship could carry. The *Anjo* had the usual passenger quarters for a few people as well as a hidden secret section of berths for additional refugees.

Max spoke with great passion about this part of his work. He explained that the Portuguese were more than anxious to send the Jewish refugees on their way to someplace else. The British Mandate administrators in Palestine, however, were not anxious to receive so many Jews into that country. There were quotas, and passenger ships were barred from unloading their human cargo without submitting complex and often impossible paperwork. Max did what he could via the legal route to get his Jews into Palestine. But when they were denied because of quotas or the wrong papers, he told Emerson and Robert that he had several "non-official ways" of getting his people into the country.

Max shared with them one of his subterfuges for unloading his passengers when they had been denied legal entry. He anchored his ship off the coast of Palestine and made contact by means of a ship-to-shore radio with his collaborators on the land. Using a code they had devised, he notified his colleagues that he had "special cargo" to unload. At night, the

Anjo's life boats were filled and quietly lowered over the sides of the *Anjo* and into the sea. There were no lights, and the oarsmen had learned to be silent as they made their way to shore. Max's Palestinian friends were ready, on the beach to receive the lifeboats full of Jews who had finally made it to the Promised Land and their chance for a new life.

Max said he worried that his contacts in Palestine would be compromised and that the British ships which patrolled the waters off the coast of Palestine would become suspicious of his activities if he showed up too often. Max told his guests how he scheduled his trips to Palestine to coincide with new rather than full moons. He was afraid he was going to have to stop his trips because the British authorities had begun watching the *Anjo* more closely.

Robert, of course, was British, and Emerson glanced at him as Max recounted how he was outwitting British officials in Palestine. It appeared to Emerson that Robert was silently applauding the young ship owner for his work. The fact that Max was defying British law did not seem to matter at all to Robert. It was obvious that Robert thought Max was a brave and wonderful young person. Emerson was in awe of Max. She found it hard to believe that someone so young could have already done so much good in a world where it sometimes seemed as if only evil reigned.

As the steaming hot dishes of Portuguese fish stew were served, Emerson felt it was time for her to propose that Max use his cargo ship for another lifesaving reason, one that did not require him to travel to Palestine. She told him that Robert would be handling the secret passage of Jewish orphans through Vichy France into Portugal. Sometimes they would travel through Spain, and other times they would arrive in Portugal by ship from Bilbao or Marseilles or other ports. She told Max about the visas and the seal she had acquired when her husband died. She told him about the network of close personal friends who would take care of everything once the children arrived in the United States.

Max asked a lot of questions. He explained that it had become much too dangerous to enter shipping lanes off the East Coast of the U.S. because German U-boats were wreaking havoc with their attacks on passenger and cargo ships along the Eastern Seaboard. He said that even though he sailed under the Portuguese flag, U-boats did not always take the trouble to find out what flag a ship was flying before they sent a deadly torpedo into its hull.

Max told them that cargo carriers in the Atlantic maintained a constant lookout for U-boats and communicated this information to each other on a regular basis so that every ship had at least some chance to know where the German submarines were at all times. Every ship's captain kept special maps on the bridge. These maps showed the constantly changing U-boat locations. All ships kept these maps, as it was a matter of survival. The alternative was to lose your ship and its crew.

Dessert and coffee were served, and Emerson asked directly if Max were willing to undertake the risk of delivering her orphans to the United States. Emerson told him that her U.S. team had designated a specific small estuary in the southern Chesapeake Bay where the children were to be delivered. The location was in a very rural and relatively unpopulated part of Virginia's Eastern Shore. There would be little if any official surveillance of the location, and hardly any notice would be paid to even a large cargo ship in that part of the bay at night. If Max could get his ship into the Chesapeake Bay, Emerson said she felt the children could be off-loaded without being discovered.

They agreed that the difficult part of the trip would be to avoid the U-boats, especially as the ship came close to United

States coastal waters. Once the ship reached Norfolk, Emerson told Max, the officials who screened ships that requested permission to enter the Chesapeake Bay would give the *Anjo* safe passage without a search and without any delays. Rachel's mother Naomi would arrange for someone she knew to be transferred to a position of authority in Norfolk. Naomi was amazing, and she anticipated way in advance every potential bottleneck and difficulty their plan might encounter.

Max wanted to see the small cove near Setubal, Portugal where he would anchor the *Anjo* to transfer the children to his ship. Emerson had learned to operate her small and ancient motor boat. The plan was that the precious cargo of children would be loaded onto the motor boat inside the boathouse. Either Emerson or Robert would take the boat full of children out into the cove and meet up with Max's ship which would be at anchor farther out to sea.

Max would already have loaded his ship's manifested and non-human cargo before it made the short trip from Lisbon to the cove to pick up the young refugees. Max said he liked their plan, and he especially supported the whole idea of saving Jewish orphans. He did not tell Emerson and Robert that by saving a young Jewish child, he felt he might be saving someone's little sister. Max was a serious and businesslike man and did not reveal anything personal about himself. Emerson was curious about him, and she wanted to know more about why he was so passionate about helping Jews reach Palestine. Max did not want to talk about himself.

They arranged for Max to meet Emerson in Setubal to look at the cove. Max wanted to evaluate the access and the possibilities for anchoring his ship to load the children onboard. If the transfer site, where the children would leave the smaller motor boat and board the larger cargo ship, was suitable, Max said he was willing to take the risk in the Atlantic. He promised to do his best to deliver the children to the safe haven of the estuary in the Chesapeake Bay. Max gave Emerson a list of questions about the precise location of Butcher's Creek in Virginia and about other latitudes and longitudes and details of the waters in which the *Anjo* would be traveling. Emerson agreed to have the answers for him when they met in Setubal the following week.

Max told Emerson she needed to acquire two shortwave radios so that they could communicate about the rendezvous of the cargo ship and the motor boat. They would need to have one radio hidden at Bacalhoa and one concealed at the boathouse. Emerson's contact in Virginia would also have to have a shortwave radio and know how to use it. Max would have to be in communication with Naomi at the end of the journey.

Max reminded Emerson and Robert about some things they already knew. They all were well aware that what they were doing was technically against the law. They realized they could be arrested and jailed if they were caught. If the Germans in Portugal discovered what they were doing, they would disappear without an arrest or a trial, never to be seen again. Emerson and Robert had already discussed these things, and they had moved beyond worrying about the danger and illegalities. The important thing was to deliver the orphans safely to their new homes in America. Emerson and Robert, and now Max, were willing to do whatever was necessary to make that happen.

Max came to Setubal the following week, and Max and Emerson drove to the small cove. Max looked at the beach, consulted some charts he had brought with him about tides and depths of water, and asked to see the motor boat and the boathouse. He frowned when he saw the old wooden boat. He told Emerson it would be necessary to find a larger, more dependable boat to bring the children from the cove out to deeper water where the cargo ship would be anchored. He told Emerson he was going to have to keep the *Anjo* farther out from the shore, depending on the tides. The boat full of children that left the cove would have to travel out into the sea to meet the *Anjo* to transfer its passengers.

Max was afraid the old motor boat would not be able to make the trip from the cove to the *Anjo* and back. He said the boat was too small and sat too low in the water. Max said it would not be possible to make the transfer of the children without a larger boat. Emerson needed to find a newer, safer, and larger launch to transport the children to the cargo ship. Max also pointed out that the *Anjo* had berths for more people than Emerson could carry in the small, older boat. He wanted to make his trips across the dangerous Atlantic Ocean as productive as possible and carry as many passengers on each trip as his ship would hold. He suggested that Emerson scale up her operation and buy a motor launch that would carry more children. If possible, Max wanted to carry as many as fifteen children on each trip.

Emerson had prepared the answers to the questions Max wanted from her. Emerson assured Max that Robert was taking care of obtaining the shortwave radios and that she would be proficient in using the radios by the time they were needed. It was agreed that Morse code in English would be their means of sending and receiving messages. Max gave a code book to Emerson so that their messages would not be intercepted by anybody who was monitoring shortwave radio traffic. Emerson knew and Max reiterated that many interested parties in Portugal were constantly listening for who was sending Morse code messages, who was receiving them, and what were they saying to each other. The radios would be used only when necessary, and they would always communicate using a cypher.

Emerson would send a coded shortwave radio message to Max when a group of children was at Bacalhoa. Max would give her an estimated date when he would arrive off the coast of Setubal with the *Anjo*. They would communicate only occasionally as the rendezvous date grew closer. On the day the children were scheduled to leave, longitude and latitude positions and approximate times would be exchanged.

No one had yet figured out how they would feed, take care of, and hide fifteen children at Bacalhoa. But if Max could carry that many children in the secret passenger compartment of his ship, Emerson was determined to have fifteen orphans ready to leave on the *Anjo* when Max arrived to take them to America.

Emerson was entering a world that was entirely new to her. It was a world filled with known and unknown dangers. She told herself she would have to begin to think and act differently if she were going to save the children and keep herself out of prison or worse. But she was completely at peace with her decisions. She was not afraid of anything her new effort might bring to her. Confronting evil and saving lives was not for the timid. Emerson had never been timid.

Emerson and Max agreed on a resonable charge for each trip and for each child who traveled. The fees were mostly for food and supplies that would be required to care for the children during the voyage. Emerson was happy to pay whatever it took to accomplish her goals, and Max was making most of his money on his other cargos, not on his small human passengers.

Before Max said goodbye to her, he asked Emerson, "Why are you doing this? You are not Jewish and have no personal stake in the effort to save these Jewish children."

Emerson had not really been asked to explain to anybody

her reasons for what she was doing until Max asked her the question that afternoon, so she had to pause and think before she answered. "I am doing this because I can. I am doing this because I have the coveted visas, and these visas can save lives. I have the letters of transit that will allow these children to go to America. I am doing this because I love children, and I abhor the Nazis and what they are doing in the world. I am doing this because, when I lost my parents, a Jewish family took me in and made me their own child. I am doing this because I am a human being and because it would be criminal and immoral for me not to do everything I can."

She continued, "I know what I plan to do is technically against the law. I acknowledge this and accept the consequences that might result for me personally if I am caught. Sometimes in life, it is necessary to make difficult choices, to choose to do the right thing rather than the safe thing. If I can possibly make this plan work, I must do it, not only for the children but also for myself. At the end of my life I must be able to come to terms with what I have done with my time on this earth. I want to be able to say that I was brave and stood up for and fought for good. I do not fear evil. I must and I will fight it to my very last breath, if that is what it takes. I will put my life on the line and do everything within my power to make sure that innocent children have a chance to live. I will give all that I have to fight this wickedness that threatens to destroy every last vestige of light in the world. I'm not afraid to die for what I believe is decent and noble."

Max looked at her for a long time. Emerson thought she saw moisture at the corners of his eyes. He almost said something, then hesitated and changed his mind. He lowered his eyes and finally looked up at Emerson and smiled. He took her in his arms and held her tightly for a few seconds. "I know there are many good people left in this world. You are one of them. Thank you." Emerson's eyes overflowed with tears. Likewise she wondered what drove this young man who did not seem to be afraid of anything. Maybe one day he would trust her enough to share his story with her.

Max left to return to Lisbon, and Emerson returned to Bacalhoa to try to figure out where she was going to find a larger motor launch and where she was going to hide fifteen children without anyone knowing about it.

Chapter 18

HIDING CHILDREN ISN'T EASY

February 1942

Pierre was thriving at Bacalhoa and had become everybody's favorite. Now that Emerson was actively planning a way for him to leave and travel to America, she understandably had conflicted feelings. Telling him goodbye would be painful. She shared with him that he would soon be leaving to go to the United States. She told him that he would be going to live with her dearest friend and almost-sister Rachel. She told Pierre about Rachel's husband who was a rabbi and Rachel's parents. She told him all about what a wonderful person and friend Rachel was and that he would be the big brother to Rachel's toddler twins. All of this seemed to please Pierre, but when Emerson finished talking, Pierre threw his arms around her and sobbed. "I don't want to leave you, Emerson. I have said goodbye to everybody I've ever known, and I don't want to say goodbye to you." Emerson had tried so hard not to cry while she was talking to Pierre, but now she broke down. She couldn't help it.

"I am going to miss you, too, Pierre, more than I can really bear. But it is dangerous for you to stay here, and the United States will be the best place in the world for you to grow up. Having my dearest friend Rachel as your mother is the most wonderful thing any child could hope for. The only thing that keeps me from being sad all the time about your leaving is that I know how happy you will be with Rachel and her family. When this terrible war is over, I will come to visit you, I promise." She held Pierre until he cried himself to sleep.

The next morning, Pierre was himself again and was running around in the small chapel that had become his bedroom. It was February, and it was too cold and damp for him to play outside in the garden. He and Lily were playing ball in the chapel although they had been told many times not to run or throw the ball there. Emerson was in her sitting room next door writing letters when she heard a loud bang. Then she heard an awful creaking noise and then another loud bang. Pierre shouted for her, and she ran into the chapel.

She couldn't believe her eyes when she saw what had happened in the small room. Made of marble and as solid as Gibraltar, the entire top half of the altar in the chapel had swung sideways. There was a huge gaping hole in the space where the top of the altar had been. Emerson was speechless. The altar had moved, but it did not appear to be broken. Emerson was almost afraid to look down into the chasm. What if this was someone's crypt and there was a body or bones inside? A body would surely be a skeleton by now. Emerson marshalled her courage and looked down into the hole. There was no body there. There were no bones. Amazingly, there was a dangerously narrow stairway along one side of the opening, and if she put her head down into the opening, she could see there was a kind of passageway at the bottom of the stairway. It was a secret something — a secret passage, a secret room, a secret staircase at least. It was too dark to see much beyond the steep stone steps. She wondered what in the world she had just discovered.

She looked at Pierre whose eyes were wide with surprise and fright. Lily was hiding under Pierre's bed pretending she wasn't there but knowing something very loud and very strange had happened. Pierre was anxious to confess. "I threw the ball across the altar. It hit the Baby Jesus. I grabbed the Baby Jesus to see if it was broken, and I stumbled. When I pushed backwards on the Baby Jesus, the whole top of the altar moved sideways like it is now. I really didn't break anything, did I? I'd never touched the Baby Jesus before, and now I have touched it for the first time and broken the Christmas altar."

A beautiful crèche made out of enameled stone had been a permanent fixture on top of the altar. Emerson had always thought the nativity scene had been carved out of the same piece of marble as the altar. It had never occurred to her that the altar could move, or that grabbing hold of the Baby Jesus would move it. She looked more closely to examine the top half of the altar that had moved sideways to reveal the hidden staircase.

She took hold of the Baby Jesus and pulled it towards her. Sure enough, the entire altar easily moved back to where it was supposed to be, closing the opening underneath. The top of the altar was on some kind of a swivel hinge and had been designed to move sideways to yield the opening which revealed the stairway. The altar was heavy. But the hinge, the balance, and the Baby Jesus as the opening lever had been cleverly, really brilliantly, deigned to operate without any motor or electricity, or even much effort. It moved quite easily if one knew the secret. It was an amazing application of physics and mechanics, and Emerson's mind immediately went wild with possible reasons about why and what it had been designed for in the first place.

"Pierre, I think you and Lily have made a brilliant discovery." Lily had come out from under the bed to sniff the scene and determine how much trouble she was going to be in. Pierre's frightened little body relaxed when he saw Emerson easily bring the altar back to its original position and then use the Baby Jesus lever to open and close the secret hiding place a few more times. Pierre was relieved that he had not permanently broken anything.

"I didn't mean to hurt anything. I promise not to run, ever again, in the chapel. Or throw the ball. Where do you think the stairway goes?"

"You didn't hurt a thing, Pierre, and we will find out exactly where the stairway goes. I want to wait until Dr. Robert can go exploring with us. It's dark down there, and we will need to take battery-powered torches with us to light our way. We will have to be especially careful because we don't know what we will find."

Emerson immediately called Robert's house to ask him if he could come over for tea that afternoon. She knew he couldn't pass up Benadina's tea cookies and the sandwiches she made especially for him when she knew he was going to be a guest for tea. Robert of course agreed to come, and Emerson hinted that she had something special to show him. They needed to talk, anyway, about the new launch and the increase in the number of orphans Max wanted to carry on board his ship.

Emerson called Magdalena into the chapel and closed the door. She grabbed hold of the Baby Jesus and pushed it away from her to reveal the opening under the altar and the staircase going down to the underground passageway. Emerson had never seen Magdalena surprised or flustered by anything, but Magdalena was dumbfounded when she saw the altar slide sideways to reveal the mystery space underneath.

After a moment of being unable to speak, Magdalena found her voice, "I have never seen this before. I have lived and worked at Bacalhoa since I was a child and did not know this about the altar or the Baby Jesus or the stairway or any of it. I do remember my mother once or twice talking about a long-held myth that there was an underground passage out of the quinta. I can't remember why she told me the story or what purpose the underground passage served. Of course, she and everyone else thought it was just a tall tale that got passed down over the years and really had no basis in fact. I can think of some reasons why such a secret place might have been built. From time to time, there has been political turmoil in Portugal's history. Nothing like in Spain, of course, but we have had some troubles. Smuggling is another thing that comes to mind, but my understanding is that everyone who ever owned this palacio was financially secure and didn't need to engage in criminal activities. Then there is always love and passion and illicit affairs of the heart. One might need a way to enter and exit unbeknownst to others. But to choose the chapel as the place to escape for a tryst is stretching my Catholic imagination just a little too much. And to make the Baby Jesus the key to opening the altar is almost a mocking point. The altar and the crèche are made out of one piece of stone, I believe, and if we could determine the age of that stone, we might be able to discover when, and then why, this hiding place was created in the first place. Of course, when we explore the passageway and find out where it goes, if it goes anywhere, we might be able to find more clues about the reason it was built. I can't tell you anything, Miss Emerson. I am as shocked as you are."

"I've invited Robert to come over this afternoon at four o'clock for tea. You know how he loves Benadina's little minced ham sandwiches and her tea cookies. I didn't tell him about the altar on the telephone, but I am hoping the three of us can go down there together after tea today. I'd rather Pierre not go with us although, of course, he is itching to know what he's discovered. Can you find some batteries and at least two torches so we can see where to put our feet as we go down those narrow stairs? This has all been sealed up for a very long time, and I am certain there was no electricity available when the secret space was created."

Robert arrived for tea, and Pierre, Robert, and Emerson ate every bite that Benadina had prepared for them. Magdalena had arranged for Pierre to go to the kitchen to help make cookies after tea. Pierre loved to help Benadina, so he would be happily occupied while the three grownups explored the mystery under the altar.

Robert was the first to climb down the narrow stairway. They were dangerously steep and dreadfully dusty. There was no railing, so he urged Emerson and Magdalena to be especially careful on the uneven steps. Robert shone his torch toward the staircase to light their way. They slowly and carefully climbed down the treacherous stairs and moved gingerly along the passageway. Emerson and Magdalena followed closely behind Robert. The passageway became a tunnel which was endlessly long and very narrow. It was so low that Robert occasionally had to bend over to make it through what was a crudely constructed underground corridor.

At some point, a long, long time ago, someone had gone to a great deal of trouble to build this primitive conduit. It seemed like the three explorers walked for more than a quarter of a mile in the tunnel that had been cut out of sandstone. Finally, they arrived in a large open space. The ceiling was higher in the irregularly shaped room. It had similar walls of stone and a floor that had been roughly finished with what looked like flagstones. The stone floor of the room was more substantial than the walls and floor of the tunnel. In the open space, there was an altar, a simple one with the remains of what had been two candles, now collapsed and broken, and a modest cross made of wood. A few ancient and primitive wooden benches were set up facing the altar, as if for some kind of service or meeting. Cloth coverings had been placed on the altar, but those had now decayed and disintegrated into a few almost invisible threads. There was a book beside the cross, and it appeared to be some kind of Bible.

The three decided to go on through the church assembly room and try to find out where the underground passage ended. Along the way, they discovered sleeping quarters and another small room that had a well in it. At one time, there had been water available in this mysterious place. The air was stale all the way along the tunnel and in the rooms they walked through. It was so dusty with sandstone particles, they sometimes found it difficult to breathe. They continued on and arrived at a thick wooden door. A secure and heavy metal latch on the door was definitely designed to keep people out. Robert lifted the latch, and the three of them pushed against the door. After several attempts to move it, the door finally swung open with a great deal of creaking and a great deal of dirt. As they pushed through the opening, the three found themselves in what appeared to be a small warehouse or a large garage with a cement floor.

Magdalena went forward into the dark space to see if there was a door or window. They sensed there was fresh air somewhere and were eager to find it as they'd been gasping for breath inside the closed and dusty tunnels. Magdalena forced open a stubborn window that was overgrown with vines from the outside, and the cold February evening air flooded in. They breathed deeply and were relieved to be out of the airless tomb that had to have been closed for more than a hundred years, perhaps longer. They looked at each other and laughed as they all were covered with reddish brown dust from head to toe. Their hair and clothes were thick with the sandy particles.

"I know where we are now," Magdalena called from a doorway that led to the outside. We are no longer within the walls of Palacio Bacalhoa, but we are on a piece of property owned by the quinta. This land is not contiguous to the main grounds. We are on a deserted part of a dirt road that leads to the Lisbon Road, and this land is quite far back into the woods. I have not been here for many years and had completely forgotten that this building existed. This property must have been on the deed, Emerson, when your husband purchased the palacio."

Magdalena continued. "The beach property and the boathouse were mentioned on the deed. The farm was also mentioned. Mr. Mullens insisted on seeing these locations. I don't know why he didn't come to see this part of his land. It is several acres of mostly woods, but I know it definitely belongs to the palacio. It could be that none of the real estate agents knew how to find this place. There used to be a dirt road out the back which winds around and around and leads to another dirt road which finally ends up at the Lisbon Road. I am certain if we were able to find that dirt road that connects to the Lisbon Road, it would be completely overgrown with trees and bushes. We would probably never find the dirt road if we tried looking for it from the other direction, that is, from the direction of the Lisbon Road."

Robert and Emerson listened closely to what Magdalena was telling them. It seemed they had found a building and a road and a church and a tunnel and a secret staircase, all in one afternoon. By now it was dark outside, and they were all tired and dusty and thirsty. They decided to call it a day and come back tomorrow when it was daylight. They secured the building and made the considerable hike on the dirt road out to the main highway.

The dirt road was, as Magdalena had said, overgrown with brush and almost impassable. It was a cold and tiring walk, trudging along the roads back to Bacalhoa, and they approached the property through the rear garden so none of the staff would see how sandy and dirty their clothes were. The three were covered with dust and had scrapes and scratches from making their way through the tangled vegetation that had blocked their way. Robert brushed himself off as best he could and got into his car to return home. As soon as Emerson reached her bathroom, she stripped off her clothes and took a long, hot bath. She washed her hair three times to try to get the dust out. She put on her dressing gown and asked to have dinner brought to her bedroom. She was exhausted.

She went into the chapel and closed the altar by pulling on the Baby Jesus. Pierre would already have eaten in the kitchen with Benadina and would be ready to go to bed in the chapel as he did every night. Emerson would read him a bedtime story, eat her own dinner, and think about what she had discovered today. Already her mind was racing with ideas about how she could use today's discoveries to help her solve the pressing problem of where to hide and take care of fifteen children.

Robert telephoned Bacalhoa later that evening. His mind had been running along the same lines, and he wanted to share his thoughts with Emerson. He did not often telephone Emerson because he was so worried that someone might be listening in on their conversations, but tonight, he couldn't wait to talk to her. "I think Providence has smiled on us, Emerson. A prayer has been answered. I know you used to be a pretty good carpenter, and I think you will have a chance to show us what you can do. I will be over in the morning. Sleep well, and don't stay up all night thinking about this." He felt he had been vague enough in his remarks that anyone listening over the telephone would find his conversation with Emerson nondescript, uninformative, and boring — just as he had intended it to sound.

"Of course, you know I won't be able to sleep at all tonight. I will lie awake, planning every detail about how to transform and 'redecorate' the space. I'll see you in the morning."

Chapter 19

THERE'S A PLACE FOR US

February 1942

Exhausted from the previous day's adventures, Emerson slept late the next day. Pierre had already eaten his breakfast and taken Lily for a walk in the garden. When Magdalena brought Emerson's breakfast, the housekeeper's eyes shone with excitement. Magdalena had been helping Robert move the Allied flyers back to England for many months now. Robert and Emerson had shared with her their hopes and plans to try to move children out of harm's way in Nazi-occupied Europe and send them to America. They had all discussed and struggled to find a solution to the problem of how fifteen children could be hidden at Bacalhoa. It was not difficult to take in one small French boy who now had the run of the entire quinta and its grounds. If strangers inquired or officials came to the door, the story was that Pierre was Emerson's nephew from Paris who had come for an extended visit.

As Emerson drank her morning coffee and ate her toasted bread spread with homemade jam, she saw that Magdalena could scarcely contain the ideas she had racing inside her own head and wanted to share. Magdalena had become a dear friend. Emerson owed Magdalena her life as she had cared for her completely over the many long months of Emerson's withdrawal from the world, the months when Emerson was so engulfed by grief that she was no longer really aware that she was still alive.

Magdalena was a partner in Robert's underground network, and she was a partner in their plans to move orphans to freedom. Magdalena was incredibly bright and knew all there was to know, or so it seemed, about everything and everybody in Portugal. She had been born on the grounds of Quinta Bacalhoa and had lived here most of her life. Someone along the way had recognized Magdalena's potential and sent her away to a private boarding school. Someone had made sure she had a good education and learned some English. Robert and Emerson felt exceedingly lucky to have her as part of their team.

"Magdalena, tell me what you are thinking, as I am probably thinking the same things. What do you have to say about the discoveries we made yesterday?" Emerson herself could scarcely contain her own desire to talk and plan and accomplish something.

"I think God has smiled on us, Emerson, and given us the solution to our problem. I knew nothing, until yesterday, about the altar or the staircase or the tunnel or the strange underground sanctuary and all of that. I still have no explanations about why that is there or who created it. I am working to find out something, but I am trying to be discreet in my inquiries. I think it is critical that we keep all of this as secret as we possibly can. I believe these discoveries are essential to our plans for housing the children we want to rescue, and no one must know anything about the underground room or the tunnels or the building in the woods. Some people used to know about that building, but I have not heard anyone mention anything about it for many, many years. I believe all of the people who once knew that building existed are now dead, except for me. I only remembered, when I saw it again, that I had been there a long time ago. I think our secrets are safe."

Emerson agreed with Magdalena about maintaining absolute secrecy. "There is no question that we must keep all of this a secret. What I don't know is how we are going to get the building ready to house the children without involving others. I haven't worked that one out yet, but I will bet your mind is going a hundred miles an hour figuring out how to do it. We will need to use the back entrance to that building and the dirt road that goes to the Lisbon Road. We need to clear the brush away to make it passable. You and I can't do all that by ourselves, and Robert doesn't have the time to devote to another project. He is too busy with his practice and his other concerns. I feel guilty asking him to help me with the orphans, but I need him. And he would never allow us to pursue this without him. He feels so strongly about it. But I don't want to overwork him so that he loses his health. Some days he looks so tired to me."

"Dr. Robert loves participating in all the projects he is working on. After his wife died, he was so depressed, he lost interest in everything except his medical practice. Thank goodness he had that to occupy his mind. He has thrown himself with great enthusiasm into moving the Allied flyers, and now he is completely devoted to the orphan project. Did you know that his wife was Jewish?"

"I didn't know that, and he doesn't want to talk to me about her. But hearing about his wife makes me understand the depth of his commitment for his non-medical work. He is not only fighting the Nazi beast that wants to destroy Britain and our democratic way of life, but he has the added motivation because he is also fighting the Nazis who want to annihilate the Jews from Europe. Thank you for telling me. He doesn't like to talk about himself, and I feel I understand him better. He was so faithful and determined to help me through my depression. I can see now that he had more than a clinician's point of view about what I was experiencing. He's coming later this morning, I think, if he can get a break in his schedule."

"He called me this morning and told me he is coming for lunch. He cleared his office hours for this afternoon so we can all go over to the 'hideout' and make plans. Benadina is thrilled he's coming, and she is making all of his favorites. He doesn't often come for lunch, and she really loves to feed him."

"Do you have some ideas about how we can make our serendipitous space habitable for the children and how we can open that road and still make sure nobody knows the road is there? Magdalena, you know everybody, and I am sure you are already planning for who can do what. Am I right?"

Magdalena laughed. "There are two men who work with us on the Allied flyer project, and I know they are completely trustworthy. One is my cousin Sandro and the other is his best friend from childhood. They are hard workers. I took some liberties, since I know we need to get this work done as quickly as possible. Sandro and his friend began working at the hideout early this morning. Robert also knows these men, so I knew it would be all right with him. I told them that we would pay them for the hours they work for us. I hope you agree with that."

"You are a wonder, and of course it's fine to offer to pay them. I would not allow them to work for us without pay. Just let me know each week how much I owe them. I am grateful they have agreed to do the work, and large bonuses will be in order for their willingness to begin in such a timely fashion. What did you tell them to do today?"

"They would have done the work for free, especially after I told them it was for such a good cause. They didn't want details but are eager to help. They're smart and skilled in a number of areas that we need, and they will work long hours to do whatever is necessary to help us get the building ready quickly. They're going to get the trash out of the building and give it a quick cleaning so it won't be so dusty when we go to look at it this afternoon. Then they will work on clearing the road, the dirt road that goes to the main road. I told them they had to make it accessible but that it also has to stay completely hidden from view. That's a tall order, but they know how to do these things. They said the road would be ready for us to drive over from the Lisbon Road after lunch. I emphasized that the Lisbon Road entrance could not appear to look any different from the way it does right now. The entrance to the dirt road must be invisible. They understand that, and they said they could easily camouflage the entrance off the Lisbon Road. We will see it this afternoon."

"Oh, Magdalena, your ideas are completely in line with what I am thinking. Thank goodness for that. We would be nowhere in this project without you. Even though my body was tired to the bone after the tunnel exploration and the hike back to Bacalhoa in the cold last night, my mind was racing with a million ideas and plans. I had a hard time going to sleep. One thing that I feel we need to find, and I don't delude myself that it will be easy, is a van or even two. Or maybe a van and some kind of truck. We need to be able to transport the children to the cove without making too many trips. Petrol is only going to become less available and more expensive as time goes on and the war continues, and driving an old van and an old truck will be better than making multiple trips in our cars. I am thinking … the older the better for the vehicles. Traveling up and down the road in old junk heaps will attract less attention than my Mercedes or Robert's enormous Bentley will. What do you think?"

"I have already put out a few discreet inquiries about finding a van and a truck, older models of both. Bacalhoa has its own farm, and with the food shortages in Europe, all farms everywhere are being asked to increase production of whatever they raise. No one will be suspicious if Bacalhoa is looking for a truck and a van to carry its increased production of farm products to markets far and wide. It is our good luck that the hideout building used to be warehouse storage where a previous owner of Bacalhoa kept his car collection. That's why it was built in the first place … for the owner's cars. I remembered there is an in-ground tank for petrol somewhere near the building. I am hoping we can find it and see if it is still serviceable. If it is still intact, I want to have my cousin fill it with petrol so we're not caught short. The warehouse building was constructed in the 1920's, I think, so it is not really that old."

Emerson wanted to know more. "I was wondering if you knew when and why this building had been built. I thought it might have been designed as a garage because of the big double doors and the cement floor. It is our good luck that there is a tank for petrol. If only it had electricity."

Magdalena continued. "The electricity did work in the building at one time in the past, but it isn't working now. The wiring is there, but it needs to be repaired and checked out to see if it is safe. I don't think it will be too difficult to get the electricity working again. Once the car collector died and his collection was sold, there was no longer any need for the additional car storage spaces. Everyone just forgot the place was there."

"As always, you are at least three steps ahead of me. Do you know anyone who can repair the electricity and put in new wiring if necessary? It would be useful to have that working before we begin our renovations. Torches and candlelight won't be sufficient for doing plumbing and carpentry work."

"My cousin Sandro can do the electrical work, and after he and his friend have cleared the road today, he's going to try to reconnect the electricity. You mentioned plumbing. That's going to be more of an issue than the electricity. I have been turning the plumbing problems over and over in my mind. We need bathroom facilities — although outhouses would probably suffice for the children. They will need to bathe. And, we need some kind of simple kitchen for warming food and washing up after meals. I am going to bring Benadina into this, but only partially. I am going to tell her that we are starting a soup kitchen for refugees outside of Lisbon. She will be thrilled to be cooking for more people. She loves to cook for parties and crowds and feels her talents are underutilized just cooking for you and Pierre and the staff and occasionally for Robert. She would love to make food for a soup kitchen. It is not exactly a lie. We will be feeding hungry children. They just won't be eating her soups and her homemade bread rolls anywhere near Lisbon. They will be enjoying her excellent cooking much closer to home. We always have extra produce from the farm, and she hates for it to go to waste. She preserves as much of it as she can in glass jars and dries the fruit from the orchards. Now she can use all those jars she has filled to help feed the orphans. "

"That solves another problem I was worried about, how to have Benadina cook for fifteen extra people without her realizing she was doing it. Brilliant, Magdalena! Truly brilliant. Now if I could just work out the bathroom and bathing issues. Maybe Robert will have some ideas. What are we going to do about Pierre? You know he wants to be in on what's happening. He wants to be allowed to explore the staircase and the underground tunnels. I don't know what to say to him about it. I don't want him to go down there, but he is the one who discovered the place and wants more than anything to climb down those stairs. Any ideas on that?"

Magdalena had already thought about what to do to distract Pierre. "I think we should tell him that Robert went down there yesterday afternoon and decided it really wasn't safe. It really isn't, with the dangerously narrow staircase and with all that terrible sandstone dust. I don't want to go down there again myself, and I don't think it is a good place for a child at all because the air is so unhealthy. I think we can distract him by taking him out to the building off the Lisbon Road. We can explain to him that we are going to help other children escape the Nazis. We will tell him that they will stay in the hideout temporarily until they can get on board the cargo ship that will take them to America. I think he might lose interest in the dusty underground labyrinth, if he has something else to think about. I want to paint the walls inside the building, and we will need to build some partitions to divide off areas for the vehicles and the kitchen and the bathroom facilities. If we ask his opinion about these things and engage him in helping us prepare the space for the other children, maybe we can keep his mind off the stairway and the tunnels."

Emerson nodded in agreement. "I am going to need more work clothes if I'm going to help with this project, and I really want to use my skills to do something useful. I have always loved doing carpentry work, and I'm terribly excited about having a chance to do something along those lines again. I want to make some measurements and some sketches today when we go to the hideout. I will draw everything to scale, and we will be able to start right away with the construction we need to do."

They all agreed it was important to leave the exterior of their building dirty and unpainted and overgrown with brush and vines. They wanted their hideout to continue to look old and abandoned and dilapidated, exactly as it had looked on the outside yesterday and for the past two decades. They decided to cover the few windows of the warehouse with blackout curtains on the inside so that any lights from the building would not be seen and would not attract attention from passersby. The hideout was so secluded they didn't think this would be a problem, but they didn't want anybody to investigate an unusual light in the woods.

When Robert arrived, the two women could hardly wait to tell him about all they had decided to do. Benadina produced a spectacular winter lunch of creamy seafood chowder, lamb stew with vegetables, her famous homemade bread rolls, and custard pastries for dessert. Robert went down to the kitchen to tell her how much he had enjoyed it. Benadina loved to cook for Robert who was one of her biggest fans.

When he returned from the kitchen, Robert commented on the fact that he had not been able to get a word in at lunch and that it appeared everything about everything had already been decided. He laughed, and they laughed with him. He was a good sport. But they realized they had completely taken over the project and hadn't bothered to ask his opinion.

As stuffed as they were from the delicious meal, they might have opted to take an afternoon nap. All three were so excited about their new project, they couldn't wait to get into Emerson's car and make the trip down the Lisbon Road. Magdalena's cousin Sandro was going to be standing alongside the road to flag them down. He would be standing at the spot where he and his friend had figured out how to open up an entrance to the hidden dirt road without its being visible.

When they reached the spot where Sandro was waiting for them, they pulled over to the side of the road, but none of them could see any place that would allow them to access the private dirt road. They waited in the car as Sandro walked up to a wall of brush and pulled on a piece of old wood. A gate covered with vines and leaves and other vegetation, and indistinguishable from the vegetation all around it, swung back to allow them to pass through onto the dirt road. As soon as the car was through the gate, it closed. They could not be seen from the main road.

They stopped the car and got out and walked back to the gate. Sandro explained to them how to open the camouflaged gate from either side, going in or coming out. The gate was a marvel of engineering and subterfuge. They two men had cleared the road such that a vehicle could travel on it, but it was still obscure enough that anyone walking in the area would not notice that it was a viable roadway. It was an amazing and ingenious solution. They continued on the winding road to reach the warehouse hideout.

Chapter 20

THE GAME'S AFOOT

March 1942

After two incredibly busy weeks, the building was ready for its small occupants. A new well was dug to provide potable water, and a septic system was created at an appropriate distance from the house, to solve one of the other plumbing issues. With enough of Emerson's cash to spread around, Magdalena's family was able to find the necessary plumbing supplies to create a simple bathroom with two stall toilets, two sinks, and a claw-foot bath tub that had its own privacy enclosure.

In addition to soap and towels, Emerson insisted that her orphans have hot water for their baths, so a hot water heater was a necessity. Bacalhoa's bathrooms used oil fired hot water tanks. Even before the war started, it had taken months for these hot water tanks to arrive in Setubal. With a war going on, another hot water tank might take years to be delivered. Too impatient to wait for a new hot water heater, Emerson's workmen borrowed the hot water tank from one of the guest bathrooms in the palacio. It was almost impossible to install it and make it work in the hideout bathroom. But Emerson was adamant that, to get really clean, the children needed hot water.

She said they had lived rough for so long they deserved one luxury, and that luxury was going to be a bath in hot water. A tank for fuel oil had to be put in the ground. It became a complicated ordeal to get a pump installed and running water going. There were many complexities of the hot water heater that had to be addressed, but Emerson was willing to pay a bundle of money for this and was determined that it would happen. She was pretty easygoing about most things, but she was not going to be denied hot water for the children. Her insistence on a hot water heater became an opportunity for the workmen to tease her. She accepted it all with good humor, but she would not be moved an inch in her quest for cleanliness.

Magdalena was able to find the linens they needed and tried to think up excuses to tell the staff at Bacalhoa about the reason for the increase in the laundry load. For security and practicality reasons, Magdalena and Emerson decided that Sandro's wife, Lindeck, would be hired to take care of the extra laundry, and Emerson was delighted to pay her to do that and to buy her a washing machine. The staff at Bacalhoa would not be involved and did not need to know anything about extra laundry.

Simple wooden bunk beds were built, enough for twenty children to sleep comfortably. Magdalena, again with Emerson's cash in hand, had procured a truckload of new mattresses and twenty feather pillows. When Emerson asked her how she had ever accomplished that amazing feat, Magdalena had made a grim face and said, "Don't ask." Emerson was afraid it might have had something to do with a railroad car that had been robbed on its way to the casino at Estoril. But she was delighted to have the mattresses and kept her mouth shut. It wasn't a luxurious camp by any means, but it was serviceable and would be perfect for the children.

Space for two still-to-be-procured vehicles was walled off from the living quarters. A simple kitchen was cobbled together from some old appliances and some new ones. Emerson and Sandro built a long table for meals that occupied the center of the sleeping room. It was a somewhat lower table than most, in order to accommodate the children. Magdalena and Robert bought and collected a motley assortment of chairs to put around the table. Emerson procured twenty wooden wine boxes. Each child would have a wooden box under his or her bed that would hold their clothes and whatever belongings they possessed. The interior walls of the hideout were painted in bright, cheerful colors. Magdalena painted a mural on one wall, a picture of a ship on the ocean flying both the Portuguese and American flags from its mast.

With Rachel's help, Emerson ordered crates of children's books in several languages as well as stuffed animals, toys, and dolls for children of all ages. She intended that each child would select one book and one other toy to take with him or her on their voyage to America. It had been a great deal of work, but the hideout was ready for the children. Emerson couldn't wait for them to arrive.

Pierre and Lily had been allowed to accompany Emerson to the hideout almost every day that it wasn't raining. Pierre approved of the bunk beds and the tiny kitchen. He especially liked the fact that there would be hot water in the bathtub. Pierre selected the colors for the walls and had tried to do some of the painting. Emerson and Pierre agreed, after discovering how difficult it was to remove paint from clothes, hair, and white dogs, that they would leave the rest of the painting to Sandro and his friend.

Pierre began asking when the other children would arrive. Emerson told him they would never know when the children were going to arrive until almost the last minute before they appeared on the doorstep. Emerson and Pierre talked about how he had found his way to Bacalhoa. He scarcely remembered anything about his traumatic journey. It was a blessing that he had put behind him whatever memories he had of the gunshot wound to his leg and his arduous hike to safety and freedom.

Robert had been able to find two shortwave radios for Emerson. He looked sad when she asked him how he had managed to acquire them. He didn't want to explain to her. Emerson guessed that the radios might have arrived with some of Robert's escaping pilots. She had the impression that something terrible might have happened to the previous owner of at least one of the radios. Emerson spent hours learning how to communicate using the radios and the codes. Robert also practiced his Morse code whenever he had some spare time, which was not often.

Using her carpentry skills, Emerson created a small secret space in the boathouse where she could safely send and receive radio messages. She copied the code book Max had given her and kept one in the boathouse and one at Bacalhoa. She sent a copy to Naomi Friedman via the diplomatic pouch. Emerson also built a secret opening in the wall of her dressing room at Bacalhoa. Always thankful for her ability to work with wood, she'd made a clever shoe rack that had dead space behind it where she installed the radio on a small shelf that provided her with a tiny desk where she could sit to send her messages. There had been much to accomplish, but Emerson's energy seemed endless. She embraced her project with love and enthusiasm. She was thrilled to be doing something constructive.

Emerson was confident that the orphans would be taken care of in every possible way once they reached the shores of

Virginia. But she needed a more efficient way of communicating with Naomi. For security reasons, they dared use the shortwave radios only sparingly. Emerson had worked out a code with Rachel and Rachel's mother Naomi Friedman based on a one-time cypher that used a favorite book, *The Spy*, by James Fenimore Cooper. Emerson always smiled to herself when she considered the irony of the title of this book that had been written such a long time ago. The story had taken place during the American Revolutionary War, and the book had been published in 1821. The women used the Cooper Code in letters and telegrams that were sent back and forth between Portugal and Baltimore and between Portugal and Boston.

The women were also developing a brief verbal code that they could use over the telephone. Emerson would call Naomi and communicate to her that a group of children was on its way. She would let Naomi know, using their verbal code, the estimated date and time of the arrival of the ship that carried the orphans. Emerson also hoped to be able to let Naomi know over the telephone how many would be arriving, specifically how many boys and how many girls and their ages, so Naomi could be prepared with transportation and housing.

Emerson decided that, if there was time, she wanted to compose a brief biographical sketch about each of the children to send to Rachel and to Naomi. Emerson intended for these biographies to arrive in the United States before the children did. That might not always be possible. The children might spend several days with Emerson in the hideout, but they also could come and go within hours. Emerson would never know how long the children would be with her; it would always be uncertain.

If she could, Emerson wanted to write a few sentences about each child — at least about name, age, gender, country of origin, and language skills. She also wanted to include a physical description and a brief statement about each child's health. If possible, she might also include a few lines about the child's personality and psychological state.

This information would help Rachel and Naomi be able to plan and better match homes that wanted to adopt children. The biographical sketches could help Rachel assign those children most likely to fit in with a particular family. Children with special needs would be identified and sent to families who had adequate financial means and access to special health facilities. Emerson wanted to give her friends in America as much information as possible in advance of the arrival of the children. Sometimes Emerson would have a chance to prepare and send the biographical sketches of the children, and sometimes she wouldn't.

Once they were safely on American soil, the little ones would spend several days with Naomi at a safe house, the Friedman's farm in Easton, Maryland. Naomi had arranged for a physician and a psychologist to evaluate the children there. Polish, Russian, and Dutch Jews had volunteered to translate for Naomi. Discretion was essential, as everyone involved realized that the entry of the children into the United States was outside the official immigration system, or at least outside the official quota system.

As each child was united with his or her new family, adoption paper work would proceed as rapidly as Naomi and her fellow lawyers could make it happen. When the adoption process had been completed, the children would be legally safe, and the rest of the transition would be up to the families, their synagogues, and their communities. Emerson had high hopes.

Robert's contacts would notify him when and where groups of orphans were going to arrive. Robert did not want Emerson and Magdalena to know about this part of the orphans' journey. Robert himself did not know many details.

He knew the fiercely brave Basque people were sometimes involved. He knew there were Catholic nuns somewhere in France who were instrumental in moving groups of children. He knew the children came from many countries. But it was always best, when using a secret network, that each part know as little as possible about the other parts. Robert was the only link between where and when the orphans would arrive at Bacalhoa, and he was adamant about shielding Emerson and Magdalena from all aspects of that facet of the operation.

Emerson sent a coded short-wave message to Max aboard the *Anjo* and told him that everything was arranged in Portugal and in Virginia. They were awaiting the first group of orphans. Max replied to Emerson that he would be returning to Lisbon in three weeks. He hoped a group of small passengers would be ready for him to transport. If it looked like there would be a group of children ready to go, he planned to take on a cargo bound for somewhere in the United States, Canada, or South America.

Max had been working with his navigation charts of the U.S. East Coast and the Chesapeake Bay. Emerson assured Max that Naomi had a shortwave radio, had a copy of the code book, knew Morse code, and had taught herself how to use the radio. Emerson told Max that Naomi Friedman could do anything. Emerson gave him Naomi's contact information. Max, in effect, would be smuggling human cargo into Butcher's Creek near Onancock, Virginia. It had to be done with as much secrecy as possible.

One day Emerson received a carefully crated and padded shipping box from a company in New York City. Inside the box were a camera and a large, puzzling, and bulky recording device. Emerson did not consider herself to be very accomplished using electronic equipment, and the recording machine was completely new to her. She read the instructions carefully and found that she could hook the recording device up to her telephone and record the coded telephone messages she sent and received from Naomi and Rachel. She could also record the words of the orphans as they told her their stories about what had happened to them on their way to Bacalhoa. She could record her own thoughts about each of the children.

The tape recording device was intriguing, and Emerson spent the time she needed to learn how to use it competently. The machine had arrived with many blank tapes which Emerson knew would not be available for purchase in Portugal. She was thankful when she realized the cumbersome recording device could be stored and transported inside one of her old valises. Hidden inside a suitcase, the recording machine could easily be carried back and forth, to and from, the children's hideout and the palacio.

The camera arrived with reams of photo paper. Emerson had lots of new things to learn. She realized that photos of the children would be useful for Naomi and Rachel in identifying and placing the children. She kept the tape recorder and the camera equipment well-hidden among the clothes in her dressing room.

Emerson knew that Robert had, in his younger days, been an amateur photographer. He'd had a keen interest in photography as a hobby and knew how to develop his own photographs. When she spoke to him about wanting to photograph the children, he was more than willing to set up a dark room at his house. Robert sometimes compounded his own medications and thought he could meld a photography dark room into his chemistry equipment.

Emerson felt guilty asking Robert to take on any more responsibilities associated with the orphan project, but he said he was excited about trying his hand at photography again. The camera Naomi had sent from the USA was an exceptionally fine one, and he was anxious to work with it. It turned out that he was quite an accomplished photographer.

Things were becoming more complex, and Emerson wondered if they would be able to keep it all a secret. It seemed to her that Germans were swarming everywhere in Portugal. They loved the Algarve with its beautiful beaches. They loved the casinos at Estoril and the absence of food rationing in sophisticated Lisbon. Rationing of all kinds was so unpleasant in the rest of Europe. The Nazis strutted around wherever they were as if they owned the world or soon would. It made Emerson sick to see them, and she didn't want to go to Lisbon anymore because they were always there in their gaudy and frightening uniforms and driving too fast in their shiny, black cars.

Emerson was not afraid of them, but she loathed their arrogance and their sense of entitlement. Portugal was a neutral country and did not deserve to have so many Nazis around with their rude manners and their menacing attitudes. Emerson felt a great affinity for her adopted country of Portugal and resented the informal invasion of the murderous Nazi goons who were bullies and thugs. They had only come to town to make trouble.

Emerson was anxious for the children to arrive. It would be a challenge of love to care for these poor souls and be sure they were sent safely on their journey. Emerson acknowledged to herself with a heavy heart that when the first group of orphans arrived and then left, Pierre, her dearest Pierre, would be traveling with them. He would travel away from Bacalhoa, away from Portugal, away from Europe, and away from Emerson. She anticipated that day with hope as well as a great deal of dread for what would be her own personal loss.

Chapter 21

BOTTLES OF WINE

1942

Mother Celine pulled the van into the rear of the Abbey. She was tired and still had plenty of work to do. Hidden among the nuns in the van were the four Jewish orphans they had picked up in Paris. The Germans had stopped and searched the van three times on the road between Paris and Beaune. The mother superior almost decided, as they were being searched for the third time, that this would be her last trip to attempt to smuggle children to safety.

Each time the Nazi soldiers demanded that the van be searched, the sisters of the convent were required to exit and stand along the road beside the van. If the children hidden inside remained completely silent during the search, they would not be discovered. The van had been brilliantly constructed with four small hiding places over the wheel wells. Each of these compartments could hide a child. When they were traveling, the children spent most of the time sitting on the laps of the nuns, but when they approached a check point the little ones had to climb back into their coffin-like hiding places.

The Nazis had been rounding up Jews in occupied France for years. Now Vichy France was becoming a lucrative hunting ground for those who were intent on implementing Germany's "Final Solution." The sisters of the Abbey had no illusions about what happened to France's Jews who were forced to leave on trains heading east. The sisters knew those who made that terrible journey never returned. It was a one-way trip.

There was a tragic irony for prescient German Jews who, seeing what the Nazis had in store for them, had sent their children out of Germany to live in France. Some had been sent to stay with relatives. Others had been sent out of Hitler's grasp to attend school in what they believed was a safe country. As they perished in the ovens of the death camps, their parents took desperate consolation in the thought that at least they had sent their children to safety. Hope was shattered when the Nazis marched into France and occupied that country as Lebensraum, more living space for the German people, the master race.

Mother Celine's order of nuns had made it their mission to try to save as many Jewish children as they could smuggle out of Nazi-occupied France. The nuns had their abbey, a few trucks, their popular wine, and other resources that could provide a safe haven for the children, as well as a way to move them around the country. Now, to save the orphans, they had to move them out of Vichy France as well. With Germans watching every border crossing, it was impossible for anybody to get into Switzerland. The sisters realized they had to take their charges south to the Mediterranean. The only way the nuns could hope to save these children was to send them on various torturous routes to Portugal.

On this trip from Paris, there were two little girls from Holland, a nine-year-old Parisian boy, and a teenager who had somehow made his way from Warsaw. They'd been hidden from the Nazis for months by Catholic families, and now they hoped to escape on the secret route that passed through the abbey outside Beaune.

The nuns ran a winery that was famous for its wine. The wine was much in demand in the region, throughout the South of France, elsewhere in Europe, and even abroad. Hiding the children at the Abbey wasn't difficult. The challenge was to move them safely and discretely from place to place on their clandestine road to a better life.

The children were fed, bathed, and allowed to sleep at the abbey. They were seen by a physician who attended to the health of the sisters. The children were deloused if necessary. They were given new clothes. Then they were loaded into a specially constructed truck that transported the wine.

The wine truck was built so that six bodies could be hidden in six compartments that were cleverly concealed among the hundreds of cases of wine loaded on the truck. The Nazis, who manned the numerous check points through which the wine truck would have to travel, would never think of making the nun who drove the truck unload all the wine stored in the back. Neither would these Nazis themselves unload the cases of wine in order to do a thorough search. That would be too much work.

It had become routine for the nuns to give the checkpoint guards a case of wine. This served as an adequate bribe, and the Nazi guards would send the nuns, their wine, and, unbeknownst to them, their small Jewish passengers, on their way.

When they reached Lyon, another driver took over from the sister who'd driven the truck from Beaune. He drove the wine the rest of the way to Marseilles, with paperwork that said the wine was being shipped to Lisbon and other Mediterranean and Atlantic ports. The little travelers, who had scarcely spoken a word during the arduous journey, were unloaded and allowed to eat and sleep overnight at a convent outside Marseilles.

Orphaned Jewish children left France by many routes — whatever ways could be found that had not yet been discovered by the Jew-hunting Nazis. Sometimes they left with Basque partisans who took them on the long and grueling road across the Pyrenees through Spain, a country still in shambles after its own terrible civil war. Although traveling through Basque territory was relatively safe, traveling through the rest of Spain was dangerous, even though it was nominally a neutral country.

Spain was now ruled by the fascist General Francisco Franco. The Nazis had trained Franco's Guardia Civil. This Civil Guard was always on the lookout for valued refugees like Allied flyers who had been shot down over German-occupied territories and were escaping to freedom through Spain. When the Germans implemented their "final solution" to eradicate the European Jews, Jews became valuable prizes. Franco's police were anxious to capture or kill any and all Jews who were trying to escape the Nazis.

The overland escape routes out of France that crossed the border into Spain might require hundreds of miles of walking through mountainous territory. This was extremely difficult for grown men in excellent physical condition, and even Allied flyers had a hard time making it to freedom this way. It was brutal and next to impossible to expect small children to survive such a pitiless land journey.

The better alternative was to smuggle the children across the border close to Bilbao or San Sebastian and put them on a boat. These boats made their way through the Bay of Biscay, along the coast of Spain, and out into the Atlantic Ocean. They could anchor at night along the Portuguese Atlantic Coast.

An alternate escape route, on a ship out of Marseilles or out of a fishing village on the Spanish Mediterranean Coast, was a longer route as the crow flies, but it was a humane way to reach neutral Portugal, especially when transporting small children. They were smuggled across the border from Perpignan or through Andorra to coastal towns north of Barcelona. There was less danger of discovery if the children were loaded onto a ship in Spain rather than in Vichy France. After sailing along the Mediterranean coast of Spain and safely navigating the Straights of Gibraltar, a ship could ultimately reach the beautiful Algarve of Portugal. At night, these remote beaches offered a number of viable destinations for putting the orphans ashore.

All of these journeys were long, convoluted, and harsh. In addition to the ever-present danger of being discovered, it was not unheard of for some of the children to die along the way. Some children began these trips with compromising health conditions, and they could succumb en route. Even the healthy ones became dehydrated and acquired a variety of illnesses. Sometimes their little hearts just stopped beating for unknown reasons. In some cases, it seemed that will and determination alone kept a fragile child alive. The sisters did their best to save each one, but they realized a few would be lost. When some of these small hostages to evil could no longer endure their pain, it was as if God took pity on them and called them home to rest.

The orphans who were transported by the sisters from the abbey in Beaune traveled through Marseilles. They were loaded onto ships, and unloaded in neutral Portugal, usually on the darkest of nights to avoid the Spanish patrol boats, German ships, and U-boats that patrolled the waters along the Mediterranean Coast. The children were picked up on the beach or in the woods and transported to whatever the next safe place was that gave them a chance to move on, the best chance to live.

The madmen in charge of the Nazis' reign of terror against the Jews, the monsters who made up one head of the Nazi snake, Himmler, Heydrich, and Eichmann, were becoming more and more aggressive and determined to extinguish the Jewish presence in Europe and everywhere. Jews were no longer allowed to escape to Palestine or other safe havens. Hitler and his henchmen wanted them all dead.

Heydrich chaired the Wannsee Conference in January 1942 which formalized plans for the "final solution to the Jewish question." Jews in all territories controlled by Germany were at risk of death. No Jews were safe. All were to be deported from the occupied territories to death camps and exterminated. The Nazi genocide of the Jews had entered a new phase, and the need to rescue Jews from everywhere in Europe became more urgent.

The sisters at the abbey in Beaune constantly received demands that they take in more children. They accepted as many as they felt they could safely hide and transport. But there were always more children who needed help than the sisters could move in their vehicles. In the late winter of 1942, word made its way through the covert network to the sisters at the abbey that a new escape route had become available. It would now be possible for a few lucky children to be moved out of Portugal and travel on to the United States. Was there any way the sisters could deliver more children to Marseilles? There were so many children who needed to leave Europe. Now there was a chance for more of them to find their way to new lives, to be saved, if they could just reach Portugal.

The sisters at the abbey decided they would increase the percentage of their winery's product that was sent to Paris and shipped to other locations in Europe and abroad.

This decision was not intended to increase their profits, and in fact their new strategy would cost them more than they could hope to recoup in revenue. The reason for the expansion of their operation was to give the nuns more opportunities to smuggle orphans out of France. The sisters found additional markets for their wine in Paris. They converted a second "special van" that would deliver wine to the city and bring children back to the abbey. The nuns ordered two additional "special trucks" to hide the children on trips from Beaune to Marseilles.

The entrepreneurial sisters were committed to disbursing their wine trucks, with the carefully designed and concealed human cargo spaces, far and wide across Vichy France, whether or not it was good for their bottom line. If they lost money on their wine operation, they knew that in God's eyes, their efforts went onto the positive side of the ledger in the currency that He was most interested in maximizing.

All children want to know they are secure, that they will not be hurt, that they will be able to sleep in the same place from one night to the next, that they will have enough to eat. They want to believe that at the end of the day, they will have a home, a safe place with people who love them. All children want and need these things. Most children who have them, take it all for granted, and that is exactly as it should be.

Born into this world through no choice of their own, the orphans that the nuns transported had lost their families in Hitler's roundup of Europe's Jews. No one had any guarantees for these children who were being hunted down because of the religion of their parents and grandparents. They were suffering through an ordeal that would be difficult for adults. It was punishing for the young. They could not be expected to grasp the rationality or the irrationality of the situation in which they found themselves. They could not possibly understand what was happening.

And, there could be no promises, no reassurances that it would all work out in the end. With the help of the good nuns from Beaune and other kind-hearted people of courage, minute by minute, hour by hour, and day by day, these children, who were lucky to have been chosen, made their way along a hazardous road in the direction of a completely uncertain future. These chosen few had been fortunate to cross paths with brave and selfless saints of God who were risking their lives to save them.

The first group of orphans to arrive at Bacalhoa was a group of fourteen who had traveled through Beaune and Marseilles. A ship delivered them to a deserted stretch of beach west of Faro, Portugal. Dr. Robert Carmichael drove his old truck with a canvas cover over the back to the lonely meeting place. He was waiting when the lifeboats arrived on shore. He lifted the children into the back of the truck and drove them north to Setubal. These little ones would be the first of many who would make the journey into the welcoming arms of caretakers at the Quinta Palacio da Bacalhoa. They would have a chance to continue their journeys to new homes and new lives, to security and freedom in the United States of America.

Chapter 22

BLESS THE LITTLE CHILDREN

March 1942

For a first run, it went more smoothly than Emerson could have imagined. They had planned well, but the unexpected is always waiting in the wings to rush on stage and cause a ruckus. Emerson had communicated with Max that there would be a group of fifteen children ready to transport during the second week in March. The plan was that they would be at the hideout for three days and would be taken aboard the *Anjo* at midnight of the third day.

The children were scheduled to arrive at Bacalhoa in the middle of the night, and Emerson and Magdalena were more than ready to welcome them. The hot water heater had been lit. Benadina had prepared a thick and hearty lamb and vegetable stew and dozens of homemade bread rolls. Butter and two kinds of homemade jam, apples, and chocolate candy bars were also on the table. There was fresh milk from the cows at the farm and lots of cookies, again compliments of Benadina.

She was thrilled to be contributing her culinary talents to the "soup kitchen."

Magdalena and Emerson waited impatiently for the children to arrive and rushed to the garage section of the hideout when they heard the truck pull in. Robert was driving, and the children were packed into the vehicle. Robert looked exhausted. The drop off on the beach west of Faro had been late, and it was now almost five o'clock in the morning.

The children had been at sea for days and stumbled shyly into the welcoming and brightly lit hideout space. They kept their eyes downcast until Emerson began to welcome them in all the languages she knew – English, French, Spanish, and Portuguese. Robert also knew German but did not want to frighten them by speaking that language, if there were any other languages that would suffice. A few of the children had already learned to communicate with each other. One child knew French, Flemish, and Dutch and could speak and explain things to the children who understood only Dutch.

It didn't take long for them to feel welcomed. The clothes they wore were filthy from days on the ship, but these young travelers needed to eat before worrying about cleanliness. Emerson insisted that they wash their hands after they used the toilet and before they sat down at the table. She communicated this through the translation chain, and the children nodded in understanding.

Soon they were sitting around the table and devouring the stew, the milk and cookies, and all the rolls that Emerson and Magdalena had put in front of them. After the meal they took turns washing and preparing for bed. Four of the children were allowed to take warm baths, as that was all the hot water the hot water heater could deliver at one time. Each child was given a clean pair of pajamas. Magdalena had found a place where she could buy sets of children's pajamas in a variety of sizes, and she handed them out to the children by estimating what size each would wear. They were delighted to have pajamas to sleep in as it had been a long time since they'd been presented with such a luxury.

Magdalena gathered their dirty clothes into several laundry bags. She would take the clothes to Lindeck who would wash them and bring them back to dry on the clothes lines that had been strung inside across the back of the "garage" portion of the hideout. Emerson washed the cups and bowls the children had used to eat their meal. She began to make mental notes about the children as she welcomed them. She was too tired to write anything down that night, but as she fell asleep her mind was already composing her notes to Naomi and Rachel about their personalities.

Sandro's wife would bring the children's breakfast to the hideout each morning. She prepared the simple meal at her house and transported it in the van. She cleaned up the breakfast dishes and supervised the children in the morning. After breakfast, a second group of children would be able to take their baths. There were games and books and cards and other things to entertain them. Magdalena brought sandwiches, fruit, milk, and cookies for lunch. The children took naps or rested in their beds after the meal. After rest hour, another group could take a bath. Emerson brought dinner from the kitchen at Bacalhoa, and she and Robert kept the children company during the evenings. Robert gave each child a thorough physical examination. Emerson and Robert alternated sleeping at the hideout each night.

Emerson made notes about every child. She brought her tape recorder to the hideout and spoke to each one — sometimes through translators. Months before, Emerson had found an old L.C. Smith & Brothers typewriter in a closet at the quinta. She'd had Rachel send a supply of new typewriter ribbons.

The bond paper and the carbon paper, also thanks to Rachel, sat beside the black machine on Emerson's desk, ready for her reports to be written. She would send these reports to Naomi and Rachel, and each report would be accompanied by a photo.

In addition to the typewriter ribbons, bond paper, and carbon paper, Rachel had sent a small postal scales and many rolls of U.S. postage stamps. After Emerson had typed her reports about the children, one copy for Naomi and one copy for Rachel, she attached a photograph to each report. She sealed these papers in oversized envelopes, weighed each one with the postal scales, and attached the correct amount of U.S. postage. The envelopes were bulky, with multiple typewritten pages and photographs. Emerson was meticulously careful to be sure she had enough postage on each envelope so her carefully prepared reports did not go astray.

Sending letters through the diplomatic pouch had always been cumbersome, but now this secure means of communication had become much too time-consuming. Emerson wanted her reports and photos to arrive in the United States before the children did. Emerson hoped that having a photograph and her written impressions about each child would help her stateside organizers better understand the children's personalities and place them with new families.

A friend of Robert's, who traveled back and forth weekly between New York and Lisbon on the Pan American Atlantic Clipper seaplane, had agreed to carry Emerson's envelopes with him and mail them when he arrived in the United States. Sending the letters via the seaplane was much faster than sending them in the diplomatic pouch.

As a back-up, Emerson also sent a coded telegram to Naomi with the age and gender and a line or two of basic information about each child. Either the telegram or the reports would almost always reach Naomi before the children did and give her some idea about who would be arriving. Emerson also made a coded telephone call to Naomi to alert her that a group of children was on its way.

The children were all so thin and terribly vulnerable. They were understandably fearful of everything and everybody. They did not smile, and they were very quiet — much too quiet. They had learned to be quiet out of necessity. If you were trying desperately not to be found, you learned to be invisible. These orphans had lost everything and had been required to live lives no adult should have to live — being hunted and in hiding.

Even the youngest child in the group, a five-year-old girl, was adult-like in the way she took care of herself, in the way she folded her clothes and gave herself a sponge bath. Emerson realized that these little people had never really been allowed to be children. It had been necessary for them to behave as grownups from the time they were very young. They'd had to learn to take responsibility for their silence and to control their childlike impulses to talk and to play. Some had been required to find their own food and places to sleep in order to survive. It made Emerson terribly sad that these children had been deprived of the gift of childhood. She was even more convinced than ever that what she was doing was the right thing.

Naomi and Rachel would be able to find, for these adult-like but nevertheless young and vulnerable human beings, families that would allow them to be children again or perhaps to be children for the first time. Naomi and Rachel would find families who would encourage them to sing and laugh and dance in sunlight. Emerson prayed that God would keep them safe and deliver them to her own free country so that they could begin to replenish their small starved souls with the things that would allow them to thrive. They needed so much

— all of the basic material things of life that were required for the body to continue to live. But beyond that, they also needed security and stability, reassurance and unconditional love, and, God willing, some fun to help their spirits soar.

On the first day, Emerson brought Pierre and Lily to meet the group of children. Several spoke French, and Pierre was delighted to be able to converse with them in his own language. There were nine girls and five boys, ranging from five years to eleven years of age. Pierre made friends quickly, and by the second night, he asked if he could sleep at the hideout with the other children.

At first this felt like a knife in Emerson's heart, but she reminded herself that it was a good sign that Pierre was preparing to make the separation from Bacalhoa. These would be his traveling companions as they made their way across the ocean to their new lives. They would be adventurers together. Pierre was getting ready to tell Emerson and Lily and Bacalhoa and Magdalena and Benadina and Dr. Robert goodbye. Pierre was acting more grown up than Emerson felt. She thought her heart would surely break. Emerson told herself that she, too, needed to work on letting go.

Emerson notified Naomi by means of a coded telegram that nine girls and six boys would be arriving on an estimated date:

> "Parcels scheduled to arrive on March 29 are nine orange and six green. Stock numbers are as follows: 5-6-6-7-7-7-8-10-11 and 6-7-8-8-9-10."

Max would be in touch with Naomi by radio when he knew more precisely the *Anjo*'s ETA at Butcher's Creek, Virginia.

Robert took photographs of the children and stayed up late to develop the film in his dark room. Many years before, he had learned to develop his own photos, and he enjoyed the process. He assured Emerson it was not difficult, that it was like riding a bicycle and never left you. One photograph would accompany Emerson's evaluations that she was sending by way of the seaplane to Rachel and Naomi. A second photograph would be attached to the homemade identity card Emerson planned to create for each child.

These small travelers would be making a trip across the ocean without birth certificates or passports. Emerson and Robert had decided that, in addition to the visas complete with the medallion and date stamps, each child would be provided with an identity card. It was something the two of them had thought up. There was nothing official about it in any way, and it was certainly not a passport. But each child would be provided with an identify card that had his or her picture, real name, date of birth, and nationality on it.

Emerson carefully chose the heavy card stock and had the identity cards printed for this specific purpose. When the photographs were finished and she had all the pertinent information about each child, she attached the photo and filled in the identity card that would accompany the visa that would enable each child to enter the United States. She went to considerable effort to make the identity card appear to be as official as possible.

The entry visa would be the basis for the adoption papers in their new country. Emerson had seen several of the real visas that Peter had signed, sealed, and stamped for people who would travel to the U.S., and she was able to duplicate these almost exactly. She had a new ink pad that had been sent from the United States. Emerson forged Peter's signature and filled out a visa for each child. Each visa was sealed and stamped and made to look legitimate and authoritative.

The visa and the identity card for each traveler were put into waterproof isinglass and oilskin packets. Robert would hand these packets, that held the official and the unofficial documents, to Max when the children were transferred to his ship. Max would in turn hand these documents over to Naomi when the children arrived in Virginia.

On the night they were to leave, the children ate an especially hearty meal. Each one carried a small rucksack with a few belongings in it. In addition to pajamas, a change of clothes, and a bar of soap and sponge, each rucksack held a book and a toy. Emerson allowed each child to select these two things for their journey. Each child was given a small brown paper bag that held a sandwich, some cookies, an apple, and a chocolate bar. Emerson knew Max had an excellent cook aboard the *Anjo*, and the children would be well fed on their journey.

After tonight, this group of children, who would accompany Pierre on the next stage of his journey, would be gone and out of her hands. During their short foray into her life, Emerson had done all she could to give these children the care and attention they so badly needed. The girls all had clean and carefully groomed hair with ribbons. Magdalena had given the boys haircuts. They were ready to leave and piled into the truck.

Emerson had stayed in touch with Max, and on the night when they were scheduled to rendezvous, they synchronized their watches and prepared to attempt the transfer of the fifteen children from a motor launch to a large cargo ship. Once Emerson had told him the specifications of the new launch they had purchased, Max said it would be no problem, and Emerson trusted him to know what he was doing. They were late enough that the road to the boathouse was almost deserted. They met a few other cars and trucks, but none of them seemed to be full of rowdy Germans or curious Portuguese policemen. The children were quiet as they'd been instructed. Bless their hearts, Emerson thought, these children had been forced to be quiet most of their lives. They moved out of the truck and into the boathouse without a misstep.

Emerson hugged each child goodbye, and her heart ached. She cried when she told Peter "a bientot." Lily was sitting in Emerson's lap, and Pierre buried his face in Lily's white hair and let the tears roll down over her head. Lily licked the salty tears from his face. He clung to Emerson, and she reassured him that he was going to have the most wonderful mother in the whole world once he got to America. It was all Emerson could do to keep herself from sobbing out loud as she said goodbye to Pierre.

The children climbed aboard the motor launch and waited silently. Emerson was on the radio with Max, and he gave her the signal that it was time for the launch to leave. Emerson gave Max's location to Robert who was piloting the launch. She waved goodbye as the small boat laden with its precious cargo pulled out of the boathouse and headed into the cove and out to sea. She blew kisses to Pierre until the children and the launch were no longer in view. She would wait until Robert returned with the launch and gave her his report about how the transfer had gone. She was alone, and she allowed herself to cry.

Emerson had to trust that things would go smoothly. She had to believe that the children would all board the *Anjo* safely, that German U-boats would stay far away from the shipload of orphans as it made its dangerous way across the Atlantic Ocean, and that they would arrive safely in Virginia. If those things happened, these special children would begin new lives in the best country in the world, under the care of Naomi Friedman, the most capable woman Emerson had ever known.

Emerson's end of things was done for now. She would grieve the loss of Pierre for a long time, maybe for always.

Lily sat quietly on her lap, and Emerson knew that Lily understood what had just happened. Lily would miss her little pal. Emerson wondered if Lily's heart was breaking, too.

Robert finally arrived back at the boathouse. It seemed as if he'd been gone for hours and hours, but when Emerson looked at her watch she realized he had been gone for just a little more than an hour. Emerson was anxious to hear every detail of the transfer. Robert pulled the launch into the boathouse and secured the lines. He had a smile on his face.

"Tell me everything, Robert. Next time I may want to go with you to see it for myself. But I need for you to tell me how you got the children on board the *Anjo*, how long it took, and if the seas were rough."

"It went beautifully. The sea was relatively calm. Max is quite a guy and had everything perfectly organized. There was a sturdy rope ladder that was lowered from the deck of the *Anjo*. Each crew member had an ingenious harness attached to his back so that the child would be secure and the crew member's hands would both be free to climb the ladder. A crew member climbed down, put a child into the harness on his back, and climbed back up the rope ladder to the ship's deck. After one crew member and one child were successfully on the deck of the *Anjo*, another crew member climbed down, picked up a child, and climbed back up the rope ladder. That continued like clockwork until all the children were on board. The loading process was smart and terribly efficient — just like Max. The children were utterly silent, and there was not a sound from the time we left the cove until the children were all on board the freighter. They waved to me as I pulled the launch away from the side of the ship. I could hear the engines of the *Anjo* starting up as soon as I pulled away in the launch. Max was absolutely right about needing the new launch. That little motor boat we used to have would never have been able to carry enough children. We would have had to make two trips, and it would have been impossible for the crew to load the children onto the *Anjo* from such a small boat. The launch must have cost you a fortune, but it was more than worth it. Without it, the transfer would not have been possible. I was terribly sad to see our little Pierre leave us, but he seemed content with his new group of friends. They were eager to explore the ship. I would say it was all a great success."

Emerson and Robert drove the truck back to the hideout. Robert delivered Emerson to Bacalhoa in his car and went home. Emerson let herself into the palacio and drew a hot bath. Every bone in her body ached, and she was physically and emotionally exhausted. She could sleep all day tomorrow — that is today.

Fifteen children who otherwise would not have had a chance to live were now on their way to a new country and to new families where they would have every opportunity for full, productive, and even happy lives. Knowing that was a good feeling. Emerson allowed herself, just this one night, to cry herself to sleep because she missed Pierre so terribly. He would soon be living with Emerson's dearest friend in the world. Pierre and Rachel would learn to love each other. It was the best of all possible outcomes. Or perhaps the second best of all possible outcomes.

Chapter 23

ARRIVING IN THE LAND OF THE FREE

March 1942

The voyage took eight days, and there were no U-boat attacks or sightings. Max was smart and careful, but danger was all around during wartime. The weather had been fine with only two days of rough seas and storms that battered the ship. Max was impressed with how well-behaved the children were. They were grateful to be provided with three meals a day and a place to sleep that was relatively safe and dry. They never complained about the days when the ship gave them a turbulent ride.

Max spent some time with them each day and was captivated with Pierre who told him stories about Lily and Emerson and things they had done together. Max felt he was getting to know the kind of person Emerson was through Pierre. The children gathered around him whenever he came down to their secret quarters. They understood the rules about what they were and were not allowed to do. They understood what had to happen if the ship was boarded by soldiers or sailors from any nation. Fortunately, the *Anjo* did not see another ship until they were almost to Norfolk.

In sight of Cape Charles and Cape Henry, Max knew the lighthouse at Camp Story had guided ships in and out of the Chesapeake Bay for over a hundred years. Since the attacks at Pearl Harbor, activity and security had increased at all vulnerable military locations. Naomi had told Max he would quickly be granted safe passage when he reached the mouth of the Chesapeake Bay. He would not be held up, and the ship would not be searched when the authorities boarded the *Anjo*. When Max presented his papers to the United States Coast Guard officials who secured the entrance to the Bay, he was given the okay to proceed immediately to Baltimore.

The manifest gave Baltimore as the *Anjo*'s destination although Max was not going anywhere near Baltimore on this trip. No questions were asked about his cargo or about anything at all. It happened just as Naomi had said it would. Max had communicated with Naomi only by radio, and he had never met her in person. He was quite impressed that she had been able to deliver on her promise to ease his way through the formalities of clearing security at the entrance to the Chesapeake Bay so that the *Anjo* could continue its journey.

After entering the Bay, the *Anjo* sailed north along Virginia's eastern shore. Midnight had come and gone by the time the *Anjo* reached the entrance to Butcher's Creek, the designated estuary south of Onancock, Virginia. It was a dark night and clouds covered the moon. Cold and windy, it was not a night for the faint of heart to be outside in the weather. Max had studied the navigational charts and the tides and knew that his ship would not be able to come in close to shore where the children were to be delivered. His plan was to put the children and two crew men into a lifeboat and lower it over the side of the ship. They had done this many times off the coast of Palestine. The oarsmen in the lifeboat would navigate Butcher's Creek and bring the children to Naomi's specified landing spot.

The children wanted to hug Max goodbye as they boarded the life boat. No one had hugged Max in years, and he felt awkward as they hung on to his legs and told him thank you. His eyes were moist as he accepted their gratitude for bringing them to this New World Promised Land. He waved them away with an unanticipated sense of loss as he watched the most valuable cargo he had ever transported being lowered into the dark waters of the Chesapeake Bay on this blustery March night. At the last minute, Max decided to go with the children. He wanted to meet Naomi and see for himself what this amazing woman was made of. Another lifeboat was lowered. The waves were choppy, but the lifeboats quickly reached the Butcher's Creek dock.

Six green lanterns stood in a line to mark the spot where the lifeboat was to deliver its passengers. Three adults waited on the shore to receive the children. The landing place had been chosen well. There was a wooden dock, recently repaired and refurbished, where the lifeboats could pull up and secure their lines. The children were transferred without incident from the boat to the dock.

Max and Naomi met briefly. Each took their measure of the other. With a perfunctory handshake, Max handed Naomi the packets that contained the critical visas and the homemade identity cards. Naomi and Max spoke a few words. Each recognized in the other a courageous and dependable partner, a person who deserved trust and respect. It did not require a lengthy exchange. Naomi was thrilled that the transfer of the children from the life boat to the dock had gone smoothly. She had not known how large the lifeboat would be or if the dock on the creek in Accomack County, Virginia would be able to accommodate it. Everything had worked, and within minutes of their arrival, the lifeboats, the oarsmen, and the captain of the ship were on their way back down the estuary of Butcher's Creek to return to the *Anjo*.

The children, always silent, were directed to a small bus. They climbed in, and before the bus began to move, each child was given a cup of hot chocolate with marshmallows on top and some chocolate chip cookies. The United States of America already looked like a pretty great place to these young travelers. They drove for more than three hours, and most were asleep when the bus finally stopped. They'd arrived inside the gates of a farm near Easton, Maryland. They would stay in the large three-story white frame colonial house for the next few days.

The children who were awake walked into the welcoming foyer. Those who were asleep were carried inside and up the grand staircase to their waiting bedrooms. Clean sheets and warm blankets greeted them. There were beautiful modern bathrooms and antique wood furnishings. There was a lamp beside each bed, rugs on the floors, and art work on the walls. In each room was a box of toys and piles of children's books. To these bedraggled and exhausted children, this place looked like heaven. They slept safe and sound in America at last.

Naomi had wanted to meet the first lifeboat full of children to be sure that everything ran smoothly, even though she completely trusted her team of organizers and caretakers. She knew they would keep the project confidential and do their jobs professionally. She'd decided she wanted to share in the excitement and be part of the welcoming committee for this initial group of children. She had not been able to wait to lay her eyes on Pierre who had arrived on the *Anjo* last night. The experience of greeting the small, frightened youngsters on the dock at Butcher's Creek had filled Naomi with such joy. She knew she would have to be there every time the *Anjo* brought a lifeboat full of children to Virginia. She did not want to miss even one of these very special arrivals.

Naomi was saddened by how thin and quiet the children were. They needed to be filled with good food and given lots of love. They would have everything they needed now that they were under Naomi's care, and Naomi had complete confidence in her own daughter's ability to find exactly the right home for each of these little ones.

Before she went to bed, Naomi called Rachel and told her briefly of their first success. Rachel was overjoyed to hear the news, especially the news that Pierre was now on American soil. Naomi sent a short radio message to Max on the *Anjo* to let him know that the children were safe at her farm. She also placed a telephone call to Emerson at Bacalhoa and told her through their coded messaging system that the children were safe in America and in her care. "Your delivery has arrived. Fifteen parcels are in good shape. We await your next shipment." Naomi slept well that night, as did her small charges. She could see a whole new role in life opening up for her.

Pierre had been asleep when he'd arrived at the Easton farm, but Naomi had watched him on the bus with special interest. He was her new grandson, after all. After telling his friends goodbye later this morning, he would be driven to Baltimore where an adult companion would travel with him on the train to Boston. Tomorrow evening he would meet Rachel and her family for the first time. He would be welcomed with open arms into their home. Because Naomi wanted Pierre to bond first with Rachel's family, she would not get to know Pierre in her current role as an organizer of the orphan project. She could hardly wait to meet him and love him in her role as his new grandmother.

Naomi was somewhat surprised that she didn't feel more guilt about what she was doing. She was essentially smuggling children into the United States. She had always been a stickler for the law, a defender of the law. And she still believed in the law. She believed that the law was what kept chaos at bay, but the war had changed her. It had changed everybody everywhere. Naomi had been infuriated in 1939 when the U.S. State Department had refused to allow a ship, whose passenger manifest was made up mostly of Jewish refugees fleeing Germany, permission to enter the United States. The German ship, the *SS St. Louis*, carrying almost a thousand desperate souls who were trying to escape the Nazi scourge, had first tried to enter Cuba. Because of the pervasive anti-Semitism on that island, the entry visas of the European Jews aboard were declared invalid, and they were not allowed to disembark in Cuba.

Appealing to Franklin Roosevelt, the *St. Louis* sailed along the East Coast of the United States, waiting to receive good news that they would be permitted to enter a U.S. port. But there was no good news. Ostensibly afraid to compromise its neutral status, the U.S. turned its back on the world's most vulnerable people. Because of restrictive quotas on Jewish refugees from Europe, the passengers aboard the *St. Louis* were refused entry into the United States. They were forced to return to Europe. Britain, Belgium, the Netherlands, and France all accepted some of the desperate passengers. Almost all of those who were lucky enough to go to Britain survived the war. Those who took refuge in countries which Hitler would conquer within the next year did not fare as well.

Naomi respected the rule of law but deeply resented the quota system which had refused to accept these people who had left everything behind in their attempt to escape tyranny and death. The decision to turn its back on them did not represent the country she knew and loved, the country she had spent her whole life defending. If the quotas were insufficient to handle the problem, the quotas needed to be changed.

In 1940 when the United States had accepted the refugees aboard the *SS Quanza*, over one hundred of whom were Jewish, Naomi had written to Eleanor Roosevelt to thank her for having compassion and allowing these desperate human beings to enter the United States. She urged Mrs. Roosevelt to intervene with her husband and his administration to change immigration laws due to the extraordinary circumstances presented by this war. She believed that Mrs. Roosevelt was an advocate for taking in the endangered Jews of Europe, but she was not so sure about the President. Naomi suspected that a number of people who had Franklin Roosevelt's ear were secretly, subtly, or even outright anti-Semitic. They did not want Europe's Jews in their country. This realization was so hurtful to Naomi and made her so angry, it caused an irrevocable change within her.

When Emerson had proposed the orphan underground, Naomi had jumped at the chance to help. The children who entered the United States would have official United States' visas, on official forms with official seals and official stamps. That the visas had been issued by someone other than the U.S. Consulate in Portugal did not seem to be an important detail when the lives of children were at stake. Naomi welcomed the chance to circumvent what she felt was a cruel and unjust quota system. Naomi was Jewish. How could she refuse to help save Jewish children?

It was not as if Naomi was participating in bringing in ordinary refugees who might become charges of the state. Every one of the orphaned children she was helping to enter the country had a family waiting to adopt her or him. Every one of them had an openhearted and enthusiastic community eager to embrace them and love them. Childless couples who had tried to have their own children, who had tried to adopt children and had failed, would now have their lives enriched by being able to adopt an orphan from Europe. Families and communities would be stronger by taking in these new members. It was a project that brought joy to all concerned. How could that be a bad thing? How could she possibly be in the wrong? It was the quota system that was wrong.

These were extraordinary times. Unbelievable things were happening in Europe. Children were being murdered by the thousands in extermination camps, and Naomi was determined to do whatever was necessary to save as many of them as she could. To do otherwise would be a violation of her own integrity and humanity. Without guilt, she went about her rescue efforts to get these children adopted. She took great satisfaction in what she was doing. How could saving lives not be the best of all possible ways to spend one's time? How could this not be her life's most important mission? The government might punish her for what she was doing, but she was certain that God would not.

Chapter 24

THE UNDERGROUND IS UNDERWAY

MARCH 1942

I*t took Emerson, Robert, and Magdalena a few days* to rest from the strain and late nights involved in taking care of their first group of orphans and getting them aboard the *Anjo* on their way to America. They were thrilled with their success and felt they would soon be ready for another group. Emerson and Magdalena, with the help of Sandro's wife, cleaned the hideout and prepared it for the next group of children. The few minor glitches in their plans, which had become apparent during the first effort, were discussed and remedied. The routine at Bacalhoa briefly returned to normal.

Emerson sanded the motley assortment of chairs she had collected and painted them in bright primary colors. She filed away, in a secret cache in her dressing room, copies of the biographical sketches she had done for the first group of rescued children. She had a picture of Pierre, which Robert had enlarged and framed for her, on the table beside her bed.

She told him goodnight every night. She looked forward to hearing every possible bit of news from Rachel about Pierre. How was he adjusting and fitting into the family? Did he ever mention missing Emerson or Lily or Bacalhoa? Emerson also wanted details about how the other children had been placed and about the families Rachel had chosen for them. Emerson had often teased Rachel that an undergraduate degree in sociology and a Ph.D. in psychology were wasted on someone with Rachel's brilliant mind. Rachel had certainly had the last laugh on that one.

Finally, Emerson heard from Rachel that Pierre had arrived safely and had immediately bonded with the entire family. Rachel was fluent in French and Pierre was learning English quickly. Rachel was fascinated to hear Pierre's stories about Bacalhoa and Lily, his bedroom in a chapel, and the Baby Jesus who had opened an entire underground passageway. Pierre was especially delighted to find that Rachel had a miniature Scottie dog named Hershey. Hershey was as black as Lily had been white. Pierre was wonderful with Rachel's toddlers and was already teaching them words in French. Rachel had fallen instantly and completely in love with Pierre, and Emerson knew that sending him into the care of her dearest friend had been the right thing to do for everybody concerned —except maybe for herself.

Emerson and Robert sent a second group of children off with Max in April and a third group in May. They wondered if their network would be forced to close down because the Nazis were becoming ever more vigilant in Southern France. Robert was worried that the increasingly intense hunt for Jews in Vichy might put them all at greater risk. Security and secrecy were always the most important factors for Robert, and he tried to impress on Emerson how vital these considerations had to be in their planning.

Robert had never wanted to share any information about his role in helping Allied pilots escape. He did not want to put anyone else at risk in case something went wrong or he was arrested. He did not want to give the Gestapo any help. The Germans were all too aware that there were a number of secret groups which helped pilots return to Britain. The Nazis were constantly trying to infiltrate these groups with their spies. They did everything they could to unmask the brave men and women of the underground who risked their lives to return these pilots to their heroic work of destroying the Third Reich from the air.

Emerson knew that Robert was sometimes called out to attend to an injury or an illness for someone who was being smuggled to freedom. Others in need of medical care were brought to Robert's clinic, secretly, in the middle of the night. Although he said he never went into Spain any more, Emerson knew that once he had driven all night to reach a remote location in Spain where he stayed for several days to attend to several wounded pilots. Only because he occasionally needed Emerson's help, to cancel his patients or to cover for him with his servants, did he ever involve her. Robert had asked her to care for Pierre out of desperation. Emerson was forever grateful that he had called on her that December night.

Robert had been conducting his underground operations for much longer than Emerson had been involved in the orphans' project. He repeatedly warned her not to become complacent about security. He knew about this from personal experience because someone in his own group had once let down their guard. If anyone in the network forgot that every step taken and every work spoken was a matter of life and death, people could be arrested and shot and disappeared.

Robert was concerned that Emerson did not take his warnings seriously enough. He was worried that she would become lax with the rules. Robert pointed out to her that initially when Pierre came to recover from his wounds at Bacalhoa, his presence was going to be known only to Emerson, Robert, and Magdalena. Within weeks if not days, Benadina and every member of the staff at the palacio knew about Pierre and adored him. Far from being hidden away, he'd had the run of the estate and the gardens and the run of the farm. Emerson pointed out to Robert that having one little French boy in the house could easily be explained and that she understood it would be much more difficult to explain away the presence of fifteen children.

Robert wanted to be specific about his concerns. "Several groups have passed through our temporary refuge here at Bacalhoa. No group has stayed for very long, and the children did not have a chance to become a problem. There may come a time when they have to stay for longer than a few days. They will grow restless staying indoors, and they will want to go outside to play. You might be tempted to allow that to happen. They will be noisier than you realize, and one of the children will throw a ball that goes outside of the safe perimeter you have established. A hiker or a random passerby will come upon the children playing and wonder why so many children are playing together at a deserted location in the woods. They will begin to ask around town about who these children could possibly be. Eventually, somebody will come to investigate that something unusual is happening, especially with all the Germans around who are constantly sticking their noses into everything. They are always stopping by my house and the surgery. They are forever asking questions and demanding to come inside and look around for I don't know what. I try to be as polite as I can be because I don't want to defy them and arouse their suspicions. That's why I hesitate to keep any really sick refugees at my house. The Germans know that some of the fliers and other people who are trying to escape need medical care. I am a British doctor. I am the enemy."

Emerson nodded in agreement. "I understand what you are saying about not relaxing security, and you are correct that I will have to guard against it. Telling the children they will have to stay inside the hideout might seem cruel in the short run, but it is better to be strict so that in the long run they stay alive and are able to move on. I appreciate and accept all of these things, Robert. I am not a fool."

"Of course, you are not a fool. But you have a soft heart and want to allow the children to have as normal an existence as possible. But things are not normal for them. What we are doing is anything but normal," Robert was adamant in his warning. "Another thing that you, that we, must always be on the lookout for is the inevitable close scrutiny from the Germans and from the Portuguese secret police. Sooner or later the word will leak out that Jewish children are being brought to this area in increasing numbers. The Germans will hear about it and will do everything they can to discover if there is any truth to the stories. A successful underground eventually becomes the victim of its own success. People will begin to talk as more and more children pass safely through our hideout. Word trickles back, and stories make the rounds. The more children we send on their way, the more chances there will be that the Portuguese, the Spanish Guardia Civil at the border, or the Germans will hear about our successes."

Robert continued. "We are fortunate that when the children leave us, they are leaving the continent. If the role of the *Anjo* remains undiscovered, the children's arrival at Bacalhoa will be the dead end. Let us hope that we can continue to keep our secret as closely held as we have done so far. I worry that gasoline shortages and serious food rationing will come to Portugal. When those things happen, the authorities may try to requisition the bounty that Bacalhoa's farm produces. We need the extra produce and animal products to feed our children. If we don't have food for them, we can't take care of them. I worry that a word to the wrong person that we need a spare part for the truck or new tires for the van will raise eyebrows and make people suspicious in these times. I am just saying that it is extremely difficult to keep anything, let alone a good thing, secret forever. Our operation has become complex. The more people we involve, the more difficult it will be to maintain confidentiality. We have to do better than our best."

"You have been working in the Allied flyers' underground for more than two years. How do you keep from being caught?"

"I really don't know how the people who organize all of this keep from being caught. They are terribly brave and so inspiring. The routes are altered regularly. The safe houses along the way are changed often, and even the people who guide the flyers out of harm's way are switched around from time to time. The routes could be discovered at any moment. The organizers have learned to react instantly and seem to almost always make the right decisions. Making a wrong decision or reacting too slowly can cost lives and has cost lives. I am a peripheral and small part of the process. The guides use me only when they have a serious illness or injury. First aid by the underground workers usually has to suffice in treating most wounds and setting broken limbs. They call on me only for the most critical cases. They know I am being watched and use great care when involving me with an injured flyer. I wish they would use me more, but they are the experts at this. I am just a professional doing medical work. One reason I am so happy to be involved with the orphan project is that I didn't feel I was doing enough because the underground was so careful and used me so sparingly."

Warm weather had come to Setubal and the orphans' network had successfully processed three groups of children. Remarkably and thankfully so far, the problems that had arisen had been small ones. Any mistakes that had been made had not been fatal. Emerson was worried about the children being cooped up in the hideout during the summer months. The building itself was made of stone and stucco, and it was surrounded by a forest. The children should not suffer from the heat. Emerson was more concerned about the children developing cabin fever.

The shorter nights of late spring and early summer caused Max some worry. There would be fewer hours of darkness. His window of opportunity, for anchoring off the cove, picking up the children, and getting back on his way across the Atlantic, would become smaller. The wind was often deathly still on summer nights. The motor launch sounded so loud that Emerson was sometimes afraid it could be heard in Brazil. The problem of the long days and short nights was also a concern when Max dropped off the children in Virginia.

They waited for word that another group of orphans was scheduled to arrive. During the second week of June, they received word that a group of sixteen children was on its way. Robert would drive to a location near Porto on the Atlantic Coast to pick them up, and it was a long drive back to Setubal. Transporting a van full of children, none of whom had the proper papers to be in Portugal or in fact to be anywhere at all, would be an enormous risk. The longer the van had to be on the road, the greater the danger.

Robert decided to take the van on this trip because he thought it would be less conspicuous on the long drive than the disreputable-looking truck would be. Up until now, Robert had driven the canvas-covered truck to the Algarve, but these trips had been relatively short. He was concerned that he would be stopped for some reason or for no reason at all on the long journey to and from Porto.

Not long after Robert left to drive to Portugal's northern port, Emerson received an emergency telephone call, in code, that told her to stand by for a shortwave radio message about an additional group of children that was on its way. Emerson's telephone number at Bacalhoa was the backup telephone number, in case Robert was unable to take the telephone call. Her shortwave radio was the backup radio in case Robert's radio was down. Robert was not at his house, so Emerson had received the call. They had briefly anticipated the problem that two or more groups of children might arrive at the same time. She had decided she would simply say no, that they could not take another group, that they already had a full house. But this communication sounded like an emergency.

She wished Robert were there to discuss it with her, but she would have to handle this one on her own. The shortwave message was full of static and difficult to understand. She heard the ETA and the latitude and longitude, the co-ordinates that let her know when and where the children would be arriving. Emerson did not have time to acknowledge that she had received the message before the radio went dead. She had not had time to tell the sender of the message that she was unable to accept the children. When she checked the map, she realized the location was close to Tavira. This spot on the Algarve was close to the border with Spain, and it would be a long drive from Setubal.

Because of the paucity of the information that was sent, Emerson worried there might be a breach in security. She decided she would try to make the rendezvous. She could not leave a group of children stranded in the woods or on the beach. These poor souls were truly homeless and without a country. She could not abandon them. She would drive herself to the meeting place on the Algarve to collect the children. Because of the way the notification had come to her and because of the brevity of the radio message, she suspected there was extra danger involved with this pick-up. She worried that she might not have heard the information correctly. She would have to play it by ear.

She asked Magdalena to accompany her. They would have to leave soon, before dark, if they were to arrive in time to meet the children. The radio message had not let her know how many children would be in the group. Emerson was hoping there would not be many, but she had no way of knowing anything. The hideout had been designed to accommodate twenty children at most. How many extras would they be able to squeeze into the secret refuge?

When they drove to the hideout to pick up the rickety truck, Emerson left a note for Robert telling him that she and Magdalena were going to pick up an additional group of children that night in the Algarve, near Tavira. Thank goodness Robert always kept both vehicles filled with petrol in case of an emergency. Even with a full tank, they had to carry extra containers of petrol with them to be able to make the round trip without stopping.

Chapter 25

BY THE SEA

JUNE 1942

Emerson and Magdalena made their way over the nearly empty highway toward the Algarve. Because of the war and the fact that Portugal was the last stop for many, the beaches were full during the day. It was as if people with no hope swarmed to this last lovely place for one final vacation from the hellhole that Europe had become. The women met a car or a truck here and there, but shortages of petrol meant that no one was out joy riding on summer nights. It was late, and it was dark.

Emerson drove the truck over roads made of gravel and dirt. Finally the road turned to sand, and that made the ride even more difficult. Emerson was glad Robert had taken the van because she felt it was safer for the longer drive to Porto, but she wondered about the reliability of the truck. Robert was exceedingly conscientious about checking out their vehicles before they picked up a group of children, but he had not known that the truck as well as the van would be called into service tonight. The drive to the meeting place in the Algarve was hours away from Setubal, and the rendezvous point was particularly isolated. This was a good thing. The more isolated the location, the less likely they were to be discovered.

There hadn't been time to prepare for this second group of children, and Emerson didn't know how many would be arriving or anything about the children's ages. It would be a surprise. Emerson asked Benadina to fix some food for Magdalena and herself so they could eat while they were on the road. Benadina also prepared a box of sandwiches and cookies for the children.

They'd all given up the ruse that there was an imaginary soup kitchen. Benadina now knew exactly what was going on. Magdalena assembled a crate that held several bottles of milk, water, and fruit juice. The women added as much fresh fruit as they could find at the last minute. They wanted to be sure the orphans had something to eat and drink when they arrived. The children would have been at sea for several days, and it was a long drive from Tavira to Setubal. Everyone would be thirsty and hungry on their return ride to the hideout. It was a four-hour drive one way with at least another four hours back to Setubal.

Emerson usually drove the van and was not used to driving the truck. She struggled with the gears as the roads became worse and worse. She had to trust that the truck would make it to the meeting place and then safely back to Bacalhoa. Robert kept both vehicles in good running condition, and she knew he had spent considerable time and money working on the truck's engine to be sure it ran well. Its body was completely dilapidated, but this was exactly the way they wanted it to look on the outside. The truck had to appear as if it was a disintegrating ruin and could not possibly be engaged in activities of any importance.

The women arrived early at the designated location and waited in the warm June night. They double checked their map to be sure they were in the right place. Everyone involved in the orphan project preferred new moons to full moons, but sometimes, that was not possible. Tonight there was not really a full moon, but it seemed as if the three-quarters moon had come up early. Moonlight poured onto the lonely stretch of beach. Working in their favor was the fact that thick fog obscured the water.

Emerson didn't like this particular location because there were so many large rocks in the water. Some were very close to the beach. These were dangerous obstacles for any small boat that was attempting to land. Usually, their young passengers came ashore in rubber rafts from larger ships that anchored in the ocean. Instructions were given to the children that as soon as the raft landed on the beach, they were to climb out of the raft and run to the truck or whatever vehicle they could see. An adult who traveled with the children would commandeer the raft and take it back to the larger ship waiting in deep water. Emerson wondered if it would all happen as planned tonight.

The arrival of the children was delayed to the extent that Emerson and Magdalena began to wonder if the emergency call for a beach rendezvous had been a mistake. Had the pick-up been intended for tonight? Or some other night? Magdalena had refilled the tank of the truck with the extra petrol they'd brought in jerry cans. Everything was ready to make as quick a return trip to Setubal as possible. They were just about to call off their watch and go home when all of a sudden, they heard gunfire. The fog that shrouded the water cleared briefly, and they could see two ships off-shore where there should have been only one.

Emerson and Magdalena had positioned the truck so that when the headlights were turned on, they faced out into the

Atlantic. This was to signal the ship carrying the children that it was safe to come ashore and indicated where the raft should land. Emerson decided the gunfire meant their usual procedures would have to be ignored, and she quickly extinguished the truck's headlights. The two women watched in horror as the drama unfolded before them.

A patrol boat of some kind was firing its guns at a small tramp steamer. The smaller boat was completely vulnerable and had no guns or any way to defend itself against the patrol boat. Emerson and Magdalena guessed that, because they were so close to the border with Spain, the patrol boat was probably a Spanish maritime police boat. If it was a Spanish patrol boat, it was operating illegally inside Portuguese territorial waters. The larger ship with guns on its deck fired several mortar shell rounds at the smaller boat. The women on shore could not see what flag the small tramp steamer was flying. Magdalena thought it might be blue.

There were no signs of any children or any rubber raft. The women knew they couldn't leave but were worried that the truck waiting on the beach road was an obvious and vulnerable target, just asking to be noticed and fired upon. The small steamer had been mortally wounded by the shell bursts from the patrol boat. Something vital had been hit, and the ship began to list to one side. It was going to sink. Where were the children? Could Emerson and Magdalena find them? Could they possibly rescue them?

The steamer was sinking, and the patrol boat fired on it several more times. It looked as if as if the patrol boat was going to pull away and abandon the steamer as it went down. The sinking ship drifted closer and closer to the shore with the waves. Suddenly the fog lifted again, and Emerson saw a rubber raft with people in it who seemed to be trying to negotiate the jagged rock formations close to the beach. The raft had drifted a considerable distance down the beach away from the truck, and the tide was quickly carrying it farther out to sea. The raft was floundering. It was turning around and around in circles on the waves. It could overturn at any moment in the turbulent water. Whoever was trying to row the raft to shore was either not strong enough or not knowledgeable enough to keep the raft headed toward land. The raft traveled farther and farther out into the ocean.

Emerson took off her jacket, slipped out of her shoes, and ran into the water. She was an exceptionally strong swimmer and knew how to swim in the sea. She wasn't sure she could do what was necessary to redirect the raft around the dangerous rocks that, along with the strong tides, were hindering its progress.

Emerson swam as fast as she could out towards the raft. The current kept pulling her away from her goal, and she had to call on all of her strength to swim against the flow to try to reach the raft. Just when she thought she was going to have to give up in defeat, she was able to grab hold of a rope that hung over the side of the unwieldy rubber boat. She struggled as she swam and pulled it behind her, making slow progress towards the shore. There were six very small children all alone in the raft. None of them were even attempting to use the oars. No wonder they had not been able to steer it or propel it forward. It was a miracle they had not all been tossed out into the water. Thankfully, each child wore a life vest, but all the vests were much too large. Working against the outgoing undertow, Emerson gave it her best shot.

As Emerson hung on to the raft, the children were calling to her and pointing to the deeper water. They were calling out names and shouting "help" in French. If it had not been for the moonlight, Emerson would never have seen the three small bodies bobbing up and down more than fifty yards off shore. These children also appeared to be wearing oversized life vests. What should she do? Should she leave the raft and go after the children? Or should she get the raft safely to shore and then try to save the children who were thrashing in the water farther out to sea.

Emerson looked up to see Magdalena wading into the water and coming towards her. Emerson gave up her hold on the rope to Magdalena, turned around, and dove under the incoming waves. She was going back out into the deep water to try to reach the children who were in terrible danger of drowning. The little ones were frantically waving and screaming as they rode the waves up and down.

Emerson was already worn out from fighting the current and trying to reach the raft and bring it to shore. She doubted she had the strength to make it to the three children who had fallen out of the raft and were being tossed around in the ocean. She did not know if she would be able to bring them all back to safety, but she had to try. She willed herself to be strong, to hold out at all costs. Finally, she reached the bobbing life jackets and realized that there were four, not three, children in trouble. All of them were so young, and it was obvious that none of them could swim. They were terrified and were wearing themselves out splashing and crying in panic. Emerson motioned and yelled in French for the two who appeared to be the oldest to grab hold of the backs of the life vests of the younger ones. Emerson grabbed the lifejackets of the two older children, one in each hand, and she began to move, swimming on her back and doing her strongest scissors kick. She urged the children to hang on tight to the life vests. She swam and swam with everything she could muster to bring the four children through the current of the outgoing tide and onto the beach.

Finally, she made it close enough to the shore that the breaking waves brought the five of them in. They had been carried farther down the beach with the current so they were a distance from the where the truck was parked. Magdalena was running along the edge of the water toward them. Just as she was dragging the four children and Emerson from the water, the steamer that was sinking exploded and burst into flames. The children began to scream and point to the burning ship. Emerson immediately grasped what they were trying to tell her.

"Combien? Dites-moi, combine!" she demanded to know how many more were still trapped on the ship. She was now more than at the end of her reservoirs of strength, but she could not leave any children to die on that ship either because they drowned or because they burned to death. The children she'd just rescued were trying to tell her that there were either two or three people still left on the steamer that had just been blown to pieces.

Emerson realized that she could go down before she was able to save anyone else, but again she told herself she had to try. She took a deep breath, stumbled back out into the waves, and dove under the water in the direction of the burning mass of wood and metal. She could not see a single living creature when she reached the flames. There were no people wearing life jackets in the water and no people to be seen on board the vessel. There was only fire and the smell of diesel oil. The fuel burned on the surface of the water, and Emerson had to swim around the burning pyres to make her way in the direction of what was left from the explosion. She swam through the burning oil and debris to the other side of the steamer that was coming apart before her eyes. An oil slick covered the surface of the water surrounding the burning ship, and by now Emerson's body was covered with oil. She heard a noise above the sound of the crackling, burning wood. When she looked up, she realized that the patrol boat was returning. No doubt, it was coming to see about the explosion and the fires.

Emerson was about to give up when she saw a young woman holding on to two toddlers and cradling an infant in her arms. The woman was standing on a piece of the deck that hung precariously from what was left of the little steamer. The young woman was about to jump from the deck of the burning ship into the water. Emerson called out to her in French and told her she was coming.

Emerson could not believe her eyes when she saw a life ring floating near her in the water. Americans called it a life preserver. Whatever it was called, it was a Godsend and gave Emerson heart and hope. She pushed the ring in front of her and told the young woman to jump off the ship close to the life preserver. The woman could not reach for the ring or swim unless she let go of at least one of the children she was trying to save. Emerson positioned the ring and told the woman to jump with the children. When she fell into the oil-slicked ocean, the woman was able to hang on to the two toddlers, but the infant fell out of her arms and went under the water.

Emerson had been afraid this would happen and had been careful to note exactly where the baby had gone down. She made sure the woman had hold of the life ring and began diving for the infant. She dove and dove and dove. Finally, farther out to sea, she saw the child bobbing on the waves. The current had swept the infant away from the shore. Emerson swam out and gathered the child in one arm. She swam towards shore with the other arm. She didn't know if the baby was still breathing, but this child was not going to disappear into the sea and die tonight — not on Emerson's watch. Emerson swam blindly back toward the shore. It seemed like the land was miles away. Emerson was far past the limits of her endurance, and she finally lost consciousness. Magdalena plowed through the waves and grabbed the baby from Emerson's arms as all three washed up on the shore with the incoming swells.

Magdalena gave the baby two hard raps on the back and then two more hard raps. Finally, the little one coughed up her lungs full of sea water and gasped for breath. The patrol boat was coming closer. The other children had run to the truck and climbed in the back. The young woman had been able to ride the life ring to shore while hanging on to two of the toddlers. One of these little ones was barely able to walk but recognized the severity of the situation and tried to run toward the truck. The young woman was holding the other toddler, who had been hurt, in her arms. When she saw what was happening, she lay the injured child down on the sand.

Magdalena was desperate to drag Emerson's limp and floundering body out of the surf. Magdalena put the infant down. The baby was still struggling to breathe. As the patrol boat began to fire at the people running for safety on the beach, the young woman helped Magdalena drag Emerson out of the water. Gunfire was exploding all around them, and they dragged her to the truck and threw her into the front seat. Magdalena ran back to pick up the baby and the injured toddler who'd been left lying on the sand. With a child under each arm, she raced for the safety of the truck's cab.

The toddler who had made it to the truck on her own but could not climb into the back, was standing beside the truck's tailgate, screaming at the top of her lungs. She was terrified. The young woman lifted the screaming toddler into the back of the truck and ran to the passenger-side door. She tried to push Emerson's limp body out of the way and climbed into the cab. Magdalena thrust the toddler and the baby she was carrying into the young woman's arms. Magdalena yelled to the children in the back to be quiet and hoisted herself up into the driver's seat of the truck. There were three adults and two babies in the cab of the old truck. Emerson, the young woman, and the two little ones were completely wet through to the skin and soaked with oil and gasoline. Emerson's head lay unconscious in Magdalena's lap as she tried to start the truck.

Soldiers with machine guns were coming ashore off the patrol boat and running in the direction of the truck that held the women and children. Magdalena almost flooded the engine, but it finally caught. She stomped down on the gas as hard as she could, and the truck took off down the sandy beach road. The men from the boat had no vehicle to follow them, but they sprayed the departing truck with machine gun fire as it sped away. There was no time to check to see if any of the children were hurt either from their ordeal in the water or from the gun fire. The important thing right now was to escape from the beaches of the Algarve, to disappear as quickly as possible and as far away as possible.

Magdalena drove the truck with her foot pressed down all the way on the gas pedal. She occasionally took a back road rather than going through the center of a town. She was taking these detours in order to be safe, but each time she went off the main road, she delayed the trip. When she felt sure that no one was following her, she stopped briefly on a back road to see if any of the children had been hit by gun fire. There were holes in the truck's tailgate, but none of the children appeared to have been hurt. None of the tires had been hit, and the petrol tank was still intact. Magdalena crossed herself and sent a thank you skyward to the Blessed Mary.

As soon as she had checked on the children's welfare, she climbed back into the truck and continued on the road. She was terrified that the PVDE might be following and looking for her. The children had helped themselves to the food, drinks, and fruit in the back of the truck. They were frightened, but their clothes were drying out from their immersion in sea water. It took almost five hours to drive back to the hideout.

Emerson never regained consciousness during the long and frantic return trip to Setubal. Magdalena had grabbed an old blanket from behind the seat of the truck and tried to tuck it around Emerson's body. The three women and two toddlers were crammed into the front seat, and this close press of human bodies and the warmth they provided probably helped to diminish the shock that would have inevitably followed Emerson's ordeal in the water. She coughed and coughed and gagged up sea water and diesel fuel. If she stopped coughing or gasping for breath for even a few seconds, the young woman whose name was Annalise, checked to be sure that Emerson was still alive.

Their clothes and their skin reeked of oil and fuel and burning wood from the sinking steamer. The smell was so strong it almost made everyone who was crammed in the truck's cab sick to their stomachs. Magdalena shuddered when she thought about what could have happened if Emerson had gone too close to the flames. Drenched in fuel, she would have been burned alive if her clothes had caught fire. Annalise's English was excellent, and Magdalena was grateful for her company on the trip back to Setubal. She was more than thankful to have Annalise with her to help with Emerson and the truckload of children.

The sun was already up when Magdalena finally pulled into the overgrown road behind the hideout. The van was parked in the garage, and she gave a small prayer of thanks that Robert and his travelers had made it back safely. There was so much to do; it was difficult to decide what to do first. Her immediate concern right now was Emerson's condition. The children could wait. Robert needed to see to Emerson and determine if she was in still alive. Then he would have to figure out how to keep her alive and deal with the shock and the burns she had sustained. Magdalena could not understand why Emerson was still unconscious. Robert had heard the truck as it approached and came running out to meet them.

"I saw Emerson's note but could not imagine what had happened to you. Why are you so late? Where is Emerson? Did the children arrive? What has happened?" As the children began to climb out of the truck, Robert could see that they had all been soaked in sea water although most of it had dried by now. The smell of burned oil and gasoline permeated everything. Annalise began to strip the oil-soaked clothing off the toddlers and the infant. She carried them into the bathroom. She filled the tub with warm water so she could begin to scrub the oil off their small bodies. All three children were screaming.

Robert ran to the front of the truck where Emerson lay stretched out across the bench seat. "What happened, Magdalena? Tell me what has happened! What's wrong with Emerson?"

Magdalena had driven much too fast away from the beach and all the way back to Bacalhoa. She was concerned that the rough ride might have injured some of the children. She tried to tell Robert what had happened while she hurried to finish unloading the chilled and frightened little ones from the back of the truck. She quickly checked them over to determine if they were all right. There were a few scrapes and bruises, but none seemed seriously hurt. Magdalena herself was dead tired, and she wished she had more hands. Whatever injuries the children might have sustained would have to wait to be attended to until Robert was able to evaluate Emerson's condition.

Robert was already making a medical assessment. "She's obviously gone into shock. I don't think hypothermia is an issue because the water is so warm at this time of year and the air was not too cool last night. But Emerson's breathing is irregular and labored, and I am sure she inhaled sea water. My concern is that she may have also breathed in oil and diesel fuel. In fact, I am sure she did. She really needs to go to the hospital, but I'm afraid to take her there. I'm going to try to take care of her at Bacalhoa. Magdalena, I know you are also at the end of your own endurance from what you have been through tonight, but you must go for Sandro and his wife. Wake them up and drive them back here. Take the van and have them bring their daughter with them. I hate to involve them in this, but we need the help. Then you need to get all of the children cleaned up, at least cleaned up enough so that I can look at their wounds. I cannot tell what is wrong with them when they are covered with oil and are wearing those ragged clothes. Bathe them and put them in their pajamas. I am going to drive Emerson back to Bacalhoa and try to get her into the house."

"If you can wait until I bring Sandro and his family back here, I will go with you. You will need help with Emerson. Please stay with her here in the truck until I get back."

Few private citizens had telephones in their homes in Portugal in 1942, especially in smaller towns like Setubal. Emerson had a telephone because her husband Peter had insisted that it was necessary to stay in touch with the American Embassy in Lisbon. He had considered it essential to his job, and they had been able to afford to pay for the costly installation and the monthly fees. Robert had a telephone in his home because he was a physician, and people called on him day and night. People who did manual labor could not afford a telephone, even if they'd wanted one. Sandro and his family had no telephone. The only way to reach them was to go to their home in person. Magdalena drove the van as fast as she dared, to her cousin's house. She did not want to attract attention and get stopped and questioned about driving too fast. That was the last thing she needed right now.

The young woman Annalise was busy bathing the children and was happy to be able to speak to Robert in English. Robert introduced himself and told her that Magdalena had gone for help and that Annalise would have to watch the group of children by herself for a while. They handed out cups of water and candy bars. In the midst of all the confusion and with a new bunch of children bursting into the hideout, the group of sixteen children that Robert had delivered to the building a few hours earlier began to wake up and ask questions. They wanted to know what was happening. Robert gave out more candy bars and told his group from Porto that they needed to help with the new arrivals. He explained to them briefly in French what had happened and why the room smelled of fuel.

As soon as he could, he hurried back out to the truck to see about Emerson who still lay awkwardly across the truck's front seat. Robert tried to awaken her, but she continued to be unresponsive. Her breathing was dangerously irregular. He piled more blankets on top of her. It was a cause of great concern to him that she had not regained consciousness after several hours of rough traveling in the truck. He was worried about smoke inhalation, and he was certain she had water in her lungs that was contaminated with oil slick. He could not yet determine how serious her burns were, but he knew they were bad. They would be terrible painful, once Emerson was conscious.

Robert spoke to her quietly and wiped the oil from her face with a clean washcloth. Her hair was stiff with oil and filled with pieces of debris from the burning ship and from the water. He held her hand and talked to her and told her she was safe now. He told her she was back at the hideout and would soon be in her own bed at Bacalhoa. He was desperately afraid that he would lose her, and he realized her recovery was entirely up to him and to Magdalena since he couldn't take Emerson to the hospital. There would be too many questions asked there about why she was in her current condition.

Robert thought he saw her eye lids flutter just before Magdalena pulled up in the van. Sandro and his wife and daughter hurried toward them. Robert began shouting orders about what he wanted them to do when they went inside the hideout. He told them he would be back after he had taken Emerson to Bacalhoa.

Magdalena told Robert what she had said to Sandro and his family. "I explained it all to them as we were driving back here. They know what they have to do. They know we are about ten or more beds short. Fortunately, the second group is made up of very small children, and two or three of them easily can sleep in one bunk. They will work it out." Magdalena climbed into the truck and tried to ease Emerson's body into a sitting position. Robert climbed into the driver's seat, and Emerson's oil soaked head rested on Magdalena's shoulder as they made the morning journey back to Bacalhoa.

Magdalena could tell that Robert was frantic about Emerson's condition, just as Magdalena herself was terribly worried. Robert attempted to hide his concern about Emerson, and he switched into his mode of being worried about security. "Do you think the Spanish patrol boat people might be able to identify you? Was the license plate of the truck covered up with mud as I have always tried to make sure it was? I think we are going to have to get rid of the truck. It has bullet holes in the tailgate and in the side. I am concerned that the Portuguese police will have been alerted about this incident and will be on the lookout for it. As soon as we have taken Emerson into the house, I need to hide the truck until I can get rid of it or do something to change its appearance. Did anybody leave anything behind on the beach, anything that might be used to identify someone in the group?"

Magdalena knew that Robert was talking about everything else in the world except the one thing about which he was most worried — Emerson's survival. "Don't worry about the license plates. No one could have read them. They were caked with mud as they always are. The Spanish patrol boat soldiers were never close enough to any of us to see our faces. They do know there were lots of children involved in this incident. I have no idea what they will be able to conclude from that observation. You've seen for yourself that the truck sustained a lot of damage from machine gun fire. It was just luck that none of the children were hurt. Emerson took off her jacket and her shoes before she went into the water the first time, but I picked them up and threw them into the truck. We left nothing behind on the beach."

"Good work. Now, tell me again exactly what happened. I want to know how long Emerson was in the water and how much time she spent close to the burning ship."

Magdalena recounted the story to Robert in detail. She told him how many times Emerson had gone back into the ocean to save more children. Magdalena told him how extraordinarily brave Emerson had been. She could see the tears in his eyes as she recounted Emerson's efforts to save the lives of others.

"We must save her now. Please promise me you will stay with her and let Sandro's wife and Annalise take care of the children at the hideout. Emerson is going to need a lot of care. Because I cannot take her to the hospital where she really needs to be, you must be with her at all times until she is out of danger. I will bring a lung specialist from the British Hospital in Lisbon to see her tomorrow. This is a big risk to take, but he is from England and knows about some of our secret work. He's a personal friend and will be happy to do this for me."

Chapter 26

FULL HOUSE

June 1942

Robert and Magdalena carried Emerson in through Bacalhoa's front door. It was light outside, but none of the staff was up and around yet, so they were able to take their patient into her bathroom without anyone seeing them. Emerson's long pants were stuck to her legs. When Robert examined her more closely, he realized that the fabric of Emerson's pants had burned into her skin. His face paled, and he clenched his jaw. He sighed with deep concern, and this worried Magdalena. She knew he cared for Emerson, but Dr. Carmichael did not usually show how worried he was, even in the most frightening circumstances.

Robert helped Magdalena get Emerson into the bath tub. "You will have to cut her clothes off her body. Her legs have been very badly burned. You will have to soak the pants' legs to get them loose from her skin. Removing the fabric will take the skin off with it. That can't be helped. At least she is still unconscious and can't feel how painful it will be. Can you handle getting her cleaned up? You must get the fuel oil out of her hair, and that will not be easy. I would suggest that you cut off her hair or shave her head to get rid of the oil, but she would never forgive us for that. And you must clean all the oil off of her skin. If you have to scrub her skin, you should do that. Scrub the skin where it isn't burned if you can. You have to get the toxic substances out of her hair and off her skin as soon as possible. The longer she breathes in the fumes of the fuel oil, the longer it will take for her to expel these poisons from her lungs. It is essential that she begin to breathe clean air. Hopefully, her lungs will clear, but she is going to be at risk for long-term lung damage. Thank goodness she was never a smoker."

Magdalena had difficulty keeping Emerson upright in the tub so she could work on removing her clothes. She propped Emerson up in the tub with towels around her to hold her steady while she cut away the clothes she could easily remove. Little by little, after letting Emerson soak in the warm bath water, Magdalena was able to loosen the fabric that was stuck to her legs. It took many minutes of careful work, but finally Magdalena had either cut away or peeled off all of Emerson's clothing. Emerson's lower extremities were in especially bad shape. Sheets of skin hung down from her legs. There was a large, jagged piece of metal embedded in her thigh.

Magdalena didn't want to touch the metal without Robert's advice. She worked around the foreign body which protruded from Emerson's leg. Emerson must have been in shock when she'd sustained the burns and the injuries from the shrapnel. Both would have been excruciatingly painful. Magdalena scrubbed Emerson's skin where she could and brushed and combed the debris out of Emerson's hair which she washed and rewashed several times. Magdalena worked to cleanse the foreign substances from Emerson's body until all the hot water was gone and Emerson's hair looked reasonably normal.

There was still a smell of fuel oil everywhere, but Magdalena had done all she could for now. Emerson was dead weight, but Magdalena was strong and made a body sling to lift Emerson out of the tub and carry her into the bedroom. She dressed Emerson in a clean nightgown and lay her head down gently on a towel that covered the pillow. Finally she had Emerson lying on her bed with a light sheet over her body. Emerson had some minor cuts and bruises on her upper body, and Magdalena treated and bandaged these. Extremely concerned about the condition of Emerson's legs, Magdalena knew her recovery would be a lengthy and painful one. Her wounds would require constant care. She wanted Emerson to regain consciousness, but she knew Emerson would experience terrible pain once she was awake.

Lily had been waiting outside the bathroom door while Magdalena worked to remove Emerson's clothing and clean off the coatings of oil and diesel fuel that had soaked into her hair and skin. Magdalena had left Lily outside the bathroom because she did not want to have to clean grease and dirt from the hair of the little white dog who would want to investigate the clothing remnants that lay in a pile on the bathroom floor. Magdalena bundled Emerson's burned and damaged clothes. They would all go into the dust bin.

Animals know when people are hurting, and Magdalena was a great believer in the ability of animals to promote health and healing. There was no doubt that Lily's arrival at Bacalhoa had helped to heal Emerson's mind years ago. Maybe now Lily's presence would be of help in healing Emerson's physical wounds. Magdalena lifted Lily onto the bed, and Lily licked Emerson's face. She sniffed her tortured legs and snuggled into the spot she usually occupied when Emerson was sleeping.

Magdalena knew that the human body could only endure so much and that people sometimes withdraw from consciousness when faced with extreme physical or mental pain as a way to cope with it and survive it. Magdalena had witnessed the lengths to which Emerson had pushed herself to rescue the children. She feared the short-term and long-term consequences of this ordeal of endurance that Emerson had put herself through, both the physical and the mental strain.

Magdalena realized that infection was going to be a real danger in treating Emerson's burns and perhaps in treating her respiratory distress. Emerson's breathing continued to be labored, and Magdalena made her as comfortable as she could. As soon as Magdalena allowed herself to sit down in the chair beside Emerson's bed and closed her own eyes, she, too, sought the restoration that only sleep can bring.

Robert drove the truck back to the hideout. He would have to leave the truck in the secret garage until it could be repaired. He drove carefully and inconspicuously along the Lisbon Road as it was now fully daylight. He did not want to be noticed driving a vehicle that the police might be on the alert for and looking hard to find. When he inspected the truck, he realized that there were many bullet holes in the tailgate, the side, and the rear wheel covers. They had been lucky that neither the gas tank nor the tires had been hit. Tires were impossibly difficult to find in this wartime economy. All rubber was conscripted into making tires for military vehicles. Civilians patched their tires and patched them again if they wanted to stay on the road. When he saw the extensive damage to the truck, Robert was even more grateful that bullets had not hurt any of the children or the women.

He checked to see if things were going smoothly at the hideout. The children were sleeping, and Sandro's wife had driven the van to her home. She would prepare their breakfast and bring the food back to the hideout. The children would be awake and hungry soon. The group from the Algarve had endured a horrifying experience the night before. All the children needed to rest as much as they could. Dr. Robert would be back later in the morning to examine them and take care of their wounds.

Robert left the truck at the hideout and drove his own car home. His clothes were covered with oil and dirt from carrying Emerson into the house. He bathed and changed and gathered bandages and creams and other medications from his clinic to treat Emerson's burns. He wanted to hook up an intravenous infusion for Emerson in her bedroom so she would not become dehydrated. The vacuum-sealed glass jars of saline solution were scarce and hard to come by. Robert Carmichael had been able to obtain a few from colleagues at the British Hospital in Lisbon. Emerson would need antibiotics, and these were also in short supply because of the war. Some of these drugs were very new and almost impossible to find. Robert would probably have to make do with whatever sulfa drugs he was able to get, but he wished desperately that he could put his hands on some of the miracle drug penicillin.

Robert decided he would have to open his clinic for appointments later this morning. He was dead tired but had to keep up appearances. He'd been out of his office all day the day before because he was driving to Porto to pick up the children. He couldn't cancel again today, or somebody might begin to get suspicious. All he really wanted to do was collapse on his bed, but he knew he had to take care of Emerson first as well as check out the children at the hideout before he could begin his regular office hours. It was going to be an excruciatingly long day.

Robert filled his bag with the supplies he needed and returned to Bacalhoa. Magdalena had dark circles around her eyes when she answered the door for the doctor, but she had cleaned herself up and was dressed in her usual crisp and spotless white blouse and black skirt.

"How is she? Has she regained consciousness?" Robert was anxious to hear Magdalena's opinion of Emerson's condition.

"She's just the same. I've bathed her and washed her hair several times. It was almost impossible to remove her trousers because the fabric had burned into her skin. I soaked the cloth until I could peel it away. She also has a piece of metal imbedded in her thigh. It's rather large, and there are some smaller pieces of metal in her leg as well, pieces I can't see very well. I didn't touch any of that as I didn't want to do anything wrong. I didn't see all the metal in her legs until I'd removed her long pants. The burns are quite serious. I didn't realize she'd been so close to the explosion and the burning pieces of timber. I had no idea she was so badly burned. She must have been in some kind of a trance state when she went into the water that last time and swam to the burning ship. She wasn't thinking about what she was doing, and I don't think she realized what was happening to her body. All she could think about was saving whoever was still in danger.

"When she came up on the beach after rescuing the four children in the life jackets, even before she went back into the water to swim to the steamer, she was already completely drained physically. I could see then that she was absolutely depleted. She couldn't even really swim anymore, and she collapsed and let the tide carry her and the children onto the beach. But when she realized there were more people trapped on the ship, she found some strength from somewhere deep inside herself and went back into the water. Her response was almost robotic, almost inhuman. She was definitely going on automatic. It was remarkable. I've never seen anything quite like it. The children were screaming at her, and she was asking them in French how many people there were still on the steamer."

Robert felt sick to his stomach when he heard about the way Emerson had punished herself to save others. He thought he understood what drove her, but his heart ached for this lovely woman who tried too hard. "It goes without saying that I will do everything I can to save her. Magdalena, as I asked you last night, you must spend all of your time caring for her. I will find others to do your work with the orphans and take care of their needs at the hideout. Lindeck can gather the laundry and make up the beds. I will find someone to take care of all your duties here at Bacalhoa. If more flyboys arrive in Setubal, I will find someone else to help me with that. I am so afraid the police will find out that Emerson is running this escape line and come after her. She must maintain a low profile. I don't want any of the staff to talk to anybody about her condition or even mention to anyone outside the quinta that she is hurt or incapacitated in any way. Can you impress on them how essential complete discretion is for her safety? There must not be even a whisper that anything at all out of the ordinary has occurred."

Magdalena could tell that even Robert was shocked when he saw Emerson's wounds. As a physician, Robert had seen everything, and still he gasped when Magdalena drew back the sheet. Emerson had been wearing long pants when they had lifted her into the bath tub. Now the extent of her burns was uncovered for him to see. He busied himself removing the shrapnel. There were several small fragments as well as the one large, obvious piece. Several stitches were necessary to close the gashes the pieces of metal had cut in her legs.

Robert hooked up the IV with bottles of saline solution, and it began to flow into Emerson's arm. He explained to Magdalena what she needed to do to change the bottles of fluids to keep the IV going. He stressed how critical it was that Emerson be kept hydrated. He gave exacting directions about how to debride and care for Emerson's burn wounds. He gave directions about the medications Magdalena was to give to Emerson. He was completely professional now that he was talking about the practice of medicine.

Finally, Robert pulled a chair over and sat down beside the bed. He took Emerson's hand in his. He brought her hand to his lips and held it there. He lowered his head against his chest as if he might be praying. Magdalena almost could not stay in the room as she witnessed the doctor's intensely intimate and emotional expression of caring. It was clear that Robert loved Emerson with his whole heart, and he was terrified of losing her. Magdalena felt compelled to say something but did not know what to say. "I know you care a great deal for Miss Emerson. I promise I will devote myself to her and do all in my power to help her recover. I will do everything for her, just as I did when she was so depressed after the baby died, when she could not function."

"I know you will take care of her, Magdalena. You have done it before, and if it had not been for your care, she would not be alive today. I know that, and I am eternally grateful to you. More than anything, I wish I could take her to the hospital. That is where she needs to be, but I'm as afraid for her safety as I am for her health. A specialist will come to Bacalhoa later this afternoon to examine her lungs. I wish she could be conscious to answer his questions and interact with him. I know how to treat her burns and her other wounds. But I'm not a pulmonary specialist, and I don't really know how to treat her for the damage she has done to her lungs." He lowered his head again, and tears came to his eyes. Magdalena touched his shoulder, in an attempt to be reassuring.

"I don't think that even I know how much I care for Emerson. The thought of losing her is unbearable to me," Dr. Robert continued to think out loud. "She has been the driving force behind the orphan project, and I know how important it is to her. But it is as if she does not care about herself or about her own well-being. I can't help but wonder if she has some kind of a death wish. From your description of her actions in the water rescues, it seems as if she had no regard whatever for her own safety."

"That is the way with true heroes, Dr. Robert. They do not stop to think about the impact their actions will have on themselves. They see what needs to be done, and they do it — even against superhuman odds that they will survive and against all hopes for success. There is no doubt that Emerson is a true hero. Whether you like it or not, that's who Emerson is."

"I do know it, and her courage is one of the reasons I love her. She is fearless," his voice broke as he made this admission. He did not want Magdalena to see him in such an emotional state. He stood and left the room and left the quinta.

By the time he reached the hideout, he had brought his emotions under control. He had another job to do, and in spite of his exhaustion and his personal distress about Emerson, he knew she would want him to make the children a priority. He'd always worried because Emerson had never once been able to bring up the subject and talk about the loss of her own baby. Robert had seen how attached to Pierre she'd become and how hard it had been for her to let him go. He knew how much she loved children, and he hoped she was not disregarding her own health and safety by attempting, in some convoluted way, to save other people's children. Was she subconsciously trying to save her own baby who had died before she was ever born?

Chapter 27

SAVING EMERSON

JUNE 1942

The lung specialist arrived that afternoon and examined Emerson. She was still unresponsive when the physician from Lisbon listened to her chest with his stethoscope and palpated her back. Robert arrived as his friend and colleague was completing the examination. Robert had spent time at the hideout earlier that day, checking the health of the new arrivals, and he had just finished his regular office hours. He had not yet had a chance to rest, but his concern about Emerson drove him to ignore his exhaustion.

Sir Arthur Ballingford asked Robert and Magdalena some questions. Had she coughed up sea water when they first rescued her? Magdalena had been busy trying to get everyone into the truck and away from the Spaniards' machine guns. A great deal had been happening all at once. But yes, Magdalena told the specialist, Emerson had coughed and coughed and coughed. She had gagged and coughed up water and foul smelling substances almost all the way back to Setubal from the Algarve. The extent of Emerson's coughing had been terribly alarming, but because she had continued to cough, Magdalena said that was one way they knew she was still alive. Sir Arthur said this was a very good thing, that she'd coughed so much. With all that coughing, she had been able to expel a great deal of the toxic oil, diesel fuel, and sea water she'd inhaled. He felt Emerson eventually would recover from her respiratory problems. She needed to be encouraged to breathe deeply when she became fully conscious and was able to follow directions.

Furthermore, Sir Arthur did not think that Emerson was in a coma. She had suffered significant injuries, but Ballingford did not believe the injuries she had sustained supported a diagnosis of coma. The specialist felt the extreme physical demands she had made on herself during the rescue of the children from the water and the burning ship had stressed her to the point of complete physical collapse. It was his professional opinion that she was not really in a comatose state but so overwhelmed with exhaustion that she was not able to rouse herself to speak. He said she had withdrawn from consciousness in order to allow herself to recover. Her body was focusing on resting and healing. She did not have the strength right now for higher cognitive thinking and conversation. He said that Robert was correct when he'd noticed that Emerson's eyes fluttered open once in a while. Sir Arthur had noticed the same thing. He thought that soon Emerson would wake up and be responsive for brief periods and then go back to sleep for many hours. Gradually, she would stay awake for longer and longer periods of time. She would retreat into sleep less often as her body returned to normal. Sir Ballingford agreed that the IV was a good idea, at least until she was able to drink fluids and eat on her own.

Robert was almost afraid to hope but agreed in theory that Emerson would regain consciousness when her physical condition had stabilized. He also thought that sleeping was a reaction to the physical extremes to which she had subjected her body. Fighting the current and swimming in the water, she had pushed her physical self far beyond its limits. She had breathed the fumes as well as the oil slicked water into her lungs, and she had suffered serious burns from the explosion. All of these things had caused her body to shut down. The pain from the burns would also keep her from wanting to be awake. Sleep was a way of coping with the intense pain.

Ballingford did not think that Emerson would suffer permanent organ damage. From listening to her lungs and hearing what had happened to her, he believed she was suffering primarily from smoke inhalation. Hopefully, her lungs would completely rid themselves of their toxic contents. She would begin to breathe normally again. He reminded them that the human body had a great ability to heal itself. The burns would need constant care and would take much longer to heal. He deferred to Robert's expertise about the burns and how to treat them. Emerson was young and strong and generally healthy. At least she had been before her ordeal on the beach. Ballingford advised Robert and Magdalena on how to care for her breathing problems and told them to have patience. Robert said he would be calling an infection specialist within the next few days.

Robert, Magdalena, and Sir Arthur shared an excellent tea prepared by Benadina. Robert was dead tired, but he wanted the chance to visit with Arthur, his good friend and medical colleague. They discussed Emerson, but Robert had warned Sir Arthur ahead of time not to ask too many questions about how Emerson had sustained her injuries. Arthur knew she had repeatedly gone into the Atlantic Ocean to rescue drowning children, but he had no idea how or why Emerson had put herself into a position that would have required her to do such a thing. Ballingford was respectful of the confidentiality that surrounded Emerson's injuries, and he asked only what he absolutely had to know to adequately treat her medical condition. He really did not want to know too much more than that.

In 1942, hardly anybody wanted to know any more than they absolutely had to know about anything. It was a time in Portugal especially when superficial explanations were usually preferred to the whole truth. Arthur sent his compliments to Benadina and insisted that she come to the drawing room so that he could meet her. She was delighted to be appreciated and flattered at the compliments he heaped on her ability to produce an English tea. He said he had never had a better tea anywhere — including in England. Benadina smiled and blushed and humbly accepted the sincere praise.

Robert's driver had brought Sir Arthur Ballingford from Lisbon to Bacalhoa and would now drive him back to the nation's capital. Robert was grateful that his friend had been willing to make the trip all the way to Setubal for a house call. It was not difficult for Sir Arthur to realize that Emerson was not just Robert's neighbor and friend but that Robert was very much in love with her. It was obvious that she was the person of utmost importance in his life. He urged Robert to call on him again if Emerson needed another consultation.

Magdalena and Robert accompanied Sir Arthur to the door of Bacalhoa to tell him goodbye. Robert was terribly grateful as he smiled and vigorously shook his friend's hand, "I am forever in your debt, Sir Arthur."

"Think nothing of it, Sir Robert. I am always delighted to help out a fellow Brit and a fellow physician. Get some rest, old man. You look dreadful. She's going to be all right."

He smiled and nodded to reassure his friend and put his arm around Robert's shoulders before he left. Then he was gone.

Magdalena always listened carefully and never missed even the most subtle use of words or looks or signals between people. "Sir Robert?" She allowed the question to hang in the air.

"It's not important. I decided when I moved to Portugal that I would not use my title. Here, I am a British doctor; I am Dr. Robert Carmichael. That is my sole identity now, and it is all anyone needs to know about me. And, no, Emerson doesn't know. Why in the world would it ever come up as a topic of discussion? And I am trusting you to keep my secret. It isn't really a secret. It just is not of any consequence at this time and in this place. It would make my life much more complicated, and my life is complicated enough. This would draw more attention to me, at a time when I am trying very hard not to attract attention to myself." Magdalena let him know she understood and would keep his confidences.

The previous day, when Robert had left to drive to Porto to pick up one group of children, Emerson had sent word to Max that there would be another group of sixteen ready for transport. It seemed to Robert that his drive to Porto had been a long time ago, not just a little more than twenty-four hours earlier. It was up to Robert to contact Max and tell him they now had twenty-eight children, one infant, and one adult ready to leave Portugal for the USA. Robert wondered if Max would be able to accommodate such a large group.

Sandro's wife and daughter were doing a good job feeding the children and keeping them occupied at the hideout. It was packed full, but somehow they were managing. Earlier that day, the young woman, Annalise had been able to speak with Robert and tell him a little about herself. She looked as if she were no more than fourteen years old, but in fact she was twenty.

Annalise was a Danish Jew and had worked with the Danish resistance against the Nazis. Her role as a member of the underground organization had been discovered, and she had gone into hiding. Her family had all died while being tortured in Gestapo custody. The Gestapo had put a price on Annalise's head. She had to leave Denmark. She'd been lucky enough to escape Nazi-occupied Denmark with several Jewish children who were being smuggled into France. From there she'd traveled through a complex secret network that promised to deliver her to Portugal. When she reached their Abbey the Catholic sisters in Beaune had asked her to take three young children with her. Two of these babies were not yet three years old and were too small to take care of themselves. The sisters also had a seven-month-old infant on their hands. Annalise had agreed to take the little ones with her and promised to care for them during the difficult journey.

The group had boarded the small Swedish steamer in Marseilles and had originally been scheduled to travel to a different destination. The voyage had been rough but unremarkable until the steamer was about to leave the waters off the coast of Spain. The Captain of the Swedish ship had confided to Annalise that he was afraid the Spanish were suspicious of his ship. He'd told her a Spanish patrol boat had been following them all along the coast of Spain. They were going to have to change their plans. At this point the captain sounded the alarm and sent his emergency broadcast. The message, that a group of children was arriving on the beach in the Algarve, had gone out to Emerson.

The captain had launched the raft with most of the children in it as soon as he thought they were in Portugal. Neither the captain nor Annalise thought the Spanish would follow them into Portuguese territorial waters, so they felt the children had a chance to reach the shore. Annalise made sure that each child who went into the raft put on a life vest, although all of the life vests were for adults, not for small children. They had not drowned because each of them had been wearing a life vest, even if it had been a vest that didn't fit.

The Spanish patrol boat had ignored the reality that it was no longer in Spain, and had pulled alongside the steamer while the children were being loaded into the raft. The waves had carried the raft with the children in it away from the Swedish steamer before Annalise, carrying the two toddlers and the infant, could climb aboard. Because of the turbulence of the rough waves and the inadequate heft of the rubber dinghy, Annalise had seen several of the children fall over the side of the raft and into the sea.

When the Spaniards came aboard the steamer to arrest the Captain, they were no longer within Spanish jurisdiction. What they were doing by boarding the Swedish ship and arresting the captain in Portuguese waters was illegal according to international maritime law. This did not seem to matter to the officials on the Spanish patrol boat. Annalise hid herself and her three small charges. After the Spaniards had taken the captain to their patrol boat, Annalise came back out on deck when she thought it was safe. She stayed on the deck with the babies even when the Spanish patrol again began to fire at the ship.

When the patrol boat continued to fire heavy mortar shells at the steamer, Annalise realized the Spanish wanted to destroy the ship and were not interested in capturing it. They did not seem to care if there were people still on board. They wanted to destroy the Swedish ship and whoever remained on to make sure there was no vessel to be seen and no person left behind to give evidence and testify to the Spaniards' illegal and immoral act. Because she had stayed on the deck, Annalise and the children she was caring for were saved when the steamer exploded. She had been about to jump off the deck into the oil-slicked water when she saw Emerson swimming towards her with a life ring.

Robert was glad to have this account of what had happened. It helped him to understand why Emerson had gone back into the water after the ship exploded. He now knew exactly what Emerson had done to save Annalise, the two toddlers, and the infant. Annalise had a few minor burns on her skin, but she had escaped most of the burning timbers. Fortunately, she had not been under the water long enough to breathe in much of the oil-slicked sludge.

Robert told Annalise they needed her help. He explained to her what they were attempting at Bacalhoa, about their efforts to transport orphans out of Europe. Annalise was willing to do everything she could do to help. Robert promised Annalise the children would all be safe and that she too would be able to go to the United States. Annalise was grateful for the chance that she and the children were being offered, the chance to escape Europe and to live in freedom.

It was obvious to Annalise that her help was needed at the hideout. Emerson was not able to do the things she usually did to keep the project running smoothly, and she would not be any help for quite a long time. Robert and Magdalena desperately needed Annalise's help — because of Emerson's absence and because there were now extra children who needed care. Robert had several specific assignments for Annalise. The first thing he asked her to do, after helping with the children's basic needs, was to write down a brief biographical sketch of each of the children she had traveled with on the steamer from Marseilles. Emerson usually attended to this task. Part of this important work would now be up to Annalise.

Robert examined each child and explained to Annalise the simple medical treatments that several of the children required.

He identified and splinted a small child's broken arm that had gone unnoticed in all the chaos of the previous night. Annalise had done an excellent job of protecting the children she'd held on to from the explosion by covering them with her body, but the one of the toddlers had lost most of her hair in the fire. All three of these youngest victims had superficial burns on their delicate baby skin.

Robert knew that Sandro's wife Lindeck was a keen observer and would have an opinion about every one of the children within a day or two. He told her he especially wanted her to get to know the sixteen he had brought from Porto. Robert explained to her that he would sit down with her in a few days and have her speak with him into a tape recorder about her impressions of each child. Robert would listen to the tapes and transcribe the information from Portuguese into English. He would type up the information to send to Naomi and Rachel — just as Emerson had done with previous groups of children. Lindeck was pleased and even excited to be asked to help. Everyone was going to have to step up and pitch in to make up for all the things Emerson had previously done. It would take a team of several people to fill the many roles she had undertaken before she was hurt.

The hideout was packed, but it seemed the women had things under control. The children were being fed. They had managed to find places for everyone to sleep, and they were taking turns helping the children bathe in the luxurious hot water. There was going to be a lot of laundry. Robert asked Sandro's wife and daughter to take over this job completely, without Magdelena's help because he wanted Magdalena to spend all of her time caring for Emerson. By the end of this unusually long day, he was completely worn out and hoped and prayed that no one from the Allied flyers' pipeline would call him with a problem. He needed to get a full night's sleep.

Chapter 28

THE WOLFRAM PRIZE

1942

Trains carrying Wolfram were always on their way from the mines of Portugal, traveling through Spain and France and on to Germany. It was a long and difficult route, but it was a journey of the utmost strategic importance to the Nazi regime. The scarcity of Wolfram, an element that was essential to manufacture extra strong and highly heat-resistant steel, was a bottleneck in Germany's overall armaments production. Moving Wolfram as quickly as possible and in huge quantities from Portugal to Germany had become a cornerstone of the wartime relationship between the two countries.

Wolfram ore, also known as tungsten, had become Portugal's greatest asset as well as its biggest headache. Because of Wolfram's special properties, this element was a vital ingredient in the steel manufacturing process. It was critical in the tool and die industry, to manufacture precision tools and to make the metal that went into producing the machines that made other machines. Wolfram was necessary to make the steel that made weapons, ammunition, tanks, and all the implements of war. The harder and more heat resistant the steel, the more powerful the weapons. The more powerful the weapons, the more efficient the killing.

Germany had no Wolfram resources of its own. It had to buy all of its supplies of this vital ore from other countries. Portugal had been blessed with significant quantities of Wolfram ore. Spain also had deposits of Wolfram. Germany sought to buy as much of it as possible from Portugal and Spain. Portugal drove a hard bargain with the Germans and demanded that they pay for their purchases of Wolfram ore with gold or Swiss francs.

The Allies had their own sources of Wolfram and consequently were not dependent on other countries to provide this essential ingredient to make their machines and munitions. They did not have to buy any of this important material to fill their own needs. But one of the obvious strategies of war is to try, wherever and whenever possible, to keep essential war-making materials out of the hands of one's enemies. Every ton of Wolfram ore that the Allies were able to beg, borrow, steal, or buy from the world's total supply of Wolfram was a ton of Wolfram ore that the Germans could not commandeer for their own use.

The game of war was a competition for natural resources. It was essential to meet one's own needs for war materials, but at the same time, it was critical to keep one's enemies from meeting their own needs for essential war materials. Oil, rubber, food, copper, uranium, and many other resources became strategic pawns in the battle for supremacy. Whichever side had control over these resources would prevail and claim ultimate victory.

Portugal had a long-standing treaty of cooperation with Britain, dating from the twelfth century, and Portugal had chosen to continue to honor that treaty. Caught between the threats from Germany and Portugal's historical allegiance with Britain, Antonio de Oliveira Salazar, the President of Portugal was forced to tread a careful path as he sought to defend his country's neutrality in the face of political pressures from both sides.

Germany desperately needed Wolfram and threatened Portugal with possible invasion if Portugal did not sell them the Wolfram ore they required. On the other hand, Britain wanted to buy up as much Wolfram as it possibly could from the Portuguese ... to keep it out of the hands of the Germans. The Wolfram market went crazy, and prices soared with the increased demand. Portuguese farmers began digging Wolfram ore from their fields and selling it to anyone who would buy it.

Since Operation Barbarossa had begun in June of 1941, Germany's armaments production had been pushed to its limits. Germany could conscript the labor it needed, and it could build more factories. But to produce more tanks, more guns, and more bullets, the Germans had to have more raw materials of all kinds. Shortages of strategic materials always constrained production in countries trying to produce the things that were necessary to conduct a war. The Axis powers and the Allied powers both suffered from shortages. Rationing was in place in almost all countries of the world during the years of World War II.

One critical shortage for the Nazis was the short-fall of Wolfram ore. Curtailed steel production, because of Wolfram scarcities, was devastating to the German war machine. Trying to buy as much Wolfram as possible, the Nazi ministry in charge of procuring resources was fighting a constant battle. This struggle, to gain control over thousands of tons of Wolfram ore, was every bit as fierce as the battle their military counterparts in the trenches on the Eastern front were fighting.

Procuring the ore was just the first step in the process. Once the Wolfram was bought and paid for, it had to be transported hundreds of miles across Europe to German refineries where it was purified. Only then could it be added to the steel which was made into tanks and bullets and heavy weapons. It was an arduous and complex logistical transportation and production process. The Wolfram traveled from the mines and fields where the ore was found on the Iberian Peninsula. In Germany it was transformed into the arsenals of war.

The Germans chose to transport the Wolfram ore they had purchased from Portugal to Germany primarily by rail and by trucks. Railroad cars and trucks loaded with the valuable ore and headed for Germany were always at risk of being hijacked or destroyed. The ore could and did disappear at any and all stages of this long journey — from the time it left Portugal until it reached Germany.

Trains loaded with Wolfram ore, that had to travel the rails through several European countries, were heavily guarded because the cargo was precious. These trains moved without stopping. All other trains pulled over to rail sidings to allow the ones that carried Wolfram to proceed without slowing down. The priority of these trains, as well as the substantial security presence which rode along to guard the cargo, called attention to themselves. These high-profile, fast-moving transports became targets for resistance groups, especially in France. Railroad tracks were blown up and torn apart by hand. Explosives were placed on the rails to destroy the engines of these trains. Cargos of Wolfram were vulnerable at all stages of the journey, and it was rumored that whole trains made up of multiple cars filled with the ore were hijacked.

Stealing an entire train is not an easy thing to do. Such a scheme requires a great deal of planning and manpower. Basque resistance groups were fiercely brave fighters and resourceful thinkers. They understood how important Wolfram ore was to the German war machine, and they knew that every ton of Wolfram they could keep from reaching German soil meant delays in Nazi armaments production.

Basque territory existed, at this time in history, partly in the nation state of Spain and partly in the nation state of France. But the Basque people did not regard either the Spanish or the French as their friends. Isolated from the rest of Europe by choice, the Basque people had always seemed mysterious to the Spanish and to the French, and the Basques wanted things to remain that way. They were a nation unto themselves, culturally and historically, if not politically in terms of contemporary geographic boundaries.

If an entire train could be stolen and hidden, it would be the Basque people who had the skills to pull off such a coup. They had blown up many trains passing through their territory, with varying degrees of success and damage. They had a track record of causing significant delays in shipments of Wolfram headed for Germany. They stole an entire trainload of Wolfram and kept it hostage until they had time to unload and dispose of its cargo. They eventually allowed the Germans to have their train back, but without the Wolfram ore. Their many ingenious plots, which challenged the imaginations of the Basque troublemakers, resulted in significant damage to Germany's conduct of the war. It was only a matter of time until they were inspired to figure out a way to hijack an entire train full of Wolfram ore and to make the ore and the train disappear forever.

The Basques knew what the rest of the world knew — that Germany was struggling with Operation Barbarossa. The invasion of the Soviet Union had not gone the way Hitler and his generals had planned. The campaign had not begun as early as it should have in the spring of 1941. Once the offensive was finally underway, it had not progressed as easily or as rapidly as the Germans had anticipated.

Russia was an enormous country, and the Russian Army was a tough adversary. Generals who had met with successes conquering Germany's close neighbors, Belgium, Holland, Poland, and even France, did not have the experience to conduct a war on the scale required to be successful in the vast Soviet Union. Conquering countries that are small and close together had not prepared German generals for the strategic thinking required to fight a war on the geographic scale which Russia presented. The gigantic land mass that comprised the Soviet Union presented a challenge these small-country generals were not equipped to master. The supply lines through the Soviet Union were insufficient to keep German armies going. The front lines of battle were too far away from friendly territory to be supported. The Germans were overextended, and this would be their downfall.

The Germans were mired in the frozen mud and snow drifts, compliments of the winter of the Russian Bear. The lines designed to provision German troops at the front were long and slow. The Germans were never going to be able to adequately equip their soldiers fighting in the Soviet Union. The farther away from the homeland the German military front lines moved into Russia, the more critical railroad rolling stock was to resupply the troops. Armies have to be supplied with guns, tanks, and bullets, but just as importantly, they must be supplied with oil, food and clothing, medications, and many other essentials that are absolutely necessary to conduct a war on foreign soil. Railroad cars were the lifeline of Germany's Army in Russia.

One glaring example of der Fuhrer's weakness as a leader was the confusion caused by his pursuit of multiple and often conflicting priorities. The German military was forced to compete for rolling stock with the demands from Hitler's other enterprises. Enormous resources were required to carry out the objectives of the Final Solution. The men, the material, and the railroad cars that served the death camps, all sucked resources away from Germany's military campaigns.

The Basque people heard the rumors, and they could only speculate, along with others in Europe, about the huge extermination camps that were being built. Was it true that hundreds of thousands of Jews were being relocated to these terrible places, from Germany and from the countries the Nazis had conquered? Hardly anyone, even those who were directly involved, could possibly realize how massive the scope of these relocations really was. Who would have dared to imagine the extent of the horror that occurred at the end of these long journeys?

What the Basques did know was that, as the war continued, the railroad cars and engines being sent to Spain and Portugal to retrieve the vital Wolfram ore were of poorer and poorer quality. The engines were older and not well-maintained. The railroad cars were increasingly decrepit and run down. There were fewer freight cars in each train that showed up to load the precious Wolfram ore. The men who operated these trains had to cope with constant equipment breakdowns. An engine part would be unavailable, and the train would be forced to sit on a railroad siding for days, waiting for another engine or for the broken one to be repaired. A railroad car would jump the tracks because a wheel had fallen off due to a rusted axle. These kinds of interruptions sometimes required unloading and reloading the ore from the car or unloading the ore from one railroad car to another. Railroad workers could either remove the car with the broken axle from the rest of the train or repair it so the train could move forward. As the war progressed, the quality of the rolling stock that was sent to procure the Wolfram ore continued its decline. This made the trains more vulnerable to all kinds of sabotage and theft.

The trains loaded with Wolfram, which had proceeded on the fast tracks to Germany early in the war, had been heavily guarded. As the war dragged on and Operation Barbarossa began to pull all kinds of resources from the Nazi military complex, fewer and fewer soldiers could be spared from the German fighting forces to ride on and guard the trains. The well-trained soldiers were needed at the front. Then the not-so-well-trained soldiers were also needed at the front.

As critical as Wolfram ore was to the German armaments industry, bringing raw materials to Germany, by default, lost its priority. It would be years before the final bell was sounded, but the German war machine was exhibiting serious cracks. The Wolfram trains were increasingly vulnerable to those who wanted to literally "derail" the cargos of Wolfram and prevent them from reaching Germany.

The Basque resistance movement had manpower, and they had mountains. Their mountains had caves where lots of things could be hidden. Basque leaders came up with a brilliant and brazen plan to try to steal an entire train full of Wolfram and hide it forever. The operation would not only deprive the Nazis of their precious Wolfram, it also would purloin valuable railroad cars that could never again be used to move anything.

In order to accomplish this audacious operation, the ingenious and bold Basque partisans decided to build their own small, well-hidden railway line inside their mountains' tunnel-like caves. They would construct enough railroad track inside the mountain so they could hide from the world the cars of an entire train. They also proposed to build a "connector," railroad tracks laid down to join the main railway line with the secret Basque rail line that lay entirely within its mountain hideaway.

These resistance fighters had plenty of lumber and could make all the railroad ties they needed. The metal track was more difficult to obtain, especially in a world at war. All countries were obsessed with salvaging and repurposing every available scrap of metal. The Basques smuggled old track into their territory from wherever they could find it. They paid high prices for the track and made deals to obtain it with countries as far away as the United States. The Basques stole some of what they needed from existing railway beds. Stealing track from railway lines accomplished two things. If the missing lengths of track were not discovered in time, fast-moving trains would be derailed and crash. The Germans and the Spaniards had to scramble to locate and fabricate new railroad tracks. The stolen track contributed to Basque stockpiles, to be used to build their own secret railway lines.

The Portuguese ship, the *Anjo* regularly delivered cargos to the Basque Port of Bilbao. Because the *Anjo* was a frequent visitor to Bilbao, it did not attract particular notice. The *Anjo* was hired to undertake mostly routine and unremarkable commercial voyages, but some of the cargoes Max Boudreaux had signed on to transport were anything but unremarkable. A shipment of uranium ore that the *Anjo* had transported early in the war from Portuguese Angola to New York City had been one such unusual and unique cargo.

From time to time, Max was hired to participate in other special cargo transfers. The time involved to execute these transactions was short, twenty-four hours, more or less. The secretive conditions surrounding the transfer of cargoes at sea were not business as usual. Max received instructions to sail the *Anjo* into the Bay of Biscay and to wait at a certain longitude and latitude to meet an unmarked ship. This ship, without a flag, would rendezvous with the *Anjo*. The world was at war, and German submarines were thick in the Bay of Biscay as they attempted to prevent ships of any kind from reaching Britain. Allowing the *Anjo* to wait in the Bay of Biscay struck Max as the height of insanity. To say the *Anjo* would be a sitting duck was to state the obvious. However, Max thankfully found that the unmarked ships from which he would transfer cargo were, without fail, already waiting for him at the designated latitude and longitude. The *Anjo* never had to be that sitting duck.

Max met the mystery ships and transferred the cargo. Max suspected that the ships were American or British ships that preferred to sail as ghost ships. They did not fly the flag of any country. These rendezvous were often with barges that were equipped with cranes. The cranes were essential to make a cargo transfer that took place in the middle of a body of water. The thing that puzzled Max most about these odd transfers was the cargo itself. It was often a cargo of old railroad tracks. The track must have been deemed unusable from whatever country it had been sent. The track was bent, rusty, and otherwise not worth transporting, except maybe for its value as scrap metal. But Max was always ordered to treat this "scrap" with particular care and to be as gentle as possible with its transfer to the *Anjo*.

The destination for these cargoes of discarded railroad track was always the Port of Bilbao, and the instructions were always the same. The *Anjo* was to come into port just after dark and wait to unload. The crew of the *Anjo* was to leave the ship and go ashore "on leave" for the night. Max was allowed to remain behind to make sure the *Anjo* was secure, but none of the other crew members were allowed to witness the transfer of the cargo from the *Anjo* onto land.

As soon as the ship's crew had left the area, a procession of horse-drawn wagons and carts pulled up to the dock. Men climbed out of the carts and began to unload the messy tangle of railroad track, the cargo from the *Anjo*, into their wagons. It was a sight to behold, a scene from the past. The men were strong and did their work quickly. They carried enormous loads of rusty railroad track on their backs. By midnight, the *Anjo* would be emptied of its metal cargo, and the horse-drawn carts were loaded with bent and rusted railroad track. The full carts were covered with canvas and went on their way, traveling on the road away from the Port of Bilbao. The men, who had unloaded the railroad tracks from the *Anjo* and reloaded them onto the horse-drawn wagons, stayed behind on the docks.

Then, another unusual thing happened. As if on cue and out of nowhere, an entire new "fleet" of horse-drawn wagons pulled up to the dock. These wagons arrived loaded with old burlap bags full of something. There might be hundreds and hundreds of full burlap bags. The Basque men, who had to be exhausted from the hours they had already spent unloading and loading the railroad track, would jump into action again to unload the burlap bags from the carts and load them onto the *Anjo*. The workers were unrelentingly focused and efficient, and in short order, they would have the *Anjo* loaded with full burlap bags.

The exhausted Basque workers climbed into their now-empty horse-drawn carts. The transfers had required all the hours of darkness to complete. After the procession of wagons had begun to move away from the docks and back along the road from wherever they had come, the crew of the *Anjo* was allowed to return to the ship. Finally, before dawn broke over the Port of Bilbao, the *Anjo* would be on its way to sea.

All of this activity happened in the middle of the night. Because Bilbao was a Basque port, Max felt safe loading and unloading cargo there. This was Basque territory, and these were Basque waters. Max was working for the Basques on a Basque operation. Bilbao was technically a part of Spain, but it was not at all Spanish. The fiercely independent Basque people called their own shots and fought wars in their own way. They feared no evil. They confronted it at every turn. This brave and ancient people, who had suffered so much over the centuries, had always found ways to fight and survive and thrive. They had outlasted many Spanish and French governments of the past, and they would outlast many more in the future.

The final stage in these odd encounters took place when Max sailed the *Anjo* to another specific latitude and longitude, a location several miles offshore from the Basque town of Irun. Always at the same location, Max's crew would unload all of the burlap bags they'd just picked up, overboard into the sea. This completed Max's mission. The financial remuneration for these bizarre transactions was excellent, and Max had grown to admire and respect the Basque people as merchants with whom to do business. They were tireless and incredibly strong. He was always paid in cash and on time, and he knew that whatever they were up to, these brave patriots were always working against the Nazis.

Max had questioned the arrangements at the beginning. He refused to dump something dangerous into the Bay of Biscay, wartime or not. Although his Basque contact would not tell him exactly what the burlap bags contained, Max was assured that whatever was in those bags would rest comfortably on the floor of the Bay of Biscay and would never be a danger to marine life or to human life. The Basques pointed out that these bags were being dumped, just off-shore from their own cherished coastal territory. Would they deliberately foul their own nest? It was difficult to argue with that.

Max trusted these people to tell him the truth, and he made the quick, mysterious, and profitable cargo runs whenever he had the chance to do so. He hoped that one day, after the war was won, he would learn the truth. He hoped that the secretive and mysterious Basque people, with whom he conducted his business, would tell him what in the world had been going on with these unusual cargo transfers of rusted railroad tracks and burlap bags full of a secret something.

Donated, purchased, and stolen track made its way by various legal, illegal, and nefarious means to the Basques' secret railroad project. Men, women, and children worked day and night inside the mountain caves to clean, rework, patch, solder, and cobble together the discarded railroad track into something that could be used again. Finally, the Basque mountain railroad was completed, and "the connector," that would deliver the stolen Wolfram train from the main rail line to the rail lines inside the mountain caves, was ready.

The location of the connector had been carefully selected to make hijacking a train possible in an especially remote area. Also, the intersection point of the connector with the main rail line needed to be as close as possible to the train's future mountain hiding place. The shorter the length of the trip from the main rail line to the secrecy of the cave, the less track would be required to build the connector and the less exposure the stolen train would have.

Basques were fiercely loyal to each other, and the secret of the railroad was never leaked to anyone outside their closed community. Their day of reckoning finally arrived. The few ragtag German soldiers who now rode with the dilapidated cars that carried the prized Wolfram ore to Germany never knew what hit them. They were taken completely by surprise when the train was attacked by well-armed men in a remote area of the French Pyrenees just over the border from Spain.

The German guards were quickly subdued, and their throats were cut. Their bodies were loaded into one of the cars with the ore. A cadre of Basque workers arrived in several horse-drawn carts, bringing with them the critical lengths of the railroad track. The track of the connector was quickly laid, and the entire train could now be diverted from the main railway line onto the rails that led to the Basque railroad inside a mountain.

It was a rough trip over the connector and into the mountain cave. The restoration of the old metal rails had been laborious and nothing short of miraculous. The rail lines of the connector had been hastily laid. The train could not proceed with any speed at all, and the trip took longer than the Basque railway engineers had anticipated. But at last, the train finally reached the cave, disappeared, and was secured completely inside the Basque mountains.

These particular train cars full of the valuable Wolfram cargo would never been seen again by the outside world. The Basque workers took up all the pieces of their crudely constructed connector line, the sections of the rail line they had laid to temporarily link the main railway to their hidden mountain tunnel-like cave. They loaded these lengths of track into their wagons and drove them away from the site of the train diversion. They brought brush and other vegetation back to hide the fact that anything at all out of the ordinary had ever occurred at this spot. As far as the Germans were concerned, this train had completely disappeared from the face of the earth. It had vanished forever.

There were several days of frantic searching before the German authorities realized that their train was not just behind schedule or off-track because of a breakdown. It took weeks for them to admit to themselves that their train was gone. They continued to believe that it was not possible for something like this to happen. They investigated to see if the train had actually left Portugal in the first place. It had. They investigated to see if the train might already have arrived in Germany. It had not. Could it have gone to the wrong destination, to the wrong city or to the wrong factory? That had not happened either. The train was nowhere to be found. Had it fallen off a cliff or a bridge somewhere? Had it run off its tracks and gone into a river, a lake, or another body of water?

It was impossible for the Germans to admit that their entire train had vanished without a trace. They sent a team to examine the route the train had taken. They retraced the journey of the lost train multiple times and found absolutely nothing. They found no signs of an accident. They found no signs of the train along the way. How could an entire train have evaporated?

Train cars as well as soldiers to guard the trains were becoming harder to find. The Swiss francs and the gold the Germans used to buy Wolfram ore were increasingly scarce. The rolling stock of France and other conquered countries had already been pressed into service to move troops and supplies through Russia to the front and to move Jews to the extermination camps. The last resort on the Iberian Peninsula was for the Germans to pay the Spanish to use their railroad cars.

Armaments factories were experiencing problems because of Wolfram shortages. Everything in Germany and in its occupied territories was in short supply and severely rationed. Nazi credit was ebbing away as the war in the East lingered on with no good news coming from German generals. Lots of lies were told, but everyone knew the truth. Maybe the public didn't know the extent of the disaster that had confronted the German military along the Russian front, but it was obvious things were getting worse for Germany, at home and abroad. The propaganda machine worked overtime to paint a rosy picture of what was happening, but the people on the home front knew the truth because they knew the conditions of their everyday lives.

To steal one or two trains of Wolfram ore may not have won the war for the Allies. But the hundreds and thousands of acts of resistance perpetrated against cruel and thuggish Germans in all occupied countries helped to punch holes in the Nazis' plan to dominate the world. Even the smallest effort helped. The Basques made at least one more German train loaded with Wolfram disappear into thin air. The Germans never found their lost trains or any of the stolen Wolfram. The Germans continued to transport more shipments of Wolfram, but it was too late to make a difference in the ultimate outcome of the war. Eventually the Nazi evil was going to go down in defeat.

Chapter 29

CHASING GHOSTS

1942

"*I want you to authorize an investigation to hunt down and punish whoever is smuggling these people into Portugal and smuggling them out again. If you don't do it, I will get the Gestapo involved and have them find whoever is smuggling Jews out of France and bringing them here. That boat full of children came by way of the Mediterranean. I am determined to find out where that Swedish steamer began its journey. I want to know who was meeting that Swedish ship, and I want to know who was driving that truck in the Algarve. I want to have a name by the end of the week. I want those children found and returned to France or wherever they came from. I am certain they were Jews, and we have a plan for that problem.*" The angry German officer, Hauptsturmfuhrer Hilmar Vater, was screaming his orders at the head of the PVDE, the Portuguese secret police.

"It is bad enough that we can't seem to crack the Basque system of transporting Allied flyers back to England. This is Salazar's fault. And, it wasn't even Portuguese law enforcement that discovered this rogue ship trying to smuggle those people into Portugal. It was Spaniards who became suspicious of the Swedish steamer. Where were the Portuguese military in this? This is your country, and you are supposed to be protecting it. Why was it the Spanish Guardia Civil that discovered this smuggling ring and mounted an operation to intercept it? They followed the Swedish steamer and destroyed it. They took the Captain of the ship into custody. Unfortunately, they never had the chance to interrogate him. I cannot even believe the story that I was told about that part of the debacle."

"Do you know what happened?" Vater paused and looked at his audience with derision and disgust. "In the confusion, the captain of the Swedish ship jumped from the Spanish Patrol boat into the water. No one knows if he drowned or swam off into the ocean. In any case, wherever he is, he's not available to be tortured and convinced to tell us what he knows about where these Jews came from and where they were going. His boat exploded and is now at the bottom of the ocean in a million pieces. There is no evidence left of the ship, nor are there any witnesses left to interrogate, other than the men from the Spanish patrol boat. It was nighttime, and they couldn't see much. The people who fled the Swedish ship were children! Children! And the only adults anyone could see on shore were a couple of women! Women!" Vater was beside himself with fury. "Find those children and find those women! Find the truck. How hard can that be? The Spanish patrol swears that there were no men involved in this farce, at least none that they were able to see. How can you let yourselves be outsmarted by a couple of women and a bunch of children? This is ridiculous. It is dereliction of duty."

The ship that had been transporting the children had been sailing under the Swedish flag, and the captain and owner of the steamer was a Swedish national. When he had been taken aboard the Spanish patrol boat, he was carrying papers which the Spaniards had not had time to examine before the Swedish captain jumped overboard. A strong swimmer, he made his way to land in Portugal. Because of his connections in the shipping business, he eventually was able to travel safely back to Sweden. He no longer had a ship, but he was safe in his own neutral country. There was no way the Germans could come to question him now, even if they somehow could find out who he was. They would never figure that out.

The origin of the ship was also a dead end. The Spanish or the Germans could probably track it down if they wanted to devote the resources to do it, but the Swedish captain doubted they would go to the trouble. The Germans were fighting the Russians now, and they probably had more to think about than a mystery ship full of children that had exploded off a Portuguese beach.

But a Nazi Gestapo officer in Lisbon, who had an obsession with not allowing a single Jew to escape Germany's Final Solution, knew Jews were trying to get to Portugal. He knew Jewish children were escaping the roundup of European Jews that the Nazis had underway. He was infuriated that Jews were evading the grasp of those who were implementing the exterminations. He wanted to find out who had collected these refugees from the beach in Portugal. He wanted to find who was behind this travesty in order to make an example of them. He felt these Jews belonged to Himmler and should not to be allowed to escape from German jurisdiction. Whoever was smuggling them out of France would face a public hanging. Or, they would be arrested and taken to a death camp in Germany or Poland. In any case, their punishment and death would serve as a warning to others not to interfere with the Nazis as they hunted down Europe's Jews.

The PVDE was constantly trying to placate the Gestapo who were in plentiful supply in Portugal. The Nazis were very busy spying in a country that wasn't their own. They seemed to feel as if they were somehow in charge of something in Portugal. The Germans made demands, and the Portuguese secret police sometimes helped and investigated. But the Portuguese did not feel it was their mission to round up Jews and turn them over to the Germans.

The Portuguese government, in fact, was lodging an official objection with the Spanish government about the patrol boat which had fired on and destroyed a ship flying the neutral Swedish flag within the safety of Portugal's neutral territorial waters. Portugal's leaders felt strongly that Spain had created an international incident. They were more concerned about the destruction of a ship on the beach in the Algarve by a country that had no business being in the area in the first place. They were less concerned with some unlikely tale that the ship which had been blown up had been full of Jewish children.

The story told by those on the Spanish patrol boat was that the Swedish ship's passengers, whoever they were, had been picked up by women and driven off in a dilapidated truck that disappeared into the night. This story was so unlikely that the PVDE did not give any credence to the odd report. The Portuguese authorities did not intend to contribute any manpower or investigative resources to help the Germans follow up on this phantom raft of children and an imaginary vehicle on its last legs.

Hauptsturmfuhrer Hilmar Vater, the Nazi obsessed with tracking down "the ring" that he imagined was helping Jews escape from Europe, intended to mount his own investigation, with or without the help of the Portuguese. He was focused on finding the truck. It was the only clue he had, the only way he could begin to track down the conspirators and find out what had really happened that night in the Algarve.

Finding one derelict truck in a country full of many thousands of derelict trucks was more difficult to do in Portugal than it would have been in Germany. The Germans were strict about the registration of motor vehicles, and officials wanted to know who owned every one. The Portuguese were much more relaxed about their paperwork and about who owned what. The Gestapo eventually would have to give up on this hunt because there was nowhere to go with an investigation. One particular German military man, Hilmar Vater, however, vowed to himself that he would not forget about the incident.

The knock at the door came when he was least expecting it. It was the middle of the night, and Dr. Robert Carmichael had just finished setting the broken and badly mangled shoulder of an American pilot who had been shot down over Nazi occupied France. The injured man, by some miracle, had been able to make his way through Spain to Portugal with the help of the resistance and was finally resting and receiving the medical care he'd so desperately needed. The pilot would now sleep and recover from his injuries for a couple of days in Dr. Carmichael's secret recovery room, until he was well enough to continue on his journey back to England. Dr. Robert Carmichael had administered pain killing drugs and sedatives to the American and did not want to leave his patient's side.

At first he ignored the banging on his door. Robert knew that whoever was outside would not be bringing good news. The people with whom he worked to send Allied pilots back to Britain had keys to his house and would let themselves in without knocking. These colleagues knew that tonight Robert was busy doing surgery to repair the arm and shoulder of a man who had been without medical care for more than two weeks. Because so much time had passed since the injury had occurred, the surgical procedure Dr. Robert Carmichael had just completed might not be able to successfully fix the American's arm. It was a long and complicated operation, and although Robert had gained a lot of expertise in fixing broken bones in the past few years, orthopedics was not his first specialty. He was sure that no one else from the flyboy rescue would be coming to his house tonight.

Robert had continued to worry about the truck because he thought it might be registered in his name. Emerson had paid for it, but Robert had bargained for it and had actually made the purchase. The Portuguese were not as careful as the British were about what traveled on the roads. When they'd bought this particular vehicle in Portugal, there had been more concern about how much money was changing hands than about how much paperwork was being completed. Robert had heard nothing about any investigation in the days since the incident in the Algarve. No one had come around asking questions. There had been not been a word about the ship that had been fired upon by the Spanish, in Portuguese waters, and had been completely destroyed. There had been no rumor that anyone was looking for a truck full of children that had sped away from the Algarve beach in June.

Nonetheless, Robert had been waiting for someone to knock on his door, asking to see his truck. He decided he would say, if anyone ever came around, that the truck had been stolen several months earlier. He had not reported it because, he would tell whoever was asking, it was in such bad shape he didn't think anyone would be able to get any use out of it or be able to sell it. He would say it really was not drivable and therefore not worth anybody's time to look for it. The truck was junk. He figured it had been stolen and sold for scrap metal. This would be his reason for not reporting the vehicle missing. He would say he'd bought it because he'd intended to fix it up, but he had never gotten around to working on it before it disappeared.

What he would not tell whoever might begin asking questions was that he had worked on the truck's engine and the suspension. He had ordered necessary spare parts, new spark plugs, and heavy-duty shock absorbers from England. He would never confess that under the hood, his truck was a champ. It just looked like a tramp on the outside.

The exterior of the truck looked as if it was ready for the scrap heap, and that was exactly how Robert wanted it to appear. It was dented, rusty, and dirty and did not appear to be road-worthy. Its canvas cover was torn, and the windshield was cracked from some long-forgotten incident. But underneath the hood, the truck ran like a top. The specially ordered shocks enabled the truck to carry more weight. Magdalena had pushed the truck to its limits when she'd driven it in the escape along the sandy roads of the Algarve beach. Then she continued to drive the truck as fast as she possibly could on dirt roads and then on gravel roads. She had driven the truck at its top speed for several hours to reach the hideout in Setubal. With all of this, the engine never overheated, and it had never hesitated. The truck had not let them down.

Vehicles were scarce everywhere in Europe in 1942, and they were likewise hard to find in war-time Portugal. Anyone lucky enough to have a car or a truck took good care of it. Spare parts were almost impossible to obtain — at any price. Tires had to be repaired rather than replaced. Robert knew he could not drive the truck anywhere in public in its current condition. Something would have to be done about all the bullet holes. But Robert did not want to get rid of the truck. It was too valuable to their project, and he had put too much time and effort into making the engine run like the engine of a much younger truck.

In addition to his concern about the truck, Robert was sick with worry about Emerson. Her condition was grave. She had suffered a number of physical injuries that would have killed a person who was not as tough as he knew she was. She had been very brave and very foolish, but her behavior had not surprised anyone who really knew her. She had saved many lives. Now if only she had the strength and the will to save her own.

The banging on the door continued. Robert told the drowsy American pilot he would have to stay hidden in the specially constructed secret place while Robert saw who was at the door. The pilot would have to be quiet, so as not to be discovered. The bandages and cast had been put on the man's shoulder and arm a long time after his injury had occurred. The orthopedic work was not up to Robert's high standards, but it would have to do under the circumstances.

Robert quickly cleaned up the medical supplies that were strewn around his surgery. After securing the secret space where the flyer was already drifting off to sleep and reminding the groggy patient again that he would have to be absolutely silent, Robert pulled on his bathrobe and mussed his hair. When he answered the door, he wanted whoever was there to believe they'd roused the doctor out of bed. He wondered if it was the Portuguese Secret Police at the door or if it was some Gestapo goon?

He opened the front door but left the safety chain on. "Who is banging on my door at this hour of the morning?" the doctor demanded through the partly open door.

"This is the Portuguese Police, the PVDE. Open up right away." Robert felt as if he had been kicked in the stomach.

This was the moment he had feared for years. The Portuguese secret police were banging on his door and demanding to be let inside his office. He braced himself for arrest. It could be that his work with the Allied pilots had been found out. It could be that his work with Emerson to move the orphans into and out of Portugal that had been discovered.

Robert Carmichael had been working for the Allied cause ever since the day the war started. He had tried to be as discreet as possible, but he also realized that he was taking huge risks with what he had chosen to do. Would he be tortured and shot? Had he been betrayed by someone who worked with the flyboys or with the orphans? If they had a traitor in one of these groups, he needed to stay alive and try to send word to the others that they were in danger. Maybe he had managed to get himself crossways with some bureaucrat in the Portuguese government? He was a British expat in neutral territory, and a terrible war raged all around his small adopted country, Portugal. He was ready to face it; whatever it was. But he was not going to give up without a fight.

"What can you possibly want with me at three o'clock in the morning? I need to get my sleep. My regular clinic will be open at nine. You will have to come back then." He expected to see the barrel of a gun pointed at him through the opening in the door. He was ready to die. He hoped Emerson would grieve for him when he was gone.

"There's been an accident on the road, and we have an injured man here."

Robert instinctively disengaged the chain and opened the door. Doctors were like that. They heard that a person was hurt and in need of their professional skills, and they didn't hesitate. Men in uniforms rushed into the office, carrying a man stretched out on a slab of wood. There was blood everywhere. The man was badly hurt. "Why didn't you say so?" Robert scolded the policemen. "Every moment counts when someone has suffered a trauma." Robert was taking the upper hand with the police, and his confidence seemed to win the day.

"We know you are an excellent doctor, and it was closer to bring him to you than it was to try to take him to the hospital in Lisbon. He's a German, and we know you are British." The senior man among the policemen was explaining the situation. Clearly, the officer was prepared to insist that the doctor treat the injured man if Dr. Carmichael objected and refused to treat him because he was a German. Technically, the critically injured German was an enemy of the British doctor in the world outside Portugal.

Robert Carmichael made his position clear. "My oath as a doctor holds me to a certain standard. I will treat anyone who needs medical treatment — no matter what their nationality or their ability to pay. If you had brought a murderer to my clinic and asked me to save his life, I would not refuse you. It does not matter that the man is a German. I will give him the best care that I am capable of giving." There was so much blood on the man's face and head as well as on his chest and lower body, Robert could not tell what had happened to him. "Tell me exactly what has taken place tonight. I need to know as much as you can tell me about the accident so that I will know how to treat him."

"We don't really know. We think his car just ran off the road and hit a tree. He was in an open convertible, and he was probably going too fast. We came along and found the car crashed beside the road. The accident can't have happened too long before we arrived on the scene. We had a terrible time getting him out of the car. His legs were tangled in the steering column, and there was so much blood, we were afraid he was already dead. But he is breathing. He had his papers with him. He is a colonel in the German Army, the Wehrmacht. His name is Stefan Weber, and he is forty years old. That's all we know. He has lost a lot of blood, but we don't know anything more."

"I need your help here. Lift him carefully and transfer him onto the table. We don't want to exacerbate a spinal injury. One of you go and get some warm water so we can clean him up." Robert gave orders to the three PVDE officials who had brought the colonel to the office. They were policemen, not medically trained personnel, but they did as Robert ordered. "I am going to need at least one of you to assist me in a surgical procedure. Which one of you would feel most comfortable doing that? I don't have a medical assistant in my office, even during regular office hours. I don't usually do surgery except by appointment. If I have to do a procedure, I schedule a nurse to come to assist me. There is, of course, no time for that tonight. So, which one of you is willing to volunteer to be my nurse?"

The youngest of the policemen spoke up, "I've done some first aid work in years past, during my school days. I don't remember too much of what I learned, but I am good at following directions. I will help you in whatever way I can."

"Stefan has a broken arm and may also have a broken leg … or two. He may also have broken some ribs. I will set and cast the arm and put splints on his legs. But first I have to stop the bleeding from the gash in his thigh and the wounds on his head and face." Dr. Carmichael spoke aloud to his volunteer assistant while he worked as rapidly and carefully as he could. "I am really trying to stop the bleeding and stabilize him so that you can transport him to Lisbon. He is badly hurt and needs a first rate orthopedic surgeon."

Robert stressed again to the Portuguese police that he did not usually do surgery, except when it was a scheduled procedure.

Carmichael had done a two-year fellowship in surgical procedures during his training, years ago in England, and he did minor operations in his medical office. He preferred to send more complicated cases to a specialist at a Lisbon hospital. Robert had been able to hone some of his surgical skills more recently when he'd treated the flyboys and other escaping refugees for broken limbs. Robert, of course, did not mention this latest opportunity to practice his surgical expertise.

Robert and the policeman worked for more than two hours. Stopping the bleeding, stitching up the colonel, setting his broken arm, splinting both legs, and stabilizing the patient had been hard work and had demanded tremendous concentration. After doing all he could to help the injured colonel, Robert felt the German could continue on to the hospital in Lisbon. An emergency car had arrived to transport Colonel Stefan Weber. Weber would survive his injuries. He would not bleed to death, thanks to Dr. Robert Carmichael who had provided him with life-saving emergency treatment.

Robert gave directions as the attendants transferred the Wehrmacht officer to a stretcher and carried him to the medical transport vehicle. The German would be at the hospital in Lisbon in a little over an hour. Robert placed a telephone call to the surgical service at the hospital where the Nazi colonel would be taken and gave directions to the surgeon who would operate on Stefan's broken femur and take care of his other injuries.

Robert had been up all night. First he had treated the American flyboy, and then he had treated the German army officer. It had been an intense several hours for the doctor, and he was past the point of exhaustion. The policemen thanked him and left. Robert went to his secret recovery room to check on the American airman. The pilot was still asleep thanks to the pain medication Robert had given him. It was a blessing the man had not awakened and stumbled into the surgery in the middle of the drama with the German and the Portuguese police. Sometimes it seemed that the only luck Robert Carmichael had was bad luck, but tonight he was thankful for his good luck that had arrived in several forms.

Dawn was breaking when Robert collapsed on his bed and slept. He would need to move his flyboy sooner than he'd originally intended. The presence of the Portuguese police had unnerved him. Two broken arms, a broken shoulder, and possibly two broken legs in one night. That went beyond all the probabilities. Robert's office hours would soon begin. Most of all the doctor longed to see Emerson and check on how her recovery was progressing.

Six weeks later, a tall, light-haired man with piercing blue eyes waited in Dr. Robert Carmichael's surgery. When it was his turn to be seen and he walked into the examining room, there was something about him that seemed familiar to the physician. The man walked with a cane, and Robert wracked his brain to try to remember where he had seen this man before. The man spoke to him in perfect, accented English, "I am Stefan Weber, and you saved my life. I have come to thank you."

"Or course, Colonel Weber. I am delighted to see that you have made such a rapid and excellent recovery. You are walking surprisingly well. Take off your shirt and let me have a look at your arm." Robert examined his handiwork and was pleased that Stefan's arm had healed so well. The colonel had regained almost complete motion.

Robert remembered that the same night he had treated Stefan Weber, he had also treated an unnamed American pilot.

The pilot's arm and shoulder had been broken almost two weeks before he'd arrived at the surgery. Robert could only hope that the American had healed as well as the German's arm had healed. "You really have the Portuguese police to thank for your life and for your rapid recovery. They found you in your car without delay after the accident, and they brought you here within minutes. My being able to set your arm so soon after the accident made it possible for you to have a good result. How are your legs?"

"The cast has just come off, and I am learning to use this cane. The surgeon at the hospital in Lisbon told me that without your care, especially because you were able to immediately stop the bleeding in my legs and my head, I probably would not have lived. He said you stabilized my broken femur and the broken tibia in my other leg, for the trip to Lisbon. He said all of that was extraordinarily well done. Because you knew exactly what to do, he said the operation he performed at the hospital was much easier, and my recovery was faster. I have been in some pain, but I am grateful for everything you did for me."

"I am delighted that you have made such good progress. You're a lucky man that your car was discovered in time and that there was a doctor's office almost directly across the street from where you crashed."

"I am lucky that I had my accident across the street from the office of Dr. Robert Carmichael. I am also lucky that you were willing to treat me when I was so badly injured. You knew I was a German, and yet you never hesitated to save my life and see to my broken limbs. Our countries are at war, and not everyone would have been as magnanimous as you were that night."

"Colonel, it never occurred to me to do anything but try to help you. My oath as a physician and my values as a human being require that my judgment not be clouded by nationalities or events or other circumstances of the moment. If my skills as a doctor are required, they are given, without question and without reservation. One day our countries may not be at war. I would like to be able to look at you and say to myself, if I were to see you walking on the street in Berlin or Frankfurt, that I gave you the best of what I had to give."

"You are a fine man, Dr. Carmichael. I hope you will understand that I am a loyal German. I would like to say that I am a good German. I am not a member of the Nazi party. I am a soldier. I do not agree with everything the current government in Germany is doing. I would like to think that in another time and in another place, you and I might be friends. I will always remember that it was a kind and skilled British physician who gave me the gift of the rest of this life that I will live. I will always be in your debt. Until that day in Berlin or Frankfurt, I say goodbye and thank you again."

Robert was moved by the German's thanks. He shook the hand of Colonel Stefan Weber and watched him limp out of the office. Robert hated the Nazis and everything they stood for and everything they had done and continued to do. He wondered how many other Germans might also not agree with what their government was doing. How difficult it would be to be torn between the love of one's country and the shame of having to support and fight for what one despised.

Chapter 30

MAX MEETS ANNALISE

July 1942

The *Anjo* would arrive in a few days to pick up the children. In addition to his medical work with the downed pilots, Robert was struggling to keep up with his regular daily office hours, his supervision of the orphans' hideout, his desire to oversee Emerson's care, and now the preparation of the visas, the photos, and the identity cards. Robert knew that Emerson had devoted considerable time and taken great care to prepare the children's entry visas — the vital paperwork that would allow them to enter the United States and be adopted by loving families. She had also provided each one, in lieu of their missing passports and birth certificates, with a personal identity card that had the child's photo on it. She had shared these tasks with Robert who had taken photos of the children and helped her prepare the identity cards. He knew what to do. He just felt inadequate to take over this task which had been so important to Emerson.

He realized that the visas and the identity cards would not be as perfectly done as when Emerson created them. There was no one else who could do it, so he would have to do it. Robert had already taken and developed the photographs of the children, as he always did. The photographs had been the easiest part of all the things he had to do.

Robert knew that the biographical evaluations of each child would not be as knowledgeable or as complete as when Emerson did them. Annalise had written out her summaries about the children who had been rescued in the Algarve. She had traveled with these children and knew them well. Robert's translations from Portuguese into English, taken from the impressions Lindeck had relayed on the recording machine, would have to do. No one else could write English as well as he could, so he had to do these reports. He did not want to disappoint Emerson.

Robert typed the biographies on Emerson's old fashioned L.C. Smith & Brothers typewriter and made carbon copies, just as Emerson did when she prepared them. He weighed and addressed the envelopes, one to Rachel and one to her mother. He would deliver the two envelopes today. His friend was taking the Pan Am Atlantic Clipper boat plane from Lisbon to New York tonight. Emerson's friends in the United States would at least have the children's names and photographs and a brief report on the condition of each child. He hoped his efforts would be useful to somebody.

Robert marveled at the ease and speed with which Emerson had completed everything she'd undertaken. She'd made it all seem effortless. Only now, as he tried to step into her shoes, did he realize how much she had done and how flawlessly and efficiently she had accomplished it. Robert was preparing the waterproof packets that included the critical U.S. entry visa and the homemade identity card for each child, complete with a photograph. These packets would accompany the children on their voyage aboard the *Anjo*. In addition to the fact that he did not feel his work was up to Emerson's standards, this time there were twice as many packets to prepare because there were twice as many children.

Word arrived that the *Anjo* was on its way, and the children were ready to go with their new pajamas and clean clothes packed in their rucksacks. Robert had spoken with Annalise, and they had decided she would join the children on the voyage. She would care for the two toddlers and the infant who realistically would not be able to make the trip without her being aboard to care for them. Annalise also would be needed to help take care of the extra children on the voyage.

Max had been notified that there would be more than the usual number of children on this voyage, and he'd not expressed any objections. Robert had sent Max a message that they would have to make two trips to the *Anjo* with the launch as all the children could not all be loaded in one trip. No one liked the fact that the *Anjo* would be anchored off the cove for twice as long as usual, but there really was no choice.

Robert let Max know that Emerson was not able to help with this transfer of children, but he'd not told him any details. Max would hear the story from the children and Annalise soon enough. Robert had told Max that, in addition to the children, he would be taking a young adult woman with him. He told Max that the woman had been forced to leave Denmark because of her work with the Danish resistance. He told Max that she was going along on the sea voyage to care for three very young children and to help supervise the unusually large number of young passengers. Max had not objected to this change in protocol. Max had long ago accepted that Emerson was a force of nature and that to argue with her when she changed the plans would be a waste of time. Even though these new instructions came from Robert, Max didn't dare object.

Robert had been so busy that he had not really had time to think about how much he missed Emerson's company. It was at the back of his mind, every waking moment of every day, but he had not been able to dwell on it. Having almost lost her, he realized he finally was going to have to tell her of his feelings for her. He could not keep quiet any longer. He knew that she liked him and respected him and depended on him. He knew she cared for him as a friend, but he did not know if she could ever love him. It had been years since her husband Peter had died, and Robert knew she had not allowed herself to think about ever loving anyone again. He had respected her grief and the time she needed to recover from the trauma of losing Peter and then the trauma of losing their baby. But Robert had loved her for a long time, longer than he would ever reveal to her.

He remembered the first time he had seen her — the night of the Christmas Party at Bacalhoa in 1938 when Peter Mullens was still very much alive. Robert had lost his own dear wife a few years earlier. Her death had completely devastated him, and he'd not thought he would ever be attracted to another woman again as long as he lived. When he received the invitation from the two newlywed Americans asking him to attend their holiday party at the quinta, he decided he would make himself attend the Christmas celebration, even though it was the last thing he wanted to do. The Mullens were his next door neighbors. He felt he had to at least put in an appearance.

When he saw the way beautiful Bacalhoa had been refurbished and how the quinta had been transformed with evergreens and the other Christmas decorations, he was glad he had decided to attend the Christmas party. The holiday cheer that had transformed the palacio had put even the sad and serious Dr. Robert Carmichael into something of a festive mood.

The night of the party, Emerson entered the lounge and walked directly up to Robert to welcome him. She was wearing a red velvet dress, and she was the most beautiful women Robert had ever seen. She glowed with joy and happiness. Robert looked back on that moment and wondered if it was the perfectly fitted long red dress with the low-cut neckline or if it was the simple but elegant diamond necklace she wore around her neck. He decided it was her sparkling blue eyes, more so than the diamonds, and her natural charisma and charm shining through that made her the center of attention in every room she entered. She was unassuming and kind and unaware of the impact her beauty and brilliant personality had on others. Robert loved her from that moment forward, but of course he knew that he could only admire her from afar. He would never impose himself on the lives of these two happy young people.

Several months later, Emerson had called on Robert, in his capacity as a physician, to examine Peter. The news about her husband's health had devastated Emerson. She had taken care of Peter and made his slow death as comfortable for him as possible. She was always cheerful and did her best to lift Peter's spirits. Robert had tremendous respect for the brave way she'd handled Peter's illness and death and the sensible way she had taken over all the responsibilities of running Bacalhoa.

Then she'd lost the baby, and she had given up on life. Robert grieved for Emerson's losses, but he also grieved for the loss of the free and full spirit that Emerson had been and was no more. In spite of the double tragedy that had befallen her, she had tried hard to hang on to her optimism and her heart. But losing her unborn child had literally destroyed her desire to keep on living.

Having suffered from depression himself, Robert was able to understand something of what she was going through. His own retreat from life after his wife had died had not been as extreme or for as extended a period of time as Emerson's. He'd had his medical practice and patients that had demanded his attention. Robert had visited Emerson weekly, fooling nobody that he was there in an exclusively professional role. He had done everything in his power to help her.

As a result of his conspiring with Emerson's dear friend Rachel, they had engineered Lily's arrival. Emerson began a slow return from wherever she had been inside her head. She attempted to embrace life again. Robert knew she was grateful to him for his constancy and caring, but gratitude could not be the basis for the kind of relationship Robert hoped to have with Emerson. Emerson and Robert had become great friends, and then they became extraordinary collaborators in their project to rescue refugee children. They worked well together. Robert did not want to endanger his friendship with Emerson, but he could no longer stay silent about his deepest feelings for her.

On the night of the *Anjo*'s scheduled arrival, it was necessary to transfer the children to the boathouse in two trips with the van. Robert was still too apprehensive about the current condition of the truck to use it on the road again, even for the relatively short distance between the hideout and the beach cove. He drove half the children to the boathouse in the van and then returned to the hideout for the other half. There would be two trips with the motor launch as well.

In the boathouse, they waited and waited to receive word that the *Anjo* was anchored offshore. Robert began to worry when Max's ship did not arrive as scheduled. The children were doing their best to be as quiet as possible. One group of children was already loaded in the launch, and they were becoming restless in their life jackets. It was a hot July night, and even with the usual breeze coming from the water, the weather was sticky and uncomfortable. Robert had hoped to be able to move the children to the *Anjo* before the moon came up and flooded the cove with moonlight. Unfortunately, Max was so late, they would be transferring the children in a bright, waxing moon.

At last, Robert received a message over the shortwave radio that the *Anjo* was off the coast. The ship's position had to be different every time it arrived. Exactly where it put its anchor down depended on the tides on the night of each transfer. Max added in his radio message that he had been detained by the PVDE and some German snoopers as he was about to cast off from the Lisbon docks. There had been closer inspections of his paperwork, and some Germans wanted to inspect the ship. Max had only allowed the Portuguese police to board. They had searched and searched, and he finally told them all to get off as he needed to leave on his voyage. The PVDE had found nothing because there was not yet anything to find. The Germans were angry that they had not been able to search the *Anjo*, but they had no legal authority in Portugal to board a neutral ship. Of course, they would not tell him what they were looking for when they examined his papers and attempted to get onto the *Anjo*.

The first group of children was transferred to the *Anjo* in the usual way, with a member of the crew climbing down the rope ladder and then climbing back up the ladder with a child strapped to his back. Robert returned the empty launch to the boathouse to load the second group of children which included Annalise, the two toddlers, and the infant.

When this second launch full of passengers reached the *Anjo*, Max was the first crew member to climb down the rope ladder. He wanted to talk to Robert. He was concerned about the extra scrutiny he had encountered when he'd tried to leave Lisbon earlier that evening. Although he had been warned, he wanted to hear from Robert why there were so many extra children. Robert did his best to answer Max's questions while the rest of the children were being loaded onto the *Anjo*. Max wanted to know what was wrong with Emerson. Robert told him to ask the children to tell him about it. He assured Max that Emerson was going to recover although it would be a long fight.

Finally, Annalise was the last person remaining in the launch. She had been completely silent and had gone unnoticed until it was her turn to climb up the rope ladder. Robert introduced her to Max. Max and Annalise looked at each other. They could have been brother and sister. Annalise's straight, almost white blonde hair and blue eyes were a match for Max's. Fair-skinned, tall, and slim, they smiled and shook hands. Annalise handed the waterproof pouch of visas and identity card packets to Max. He continued to stare at her, his usual confidence and brusque, businesslike personality set aside for a few moments.

Robert reminded himself that Max was actually quite a young man at age twenty-three. Max was so competent and had taken on responsibilities and achieved success way beyond his chronological age. Sometimes one forgot how young he really was. He asked Annalise in perfect French how old she was. Annalise looked fourteen but was in fact twenty years old. Max was visibly taken aback when he heard that Annalise was nearly his own age. He took her hand and helped her climb ahead of him up the rope ladder. Watching these two as they met each other for the first time, Robert realized that this voyage would be unlike any of the previous ones and for more than one reason.

Chapter 31

ABOARD THE ANJO

July 1942

Annalise's duties taking care of the children and getting them settled into a routine aboard the *Anjo* occupied most of her waking hours during the first two days of the ocean voyage. Max checked in frequently to be sure everything was going smoothly. Were there enough beds? Was the food satisfactory? Max and his crew had managed the care of the children during previous crossings, and he was trying to be careful and considerate in his new role of not being completely in charge. He knew that with so many children aboard, Annalise needed his help. But he wanted direction from her about what she wanted him to do. Annalise was not a shrinking violet and readily gave directions to Max and everyone else about what they were to do and when they were to do it.

Annalise looked so young; it was surprising how she could organize them all into schedules for watching the children and supervising their activities. By the third day everyone was fully briefed and following orders issued by Annalise. She had a charming and diplomatic leadership style, so everyone was more than willing to go along with her program.

It wasn't that Annalise and Max had failed to recognize the electricity that had passed between them at their initial meeting. It was just that there had been so many other things to think about. Annalise was occupied with the care and feeding of the children, and Max was diligent about his responsibilities to navigate a safe course for his ship through a dangerous ocean full of German U-boats.

On previous voyages, Max had been in the habit of spending some time alone each evening on deck after dinner looking at the stars and thinking. The crew was respectful of his need to have this quiet and contemplative hour and tried not to come to him with questions during these few moments he took for himself. He was sitting in a deck chair on the third night of the voyage when Annalise joined him and pulled a second deck chair up close to his.

"So, Captain Max, tell me about yourself. How it is you happen to own this big cargo ship when you are scarcely older than I am?"

Max smiled and in fact had been secretly hoping that it would not be too long before he would have a chance to talk with Annalise and get to know her better. "I will tell you about myself, but you must also tell me what a young woman like yourself has been doing for the Danish resistance and how you have happened to turn up on the *Anjo*?"

"I don't speak Portuguese. I also don't speak Russian, Spanish, or Hungarian. You aren't Portuguese, so how do you happen to know how to speak it? And how did you learn to speak such good English and perfect French? I heard you speaking with the children and know that you speak French like a native."

"My mother was a French teacher, and she insisted that my sisters and I speak French from the time we learned to talk. You have told me what languages you don't speak, so tell me which ones you do speak."

Annalise noticed that although he had answered her question, he did not seem to want to elaborate with more information about his family. "I speak Danish, Norwegian, and Swedish the best. I also know English, French, German, Dutch, Polish, and some Finnish. You still have not told me how you came to learn Portuguese and live in Portugal."

"How does it happen that you know so many languages at such a young age?"

"You are not answering my questions, and I am answering yours with more questions. I want to get to know you, Max, and you are going to have to be honest with me if you want to get to know me, too. My parents are both dead, killed by the Nazis. My sister was also killed by the Gestapo in Denmark. They all worked in the Danish resistance. That is how I came to work in the resistance. We are Danish Jews although we are what one would call "secular Jews," more cultural Jews than religious Jews. There was a rabbi way back in our family history somewhere, but I couldn't tell you anything about him."

Max held a French passport. He had never revealed to anyone, since first signing on to sail with Captain Sousa years ago, that in fact he was Jewish or that he was German. He never spoke German and even pretended that he did not understand it when he heard it spoken. This had been his closely held personal secret information that no one else had needed to know. He suspected that Captain Sousa had guessed he was a German escaping the Nazis, but he'd never asked Max any questions about his previous life. Now Annalise had revealed herself honestly and openly to Max, and he had to decide if he was willing to open old wounds and respond to her with his own honest answers. He had kept his pain locked inside himself for so long, he didn't know if he would be able to tell Annalise what she wanted to know, even if he decided he wanted to expose his vulnerability to her.

They met each evening after the children were in bed. They talked about themselves, and they talked about the world they lived in, sharing the past and their hopes for the future. Max finally told Annalise his story in all of its horrible detail. He told her about the deaths of his parents and two sisters. He told her of his escape from the house of death and his escape from Germany. She cried with him and held him in her arms, as she moved into his world and gently held his sad heart. She told him of her own parents' deaths in front of a Nazi firing squad. She told him of her sister's rape and torture and eventual blessed death.

They laughed together, and they cried together. Their lives intertwined in a way that might be able to hold them together as they faced an uncertain future. Would they see the next year? The end of the war? What kind of a world would it be? Could these two wounded souls, both of whom had been forced to be adults before their time, have a future together? They made love in Max's quarters, a desperate expression of their sharing, their youth, their hopes that they might survive this terrible time in history. In the midst of the insanity of their current lives, they both needed to hang on to the possibility that life might once again be worth living.

A network of communication among merchant ships in the Atlantic Ocean had developed during the early months of 1942. German U-boats seemed to be everywhere off the Atlantic

Coast of the United States since the U.S. had entered the war. Hundreds of merchant marine ships had gone down, and thousands of sailors' lives had been lost. The German U-boats and their torpedoes were a constant threat, and the U-boats often left underwater mines behind when they returned to France. Even though the U-boat itself was no longer in the area, there was no guarantee that the waters were safe.

In mid-June of 1942, a German submarine had surfaced at night off the coast of Virginia Beach. U-701 had left Brest in France the previous week, and its mission was to leave underwater mines at the entrance to the Chesapeake Bay. Lookouts on the enemy submarine could see the lights of Virginia Beach and the headlights of the cars as they drove on the surrounding highways. The U-boats were that close to the unsuspecting shores of the summer resort town. With the Cape Henry lighthouse to its port side, the submarine launched fifteen underwater mines.

The German submarine was already on its way back to Nazi-occupied France when the mines exploded. The underwater mines that had been deployed would explode when they collided with an unsuspecting ship. Three days later, just four miles off the Virginia Beach boardwalk, the American tanker *Robert C. Tuttle* was hit. Thirty minutes later a mine detonated underneath the tanker *Esso Augusta*. Initially, it was thought that a German submarine was in the area, but a few days later, it was determined that underwater mines had been planted by a long-gone German U-boat. Minesweepers were called in to search for and destroy the mines, but there was no certainty that all of the German mines had been found. It was an impossibly dangerous time to be on a ship of any kind in the waters near the East Coast of the United States of America.

Two nights before they were to meet Naomi in Butcher's Creek, Virginia, Max received word on the ship-to-shore radio that there was a cluster of U-boats in the area off the coast of North Carolina. Although he didn't want to be late for a rendezvous, he always erred on the side of caution. The *Anjo* had planned to approach the mouth of the Chesapeake Bay from the south. Max decided to set his ship's course for farther out to sea, rather than follow along the coast of the Carolinas into the Chesapeake Bay. He continued sailing north while he was still far out in the Atlantic. When he arrived off the coast of Delaware, he intended to turn west and follow the Delaware and Maryland coasts south to Norfolk. He had not received any reports of recent U-boat sightings in that area. He let Naomi know he was probably going to be at least a day late. He continued on his new indirect course and hoped for the best.

Off the coast of Cape Henlopen, Delaware, Max made his turn to the west. He stayed fifty miles out to sea as he followed along the Delmarva Peninsula south towards Virginia Beach. When he reached the waters off the Eastern Shore of Virginia, he headed toward the mouth of the Chesapeake Bay. At four o'clock in the morning, in a totally unexpected attack, the *Anjo*'s cargo bay was damaged by a stray underwater mine.

The *Anjo* was lucky. The mine had not dealt the ship a fatal blow. The crew made sure no one was hurt and assessed the damage to the ship. The children were frightened, but there were no injuries. At the beginning of each voyage, Max told his group of small passengers that being hit by a mine or a torpedo from a German U-boat was always a possibility. The children rehearsed putting on their life jackets and practiced what they would do in case of such an emergency.

The children had put on their life jackets and assembled on deck as they'd been instructed to do. Max explained to the assembled group that the damage from the mine was not serious enough for them to get into the life boats and abandon ship. The *Anjo* was taking on water very slowly, but the destruction was so slight that Max decided the *Anjo* could make a run for it. They would try to reach the rendezvous point to deliver the children before the ship took on a dangerous amount of water.

The crew of the *Anjo* did their best to patch the holes in the cargo bay. Although Max felt the *Anjo* could safely make it to the rendezvous at Butcher's Creek, he was not sure his ship would be able to continue on and reach the Port of Baltimore where it could be repaired.

Traveling as fast as he felt was prudent, Max sent a radio message to Naomi that his ship had been damaged. Max was scrupulously careful about always sending his messages in code, and Naomi decoded the message twice to be sure she had not made a mistake. Max told her the *Anjo* had been struck by a mine off the coast of Virginia. They'd taken a hit in the cargo bay, but the ship was not badly disabled. Max was continuing the voyage and would be delivering the children as usual to Butcher's Creek. He would be delayed by two days because of the damage to the *Anjo*, and he would be using two lifeboats to bring the children up the creek to meet Naomi.

Naomi trusted Max to know his own ship, but she did send back a coded message to ask if she could arrange for repairs to be made to the *Anjo* in Baltimore. She knew many people in that city, and she might be able expedite the repairs. She understood, without Max having to say anything, that he could not bring the ship into Baltimore while the children were still on board. They had to be unloaded before Max could even think about taking the ship into a U.S. port. Max sent a message back that he thought the *Anjo* could made it to Baltimore, and yes, he would be forever grateful if Naomi could find him a berth where he could take his ship to be put back together.

Because it was wartime and because of the U-boat traffic off the East Coast of the United States, there sadly were a great many damaged ships. Those that were burned or sunk could never be repaired. There were countless ships that had been completely destroyed. Naomi was enormously thankful that the *Anjo* had not been harmed more seriously, or worse, was not sitting at the bottom of the Atlantic Ocean with its precious cargo. The risk of going down was a fact of war and an ever-present danger to ships that chose to approach the shores of the United States in 1942.

Max knew he could not go into a port with the children on board. There would be officials all over the ship, and he would be arrested. Even though each child had a visa which allowed her or him to enter the United States legally, neither Max nor Naomi wanted to test the veracity of those visas if they didn't have to. They did not want to set off an investigation in Portugal — an investigation that would look into Emerson as the person whose dead husband's signature was on each visa. It would be better to avoid all ports until after Max had delivered the children safely into Naomi's hands.

Annalise had decided she did not want to leave Max when the ship arrived in Virginia. She had a visa which allowed her to enter the United States, but her passport and her birth certificate were Danish. Would the State Department or the Immigration Service want to know how she had arrived in the United States? Denmark was now under Nazi rule. Did that mean that Annalise would be considered a citizen of a country that was an enemy of the United States? The children would be adopted within weeks or months of their arrivals, and they would take on the names of their new families. The adoptions would be scrupulously legal, and no one would ever need to know where a young adopted child had actually been born or where he or she had spent the first few years of their lives.

Annalise's situation was a different story. She had no adoptive family waiting for her when she arrived in the United States. Naomi knew Annalise was among the passengers who would be arriving soon, and she was working to find a way to get Annalise the papers that would allow her to stay in the USA legally. Annalise wanted to stay, of course, even more so now because she wanted to be with Max.

The crew dealt constantly with the threat that the *Anjo* might not make it to the transfer point at Butcher's Creek. The reception the *Anjo* received at the mouth of the Chesapeake Bay, at Norfolk, Virginia went pretty much as it had gone on previous trips. The Coast Guard officials looked at Max's papers, consulted a list, and waved him through on the ship's channel that ran between Cape Henry and Cape Charles. Max was always amazed with the efficiency of these procedures and thanked Naomi's powerful and influential reach which had facilitated what might have been a prolonged and maybe even a futile wait to enter the Chesapeake Bay.

No questions were ever asked when Max's ship entered the bay. No one ever suspected that on most of these trips, he would not continue on to Baltimore and deliver his declared cargo as the manifest indicated he was supposed to do. This time he hoped he would actually be able to make port in Baltimore, that he and the *Anjo* would be lucky enough to reach that destination. Baltimore shipwrights would be able to make the necessary repairs to his ship. Max's goals were first to deliver the children to Naomi at Butcher's Creek in Virginia and then to deliver the *Anjo* to Baltimore.

Max did not want to think about leaving Annalise. Before the *Anjo* had been damaged by the mine, Annalise had insisted that she did not want to leave the ship when it arrived in the United States. She wanted to stay on board with Max. Max and Annalise had discussed every possible scenario about how they could manage to be together. If Max could get the ship to Baltimore, they might have more time to discuss their options. Max did not want to be separated from Annalise for even one day, but he wondered if there could ever be a place for her aboard the *Anjo* on a permanent basis. His life was committed to the sea and to his ship. The question about how he could fit Annalise into his life was continually on his mind.

Chapter 32

TROUBLE IN VIRGINIA

June 1942

Naomi had received word several days earlier that twenty-eight children would be arriving this time when the *Anjo* unloaded its valuable cargo at Butcher's Creek. She commandeered an additional van because she knew her passengers wouldn't all fit into the small bus. The voice on the telephone call from Portugal had been a man's voice, and he'd said all the correctly coded things to prove it was a legitimate message. But it was not Emerson's voice, and Naomi wondered why Emerson had not delivered the message as usual. Their agreement was that the person receiving the message would not ask any questions, and Naomi had respected this rule although she was worried about why Emerson had not been the voice on the overseas call. There was a count of twelve males and eighteen females, including one female infant. There was also an adult female who would come aboard. The telephone message did not reveal their ages as Emerson's communications did.

Naomi wondered if the biographical sketches would be arriving, as usual, by way of the Pan Am Atlantic Clipper boat plane and the U.S. mail. Emerson's brief but on-target biographies had been a great deal of help to Naomi and to Rachel in preparing for the children's arrival. Knowing some things about them in advance had given Rachel an idea about what their personalities were like. This information had proven to be invaluable in placing the children with their future families. Naomi knew that Max would radio her with a full accounting including genders and ages when he told her of his arrival plans. But both Naomi and Rachel had come to depend on Emerson's opinions about the children.

A few days before the children arrived, Naomi was relieved to find the anticipated envelope with the biographical sketches about the children in the mail. It was obvious to Naomi that these sketches had not been written by Emerson. They were well done but were much more clinical than Emerson's had been. They lacked Emerson's special insight and descriptive touch.

Naomi was now convinced that something had happened to Emerson and was anxious to find out from Max what was wrong. Emerson was not making the telephone calls from Portugal as she usually did, and she had not written the biographical sketches about the children. Someone had taken over Emerson's duties and was doing a good job with them. But Naomi thought of Emerson as another daughter and was terribly concerned about her.

The weather was not cooperating with this latest transfer of children. A bad thunderstorm was predicted for the night they were to arrive, and even though the weatherman was wrong at least half the time, this time he seemed to be certain about his forecast for heavy rain.

Naomi anticipated that most of the children would not have rain gear and would be soaked to the skin after riding in the life boats from the *Anjo* to the dock on Butcher's Creek. They would be cold and wet and would need towels and dry clothes and blankets. They would need hot cocoa and more. They had already been through so much. She certainly didn't want any of them to become ill because of bad weather.

Naomi was eternally grateful to her good friend who owned two thousand acres of land on the Eastern Shore of Virginia. Virginia's Eastern Shore was underpopulated and rural. There were lots of crops, a few animals, and not many people. Naomi's friend had purchased this land as a long-term investment, and he'd built a small, primitive hunting lodge on the property. He was delighted to allow Naomi to use the dock on Butcher's Creek to transfer the orphans from their ship to road transportation heading north. This generous benefactor had made certain the dock was in good repair and assured Naomi that the area was so desolate that no one would ever see the children arriving in the lifeboats. He was the one who had chosen Butcher's Creek as the best spot to transfer the children. It was the deepest and most obscure of several inlets on his property, and the water was deep enough and wide enough to accommodate the lifeboats. The best thing about Butcher's Creek was that it was completely on Naomi's friend's land. There would never be a reason for anyone else to be remotely close to the transfer point. If there was anyone around the dock at Butcher's Creek, they would be trespassing.

Once the children were in the bus and traveling on the road north to Easton, Maryland, the situation became another story entirely. Because gasoline was rationed, any vehicle that was on the road after dark was suspicious. Whoever was driving might be stopped and questioned about why they were traveling so late at night. Gasoline rationing had begun in May of 1942, and Naomi was very afraid of being stopped and asked how she happened to have enough gasoline ration coupons to drive a bus any significant distance. And, what was she doing out on the road in the middle of the night?

Naomi had connections of many kinds. In addition to the friend who had provided her with the excellent landing spot at Butcher's Creek, another of her contacts had been able to find extra gasoline rationing coupons and some spare tires for her small bus. No one really wanted to know the details or the exact nature of the reason Naomi needed the extra gasoline and the extra tires. They knew that if Naomi asked for it, it was for a worthwhile cause. No one ever questioned her motives except to ask what else they could do to help. She knew she was fortunate to have all of these resources available to her. But she constantly worried about being stopped in the middle of the night with a bus full of children by an overly zealous policeman on the road between Onancock, Virginia and Easton, Maryland. None of these children spoke any English. The jig would indeed be up for her if she were stopped in transit. It was essential that she travel incognito and not attract attention to her bus.

This particular night she would be traveling with a bus plus a van. Both vehicles were necessary because of the additional children. They would all be tired and would want to go to sleep. It was a three-hour drive to the farm in Easton, and that was in good weather. Three hours was already too long for her vehicles to be exposed on the road. Things had gone very well up until this trip. She had been lucky so far, but there were never any guarantees that her luck would continue.

Unfortunately, the weather prediction was quite accurate this time, and the rain poured down on the bus and the van all the way from the Easton farm to Butcher's Creek. The wind was fierce, and Naomi was concerned the weather would interfere with the transfer of the children from the *Anjo* into the lifeboats. Naomi was well-protected in the waterproof foul-weather gear she wore for sailing on the Chesapeake Bay, but this was a bad storm with thunder and lightning and sheets of unrelenting rain. She worried about how wet the children would be when they arrived and about the low places in the road.

Each of these transfers was difficult and stressful — even with perfect weather, a new moon, and favorable tides. One never knew what might happen. Max's knowledge of currents, tides, and weather was excellent, and he understood the conditions of the water. Under normal circumstances, he knew what his ship could and couldn't do, but this time the *Anjo* was limping along at much less than one hundred percent. Naomi always prayed and kept her fingers crossed, but this time there were so many more things that could go terribly wrong.

Naomi had allowed extra time because of the weather, so she arrived early. And of course, Max was late because of the damage to his ship and because of the storm. He was moving more slowly up the Chesapeake because of the hole in his cargo bay, and the weather and winds made navigation more difficult than usual. At three o'clock in the morning, the children finally arrived at the dock. There were two lifeboats full of passengers. Naomi was heartened to see that someone had bought or made small, waterproof ponchos and put one on each child. They were at least partially protected from the terrible rainstorm. The transfer seemed like it took forever with all the extra children, and Naomi wondered if they would ever be safely aboard the bus and the van.

As the last of the children stepped onto dry land, a lovely young woman, carrying an infant in a sling across her chest, stepped out of one of the lifeboats and up onto the dock. Annalise introduced herself to Naomi and said she hoped they had room for her. Then Max stepped up onto the dock behind Annalise and handed the packet of official documents to Naomi as he always did. He told Naomi that Emerson had been hurt but was going to be all right. Annalise would tell her all about what had happened.

Max and Annalise held each other and kissed goodbye. Neither one wanted to let the other one go, but they finally separated. Annalise was crying, and Max looked at the ground. Max climbed back into one of the life boats, and both boats disappeared into the deluge of rain and fog, headed back to the *Anjo*. Annalise boarded the bus and lifted the youngest child in the group onto her lap. She still had the infant secured close to her chest. Naomi was anxious to hear Annalise's story and was even more anxious to ask her about Emerson's health. But Annalise was so obviously upset at leaving Max behind that Naomi realized this was not the right time to ask her anything.

Naomi had come prepared with hot cocoa and cookies as usual. She'd also brought boxes full of sandwiches. Towels, blankets, jackets, and sweaters in a variety of small sizes appeared. The children could dry out and warm up as they traveled for hours in a not-very-well-heated bus or van.

The two vehicles struggled along the primitive dirt road heading away from the dock. Previous trips in good weather had challenged the bus to make it down the private roadway to the public road. The treacherous sandy track, that was little more than a footpath, had now turned to mud. Naomi found something else to pray for — that the van and the bus would be able to slog through and make it to the paved road. Once on the paved road, she would worry about making it to Easton without being stopped.

The children had been instructed that if the bus was stopped for any reason they were not to speak or say anything at all. They were to remain completely silent. Naomi would explain to whatever authorities might stop the bus and inquire about their middle-of-the-night journey that this was a bus full of children who were deaf and mute. They were being transported to a home for deaf mute children in Baltimore. With that excuse, whoever questioned their presence on the road late at night would be given a reason why the children did not speak.

Naomi had chosen her cover story about the children being deaf and mute because it was a story that could make sense. She'd had a sign made and posted it on the side of the bus that read "St. Augustine School for the Deaf." She hoped that no policeman on the Eastern Shore of Virginia would go to the trouble to try to find out where the St. Augustine school was located. If he or anyone else tried to locate the school, they would not be able to find it. There was no such school in Baltimore or anywhere at all in the world, as far as Naomi knew. Naomi hoped that she and the children would be long gone if such an inquiry was ever initiated. Tonight they also had the van, and it did not have a sign of any kind on its side.

Naomi had felt she could pull things off if the bus were stopped, but on this trip with two vehicles, things were more complicated. Naomi was driving the bus. Naomi had instructed the driver of the van, a close and trusted friend, to wait to get on the road and to allow the bus to travel on ahead. She told her friend to allow plenty of space between the two vehicles. Naomi felt that two vehicles traveling separately would be less conspicuous than two vehicles traveling in tandem.

They were on their way, but Naomi was worried as they passed through the small towns of the Eastern Shore during the early hours of the morning. They could not travel very fast, and because the transfer of the children had been delayed, this would be the first time they would not be able to arrive safely at the farm in Easton before daybreak. There were still too many things that could go wrong with this trip.

About an hour south of the estate in Easton, a tire on the van blew out. It was wartime, and tires were at a premium. Naomi tried to keep the tires on her vehicles in good repair, but one could only put so many patches on a tire before one was driving only on patches. Naomi had known it was just a matter of time before the van broke down or a tire went bad. She had worked some miracles to obtain the gasoline she needed to transport her small passengers where they needed to go, but car parts and new tires were more precious than gold in the world where she and everyone else lived these days. There were some problems that money could not always fix.

They had a spare tire but it was worse than the tire that had gone flat. It would have to do, and Naomi could only hope and pray that the driver of the van would be able to switch the tires before any law enforcement people appeared on the scene to see what was happening. She hoped no friendly sheriff would stop by to help change the tire. The rain continued to pour down as the van sat on the side of the road. Naomi's heart pounded as she stayed on the bus and waited while her friend changed the tire on the van.

Before she'd become involved in the orphan's project, Naomi had lived her life absolutely and completely on the right side of the law. It had never occurred to this highly moral and conscientious woman to live any other kind of life. Now she was smuggling children into her own country. Everything this unconventional mission entailed was a completely new experience for her. She had been a fierce prosecutor and all about justice and punishing those who broke the law. She wondered if she would be able to tell a convincing lie to a local sheriff who might stop to help them. She knew this delay would put them even further behind schedule. There was no way to call her farm in Easton to tell them not to worry. They would get there when they got there.

Naomi's life had been so well thought out and planned, so well-prescribed before the war. She knew now, without any doubts whatsoever, that she was doing the right thing by helping save these children who otherwise would die. With each lifeboat that arrived at Butcher's Creek, she became more certain that she had chosen the correct path. How could she not do what she was doing? There really was no choice in the matter. Naomi was brave. She was not afraid for her own safety. She knew that in order to fight the evil that existed in her time, she could not stop to think about whether or not she had anything to fear.

Just as the rain was ending, fog descended on the convoy of two vehicles. In spite of attempting to keep some distance between the two, the small bus and the van were now traveling together. Neither driver could see much of anything ahead on the road, but at least they were hidden by the fog. Eventually the bus and the van made it to the house in Easton. It was mid-morning, and the children were exhausted. Most of them had fallen asleep during the journey and had to be carried to their beds. Once again they all had made the trip safely, and Naomi did not forget to thank God for protecting them on their way. Naomi called her daughter Rachel in Boston. They never discussed the orphans over the telephone, but Naomi always called Rachel to let her know, through carefully coded words, that the group had arrived and were safe.

Naomi did tell Rachel that Emerson had been hurt, but she assured Rachel that Emerson would be all right. Naomi hoped she was telling Rachel the truth when she reported this to her daughter. Naomi had not yet heard the story of Emerson's heroic rescue of the children from the beach in Portugal, so she did not know how serious Emerson's condition really was. Naomi promised to tell Rachel everything once she herself found out what had happened to keep Emerson from her participation in their project. Both women were well aware of Emerson's passion for what they were doing. They realized that only something terrible could keep Emerson from her duties.

Annalise eventually talked to Naomi at great length about Emerson. She told her every detail of the amazing night when Emerson had saved her life and the lives of so many children. The irony of the situation was that Emerson and Annalise had never actually had a conversation. Emerson would not know who Annalise was if she saw her at Naomi's house. Everyone was praying that Emerson would be able to survive her ordeal.

Chapter 33

THE TREASURE OF SHINKOLOBWE

1942

M. *Edgar Sengier was a Belgian mining engineer,* and he was also a businessman who could tell which way the wind was blowing in the late 1930's. He didn't think he was necessarily a brilliant man or that he had especially accurate prophetic powers. What he saw, when he looked into the not-so-distant future that was playing out in front of him on the European continent, was there for anyone to see. What he knew would happen with some certainty was what any clear-headed person with a modicum of intelligence ought to be able to predict. He blamed people who didn't see what was coming in the years ahead on the fact that too many of them lived in a world of denial and wishful thinking. They so desperately wanted to believe what they wanted to believe that they ignored the facts which dictated what was actually going to happen. Edgar Sengier was a realist.

Sengier managed the Union Miniere du Haut Katanga or UMHK in the Belgian Congo, one of Belgium's African colonies. Union Miniere had a monopoly to mine the rich resources of this extraordinary place. In 1915 a unique and unusual discovery was made in the midst of the African bush at the Shinkolobwe mine in the Katanga Province. Five million years earlier a bubble of radioactivity from deep in the earth's crust had made its appearance on the surface, and the purity of the ore that had erupted was more than 200 times that of most uranium deposits.

At the time the uranium was discovered, what had made these superbly rich deposits of pitchblende ore so important was that they contained high concentrations of radium. Discovered by the French scientists Marie and Robert Curie, radium had become the latest and most effective method for treating cancer. Radium was the miracle cure. The Shinkolobwe mine opened in 1925 and immediately became the world's primary source of radium. The radium had to be separated from the pitchblende, and what was left over after the highly valued radium was extracted was uranium ore. In the 1920's uranium ore was merely a by-product of radium mining and of little value.

In the 1930's, this residue, these leftovers from the processing of radium, became potentially important. The importance of the uranium from the Shinkolobwe mine eventually would completely overshadow the importance of the radium that originally had been produced there. What made the pitchblende at Shinkolobwe extraordinary was that it was so rich in uranium ore, rich specifically in the highly-sought-after U-235 ore. The concentrations of the high grade uranium ore found at Shinkolobwe were unique. No deposits of ore with such unbelievably high concentrations of uranium had ever before been discovered. No deposits with as high a percentage of uranium ore would ever be found again, anywhere in the world. The Shinkolobwe mine pitchblende ore deposits were blessed with such a high percentage of uranium that they were deemed to be a "freak of nature."

Edgar Sengier, managing director of the Union Miniere, understood the implications of what had been discovered in the Katanga mine. He had learned from colleagues in both England and France about the vital importance of high grade uranium in the research that was being done by physicists who were working to "split the atom." Sengier knew he had under his control one of the world's most valuable potential strategic resources. He realized that if this precious ore fell into the hands of an enemy, it could bring catastrophe upon the earth. The ultimate value of this prize might not be realized for years to come, but Edgar Sengier intended to secure and guard his ore with an eye to that fateful future day.

Sengier remembered the horrors of the 1914-1918 War in Europe. He had hoped that Belgium and the other countries of Europe could live in peace without a bellicose Germany rattling its sabers again. He feared and despised the Nazis as he watched Hitler rise to power in Germany. He saw the handwriting on the wall when Germany again began to threaten its neighbors. With the remilitarization of the Rhineland in 1936, Sengier could see what was going to happen.

As Hitler consolidated his power, Sengier knew things would only get worse. He was full of dread for his own beloved Belgium, for France, for the Netherlands, and for all the free countries which had suffered so horribly and lost so many brave young men fighting German aggression in The Great War. Germany's recent behavior had been an arrogant and offensive slap in the face to the treaties that had ended a terrible war. The treaties which had been put into place so that Germany could not plunge the continent into chaos and death again, had become worthless hopes and hollow memories. The buildup of the German military machine was obvious to all — even though no nation wanted to admit it, let alone confront it.

Sengier knew Germany was working on the problem of atomic fission. Other nations were also at work to solve the atomic puzzle. Physicists who understood these things predicted that one day, the country that was able to first harness the power of the atom and was able to build an atomic bomb, would unleash a demon never before seen in the world. It would be a force so powerful and so destructive that all existing weapons would immediately and instantaneously be rendered pitiful and obsolete. The previous world order would be ended forever, and power among nations would be rearranged in dangerous and unpredictable ways.

Sengier was determined that, no matter what, Germany would never take possession of the potentially valuable uranium ore at Shinkolobwe. Sengier wanted to be certain it could never fall into the hands of the Nazis. He realized with a great deal of sadness and loathing that Belgium would again be conquered by the German war machine, just as it had been in The Great War. He grieved for his country that it would once more be forced to struggle under the German boot. This time his beloved Belgium would be oppressed by an even worse tyrant than the tyrants of previous wars.

Sengier realized the Nazis would be more brutal in every way than former German invaders had been. He knew that Belgium would fall, and this broke his heart. But what he feared, perhaps even more than he feared Germany's takeover and destruction of Belgium, was that Belgium's colonies all over the world would be conscripted by the Germans. He was terrified that the Germans would expropriate the Belgian Congo and with it the Shinkolobwe mine.

In October of 1939 Edgar Sengier had, just weeks after Hitler invaded Poland, moved his mining headquarters to the United States. He founded the African Metals Corporation as a subsidiary of Union Miniere with offices in the Cunard Building at 25 Broadway in New York City. Sengier realized that money was to be made during the war, and he knew that the United States would need to buy cobalt, an element essential in the assembly of airplane engines. Sengier's mines in Africa produced a great deal of cobalt, and he was happy to sell it to the Americans who quickly became the world's largest consumers of that element. Sengier also knew that the United States offered a safe place to do business which neither Britain nor any place on the European Continent could provide with certainty at that time in history.

Falling radium prices had been the deciding factor in Sengier's choice to close the Shinkolobwe mine in 1939. This pit mine in the Belgian Congo was abandoned and eventually flooded with water. Mining equipment and men were transferred from Shinkolobwe to the more profitable copper and cobalt mines.

But Sengier knew that he had a potential treasure in Shinkolobwe, and he rescued tons of the uranium ore which he knew would be of considerable value at some time in the future. He sent some of the pitchblende ore to Belgium, hoping to be able to transfer it out of the country before the Germans reached Belgium. But he'd waited too long. When the Germans marched through Belgium on their way to France in 1940, the ore was sitting on the Antwerp docks awaiting shipment to a haven outside of the grasp of the Nazis. It was too late to keep that uranium ore out of German hands. When the Nazis subjugated the country of Belgium, they assumed ownership of the Antwerp uranium. But Sengier had been able to successfully rescue a much larger cache of uranium ore from

Shinkolobwe, a trove of treasure which would escape being taken by the Germans.

Sengier's plan for safeguarding the remaining inventory of uranium oxide or "yellow cake" from the Shinkolobwe mine meant that some of that ore would soon be on its way to the United States. Massive amounts of uranium ore still lay on the ground around the Shinkolobwe pit mine, residue from the radium extraction. In May and June of 1940 1,250 tons of uranium ore were put in barrels and sent by rail to the port of Lobito in Portuguese Angola. From there the barrels were loaded on two freighters and sent across the Atlantic to New York City. To throw off possible Nazi informants, this was accomplished quickly and quietly and without fanfare. Edgar Sengier did not want the Germans to suspect that he had possession of a valuable store of uranium ore or where that ore was going.

Sengier's deputies in the United States, forced to find a place to store the barrels of yellow cake that were arriving on short notice, could find only a three-story warehouse on the site of a former vegetable oil plant near the southern footing of the Bayonne Bridge at Port Richmond Terrace on Staten Island. The barrels, each stamped with the unremarkable label "URANIUM ORE — PRODUCT OF BELGIAN CONGO," would wait, hidden in plain sight in the Staten Island warehouse, until it was time for them to play their central and unique roles on the world stage.

In 1942, United States military personnel, who were tasked with developing an atomic weapon, approached Edgar Sengier and offered to buy his uranium ore. In addition to the ore Sengier had stored in the warehouse on Staten Island, there were an additional 4,000 tons of uranium ore lying in waste piles at the Shinkolobwe mine in the Belgian Congo. The United States Army purchased both the ore that was already in the U.S. as well as the ore that remained in the Congo. In 1942, the ore that remained in the Congo was loaded into whatever containers could be found and brought to the United States aboard special rapidly moving cargo ships that could outrun the German U-boats. Only one shipment of the precious Shinkolobwe ore was ever lost to a German U-boat torpedo.

In addition to purchasing ore that was already in the United States as well as the ore that was available to ship from the Congo, the U.S. was anxious to procure, from every possible source, as much uranium ore as possible. The United States wanted the supplies of uranium ore for their own atomic weapons program. And wartime strategy demanded, of course, that as much of this valuable ore as possible be kept out of the hands of current and future enemies.

If it had not been for Edgar Sengier's deposits of high grade uranium ore from the Shinkolobwe mine in the Belgian Congo, the atomic bomb that destroyed Hiroshima, Japan on August 6, 1945, and hastened the end of the war in the Pacific, would never have been built.

Chapter 34

VISITING THE PAST

1942

Max had a huge hole in his heart as he left Annalise on the dock at Butcher's Creek. He'd anticipated that it would be difficult to tell her goodbye, but he hadn't realized how deeply it would affect him. He had other things that demanded his attention now, and he tried to relegate his thoughts of Annalise to a dull ache in the region of his chest. He had to get the *Anjo* repaired and back out to sea, and he had a crew to take care of. These had to be his first priorities. He had a cargo on board that he needed to deliver to Cuba. He had another cargo waiting to be picked up in Brazil.

Max was always worried that his past would catch up with him. He had legally changed his name, and his French passport and papers were very good. In spite of the fact that he had officially and legally become another person, he was Maximillian Boudreaux in name only. He felt the *Anjo* was above reproach because it had always sailed under the neutral Portuguese flag.

He felt he was safe because most people believed him to be a Portuguese national. Max had done everything he could to distance himself from his German origins. The word had been spread around both in Lisbon and in the international shipping community that Max had grown up in Brazil and was the nephew of the previous owner of the *Anjo*, Captain Bruno Sousa. The story was that Max's mother was Bruno Sousa's sister, and his father was a Frenchman who had emigrated to Brazil. Max's last name was Boudreaux, his father's last name. According to his mythical background, Max carried dual citizenship, both French and Portuguese. He preferred, for whatever reason, to use his French passport.

Max had always been excellent with languages, and he now spoke Portuguese like a native. Any questions about his accent were explained by the fact that he had learned his Portuguese in Brazil, one of Portugal's colonies. Supposedly, Max had come to Lisbon to learn the shipping business from his uncle because his uncle Bruno Sousa and his uncle's wife, Inez, had no children. The nephew had elected to purchase the ship after his uncle's death. It was widely known that Max and his uncle's widow were extremely close and that he took care of all of her financial needs.

Now Max was faced with an additional dilemma — his feelings for Annalise. He loved her and wanted to be with her. But the life of a merchant seaman was no life for a married man. The wife of a ship's captain was a lonely life. She stayed at home alone and raised whatever children the couple might have. She would never know, even if it was not a time of war, whether or not her husband would return safely from one trip to the next. It was not an existence that made for a happy marriage.

Annalise had suggested that she accompany Max on the *Anjo*. She proposed that she could help with the children when

Max transported them to Virginia. She said she could teach English to the children and relieve the other crew members of their childcare duties during the trans-Atlantic voyages. Max was turning all of this over in his mind. He had never thought he would want to marry. He had never thought his hardened heart would ever allow anyone inside. He thought he had forever lost his ability to love or trust. Annalise had proven him wrong, and now his life, about which he had come to be so certain, was turned upside down. This time the impact was a positive one, but loving Annalise presented many new questions and uncertainties that Max had never thought he would have to consider.

He pushed the *Anjo* on through the Chesapeake Bay in the direction of the Port of Baltimore. Once in that city, Max would have his ship repaired and made whole again. He had always thought the *Anjo* would be his only love, taking the place of wife and child. He was devoted to the *Anjo*'s well-being, and his first thought had always been to take care of the ship and its crew. Now he served two masters. He wanted to hurry the *Anjo*'s passage to safe harbor in Baltimore because he was anxious to begin the necessary repairs to the holes in her cargo bay. But he also longed to arrive as quickly as possible because he knew that in Baltimore, he would see Annalise again. She was staying with Naomi. Max had narrowed his life so that he minimized the ambiguities with which he had to deal. Meeting and falling in love with Annalise had changed all of that forever.

The ship finally arrived safely in Baltimore. Naomi had once again worked her magic and prepared the way for work on the *Anjo* to begin immediately. Max made arrangements for his crew to be housed and fed during what might be a lengthy stay in port. Many of the crew did not speak English, so he wanted to be sure they were comfortable and safe.

These men who sailed on the *Anjo* had been Max's family for the past few years, and he cared very much about them.

When all the arrangements had been made, Naomi sent a car to collect Max from the shipyard and bring him to her Baltimore home. When the car stopped at the front of the stone mansion, the door of the house flew open, and Annalise ran into his arms. Max buried his face in her soft blonde hair that smelled of lilacs. He felt her slight body clinging to his. At that moment, Max realized his entire life was going to change dramatically. He could not imagine a future that did not include Annalise. He understood now what other people meant when they said "he could not live without her." Whatever changes he had to make, he would make them. Whatever accommodations had to be undertaken, that would happen. Indeed, he realized he could not live without Annalise and that he was only half a person when he was not with her. He hadn't asked for this gift, but he suspected that God had sent Annalise into his life for a reason. He was going to cherish her and share the rest of his days on earth with her, no matter what else life might throw his way.

The restoration of the *Anjo* was going ahead, and Max and Annalise were staying with Naomi. Max checked daily on the progress of the repairs and on the welfare of his crew, but most of his time was spent with Annalise. The lovers did not know what their future might hold, so they treasured every moment they had together as if it might be their last, which it well might be in this uncertain and dangerous world at war.

Annalise had told Max and Naomi every detail about the night Emerson had rescued her and the children from the waters off the coast of the Algarve. They now were fully aware of what Emerson had sacrificed to save so many. They knew she had sustained serious injuries and was badly burned. What none of them realized was how her psyche had been impacted by the events of that night. Everyone had always known that Emerson was the heart and soul of their mission, the driving force behind the orphans' rescue project. Robert had done a valiant job of stepping in and shouldering Emerson's responsibilities, but for the project to continue, it would require Emerson to be in good physical and mental health. No one knew, at this point, if that would ever again be possible.

Naomi never mentioned Emerson. Max knew Naomi was in contact with people at Bacalhoa, and he had hoped Naomi would tell him that Emerson was recovering from her terrible ordeal. One day he decided to ask Naomi what she'd heard from Setubal. When Max asked, Naomi's face took on an uncharacteristically sad expression, and she told him she had not heard any news. As long as the *Anjo* was in dry dock and under repairs, there would be no way to transport the children anyway. Emerson was never far from any of their thoughts and prayers.

Naomi was a busy woman and had her fingers in many important pies. She was often absent from Baltimore, traveling for one of her numerous causes. Max and Annalise might not see her for days at a time. One afternoon, Naomi called Max to say she needed to talk to him as soon as possible. She would be home for dinner at 7:30 that evening, and she told him she had an enterprise of the utmost importance to discuss.

Max and Annalise were having cocktails in the living room when Naomi rushed in. She kissed them briefly and told them that she needed Max's help.

"I have an urgent need for a dependable merchant marine crew — preferably from a neutral country. Max, do you have any idea where I could find such a crew on short notice?" Naomi wasn't one to beat about the bush with unimportant small talk. She smiled a conspiratorial smile, and her eyes were sparkling with excitement as she looked at Max.

"Naomi, you know that I have the most excellent of maritime crews sitting idle in a rooming house in this very town, at this very moment. What is this all about, and what do you need from my crew? Of course the answer is 'yes' to whatever you are going to ask me to do. How could I ever turn you down for anything, after you have done so much for me and for Annalise and for so many others?"

"I need to have you and your crew at the harbor in New York City by tomorrow night. There is a top-secret war-time emergency that is unfolding as we speak. My only question is, how quickly can your crew learn to operate a new, unfamiliar, and exceptionally fast freighter?"

"My men are smart and skilled. I cannot imagine there is a ship of any kind that they would not immediately be able to take control of and sail to any place in the world. I put my men up against any crew anywhere — for ability and for learning quickly. What's this all about, Naomi?"

Max and his crew were being recruited into a project for the Americans which ultimately would change the world. In 1940 Max had transported uranium ore from Africa to New York City. The operation had been a highly secret one to which Max's mentor Captain Sousa had committed the *Anjo* before he died. After the captain's death, Max and the *Anjo*'s first mate had decided to honor Sousa's agreement. Once they had fulfilled the contract, they had not thought much more about it. But the secret voyage had not been forgotten by the man whose uranium Max and the *Anjo* had transported.

"I can't really tell you, Max. I don't know that many details myself, but I will tell you all I know. A good friend of mine, a colonel in the United States Army, has contacted me and asked specifically for you by name. Don't ask me how he knows your name or how he connected you with me. I suspect it has something to do with the fact that the *Anjo* is in for repairs at the Port of Baltimore. I pulled some strings to arrange for a rush job on that. Consequently my name is linked to the *Anjo* and therefore to you. My friend, Colonel Nichols, knows you own the *Anjo*. He knows it is temporarily out of commission here in Baltimore while it's being repaired. Nichols has told me that back in the spring of 1940, the *Anjo* and its crew transported a special shipment for a Belgian mining company, Union Miniere. He said this transaction had been handled discreetly, and the cargo was surreptitiously moved out of Porto Lobito in Portuguese Angola and sent to New York City. You followed instructions to the letter and there was never a word leaked from your crew about this secret and unconventional cargo transfer. Edgar Sengier, the man for whom that cargo was transported from Africa to the United States, spoke highly of you, your discretion, and your ability to follow orders. He admired your ability to load your ship quickly and efficiently. He said you have an excellent crew that works like 'a well-oiled machine.' Sengier recommended you to Nichols, so Nichols trusts you and your crew to maintain secrecy. Nichols needs skills, but he also has to have people he can trust. He could not believe his good luck when he learned that the crew of the *Anjo* was here in Baltimore."

"That was an unusual and mysterious cargo, from the Belgian Congo. We loaded barrels of something called uranium ore in Porto Lobito in the middle of the night, directly off the railroad cars. At least it was stamped on the barrels that they contained something called uranium ore. Who knows what might really have been inside those barrels?"

"It was exactly what you said it was, inside those barrels, I mean. And that is another thing. You must never mention what was in the barrels you transported in 1940, and you must never mention what will be in the containers you will pick up on this new assignment. You will again be loading cargo in Porto Lobito and taking it to someplace in the United States — maybe to New York, maybe someplace else. I know you are trustworthy, Max, but this is an absolutely critical and top-secret assignment. I hope you will agree to take on the job which I have been told is essential in determining the course of this war. If the wider operation is successful, it will guarantee victory and an earlier end to the war. Furthermore, the results of this project will dramatically change future history, what comes after the end of the war."

"If it means helping to defeat the Nazis, Naomi, you know I am on board. Tell me what I have to do and where my crew and I need to be by tomorrow night. My men are bored and unhappy sitting and waiting for the *Anjo* to be repaired. They will jump at the chance to do get back out to sea, and I am confident they will be able to handle whatever ship we are given."

"Colonel Nichols stressed to me that your knowledge of Portuguese and your familiarity with Porto Lobito are of particular importance to this mission. You will meet with him tomorrow night before you sail, and he will give you the details. Briefly, in addition to loading the ship your crew will be operating, he wants you to supervise the loading of other ships with the valuable cargo from the Congo. All of these ships are exceedingly fast moving and smaller than the *Anjo*. They can outrun German U-boats, which is why they were chosen for this mission. Several of them have been conscripted from other uses and from other places for Nichol's special project, specifically for the purpose of transporting this valuable ore. You can see that this mission is top priority for the Americans."

"I will make a call to the *Anjo*'s first mate. I will tell him only what he needs to know and that he is to get the crew packed up and ready to move out in the morning. Will we take the train? How will we get ourselves to New York?" Max was eager to tell his crew that they had work to do.

"Make your telephone call, Max. Transport will be taken care of by Colonel Nichols and the U.S. Military. Tell the men to get a good night's sleep. They will be leaving their boarding house at six tomorrow morning. A bus will be there to drive them to New York. They will be going to sea again. Tell them you don't know when they will be back to Baltimore or when they will see the *Anjo* again."

Max frowned at Naomi. "What do you mean? You don't know when they will see the *Anjo* again? I can't tell them that. We'd all better see the *Anjo* again, Naomi."

"Of course you will, dear heart. But it's a war. We all have to play to our highest and best calling. Your highest and best is something other than navigating the *Anjo*, at least a for the next few weeks. I'll take excellent care of the *Anjo*. Sitting in Baltimore Harbor is the best and safest possible place for her to be in 1942 while German U-boats are creating havoc along the Atlantic Coast. Call your crew. My blood sugar is low, and Annalise has not been able to get one word in with the two of us yakking. I will meet you in the dining room. It is roast leg of lamb with mashed potatoes and gravy tonight. The lamb comes from our farm in Easton. I have been looking forward to this meal all day."

Early the next morning, Naomi's driver delivered Max to the rooming house where his men were waiting. When the olive drab military transport bus arrived, the crew of the *Anjo* loaded their duffle bags and themselves into the vehicle. They were on their way to the Port of New York. The crew trusted Max. He had told them the United States and the Allied cause needed an experienced crew that was familiar with Porto Lobito for a special mission that was critical to the war effort. That was all these good and loyal men needed to hear. They had carried Jews to Palestine and helped to smuggle them into a country that really didn't want them. They had transported small children, lifting them out of a motor launch one at a time strapped to their own backs, from Portugal and delivered them in the middle of the night to a remote creek off the Chesapeake Bay in rural Virginia in the United States. How difficult could this next adventure be? They were not going to be transporting people, just some kind of strange material nobody had ever heard of or knew what to do with. It was mysterious, to be sure, but it wouldn't be difficult for this experienced crew.

Max and his men boarded their rapid transport freighter late that evening. There were some things that were new to the crew, but for the most part, they were excited to learn the ropes and have a chance to operate this very fast ship. Max's men were sailors to the core and were thrilled to be at sea again. It was all going to work out fine. Max and his crew left New York Harbor as soon as it was dark. This ship, which had no name, flew the Portuguese flag. It would be the first of several ships without names to arrive in Porto Lobito. All of these ships would be flying the Portuguese flag. Max would make sure his ship was loaded discreetly, quickly, and always at night. He knew how to speak Portuguese and he knew Porto Lobito. He would supervise the loading of the other fast ships. He would sail back to the United States with the first load of uranium ore and supervise its unloading at an as yet undisclosed location. He would return to Porto Lobito for a second cargo of uranium ore. His crew would continue to sail the fast ship back and forth across the Atlantic. Max would continue his trips to Porto Lobito until all of the important strategic material was loaded onto ships and delivered to the United States. There would be more than 4,000 total tons of uranium ore transported during this operation.

Max knew his work out of Porto Lobito was of the utmost importance to the war effort, and that under any circumstances, it would take priority over rescuing the children. After his assignment in Africa was completed, Max would return to Baltimore and to the *Anjo*. He prayed that by that time, his ship would have been made seaworthy again. He hoped Naomi would have news that Emerson had recovered her health so that the orphan rescue could resume. Most of all, returning to Baltimore meant that Max would be returning to Annalise.

Chapter 35

HEALING EMERSON

September 1942

Emerson's *physical recovery followed a better-than-expected course*, and everyone was thankful for that. Magdalena was once again the ever-faithful caretaker and friend that she had been years earlier when Emerson had withdrawn from the world in grief and despair. Magdalena had talked constantly to Emerson during the many months of her severe depression after Emerson's husband and baby had died. Magdalena had spoken to an unresponsive Emerson about Bacalhoa, about her own life growing up in Portugal, and about what was happening in the European war. Afterwards, Emerson probably hadn't remembered much of anything that Magdalena had said to her, but Robert was convinced that just continuing to hear another human voice had kept Emerson alive.

Magdalena talked to Emerson again as she struggled to recover from her recent injuries and burns. Magdalena told

Emerson she had done some discreet investigating about the secret underground stairway and tunnel beneath the altar in Bacalhoa's chapel. Pierre's bouncing ball had led to the discovery of the former garage for extra cars which had become a hiding place and refuge for the children.

No one had been able to give her a satisfactory explanation for how or why the top of the altar in the chapel slid sideways to reveal its hidden opening. The best answer Magdalena had been able to determine was that the sliding altar had been part of the chapel since the chapel and the altar had been built. The baby Jesus, an integral part of the nativity scene on top of the altar, had always been the lever to open it. Magdalena's own theory was that originally the sliding altar top concealed a relatively small repository for communion supplies, valuables, or secret papers.

She was guessing that it was only later that the space under the altar had been excavated. The narrow stairway had been built, and tunnels had been constructed that led to a much more extensive underground maze. Magdalena was convinced she knew why the tunnels had been dug and the stairway had been built. She also thought she had discovered what the explanation was for the sanctuary room that was part of the underground network. At one time, she believed the sanctuary room had been a religious gathering place.

In 1755 a devastating earthquake had struck Lisbon. The epicenter of the earthquake was located off the coast of Portugal, but the quake was so powerful that Lisbon had been almost completely destroyed. The earthquake triggered a tsunami so huge it was believed to have wreaked havoc from the shores of Portugal to the shores of Brazil, all the way across the Atlantic Ocean. Although Bacalhoa had not been damaged in the earthquake, in its aftermath, the owners of Bacalhoa decided they needed an escape route from the quinta and from whatever devastation another earthquake might bring. They had seen the destruction in Lisbon and heard stories of people being trapped for days beneath the rubble after their homes collapsed on top of them. Those who lived in Bacalhoa at the time believed that an underground passageway would be a way to get away from the palacio and provide its occupants with an escape into the countryside. The tunnels originally had probably exited the underground escape route through some kind of rudimentary structure in the woods. Bacalhoa's owners felt, rightly or wrongly, that they would be safer outside when another catastrophic earthquake hit.

Magdalena explained that, to the best of her knowledge, the stairway, the tunnel, and the exit in the woods near the Lisbon road had been built sometime after 1755 as a possible way to escape for the people who lived at Bacalhoa. Originally, only the tunnel to the outside had been built. Magdalena had discovered that there were other quintas and palaces in Setubal and in the wider Lisbon area that had built similar tunnels to the outside. Most of these had been dug in the aftermath of the 1755 earthquake, as a means to escape through an underground passage if one's castle was destroyed.

The effort and expense to dig out the tunnels from the sandstone had been enormous. In the case of Bacalhoa, it would have required many years and a great deal of manpower and money to build a tunnel that would reach the location in the woods. There had been no hideout building in the eighteenth century, of course, just a rough exit at the end of the long tunnel complex. The tunnel would never be needed because there was never another terrible earthquake like the one which had occurred in 1755. The underground "escape route" was all but forgotten until it was again pressed into service at the beginning of the nineteenth century.

The room that had been carved out in the center of the system of escape tunnels, had been created, as far as Magdalena had been able to determine, during the Napoleonic Wars when the French had invaded and occupied Portugal. French rule did not last very long, but the early nineteenth century inhabitants of Bacalhoa were afraid of Napoleon's generals. The family that lived at Bacalhoa had built themselves a safe and secret place of worship below ground.

A devout Catholic family, the owners of Bacalhoa had created a secure place where they could continue to practice their religion without fear. They did not trust the French emperor's occupying forces to respect their religious rights. This Catholic family had built the sanctuary. They had provided a well for fresh water and even a primitive kitchen in their sandstone hiding place. Magdalena told Emerson that she could not verify, with any degree of certainty, the information she'd discovered about the underground rooms and tunnels. But she wanted Emerson to know the gossip and rumors she had uncovered about the secret spaces underneath the altar.

Emerson was awake for brief moments. At one point Magdalena thought Emerson even smiled when she looked down and saw Lily snuggled beside her in the bed. Lily had been another faithful soldier who was by Emerson's side twenty-four hours a day. She licked Emerson's hand. She put her head on Emerson's arm and stared at Emerson — searching for any kind of recognition in Emerson's face, some kind of acknowledgement that Lily was there or that Emerson was there. Finally one day, Emerson opened her eyes and began to talk to Lily. Lily was beside herself with joy and was ready to play ball and run and go for a walk. It would still be long days before Emerson would be able to match Lily's energy and enthusiasm, but it was the beginning of Emerson's road to recovery.

One day, Emerson looked up at Magdalena and tried to smile. "I am so tired. I can't even sit up; I am just so tired." Magdalena had expected Emerson to immediately ask about the children and demand to know if they had all been safely rescued. When Emerson's first words made no reference to the events on the beach in the Algarve, Magdalena realized that perhaps Emerson had no recollection of what had happened that night. Magdalena would ask Robert about it, but she thought Emerson might be suffering from something called "selective amnesia." Maybe it was for the best that Emerson had no memory of what she had gone through to save the children. Magdalena didn't know whether to hope for the amnesia to continue or to hope for Emerson to recover her memories.

Magdalena continued to wake Emerson to try to convince her to eat and to take her to the bathroom. She was drinking sips of water and orange juice so Robert had discontinued the IV. He was concerned that Emerson's burns would become infected, but Magdalena had been scrupulously conscientious about caring for the wounds with the healing ointments and creams that Robert had taught her how to use on Emerson's skin. Robert had researched the best and most recent remedies for treating burns, and he had somehow procured these medications.

Together Magdalena and Robert cut away the dead skin from the wounds and cleaned them thoroughly. Magdalena changed the bandages twice a day. She wondered when Emerson would ask her how she had sustained the burns on her legs. Emerson's breathing had returned to normal, and her body began to heal. Magdalena wanted Emerson to start eating again. It had been weeks since she had taken any solid food.

Emerson began to stay awake for longer and longer periods of time. Magdalena urged her to eat some of Benadina's delicious chicken broth which she knew Emerson loved.

Magdalena sat in her chair beside Emerson's bed until Emerson had finished eating the broth. The next day, Magdalena had Benadina add homemade dumplings to the broth. The next day chicken was added, and the day after that, vegetables appeared in the soup. Soon, Benadina was sending full plates of food to Emerson's room.

Magdalena insisted that Emerson get out of bed, sit in a chair, and eat her meals at a small table in the bedroom. Emerson gradually regained her strength and began to take walks around her room. She still had not asked about the night on the beach or anything about the orphans' project. Finally, one day she asked Magdalena about how she had received the burns on her legs.

"You don't remember what happened the night you were burned, do you? Do you remember anything about our last rescue of children from the beach in the Algarve?"

"Rescue of children? What children? I don't remember any children. Why were we rescuing children?"

Magdalena realized that Emerson's unusual situation-specific amnesia was far more serious than anyone had imagined. She needed to talk to Dr. Robert before she dared try to bring Emerson up to the present day and force her to remember. "You do know that the world is at war, don't you Emerson? Do you remember that the United States entered the war in December of 1941? It is now September of 1942. Do you remember any of this?"

"Of course I know we are at war. How long ago did I get burned? Is Portugal in the war now? How long have I been recovering from whatever caused these burns? How long have I been sleeping?"

"It has been a few weeks, but you have wiped from your memory everything that happened the night you were burned so badly. You don't seem to remember anything at all about how you were hurt." Magdalena could see that Emerson was suddenly quite tired, and Magdalena helped her get back into bed. Full recovery was going to take more time than they had thought it would take. Robert and the specialists had been so focused on Emerson's physical health that no one had paid much attention to what the impact of the night on the beach might have had on her memory and her mental state.

Robert came to visit Emerson every day and helped Magdalena with the bandages. At first he came and sat beside Emerson's bed, hoping she would open her eyes or begin to talk. Robert talked to her constantly while he sat beside her. Once she did begin to speak again, Robert kept the conversation about the current moment. Was Emerson drinking enough water? How was her appetite? Was she getting out of bed and walking? Did she think she might want to go out soon for a ride in the car?

Robert, too, was waiting for Emerson to make a reference to the orphans' project. He was at a loss about how to bring up the subject. He did not want to trigger a relapse into silence if the memory of the night on the beach was so traumatic that Emerson could not bear to remember it. Likewise, having made the decision to declare his love to Emerson, he was also afraid that the right moment for this admission would never present itself.

No more children could possibly come to Bacalhoa at this time. The Anjo was out of commission. Maybe they should discontinue the project completely? One evening Robert decided he would ask Emerson about Pierre. Maybe the memory of Pierre would trigger something for Emerson.

"Emerson, do you remember a little boy named Pierre who came to stay with you at Bacalhoa for several months. You and Pierre were very close, and you were terribly sad when he had to leave." At first Emerson's face looked blank, and

Robert thought she must have no memory at all of the little boy. "He was from France, and he'd been shot in the leg. He stayed here and slept in the chapel, just off your bedroom." Emerson's eyes suddenly opened wide. It was as if a door had opened in her mind. She was looking through the door and was surprised, even shocked, to see what lay on the other side. Tears streamed down her face, and she began to sob.

"My darling Pierre. I miss him so much. He took the place of my own baby that I lost. And then I sent Pierre away, too. How could I have done that? Why did I send him away?"

This was the first time Emerson had ever spoken aloud about the loss of her own child. Robert knew to tread carefully. "You sent Pierre to live with Rachel in America. She has adopted him as her own son. Pierre could not stay in Portugal. He didn't have any papers and could have been arrested and sent back to France. You have made it possible, with the blank visas that Peter left for you, for Pierre and many other children to be saved and find new lives in the United States."

Sobbing uncontrollably, something connected in Emerson's mind, and she reached her arms out toward Robert. She pulled him close to her and let him hold her as she cried. He sat on her bed and stroked her hair and rocked her back and forth as she clung to him. Emotions she had kept at bay for so long had finally overwhelmed her defenses. Robert knew that her grief and this emotional release were for many things that she had never been able to express before. She was weeping for the loss of her husband Peter, for the death of her unborn baby girl who had died at six months gestation, and for having loved and then having given up Pierre.

Some of her grief might even have been for the shocking loss of both of her parents on the same night in a car accident when she was a nineteen-year-old college student. She had suffered so many losses, and she had never really acknowledged how much these tragedies had taken from her. She had been strong and had tried hard to be brave and absorb all these deaths without allowing herself to fully accept them.

Robert knew she needed to go through this painful catharsis. He hoped that she would come out whole on the other side of it. He hoped that when she finally confronted and then let go of the past, she would realize that she had a future, a life to live, in front of her. He hoped against hope that she would see him through a somewhat different lens, not as clouded by the burdens of the past that she had heartbreakingly carried for so long. He kissed her gently. "I love you, Emerson. You must know that. I will always be by your side no matter what happens." He didn't know if she had heard what he'd said, but he hoped she'd understood him at some level and believed him. He was glad he had finally told her how he felt. He lay her head down on her pillow and kissed her again. He put his hand on her cheek and pulled the sheet up around her shoulders. He left her to whatever dreams and demons she might find in her fitful sleep.

Emerson almost slept the clock around after regaining her memory with its accompanying emotional release. It had been exhausting for her to confront so many things from her past after having kept them bottled up inside for such a long time. Gradually, she began to remember the children and the organization she and her friends had created to save them. Then she started to remember bits and pieces of the night she had rescued so many children and how she had sustained her burns. Magdalena and Robert helped her through the process of remembering. Robert again called in his psychiatrist friend Dr. Benjamin Meyer, who met with Emerson for several hours every week.

One day in October, Robert arrived at Bacalhoa, just as one of Emerson's sessions with Dr. Meyer was ending, and

Robert heard her laughing out loud. It had been months, years even, since he had heard her laugh like that. The wonderful sound thrilled him to the core of his being. Emerson came out of her room to greet Robert with a big smile on her face. She put her arms around him and held him for a few seconds. She had never hugged him quite like this before, in such a warm and spontaneous way. Robert looked questioningly at Dr. Meyer over Emerson's tousled head. "She is ever so much stronger. She has been telling me about the orphans' project and how she can't wait to get back to it," Meyer was pleased to report.

Robert had told Dr. Meyer that Emerson was doing work for the resistance but had not been specific. He'd told the psychiatrist that her burns and her amnesia were the results of a boating accident and water rescue that had happened in the Algarve. It had been difficult for Emerson to accept that she had been such a hero and had saved so many children's lives. She had tried to minimize her heroic feats from that night. Dr. Meyer had told her she must face what she had done to be able to fully acknowledge who she really was. Emerson was gradually able to realize and accept what that night had meant for her.

"Have you been able to talk to Dr. Meyer about what you remember from the night you saved so many lives?" Robert wanted to press her to talk about what an extraordinary thing she had done.

Emerson looked down at her feet, as if she were almost ashamed or embarrassed. "I don't think I did anything anybody else would not have done — given the circumstances. I am just so thrilled that we saved them all, that no one died."

"You saved them all Emerson. It was *your* doing. *You* were the one who dove again and again into the ocean to save the drowning children. *You* were the one who swam into the wreck of a burning ship to rescue a woman, an infant, and two toddlers. It was not a 'we.' It was all *you*." Robert was anxious that she honestly accept her own bravery.

Emerson changed the subject and said she had invited Dr. Meyer to stay for dinner, but he had refused. "I guess it's going to be just the two of us tonight, Robert. I want to eat outside on the loggia. I have asked Benadina and Magdalena to set the table there for us." Emerson's eyes were shining with enthusiasm, almost with excitement, even joy. Robert remembered the last time he had seen that look in her eyes. It had been at Emerson and Peter's Christmas party so many years ago. He never expected to see that light in her eyes again, and here it was. He wondered selfishly if any of her happiness was because of him. A man could hope.

Dr. Meyer and Robert had a drink in the lounge while Emerson dressed for dinner. Her hair had grown out after it had been burned in the boat rescue. Emerson appeared in a navy-blue, silk dress that hugged her body like a glove. It had a low-cut neckline, and her long pearls fell into the bodice of the dress. She was dressed in a way Robert had hardly ever seen before — in all the years they had been having dinner together. She carried herself differently, with more confidence and maturity. They said their goodbyes to Dr. Meyer, and he gave Robert a special nod of his head as he went out the door.

During dinner on the loggia, Emerson and Robert laughed and talked like the good friends they were. The candles shimmered, and Emerson's face glowed with health and happiness in the light. Robert was so thankful to have Emerson well again. He decided that even if their relationship never progressed beyond their current friendship, it would be enough for him. To have Emerson restored to herself was more than enough, more than an answer to his prayers.

Emerson knew she looked attractive that night. She knew that Robert loved her and that he had loved her for a very long time. She knew that she had not been able to move beyond her own grief from the past to appreciate Robert for the extraordinary man he was. He had been Emerson's own physician and the physician who had cared for her dying husband. He had been her comforter. He had supported completely and with his whole heart her project to save the lives of the Jewish orphans. He had always been there for her. She might have taken him for granted. Finally, she saw herself so much more clearly and was able to acknowledge and move beyond the tragedies of her own life.

She had always known what a fine human being he was — how generous and caring he had always been, how dedicated he was to his profession, and how fiercely devoted he was to his country. She knew without a doubt that Robert Carmichael would do the right thing, under any and all circumstances. She had always admired so many things about him. She knew that he was brave and strong.

What was different now was that she also saw him as the very handsome and appealing male that he had always been. He was only a few years older than she was. He had lost his wife; she had lost Peter. Emerson knew that for too long she had retreated into her own sadness and had not thought she would have a future life that included happiness, let alone ever loving someone again.

She realized as she looked at Robert with fresh eyes and a heart not overwhelmed with sorrow, that she loved this man. She liked him and respected him and always had loved him as a dear friend. She was beginning to realize that she also loved him as an attractive man who had fallen in love with her. She had not wanted and had not believed it was possible that she would ever have another lover after Peter died.

She now realized that Robert was a man worth loving with her whole heart. He was a complete gentleman and would defer to her to make the first move. She could see in his eyes as well as sense his desire as he looked at her in the candlelight that evening. She decided it was time to tell him how she felt about him. This beautiful, wonderful, loving man had waited long enough to hear from her.

Emerson reached for Robert's hand and raised it to her lips. She kissed it gently and began to tell him what was in her heart. She leaned against his shoulder and put her arms around him and pulled him close to her. She left no question in his mind exactly what she hoped their future together would be like. She told him she loved him. She gently wiped away the tears that formed at the corners of his eyes when she declared her love. She knew she could do anything with Robert at her side. She knew that she would always be brave and independent and that she feared no evil. She was completely confident in herself, but she also knew that her life would be richer and a lot more fun with this good man's love surrounding her.

Chapter 36

PREPARING THE TABLE

November 1942

When *Emerson got the call from the United States* Embassy in Lisbon, she was worried. She was afraid the reason someone from the embassy was calling her had to do with the blank visa forms she had in her possession, the forms that Peter had left her. These precious pieces of paper had been the starting point, the sine qua non, of the project to save the orphans and give them lives in the United States. Emerson did not worry about whether or not she would be in trouble for how she had used the visa forms. She had come to terms with the consequences of that decision long ago, even before the orphans' project had become a fully formed idea in her mind.

Thankfully, the call from the embassy had nothing to do with the visas. The man who was calling made a brief, polite reference to Peter and what an extraordinary human being and American patriot he had been. Emerson felt a sharp pang of grief. She momentarily lapsed back in time as she recalled the memories of her life with Peter. It had been so sweet. It had been so brief. It had been such a long time ago.

"Mrs. Mullens, we have a somewhat unusual favor to ask of you. We hope you will not consider it presumptuous of us to ask, and of course we understand if you want to decline our request. But, above all, our hope is that you will choose to agree, not to turn us down."

Emerson was thinking to herself, am I really Mrs. Mullens? No one has called me that in so many years; I had forgotten that is who I am. She was frustrated with the man on the phone and wondered what was with these diplomatic types and their beating around the bush? Why don't they just spit it out? Emerson remembered Peter had always told her that her directness was one of the things he loved about her. She got right to the point and didn't talk around a subject before saying what was on her mind. Peter had confided in her that his work with diplomats, the prescribed way they conducted business, and their "diplospeak" sometimes drove him crazy. Apparently Americans were better about this than diplomats of other cultures, but it had always put Peter's teeth on edge when people wouldn't say what they meant.

"Your indulgence and hospitality could be instrumental in the war effort to which we as American are of course completely committed. I am sure that you are willing to do whatever you can to help defeat our enemies and to be sure that democracy prevails in the world."

Emerson was now gritting her teeth and wondering if this guy would ever get to the point. "Of course, I am willing and eager to do whatever I can to help the Allies win the war. In what way can my indulgence and hospitality aid the cause of democracy?" Emerson hoped the fact that they were talking over the telephone would keep the irony, maybe even the sarcasm, in her voice from being too obvious to the man on the other end of the line.

Now he was fawning. "I knew that you would be willing to help us. Some of the people at the embassy feel they dropped the ball after Peter died and didn't adequately reach out to you in your grief. Some people thought you would hold that against us and would not want anything to do with the embassy."

Now she was becoming disgusted with this fellow on the telephone. She remembered this type was one reason she hadn't been fond of attending embassy events with Peter. "Don't be silly. Peter's life was devoted to his diplomatic service. He loved his country beyond reason. I am anxious to do whatever I can to help out, although I can't imagine what in the world I could ever do that would be useful to the embassy."

"That is exactly what I was hoping you would say, and I assured the ambassador that you would respond exactly as you have done. Can I speak to you directly and confidentially?"

Emerson was thinking to herself, oh, yes, please, please speak to me directly! "Please, I appreciate directness, and of course, I consider that anything you say to me will be kept in confidence. Now, please, tell me what you'd like for me to do."

"The embassy needs Bacalhoa. I mean, we need to use Bacalhoa for a week or so — for a meeting, an extremely important meeting. We need your home to hold this critical meeting, a meeting that could lead to a turning point in the war. We want to gather together a number of exceptionally high profile military and civilian war planners. They need a place to talk to each other with complete confidentiality, but they cannot be seen talking to each other — seen publicly, that is. This meeting has to be conducted with the utmost secrecy and security. We need a location that is close to Lisbon, but not in Lisbon. Bacalhoa is the perfect place for our meeting. We know this event will be an imposition on you and an inconvenience for you. But your country would be eternally grateful if you would take it upon yourself to agree to let us use your estate to help us win the war."

Emerson laughed. She didn't know what she was imagining the man from the embassy would ask her to do, but this seemed like such an easy thing. "Of course, I am happy to lend Bacalhoa to the Allied cause — for however long you need to use it. I am delighted to have my home participate in the war effort. Peter would have been thrilled that his beloved Bacalhoa would be called upon to be a soldier in the fight. Just tell me what you need for me to do. I am at your service and the service of my country."

"The ambassador will be delighted to hear that you are on board. We have already begun our plans to get all of these important people together, which is not an easy job in the first place. But we were stymied as to where we could possibly house the participants and hold our meetings. We can't have them meeting together any place in Lisbon, but we also don't want them to have to travel long distances all over Portugal. It would be very dangerous if anyone, especially the Germans, found out that even one of these individuals is in Portugal. There is great risk to each of these people who will be attending the conference. There is danger in the travel that is involved as well as in the fact that they will all be gathered together in one location. But they have to be gathered in one location to plan and talk and make decisions. I am saying too much. We have to take this chance. Portugal is the only possible place in Europe that this important meeting can take place. Great Britain and Switzerland were the only other possibilities, but they are really not appropriate for these circumstances. Holding the meeting in a neutral country is ever so much better. Switzerland is neutral, but it is full of Nazis. Well, I guess Lisbon is full of Nazis, too, but Setubal isn't.

It will be an extraordinarily complex assembly. We are very grateful, Mrs. Mullens."

"As I've said, I am happy to have Bacalhoa join in the war effort. Whatever we can do and I can do, you only have to ask. I will offer my home, my staff, and myself completely, to help make your meeting a success. Just let me know what you need and when you need it."

"We will have a liaison team out to speak with you tomorrow, if that is all right with you. I know this is short notice, but a window of opportunity has opened up for us to be able to get these people together. That window is coming up week after next. We need to finalize the arrangements so that our special guests can get on with their meeting. I will be back in touch with you about exactly what time our representative will be out to Setubal to meet with you tomorrow. Again, we are so grateful for your generosity."

"I am free all day and look forward to meeting with your liaison team."

Emerson was intrigued and excited. She wondered who the "important people" were who would be meeting to make plans for the war — at her home. She was delighted to offer Bacalhoa as a place for this significant and secret conference. She would turn Bacalhoa over entirely to the conference and move into the secluded orphans' hideout. She wondered if the embassy would use Bacalhoa's own staff or if they would be bringing their own. She sincerely hoped that the liaison people the embassy was sending to talk to her would be more direct than the person with whom she had just spoken on the telephone. She had already forgotten his name.

The liaison team from the embassy was composed of two people, a no-nonsense organizer and his secretary. Thank goodness, from Emerson's point of view, these two knew how to get to the point. They knew what had to be done to get ready for the up-coming meeting, and they got right to it. Preparations had to be made in a hurry, and this no doubt was a motivating factor in their decision to "cut to the chase."

They all agreed that Emerson's staff would remain in place and additional help would be brought in to assist. There would be a great deal of extra meal preparation, security details, laundry, and a myriad of other things that would have to be provided for the attendees. Emerson's staff would be in charge, but additional people would be needed so that the week-long meeting would not be too much of a burden on those who took care of Bacalhoa. Emerson appreciated the acknowledgement that the up-coming conference would be a lot of work and that Bacalhoa's staff would not be expected to carry all of the responsibility.

Magdalena and Benadina were both known to the embassy and had already been fully vetted. To provide additional security, the participants who attended the meeting would not use their real names. They would all have code names and would use these names during the entire week. This seemed excessive to Emerson, but apparently it was a tried and true way of keeping a snoopy cleaning person or a talkative gardener from leaking important information, even by accident.

Emerson asked if she could confide in her close friend Dr. Robert Carmichael about the meeting. The embassy liaison organizer laughed and said that of course she could. Robert Carmichael was already an integral part of the meeting plans. The British Embassy had prevailed on Robert to house several of the meeting's participants. A few of them would be British nationals after all, and Robert's villa was next door to and within walking distance of Bacalhoa. Robert and Emerson would be conspiring in yet another secret mission.

Magdalena and Benadina were briefed, and they were also excited to be participating in doing something positive for the war effort. Emerson, Magdalena, and Benadina would all put their best foot forward for the sake of Bacalhoa. They wanted to make sure that everything was comfortable and first rate for their important guests. They spent a lot of time discussing menus and meals. Benadina was happier than Emerson had ever seen her. She loved to cook for a crowd. Afternoon tea would be offered every day. A variety of wines and spirits would be available. They pulled it all together quickly. Emerson was once again thankful that her farm, with its plentiful vegetables and livestock, would allow her to provide a more lavish spread for the meeting than might otherwise have been possible, especially considering the rationing that was now the norm throughout Europe. Scarcities were beginning to appear even in Portugal.

The week of the conference, its participants arrived in various disguises and means of conveyance and on different days. There was no grand procession to the front door. There was no parade of limousines making its way up the driveway of the quinta to discharge distinguished visitors. All arrived discreetly, and if anyone had been watching Bacalhoa, they would never have noticed that anything out of the ordinary was happening. Two participants arrived in a bakery truck with a delivery of pastries. They brought trays of croissants and cakes into the kitchen and remained at Bacalhoa. The driver of the bakery truck drove away. Two more members of the group, dressed as bohemian students, walked from the train station and entered Bacalhoa's grounds through the garden gate at the rear of the property. Pretending to be patients, a man, accompanied by a woman with her arm in a sling, entered Robert's house. The participants' luggage was delivered after dark.

The embassy might be really bad at getting to the point when you were speaking with them over the telephone, but Emerson had to admit they were quite good at moving people around in surreptitious ways. There were four women in the group. Everyone used his or her "code name" identity adopted for the conference only. No one wore a uniform, and everyone dressed in casual clothes. It was obvious which people were military from their posture and the way they walked. Emerson wondered about the women. She overheard two of them talking about the Red Cross and refugees.

A large conference table and twenty chairs, brought in by the embassy, had been set up at one end of the lounge. Embassy people moved the furniture around to make room for the table. The lounge was where the main discussions of the week would occur. Pens and tablets and pitchers and glasses for water were on the table. All the chairs for the dining room were brought in, and the dining table was full at every meal.

Benadina was in her glory with two sous chefs. She loved to show off her culinary skills. Her tea sandwiches, cookies, and scones had become legend by the second day of the meeting, and she was basking in the praise. Magdalena was working too hard, and Emerson offered to help with some of her duties. Magdalena wanted it all to be perfect. She was proud of Bacalhoa and wanted to be sure the conference attendees remembered their visit with fondness. Bacalhoa's reputation was important to Magdalena.

Several of the attendees were staying at Robert's home, and Emerson and Robert were invited to join some of the evening meals and an occasional tea. Most of the meals were working lunches and working dinners, and these were for the attendees only. But the planners had imposed upon themselves a rule that during certain meals and on certain evenings, there were not to be any discussions about the matters under consideration at the conference. It was all right to discuss the war in general, music, art, history, literature, or any other subjects. Whatever "matters of utmost importance" these people were planning, it was decided they needed a break from their intense discussions. Forcing their minds to think about other things was intended to refresh their "little grey cells."

Emerson loved the dinners with these people she assumed were influential leaders in their non-conference lives. A few of them looked familiar to Emerson, and she thought she had seen some of their photos in the newspapers. The participants thanked Emerson individually, and on their last night at a special dinner, they stood and gave short speeches of thanks to Emerson and Robert and the staff.

Many months later Emerson realized what had been taking place at Bacalhoa. Peter would have been so proud that the home he had loved so much had been able to play a role in helping win the war. One speech in particular that was made the last night stuck in Emerson's mind. The military man who seemed to be the chairman of the group spoke specifically to Emerson and Robert as well as to Magdalena and Benadina. He raved about the food and said they could never have reached the consensus they had achieved without the excellent food and wines. Benadina blushed and beamed.

The group all had come to love Bacalhoa, and it had been the perfect place for their work. They particularly mentioned Magdalena who had so masterfully managed every detail of the complicated logistics and at the same time had made it all seem effortless. The chairman said they could all take a page from her book about how to run an operation. Because of her extraordinary skills in managing the conference, they had decided to give her an honorary "code name." The chairman explained how the group had labored over what code name to bestow upon the exceptional Magdalena. They had rejected the titles of boss and house manager as too mundane and ordinary. In deference to the fact that she was the force behind making what had at one time been a royal palace run so smoothly, they decided that she should be referred to as the "Overlady In Charge of Operations."

This drew huge laughter and much applause from the conference participants. Emerson and Robert looked at each other and were somewhat puzzled. At the time, they felt as if they were missing part of the joke. In the late spring of 1944, they would finally understand that Magdalena's code name was a very clever play on words. The guests at the quinta had given them a hint on that November night about what they had been planning during their week at Bacalhoa. When they had named Magdalena "Overlady," the great organizer of operations at the quinta, they had hinted at the codename for D-Day — "Operation Overlord."

Chapter 37

GOODNESS AND MERCY

December 1942

Emerson and Robert discovered that their orphans' project operation could handle, with some alterations to the hideout, twice as many orphans as they had originally thought they could accept and send on to America. The serendipitous arrival of the "double" group of children the night that Emerson had saved so many lives and was so badly hurt had made them realize they could do it. They'd expanded the hideout by converting the existing garage area into a second bunk room and an additional bathroom. They even were able to find an additional hot water heater. They built a new, larger garage addition onto the back of the hideout.

Robert had found someone to repair the bullet holes that had riddled the exterior of their pick-up truck. The truck had been painted a different dark color as a precautionary measure, and it still looked decrepit. Robert preferred to drive it only after dark — just in case. They acquired another old vehicle which looked terrible, but after Robert had worked on its engine for several weeks, it ran beautifully. It appeared to be wonderfully disreputable on the outside, like it was well past the end of its years of service.

They bought an additional launch, at great expense and under circumstances that strained the parameters of legality. They kept the boathouse locked at all times now that it held two sizeable boats. The transfer of the orphans to the *Anjo* could be completed in one trip using both launches. Having two launches made delivery of the children to the *Anjo* safer because they no longer had to make two trips from the boathouse. There was no need to send the launch back for a second load of children. It was a busy and chaotic time when they had a full house, but as long as Rachel continued to find homes for the children in the United States, the *Anjo* would continue to make trips across the Atlantic.

The *Anjo* had been repaired. Max and his men returned from their special assignment transporting uranium ore from Africa to the United States. As soon as they had completed that mission, Max hurried to be with Annalise. He told her he wanted to marry her and wondered out loud if he was insane to be so presumptuous. Given the war and the uncertainty of his occupation as a sailor, he told Annalise he did not feel as if he should be asking her to sign on for the kind of life he had to offer. Annalise told him that it was precisely because of all these same reasons, she could never refuse his proposal. She said that the war and the life Max lived at sea made him even more precious to her. She pointed out that many people these days were seizing whatever brief moments of happiness they could find. Annalise told him that even if they only had a few days or weeks to be together, their love was worth it.

She told him she was expecting their child. Max cried when he heard this news. He had written off so many things that he had never imagined his life would allow him to have. He had never wanted to take the risk of allowing himself to love a woman, and then Annalise had come into his life. He had never wanted to take the risk of having a family and becoming attached to a child, and now Annalise had told him that he was going to be a father. Yes, Naomi knew about the pregnancy, and she wanted Annalise to stay in Baltimore with her until after the baby was born. She knew the chairman of the Department of Obstetrics at Johns Hopkins Hospital.

Max and Annalise were married in Naomi's garden. The October afternoon was warm, and the crew of the *Anjo* were all there. Rachel came from Boston and brought Pierre with her. They heard first-hand from Annalise and Max about their much-loved and brave friend Emerson. Naomi provided a wonderful wedding feast with champagne to toast the couple. Everyone was happy that night and held on to the joy of the celebration. That was what one did during wartime. Chances for happiness were rare and fleeting and all the more cherished because of that. There were still years of war left to endure, but these brave civilian soldiers had learned that they could find occasional moments of light in the darkness.

One night in early December, Emerson and Robert had just finished loading the children into the launches which were moving slowly and quietly out of the boathouse into the cove. It was warm for December. On this partly cloudy night, the moon was brighter than they would have liked for it to be. The schedule was such that the transfer of the children to the *Anjo* had to be made at this particular time. Clouds were moving back and forth across the moon, and the clouds would give the launches brief moments of cover as they made their way from the boathouse. There was silence except for the low hum of the engines and the sound of the waves slapping against the sides of the boats. The first launch was in the cove on its way to the *Anjo*. The second launch was about to leave the boathouse. They heard a noise from the road; a car was coming. The launches turned off their engines and were silent.

A large Mercedes, the kind that high-level German officers in Portugal liked to drive, was passing by the boathouse on the road. Hardly anyone ever drove on this road, so it was an unusual as well as an unwelcome thing to happen. The Mercedes slowed when it came in sight of the boats which were just heading out into the cove. As the clouds cleared the moon, the entire scene was bathed in bright moonlight — for all the world to see.

Robert was just about to jump into the second departing launch when he saw the man who was sitting in the driver's seat of the large Mercedes. He thought the man looked familiar. The German officer got out of his car and walked towards the water to have a closer look at what was going on here in the middle of the night, south of Setubal. There could be no question in anybody's mind exactly what was happening. Children were being smuggled out of the country by boat. Robert's throat constricted. Then he realized he recognized the German officer who was standing beside the water. Robert was certain it was the German Wehrmacht officer whose life he had saved and whose arm he had repaired after a bad traffic accident. This was Colonel Stefan Weber.

Robert took a chance and waved at the German in the uniform. The officer was tall and erect and wore his military regalia with distinction. He walked with a slight limp, and his gun was entirely visible in the holster at his side. Colonel Weber watched with great interest what was so obviously unfolding before him. He stood very still for a while and took in every detail of what he saw. He seemed to recognize Robert when he waved to him. Emerson was in the first launch, bobbing in the waters of the cove. Robert stood next to the second launch, filled with small children wearing life vests. The children held their breaths and wondered what would happen next. There was a gun. Someone could be shot. One of the children could be hurt. This German soldier could report them to the Gestapo. This German officer could be the Gestapo. Any number of bad things were possible.

Finally, the German officer gave a casual tip of his military cap in Emerson's direction. He spoke in his accented English — loud enough for them all to hear him, "It's a fine night for a drive and a fine night for a sail as well, I see. Have a safe journey. God's speed, Doctor." Colonel Stephan Weber gave a small bow in Robert's direction. He climbed back into his car, waved his hand, and drove away.

They all began to breathe again. Robert knew Emerson was completely puzzled by what had just happened. He told her he would explain later about the Wehrmacht officer. Twenty-seven children were successfully transferred to the *Anjo* that night, and they made their way to America as planned.

Robert later told Emerson the story of how he had saved the life of Colonel Stefan Weber. Robert shared with Emerson his belief that, even in the midst of catastrophic and overwhelming evil in the world, there could be moments of forgiveness and redemption. He believed that, even in the presence of one's enemies, it was possible for one's cup to runneth over.

Emerson and Robert both believed that, in spite of everything, they were the lucky ones. They were totally committed to their mission to save lives. They were thankful they had been born at a time in history when they could make a difference. They were doing all they could to fight the evil that had engulfed the world. They had each other, and they had courage. They could do anything.

AUTHOR'S NOTE

Once in a while, fortune really smiles and delivers a wonderful surprise in the form of an experience which surpasses even your highest expectations. Such good fortune came into my life when I decided to travel to Portugal in 1998 and made the acquaintance of the fabulous, intriguing, and incredibly beautiful Quinta Palacio da Bacalhoa near Setubal. This chance of a lifetime came to me when a friend invited me to participate in a fund-raising auction that was being held at the Washington, D.C. school where she was a teacher. A parent was donating a week at a "really wonderful place" in Portugal. Four couples had already committed. The quinta slept ten, so, if my husband and I were on board, we could get our bid together and try to win the vacation week. I'd never been to Portugal.

My father had died the previous year, and I'd moved my mother to an assisted living facility near my home in Maryland. I was cleaning out my parents' house in Columbus, Ohio and had made many road trips to Columbus to sort through, pack up, and deal with a lifetime's worth of my parents' household belongings. Repairs, painting, and staging were required to get their house ready to put on the market. I had made so many difficult decisions about so many things during the past year, the decision to go in with a group of friends for a trip to Portugal was an easy one. I wanted to do something fun.

My husband decided he didn't want to participate in bidding on a vacation in Portugal. I could afford to do it on my own, so I decided I would. We won the week in Portugal. As I talked more and more about the place where we would be staying, my husband couldn't stand to miss out and decided he wanted to go along. He had never been to Spain and wanted to combine the week in Portugal with an additional week in Spain. We planned our Iberian holiday.

We drove out of Madrid and visited Toledo, Seville, Granada, and The Alhambra in Spain on our way to Portugal. It was March, and in spite of the delightful weather, I became ill with bronchitis. Some of that drive was hazy. We kept our eyes open for windmills. When we reached the Algarve, we were shocked to find that the Mediterranean beaches were packed in March. Following our maps, we found Setubal and drove up the driveway to what we thought was our Quinta da Bacalhoa. We weren't certain we were in the right place. It really was a palacio, and it was quite large. Thinking we had happened on a hotel of the same name, we waited in the car until we saw someone we recognized. Our friends had been out sightseeing all day, but when they drove into the courtyard in the late afternoon, we knew we had arrived at Bacalhoa. They said they had expected us the day before. We had been assigned the bedroom with the chapel. I still was not feeling well and thought I might go straight to bed without dinner. But the wonderful food prepared by Bacalhoa's cook convinced me not to skip any meals.

As impressive as Bacalhoa was from the outside, discovering its many layers, as we did over the course of our visit there, proved to be an unforgettably rich experience in several unexpected ways. The architecture and the history of its ownership during more than four centuries was fascinating to the architect, the art historian, and the historian in me. The gardens and the vineyards and the food we enjoyed endeared the cook in me forever to the palacio and to Portugal. Two evenings of Fado performed and sung by one of the staff touched everyone who loved music or who had ever suffered a loss. The warmth of the staff and the hospitality they extended to us were extraordinary.

As we learned about the massive restoration Bacalhoa had undergone under the capable and tireless hands of Orlena Scoville, the grandmother of the current owner, her story inspired the artist and creator in every one of us. This decades-long, meticulous, labor of love explained the heart and soul of Bacalhoa, and I understood why this brick and stone artifact of history was so full of life and fun and good feeling. I was in love.

As we explored Bacalhoa and Portugal, the faces of the beauty, the faces of the art and the extraordinary craftsmanship, and the faces of the culture revealed themselves. When I stood in front of a spectacular tile fresco at one of Bacalhoa's entrances, I said aloud to myself, "I will never, as long as I live, be as close to a work of art as beautiful as the one I am looking at right at this moment. I can even touch it." Fortune had indeed smiled on me when I decided to visit Portugal and Bacalhoa.

I knew, when my train left Lisbon at the end of the week, that Bacalhoa would be the main character in a book I would write one day. We'd read the guest book the Scovilles kept over the years in which visitors to Bacalhoa had listed their names and addresses and written remarks about their visits to this magical place. I was especially interested in the names I'd read of those who had visited during World War II.

I knew that Portugal had been a nominally neutral country during that war. I realized that travel visas to Lisbon had been scarce during those days. *Casablanca* had been my favorite movie for many years, and I knew how dear were the "letters of transit" which Humphrey Bogart's Rick had been willing to give up to his rival in love for the heart of Ilsa, Ingrid Bergman.

I recognized some of the famous names who had signed the guest book during World War II, and my imagination went wild plotting intrigue and the meeting of generals and the planning of D-Day and what all must have happened in this home during those years of war. I knew the book I would write about Bacalhoa would be set during the time of World War II. The heroine of the story would have to be brave, adventurous, strong, smart, and dedicated and exemplify all the virtues that I knew had to have been present in the personality and character of Orlena Scoville who had rescued Bacalhoa from the ruins of history. I knew that the story I would write would be about rescue and trying to save what might otherwise be lost.

I was so inspired that I began writing that story on the plane as I flew back to the United States. I wrote a few paragraphs in a notebook and sadly lost the notebook somewhere on the plane that day. My real life took over. My daughters got married; my mother died; my grandchildren were born; and I moved. All the other things that take precedence over creativity overwhelmed me and took priority. I put writing lower on my long-range to-do list. My precious canine pal, Piper, the perfect West Highland White Terrier and soulmate of seventeen years, died. I experienced several very serious health events. I attended my fiftieth high school reunion. I realized that if I ever intended to write anything, it was time to get on with it.

In 2014, I wrote *Traveling Through the Valley of the Shadow of Death*, a book about my mother's trip to Germany in the summer of 1938. I became so fond of some of the fictional characters I'd created, I did not want to let them go. While doing research for the book about my mother's trip, I'd read extensively about the Spanish Civil War, Guernica, and the Holocaust. Memories of my trip to Portugal came back to me, and I knew it was time to write my story of love and loss and beauty and war and rescue and Bacalhoa.

AUTHOR'S NOTE

Orlena Scoville bought Bacalhoa in 1936. She wrote a wonderful article, "Foreign Gardens: A Palace in Portugal," by Mrs. Herbert Scoville, published in the <u>Bulletin of the Garden Club of America</u>, September 1937, in which she describes her first visit to Bacalhoa and her impressions of this special place she would later be lucky enough to call her home. Orlena writes beautifully and lovingly about Bacalhoa, and I highly recommend that you access and read her excellent article which is available on the internet. This article is a must if you want to know more about Quinta Palacio da Bacalhoa. Orlena spent the rest of her life rehabilitating and caring for her treasured quinta.

When we visited, the staff was full of stories about the lengths to which Orlena would go in order to locate the historically correct tile to replace a missing one or to patch a broken one. She would travel all over Portugal to find the perfect tile. Her dedication was extraordinary. She had known a great deal about tiles even before Bacalhoa became her home, and she learned everything there was to know about Portuguese tile during her meticulous restoration.

A red leather book of "before and after" photos was made available to us when we visited, and now this book is available to everyone on the internet. If you have any interest in architecture, art, history, archaeology, or life, please look at these pictures. When you see the "before" pictures, you will understand what a prodigious task Orlena undertook and what a magnificently orchestrated result she achieved with her brilliance and hard work. It took decades to restore Bacalhoa to the condition in which we found it in 1998.

We begged to be able to return to Bacalhoa in 1999 and bring our children, but the Scoville Family had sold the estate after our visit in 1998. I feel so privileged that I had the chance to visit and be a guest at Bacalhoa. I hope the story I tell about this historic palace and beloved home will honor it and express some of the affection I feel for the old building, for the time I spent there, and for the woman I never met but in some way feel that I know, Orlena Scoville.

For the purposes of my plot and my characters, I have set my story in the Bacalhoa I visited. In 1938, when my fictional characters buy and move into Bacalhoa, Orlena's restoration in the real world and in real time would have been in its very early stages. It would have looked nothing like the stunning and well-appointed place it had become by 1998. Sixty years of restoration work is quite a leap to make, and I hope the reader and Orlena will forgive me for taking the luxurious and completed Bacalhoa I visited in 1998 and allowing it to exist in the 1938 world of *I Will Fear No Evil*.

When I think of Orlena living at Bacalhoa in the years just before the beginning of World War II and during the years of the war, I greatly admire her courage. In 1936, the brutal Spanish Civil War was raging in neighboring Spain. Portugal shares its only land borders with Spain. During the Spanish Civil War, safely traveling to and from Portugal was possible only by air or by water. Living as an ex-patriot in Portugal during World War II, before the United States entered the war and even more so after Pearl Harbor, had to be a challenge. Because of German U-boats, it would have been extremely risky to cross the Atlantic Ocean by ship between October 1939 and May 1945.

My characters and the staff who live and work at Bacalhoa in the story are made up entirely from my own imagination. Likewise the other characters who live in Portugal and England during the years in which *I Will Fear No Evil* takes place are fictional — with some exceptions.

Katherine Stuart-Ramsey (Kitty), the Duchess of Atholl, was a very real person and was one of several driving forces who worked against the odds to bring the displaced Basque children to England. I have used her name and a little that I know about her efforts in the "Beret Project." She was an amazing woman and one whose determination to do good we all must admire and strive to emulate. I have made up thoughts, words, and deeds about this woman, and I hope I have done her even a fraction of the justice she deserves.

The children of Guernica are also very real. Their tragedy is known through Picasso's conscience-shattering work *Guernica*. The story of the Basque people and their suffering during the brutal days of the Spanish Civil War and subsequently for many years under the reign of Spain's fascist ruler Generalissimo Francisco Franco, has largely been ignored by the world.

Edith Pye, Leah Manning, M. Edgar Sengier, Antonio Salazar, and Colonel Ken Nichols are all real people who existed in the past. The roles they play in my story may or may not be historically accurate. I have brought them into the narrative to add historical context. However, any thought, word, or deed I have attributed to these people in *I Will Fear No Evil* is entirely fictional. Any and all attributions made to these people are completely made up by me and are strictly figments of my imagination. All other characters are fictional and have never existed in real life. Any resemblance they have to anyone living or dead is purely coincidental.

I have used a number of real historical events in my story. The Spanish Civil War, the destruction of Guernica, and the Beret Project were all real historical events. The *SS St. Louis* and the *SS Quanza* were real ships which carried refugees to the Western Hemisphere. The discovery of uranium in Shikolobwe and its transport to and storage in the United States are true events. The ultra-rich uranium ore made possible the production of the Hiroshima atomic bomb. Tungsten, aka Wolfram, was an important resource in the manufacture of extra-strength steel during World War II. I have tried to weave actual historical events and a few real people into my story which is primarily a work of fiction with fictional characters. This mingling of truth and fiction is not meant to deceive but to create a more interesting storyline with some historical touchstones.

I hope that reading my story which is set primarily at Bacalhoa will endear this amazing place to you. The Quinta da Bacalhoa is the inspiration for the setting of the story. My "underground railroad" for orphaned Jewish children is entirely fictional and not based on any known fact. However, I have a wish that perhaps, unknown to everyone except those who accomplished these good deeds, networks of this kind might really have existed and operated to save a few from the Nazi ovens.

There have always been people in the world who do not fear evil and who engage in acts of great courage, in spite of the potential dangers to themselves. Through my characters in *I Will Fear No Evil*, I have tried to imagine and bring to literary life some of these brave heroes.

ACKNOWLEDGMENTS

My first thanks always goes to my readers: Jane Corcoran, Peggy Baker, Robert Taylor, and Nancy Calland Hart. Nancy Hart and my husband Robert Taylor also edited and proofread *I WILL FEAR NO EVIL*. I am indebted to their sharp eyes and critical scrutiny.

I am beholden to Martha and Edward Jenkins, from beginning to end. Their connections to the Scoville Family made possible the trip to Portugal that inspired this novel. Their photographs from that 1998 trip form the basis for the covers of the book. They were kind enough to share their photos with me and give me permission to use them for *I WILL FEAR NO EVIL*. I am forever grateful to Martha and Ed for the chance to spend a week at Bacalhoa and for their generosity in making these photographs available to me.

Andrea Burns, my brilliant photographer, prepared the photographs so they could be used as the covers.

Jamie Tipton of Open Heart Designs used the Jenkins/Burns photos to create the amazing covers for this book. Jamie also formats the interiors of the hardcover, the paperback, and the ebook. She does everything that is necessary to turn my manuscript into a printed book. She also holds my hand. I could not possibly produce a book without her professional and patient expertise.

I am very grateful to all those who contributed their help to make *I WILL FEAR NO EVIL* a reality.

The first question Elizabeth Burke, M.D. always asked me when I saw her in her office was: "What's new and exciting in your life?" I promised myself that one day I would have a good answer for her. Thank you, Dr. Burke.

ABOUT THE AUTHOR

MARGARET TURNER TAYLOR *lives on the East Coast in the summer and in Southeast Arizona in the winter. She has written several mysteries for young people, in honor of her grandchildren. She writes spy thrillers, stories of political intrigue, and all kinds of mysteries for grownups.*

CPSIA information can be obtained
at www.ICGtesting.com
Printed in the USA
BVHW041742010321
601356BV00010B/28/J